Mary Hargreaves is from Manchester and enjoys writing and reading things that cleverer people have written. She hates waiting, musicals and Pinot Grigio. *This Is Not a Love Story* is her debut novel.

THIS IS NOT
A LOVE STORY

Mary Hargreaves

A Trapeze Paperback
First published in Great Britain in 2020 by Trapeze,
an imprint of The Orion Publishing Group Ltd
Carmelite House, 50 Victoria Embankment,
London EC4Y 0DZ

An Hachette UK company

1 3 5 7 9 10 8 6 4 2

A CIP catalogue record for this book is
available from the British Library.

ISBN (Mass Market Paperback) 978 1 4091 9465 1
ISBN (eBook) 978 1 4091 9466 8

Typeset by Born Group
Printed and bound in Great Britain by Clays Ltd, Elcograf S.p.A.

www.orionbooks.co.uk

For Stef, who will probably never read this book, but without whom it would never have been written in the first place.

1

I am wide-awake at 6 a.m., listening to a furious scratching sound filtering through the paper-thin walls of my bedroom.

I know exactly what this is.

Gazing up at the ceiling, I attempt to curb my rage for approximately ten seconds before swinging my legs out of bed and stomping through to the kitchen.

What I really need, I know, is a cigarette. But what I'm probably going to do is start a nicotine-craving-fuelled argument with my boyfriend that I'll regret for the rest of the day.

Martin is hunched over the sink, viciously scrubbing a pan that I washed last night. I now have a choice. Tell Martin to please save his sanitising for when I'm not savouring my sleep hours due to a wild night of back-to-back episodes of *The Office*, or keep my mouth closed, roll a cigarette and begin my day with peace. I am weighing up my options when he turns around and smiles at me.

'Morning, lazybones!'

'I washed that pot last night, Martin.' I attempt an amenable tone, but it comes out as a sort of screech, so I plaster a grin on my face to mask it.

'I know you did, my love, and you did it very well! It's just there was this *teeny* little piece of spaghetti sticking to the rim, so I thought I'd just rinse it off.' He holds up the pan and it glints at me sadly, not used to such a violent cleansing.

'You need to look up the definition of "rinse", Martin.' The grin is sliding off my face at alarming speed. *Stay calm.* I clench my teeth. 'Would you mind saving the more aggressive scrubbing for after I've woken up next time?'

I leave the room again before he can answer and, more importantly, before I explode, and head back to the warm sanctuary of my duvet. Martin is undeterred and I hear him padding to the bathroom, no doubt to floss the toilet roll holder or something.

I reach my arm across the thirty-centimetre space between my bed and the window and swing it open. I'm just licking the edges of my rolling paper when Martin hurls himself into the room.

'Maggieeeeeeee . . .' he sings, 'look what I've found!' He holds out his hand, his thumb and index finger clutching something invisible. I lean forward and strain my eyes.

'A hair?'

Oh, for god's sake.

'They really are everywhere, aren't they!' He waggles his finger on his free hand. 'These can be a real nightmare if they build up, remember? You should always try and lift up the plug after you've had a shower and just pull them out – easy peasy. I can show you, if you like?'

What life Martin believes I lived until I met him I do not know. He seems to think that, as a single woman, I spent my days eating from soiled plates and defecating on the floor for fun, with absolutely no idea how the world *'actually works'* (his exact words). I have restrained thus far from reminding him that I have lived independently in the centre of Manchester for the past nine years, whereas he still technically lives with his mum in a semi-detached house in Rochdale.

'I know how to unclog a plug, Martin.' I try to keep my voice level. *He's only trying to help, he's only trying to help.* In his defence, the plumbing system in this place has worked impeccably since he moved in.

2

'I'm sure you do, sweetheart,' he wrinkles his nose, 'it's just that you weren't too clued up about emptying the bin last week, were you?' He wiggles his horrid, horrid eyebrows.

I put my cigarette to my lips, flick the lighter and inhale slowly. Blowing plumes of smoke through the room, I gaze at him steadily.

'Fuck off, Martin.'

2

I must get rid of Martin. I am walking to the bus stop and with every stomp on the wet ground my resolve hardens. He utterly, totally infuriates me. If someone utterly, totally infuriates you after only six months, I don't believe it is necessary to consult the self-help books to conclude that he is absolutely not 'The One'.

I must dissect this issue.

What *do* I like about Martin? I stop dead in the middle of the street as I rack my brains and the homeless man at my feet looks up excitedly. There is literally nothing I like about Martin. Or, at least, the things I thought I liked are now tainted with the fact that he's so bloody irritating. It's seeped into everything; he can't even yawn without making me want to throw myself out of the window.

I look down. 'I don't like anything about him!' I shout happily. The homeless man frowns.

'Who?'

I drop a pound into his cup and keep walking. If I don't like anything about him, this will be very, very easy. There will be nothing to keep me holding onto him! Nothing to cry over; just the sweet, free feeling of relief. I can wake up each morning to the sound of silence, watch films without him constantly correcting the 'corporate Hollywood bullshit' and eat foods that haven't been fortified with extra protein for his 'guns'.

I think I definitely *used* to like Martin, at the start. I definitely did. Maybe. We met in a really boring way (should have been a sign, really) at an awful club called 42nd Street just off Deansgate. I went with my best friends Cecilia, Anna and Sophie; we used to visit this place all the time while we were students, and thought it'd be fun to go back and relive it now that we were all grown-up with jobs and things. In case you're considering emulating this idea, I can assure you that it is not fun. It isn't even *funny*. It's just very, very sad.

Anyway, I spotted Martin standing moodily next to the toilets, and he looked so mysterious and brooding that I just had to go and talk to him. He told me that he hated clubbing (and, it turns out in the end, all types of fun) but had gone along with his brother who was getting over a pretty nasty breakup. We didn't really have anything in common, but, like all nightclub romances, it didn't really matter, and he came home with me anyway.

Two years later, he still hasn't left.

Right, come on, there must have been *something* I liked about him. *Think.* Oh, his eyebrows! I used to love his eyebrows. They were so . . . expressive. And he made me laugh, sometimes. Mainly *at* him, rather than with him, but I'm not sure I could really tell the difference at the start. I probably thought he was being ironic. In any case, his eyebrows now piss me off to the extent that I often fantasise about waxing them when he's asleep and then overdosing him with botox so that even the bald space where they *used* to be wouldn't twitch, and I haven't so much as smiled in his company for months. If I'm honest with myself, I think anyone could have walked into the club that night and I'd have done the exact same thing. I was twenty-five and people were starting to get their shit together; it seemed like the time for me to do the same.

After only a thirty-four minute wait (winner) I'm on the bus, wedged next to a man who has an oozing, shiny scalp and smells like compost. My hair is dripping onto my knees and I can't feel my toes. If I won the lottery, I would buy a chauffeur. Not a car, because driving is boring and if you're out somewhere and someone offers you a drink, you have to say no. Driving is the antidote to spontaneity.

I would really prefer to be sat by the window, because weirdly it's a lot easier to think when you can see things moving past, even when your only view is the bowels of Salford. Instead I make do with focusing on the greasy smear on the 'STOP' button in front of me and contemplate how to remove Martin from my life and, most pressingly, my apartment.

What I think I should do is sit down with him with a nice cup of tea and kindly explain that I think he's a wonderful person (he isn't) but that I just need to focus on myself and I hope we can still be friends. An offer that I pray he will not take me up on. That way he can move on, I can move on, and there will be no animosity or ill-feeling when we each reminisce about our pasts. He can look back fondly on our six months together and, with the rose-tinted glasses of time, he will probably begin to wistfully dream of me as 'The One Who Got Away'. Perhaps even I, with a great deal more time, might one day think of his eyebrows with a smile, and be grateful that we were so mature and dignified about our incompatibility.

What I will probably do, I concede, is start an argument until he storms out and then change all the locks.

The bus has pulled up outside my office block; a pebble-dashed, diarrhoea-coloured monstrosity, currently looming down on me from its rain-grey backdrop and making me wish I'd never been born. I pull my swipe card from my pocket and wonder, as I do each day, why we need one when really, who in the name of god would ever want to break into this place? I spend around eighty-two per cent of my working day (calcu-lated by an Excel spreadsheet last Tuesday, so yes I *do* use the full Microsoft Office package I asked for, Theo) devising plans to escape. So far, setting the place on fire seems to be the only feasible option.

It came to me on a particularly mind-numbing Monday afternoon, when the office radio asked me, 'have you had an accident in the workplace that wasn't your fault?' and I thought, *no . . . but I could.* I toyed with electrocuting myself, but then the soul-sucking building would still be standing, and I'd probably die, so now I spend most of my time wondering which part of my body I wouldn't mind getting minor burns on for the sake of compensation. No more job, no more hideous poo-toned prison, pocket full of cash. Sorted.

It wouldn't even be that hard, I realise as I'm walking down the stairs into my basement dungeon. For all the state-of-the-art security in this place (a swipe card and a man named Leonard who is permanently asleep at the front desk), health and safety here is non-existent. The fire doors are constantly pegged open, wires poke out of most of the walls and the huge thirteenth-floor windows open fully, which is incredibly risky in a place like this, where quality of life is at about 0.01. Not to mention that everyone smokes in the toilets, so all it would take would be one unextinguished cigarette and POOF, bye-bye bane of my life. It did cross my mind once, very fleetingly, that I could perhaps get another job. But I was quite hormonal at the time and I wasn't thinking straight.

I reach the bottom of the stairs and shoulder the cheap, wooden door onto my corridor three times until it swings open and smacks the wall. Apparently our department can't stretch to a new doorframe, although I'm sure there'd be a couple of grand in it for me if I dislocated my shoulder. Every cloud.

The corridor is deserted as usual; it's ten past nine and I'm ten minutes late, but I've been here for six years now and have yet to arrive after anyone else on the entire floor. Every morning I consider breezing in at 10 a.m. like my colleague Kelsey, and I sit in front of the news in my pyjamas with a cup of coffee, watching the minutes inch by in the corner of the screen, trying to relax. And every morning, without fail, Louise Minchin says 'it's eight a.m., up next—' and I leap off the sofa, shove on my clothes and run out of the house. Because what if today was the day someone came in *on time*? And they thought that every morning I swanned in late too? And so, every day, I enter my department at roughly 9 a.m., turn on all the lights and sit here seething and online shopping until someone comes in and their presence forces me to actually work.

Amazon has got some absolutely *incredible* deals today. A hand blender for a tenner! A sausage maker for only thirty quid?! Am I dreaming? I already have two hand blenders (thanks Nana, two Christmases in a row) and would not know where to buy sausage meat to save my life but *really*. This new world we're living in is fantastic.

It's 10.45 and I've already restrained myself from buying a Cinderella pug costume for the dog I don't own and have opened a Word document and typed 'TO DO' at the top. I'm just typing 'best shampoo for frizzy hair' into Google when I hear familiar quick, light footsteps trotting down the corridor.

'For the last time, Bernadette, Romulus is *incredibly* sick! I will not have you dismissing his fragile condition like this! He needs warmth, love and someone who cares, and quite frankly you sound as though you don't give a flying fuck. Now you give him a bath and get him into bed *this instant*, or mark my words, you will hear from my lawyer.'

Oh, kill me now. It's Theo.

My boss.

3

Theo sweeps into my office and his eyes settle on the empty chair beside me.

'Where's Kelsey?' He gasps. To be honest, I feel like gasping too. This is a rare and sacred moment; Theo has arrived before the personal assistant he really doesn't need. I would like to take a picture.

'In the bathroom,' I lie, covering for her. 'Problems with . . . her uterus.'

'Oh my goodness me.' Theo brings his hand to his chest and sinks down into Kelsey's empty seat. 'What I wouldn't give to have a uterus. You're so *lucky*.' He leans forward and links his hands in prayer, gazing up at me.

'Right, yep, but erm, I think she might be in a lot of pain, so—'

'Pain is the price, Margaret!' he shouts. I cringe. Reason number one why Theo is my least favourite person: he calls me by my full name. Also, incidentally, a reason why Martin and I are doomed for failure. Margaret and Martin – absolutely *not*.

Theo has taken to leaning back in his chair and sighing theatrically, the back of his hand flung across his forehead. By all accounts, Theo was born dramatic. At any given opportunity, he will tell the story of his birth (he ripped his mother in

9

two because he just couldn't *wait* to get out and start living) and how he cried for the first four days of his existence until his cot was kitted out with 800-thread count Egyptian cotton bedding. Theo lives in Chorlton and likes to think that makes him well-to-do with an edge, but if it weren't for his semi-successful, Boohoo-model husband he'd be living in a decomposing one-bed somewhere non-specific like the rest of us.

I want, more than anything, for him to leave before we enter into his favourite subject: *the beauty of periods*. I brought this on myself with my excuse for Kelsey, I realise. I should know better. Unfortunately, he's in a talkative mood this morning, so I'll need to change the topic myself if I want to win.

'Romulus not well again?'

Theo takes a sharp intake of breath and runs his hands down his cheeks. 'Oh, no. Not well at all. I'm at a loss with what to do, Margaret.' He begins to well up. 'He's had this cough for three days now, and his breathing is so *laboured*, I —' His voice breaks and I hand him a tissue from my desk. 'Thank you.' He clears his throat. 'It's such a difficult time. Christopher and I are out of our *minds* with worry. I've had to leave him with Bernadette from next door. She thinks I'm being dramatic. Dramatic! Like she knows anything about what I'm going through. I'm slaving away here every second of every day –' (I also used my spreadsheet to calculate that Theo spends an average of twenty-two hours per week at the office) '– and she just dallies around her kitchen making pies and cakes and taking them to everyone in the bloody village. She doesn't even try to get to *know* Romulus. To find out what he likes, who he *is*. She won't even give him a gentle kiss on the head when she puts him to bed. She says it's *weird*. Weird! It makes him feel safe and comfortable, and I've already told her it's not a problem with me; I know she's not some creep who'll get off on it or something. But oh *no*, Bernadette won't do it because it's *weird*, and of course Bernadette knows *everything*, but has she ever even *owned* an iguana?!'

10

Oh, yes. Romulus is an iguana. And Bernadette, I happen to know, raised five boys on her own whilst working two jobs. I wish I'd chosen *the beauty of periods.*

Kelsey, whose timing is notoriously shit (I could hear her standing outside waiting for the tirade to end before she entered), chooses this moment to grace us with her presence. She sweeps in, flicks her hair back and gazes pointedly at her seat, which is still occupied by Theo and his heavy breathing.

I'm quite pissed off, because I followed the rules of the 'sisterhood' or whatever and saved Kelsey with the story of her mangled womb, and now she has betrayed me by making me today's recipient of Theo's iguanine infatuation.

'Kelsey, you're back!' I etch concern upon my face. 'I hope your, erm, *pains* –' I gesture to my lower stomach, '– are a little better?'

Kelsey's face registers confusion, realisation and then anguish at an alarming speed. 'Oh, yeah, I'm really suffering today. I'd rather not talk about it, though. I've actually got some emails I need to go through . . .' She eyes Theo again, who still hasn't moved.

I wouldn't wish it on my worst enemy, but I'm going to have to drop Kelsey in it if I want to escape. When it comes to Theo, it's every man for himself.

'I need to nip to the bathroom myself, actually. Theo was just telling me about poor Romulus and it's made me quite sad.' I skirt around her and up the corridor as Theo launches into an in-depth analysis of Romulus's bowel movements.

Twenty minutes and two cigarettes out the bathroom window later and I'm back at my desk. Kelsey is determinedly ignoring me, presumably in retaliation for landing her in it earlier, so I am clicking my mouse extra loud in the hope that she'll chat to me and distract me from my work. My task for the morning is to write a pitch for a new weight-loss drug, which I'm ninety-nine per cent certain is just capsules of salt. I have to read the information leaflet, past research and statistics before translating it into normal English and picking out all the best bits. Then I have to write a really moving speech about how great and life-changing it is, based on the 0.0001 per cent of success stories it's produced. This is where a biology degree takes you, folks.

'Maggie?' Rachael from upstairs winds her skinny, annoying neck round the door. 'Have you got Loss-A-Lot?' She taps her fingers impatiently.

'He's riding his horse back from Camelot as we speak.' I don't look up.

'What?'

'Loss-A-Lot? Lancelot? No?' She stares at me blankly. Never-bloody-mind. 'Just finishing it now. I'll bring it up in ten.'

She totters back out and up to her palace, where she resides with Ben and Mohammed. *The dream team.* Basically, they sit around slurping skinny lattes all day and wait for me to bring them their briefs, then swan off in their company cars and try to sell drugs to doctors. The official title is 'sales rep', but I prefer 'wanker'.

Rachael is one of those social media queens, with an unteach-able knack for posting every single aspect of her life at *exactly* the right angle. She once spent half her month's wage on a decorative bed cushion and went on about it for weeks like it was something she was proud of. Secretly, I think she hates me because my Instagram is made up of blurry photos of Domino's pizza and fish I've spotted in the canal, and that must say something about me. She followed me once for about two hours, and then abruptly disappeared from my followers list as quickly as she came.

My phone vibrates on my desk and I flip it over. A text from my sister, Verity: *Mum says I haven't checked on you for too long. Will be at yours Friday p.m.*

I resist the temptation to text her back and ask her if she'd considered that I might have *plans* on a Friday night (I don't), and to call my mother and ask her why she constantly thinks I need 'checking on', and push my phone between the four dirty mugs on my desk. Veri is always the last person I want to see, but if I get it out of the way she probably won't bother me for another couple of months.

I finish off the Loss-A-Lot brief, checking that all the facts are vague enough to be uncontentious, print three copies and make my way up to the first floor. I tap on the door and wait until I hear Mohammed say 'enter' (*enter?!*) before going in. Rachael is sat on the edge of her massive desk, her slim, waxed legs reflecting the light coming from the window behind her. Mohammed and Ben are lounging on two giant beanbags, sniggering at something on one of their phones. Probably porn. Saddos.

'Finally.' Rachael snatches the papers from my hands.

'I said ten minutes like . . . five minutes ago?' I say petulantly.

'OK, Maggie, well you let us know when you've got a job where people actually depend on you, yeah?' Mohammed pipes up.

I look at him for a second and then turn on my heel, slamming the door behind me.

I head back down to my office and stare at my blank screen for a moment. Kelsey doesn't look up from her computer.

'I can't believe you don't make more of an effort with them.' She types as she speaks.

'Who?'

'The sales reps.'

'Because they're awful people?'

She laughs like a manic toad. 'They make a *lot* more money than you.'

'And more than you . . . doesn't mean I have to get on with them. They don't control my salary.'

'The company's growing, Maggie.' I really don't like her tone.

'And?'

'And when they need more sales reps they'll be recruiting internally first. Don't think Rachael won't have a say in who gets hired.'

'I'm not going to suck up to them, Kelsey. I honestly couldn't give a shit.'

She snorts and we lapse into silence. When I glance over at her, she's peering at me over her 'designer' glasses (I saw an identical pair in Primark last week for £2.50), 'That's why you'll always be stuck at the bottom, whilst everyone else makes an effort and actually gets somewhere.'

I gape at her in shock. I cannot believe she just said that to me. She glances over at the empty seat on the far side of the office. Mohammed's old seat. He used to do what I do, before he applied for one of the rep positions. He trained me up a bit when I arrived and then moved on up to his kingdom upstairs. He actually used to be an OK guy before the status went to his head. I even considered shagging him. Rank.

I'm really riled up now. 'Believe it or not, Kel, running around the city with a superiority complex and a sushi meal deal isn't my number one career goal. But I'm thrilled for you, your dream of spending the rest of your life in this building isn't a hard one to achieve.' I can't believe it. How can she sit there and tell me I'm going nowhere, when last week we were both crying over a bottle of wine, talking about how much we hate our jobs?

Kelsey and I have the kind of forced friendship that springs from a shared office and a mutual demographic. We're both twenty-seven, struggling to pay city-centre rent and wondering when the ladder out of here is going to appear. Apart from that, we have very little in common, and our collective dissatisfaction with our lives brings out the worst in us most of the time.

She says nothing.

'If this is some tough-love tactic you're trying out, it's not working.'

She sighs. 'No, you're right. I'm sorry. Ignore me. Bad day.'

'Me too.' I'm annoyed with myself for mouthing off at her and not being the bigger person. It isn't her fault I'm unhappy, nor is it mine that she is. Self-consciousness and hopelessness

14

are making me bitchy, though, and I need to reign it in. There's enough misery around here without the two of us turning on each other, and I really don't want people to start thinking I'm a nasty cow.

'What's up?' I scoot my chair round to her side of the desk. 'Anything you want to talk about?'

'It's nothing, really.' She rubs one heavily made-up eye with her little finger, niftily scratching an itch whilst keeping all her eyeliner in place. I watch in awe. 'Just an interview I didn't get. Again.'

Theo flings himself into the office before I can delve further, his bag swinging from his shoulder. 'Ladies, this place is giving me a migraine. I'm going to work from home.' He notices Kelsey's bowed head, my hand on her arm. 'Feel free to do the same, both of you. You've worked hard this month.'

4

Home, home, home. At midday! This is incredible. And it's four hours until Martin gets back so I actually have some time alone for the first time in months. One of the worst things about Martin is that he only works six hours a day – he's a Personal Trainer at PureGym – so he leaves the house after me and gets back before me. He also never goes back to his own house, although I pray every day that he will; he just trots back here every afternoon like a homing pigeon. His mum probably thinks he's dead.

So, you see, it's not like I'd be leaving him *homeless* if I kicked him out. His mum's house is lovely and she has very thought-fully kept the Busted duvet cover on his single bed just in case he ever fancies a visit. Unfortunately, Martin clocked pretty quickly that a ten minute walk to work was much more convenient than a twenty-five minute train journey, so he stopped going home almost as soon as we met. It was fine with me, at first; I actually looked forward to coming home to him during those first few months, when I really thought I'd hit the jackpot by settling down and finding someone. I honestly don't know what I was thinking.

I'm boiling myself in the bath and my skin is the colour of chicken tikka marinade. I'm making myself hungry. If I want curry for dinner I'll have to make it myself because Martin doesn't 'do' takeaway, as he is so fond of telling anyone who so much as breathes in his direction. He keeps saying he's going to write a book about his 'lifestyle', which as far as I can see consists of lifting weights and being an annoying twat. It'd probably be quite popular.

God, I'm horrible. Why am I thinking these horrible things? Martin isn't a bad person, he's just not *my* person. He's custom-made for an organised, health-conscious gym bunny, which is about the least fitting description of me you could possibly come up with. I can't blame him for how I'm feeling, though. It really isn't his fault, and he's totally clueless as I never talk to him anyway.

I sense the tide of unhappiness and self-consciousness lapping at my skin in time with the bath water. I squeeze my eyes shut. I don't want to lash out at people I care about. I just need a little pick-me-up, that's all. A nice curry will do the job. I can already feel the endorphin rush of that first bite of greasy garlic naan.

I could order it now . . . I haven't eaten since breakfast. I shouldn't, though. It's only midday, and I'm already toeing the overweight line. But why is there so much shame attached to ordering a takeaway in daylight hours? If I wanted to eat a 14-inch Domino's at 9 a.m., why on earth couldn't I? It's *open* at 9 a.m., so surely there are people who swim against the tide.

Sod it. I'm young, free and only a stone overweight; I won't be able to order Indian food when I've got three kids and a mortgage, will I? Although god forbid that ever happens because I can't even look after myself.

OK, according to JustEat, only one of the thirty-seven Indian restaurants in my area is open. It's a sign! Other people do this too. Holding my phone carefully above the water, I place my order – which could feed an obese family of four with lefto-vers – and heave myself out of the bath. I empty the water and watch three of my hairs coil themselves around the plughole. Something to occupy Martin later. *Stop it, Maggie!* I fish them out and toss them into the bin.

Waiting for a takeaway is the worst feeling in the world. I've put my phone on maximum volume but I keep checking it anyway, because if I miss the call and my onion bhajis get cold I will die. You can't microwave a bhaji. I distract myself by sitting on my bed in my wet towel and flicking through Instagram. God, Emma Penton's in Santorini. There's loads of pictures of her standing outside white-washed buildings in bright, flowing dresses with the kind of shoes you wouldn't *expect* would go with the outfit, but really do. Katie Sandhurst is travelling Asia with her model boyfriend. They upload these montage videos to Facebook with amazing backing music and it all just looks *so good.* Jess Benham's having brunch in London. Why is it always so bloody sunny in London?

I haven't spoken to any of these people in over fifteen years. When I got Facebook in 2005 I was seriously lacking in high school friends, so I just added everyone I knew, including people from primary school who I hadn't seen since I walked out of the gates on the last day of year six. How did they all get so beautiful and successful? I bet none of them work in a basement dungeon. I bet they all carry themselves with absolute professionalism and never get curry at midday. Perhaps I should have listened to Kelsey. Maybe I've been so determined to hate Rachael that I didn't realise she was actually winning? I can't pretend I'm living my best life as an overweight sofa dweller whose idea of a good time is getting a free cheeseburger with my out-of-date student ID. It seems like every single person I know is doing something incredible – getting engaged; travelling; experimenting with Scandinavian interior design. The last holiday I went on was a weekend in Dublin with Martin where it rained the entire time, so we just spent most of it holed up in the hotel room (not shagging, I was miserable enough as it was).

I bet people think I'm drab and scruffy. I wonder if the girls ever roll their eyes when they talk about what we'll all wear on our nights out: *well, we all know Maggie will be dressed the same as she always is.* No, they wouldn't be that horrible. But I need to up my game. I need to buy some sunglasses and start getting brunch. I jump up from the bed and start pulling my clothes from the drawers, throwing them on the floor. Perhaps I can make some chic outfits from some of this. No. All of it will have to go. I need long dresses, ankle boots and shoulder bags. I need to say goodbye to Rimmel and spend three days' salary on some Estée Lauder foundation and a mascara. I could even start contouring. In fact, I've got the afternoon off (working from home, yeah, yeah); I'll go now.

This is it! I'm so full of energy, I'm shaking a bit as I pull on a scabby bra and a greying t-shirt. I'll get out there and buy stuff until I become the best version of myself. It's a tried and tested, fail-safe way to solve problems.

The doorbell rings.

Oh. The takeaway.

Well, I have to *eat*, don't I? No one ever had a successful shopping trip on an empty stomach. I'll eat this giant curry, and I'm sure once I've got a belly full of rice and naan I'll feel even more energised and ready to go and raid the shops. I'm sure I will.

I open the door and there's an elderly man with a JustEat bag.

'Hot Flavas?' He squints at me.

'Yep! Thanks so much.' I reach for the bag.

'Thirty-two pounds please.' He pulls the food back out of my reach.

'Sorry? I paid by card?'

'Card declined. Thirty-two pounds please.'

This is just not happening. I scrabble for my phone and check my online banking app. Sure enough, only £29 left of my over-draft. *Shit.* I run to the bedroom and pull out my emergency money sock. Situations like these are the exact reason I have this secret stash – this is an absolute Grade A emergency. The man stands and watches sadly as I dig notes and coins out of the sock, which is grey and has a picture of the Spice Girls on it.

'Here, sorry about that.' I thrust two twenties in his hand and he passes me my change and my food. He looks at me with concern.

'You take care,' he says eventually.

'Yep, yep, you too, have a great evening, hope the weather's good to you, bye-bye.' I shut the door in his face.

I gaze miserably into my sock. Just twelve pounds left in there now. Maybe I could ask Theo for a payrise? I laugh out loud. That's about as likely to happen as Oasis getting back together.

I grab a plate and a spoon, go into the bedroom and close the door behind me. Dragging my laptop onto the bed, I bury myself in the covers and load up *The Office* on an illegal streaming site I'm sure I'll be arrested for using one day. Season bloody seven. How has it come to this? I'm trying to calculate how many hours of my life that totals, but I don't have my Excel spreadsheet and it's hard to do maths whilst concentrating on not spilling lamb madras all over the bed.

The rush of that first bite is like nothing else. Total ecstasy. But there's still that little voice in the back of my mind: *what are you doing?* Two years ago, all I wanted was to find someone; do cute things, get engaged, be a unit. Yet here I am, alone in the middle of the afternoon, stuffing my face with curry. I suppose the upside is that I'm no longer bothered by the idea of being with that perfect partner; I just want to be on my own in my space. The downside, however, is that I now seem to have fifty thousand more problems than I did two years ago. I peel the lid off the rice and shovel a huge spoonful into my mouth. The voice quietens a little.

I'm dunking my second garlic naan into the chicken tikka masala when I hear a key in the front door. *Fuck*. Is that Martin?! It's only two-thirty, what's he doing here? Or maybe it's a burglar? But a burglar wouldn't have a key . . . Or maybe he would, if this is a premeditated, extensive operation? Maybe I've been targeted. Someone's been following me for weeks, waiting for the right moment to steal and copy my key. Working stealthily to gain access to my apartment so they can – what? Steal my second-hand NutriBullet and five-year-old vibrator?

The person in the apartment starts whistling the *Lord of the Rings* theme tune. Oh Christ, it *is* Martin. I'd have preferred a burglar. If he finds me with this curry in bed he'll flip. I'm not going out there. I've finally got an afternoon to myself and I am *not* spending it discussing how many grams of saturated fat are in a prawn korma. I'm just going to stay here and finish my curry. Curries. There are four. I'm actually quite full now, but I feel like finishing this would be a protest against chic brunch-eaters, my job and the society that frowns on midday takeaways.

Martin has settled himself in front of the TV. He doesn't know I'm here; I'm not supposed to be back until five thirty. I keep the volume on low and lay my head on the pillow, lazily feeding myself pieces of saucy lamb with my bare hands. I sort of need the bathroom, but Martin's out there and I think I'm in a food coma. I'll close my eyes for ten seconds and then I'll have to go and face the insufferable music.

God, I'm so comfortable. Life is so nice without work. I can't believe I've got to go back there tomorrow and write more briefs, smoke more bathroom cigarettes, feel more pathetic. I'll think about that later.

5

'OH MY GOD!'

I jerk awake, blinking madly at Martin, who is clambering across the bed.

'Maggie! Maggie, oh my god, are you OK?' He grabs my face and flits his eyes across my body. I look down. I am covered in chicken tikka masala.

'Martin, hellooooo.' I rub my hand across my stomach and watch as a huge gloop of curry slides onto the bedsheet.

'What the hell happened? Why are you here? What's . . . this?' He's gesturing towards my general situation.

'I got sent home from work and I was hungry, so I—' I stop as I notice a flickering coming from the hallway. 'Oh my god, Martin, is something on fire?!' I jump up from the bed and a naan bread hits the floor with a *splat*. I run into the lounge and skid to a stop. There are tea lights on every surface and petals are scattered all over the sofa and floor. In the middle of the dining table is a bottle of champagne in an ice bucket. I turn around. Martin is standing in the doorway looking sheepish.

'What the hell is this?'

'Don't you like it?' He pouts.

'Well, I mean . . . are we celebrating?'

'Maybe.' He takes my crusty, garlicky hand and leads me towards the table. I sit down and he disappears into the kitchen.

'Stay there!' he shouts.

I look around the room. There must be over 100 candles in here. They're probably the paraffin ones that give you cancer, too. What is going on? How long was I asleep? I peer at the label on the champagne bottle. Right. So *this* is where he spends the rent money he never gives me. *Be nice, Maggie.*

'Ta dah!' Martin is wobbling into the room carrying two steaming plates of something which smells suspiciously like farts. He places one down in front of me. Grilled chicken, broccoli and sprouts. The curry in my stomach swirls in protest.

'Now, I didn't want to break my diet, but as this is a special – well, potentially special – occasion . . .' He reaches into his back pocket and pulls out a squeezy bottle of extra light mayonnaise. 'Let's be naughty, shall we?' He winks.

'Martin, this is really great, but—'

'Shhh. Let's eat.'

I'm really not awake enough to play detective right now. I smother a sprout in mayonnaise and force it into my mouth. I gag.

'Careful, it's hot! You OK?'

'Yes, yeah, I think I just need a glass of this to cool my mouth down.' I reach for the champagne and rip off the foil.

'Wait, I wanted to save that for—'

POP. I fill my glass to the brim and take a huge gulp before pouring some for Martin.

'Oh. Well . . . cheers.' He clinks his glass glumly against mine and I smile brightly. I need a distraction so he doesn't notice I'm not eating his sulphurous food. I could break up with him . . . he wouldn't notice I wasn't eating then, would he? I stare at the line of tea lights precariously licking at the space under the curtains. No, probably not the best time. Later, when we've blown all the candles out.

I feel my eyes threatening to close again. I blink hard and look down at my plate, but I'm saved from eating any more because Martin is inexplicably on the floor next to me.

'Have you dropped a sprout again?' I peer my head under the table.

'No, Maggie, look at me.'

'OK . . .'

'Dear, sweet Maggie.' *What?* 'My life has changed in so many ways since I met you. This apartment, our home, has become a haven for me with you in it.' *WHAT?* 'You are the most beautiful, sweet and kind person I know.' I am none of these things. OK, maybe a bit beautiful. Gotta be your own cheerleader. 'I can't put into words how much you mean to me, but hopefully this will show you.'

He reaches behind him and as he turns I notice that he isn't just on the floor. He's on one knee.

ONE.

KNEE.

Oh my god, no.

No, no, no.

This is not happening.

Abort.

ABORT RIGHT NOW.

'Are you proposing on a *Wednesday*?' I screech. I have no idea where that came from.

He pauses. 'What's wrong with Wednesdays?'

'I can't believe you've just asked me that. I cannot *believe –*' I scrape my chair back, '– you just asked me that.'

'What's the matter?! I don't understand.'

I down the rest of my drink, buying time. *Be patient. Be nice. This is nice. This is a lovely moment.*

'What?' he repeats.

'Do you even *know* me?' I don't know what I'm saying. I need to be sensitive and say no politely, but I can't. I just need him to shut up so I can think. My brain can't process what's happening, never mind generate appropriate proposal rejections.

He blinks at me and my eyes travel to his hand, which is holding the most beautiful ring I have ever seen. A thin, silver band with three delicate, perfectly round diamonds nestled together.

Jesus.

I pause for a second. Martin looks up at me with big, wide eyes. Oh, god. That would look *so* good on my finger. We could have the wedding on the beach in Santorini; me in a flowing, cream gown, barefoot with flowers in my hair, three bridesmaids trailing behind in different pastel shades. A honeymoon in the Caribbean; that place where you can swim with pigs. Me laughing on the sand, my head flung back, salty hair billowing in the breeze. A photo-montage that would lift my depressing social media presence and gain me a thousand followers. And then back to England, to Manchester, relaxed and tanned, back to work and this apartment. Coming home to Martin every evening, poached salmon and green beans for dinner, never having any time alone again. Getting pregnant, trapped working for Theo forever to pay off the mortgage, the boiling hatred for Martin growing inside me every day until I eventually snap and burn the house down.

'Maggie?' His eyebrows are drooping.

No. *NO.* I will not trade my soul for a pretty ring.

'I can't.' I shake my head violently. 'No.'

I grab the bottle of champagne and take a swig. Martin watches me.

'That was supposed to be to celebrate . . . if you'd said yes. I could have saved it if you hadn't opened it.'

'Oh my god, Martin, for *what*?'

He shrugs. 'I don't know. For next time, maybe.'

'There won't be a next time.'

'You don't know that. I could meet someone else.'

'Oh. Right.' I'm not surprised to find that doesn't upset me in the slightest. The idea of Martin with someone else actually makes me feel relieved. Although I am slightly offended.

'Great. Yeah, no, that's great. Save the champagne and the ring for the next one.' I grab the bottle again. 'Oh, except you can't, because I've drunk most of it.'

'Yeah, exactly. I'll have to buy another one.' He's completely serious.

I can feel the rage bubbling in my veins. There's no point even trying to filter my responses.

'Don't worry, I'll pop a stopper in the top and it should last another week or so. That should be enough time, shouldn't it?'

'That's silly. I couldn't propose to someone with half a bottle of champagne.'

I cannot believe I'm having this conversation. I grab my half-full glass from the table and messily pour it back into the bottle.

'Better?'

He frowns. 'That was really expensive.'

He's pouting at me miserably. I suddenly want to suffocate him with the rose petals. I am so angry. How has it come to this? I grab a handful.

'Would you like these back, too?'

'No, they go off really quickly.' He tuts. 'The food's gone cold now as well.'

'Thank god for that.'

'It was a bit too hot, wasn't it?'

Right, that's it. The gloves are off. 'No, Martin, it was disgusting. And I just ate four curries, so I'm not all that hungry to be honest with you.'

'*Four?*' He gasps. For the first time this evening, he looks devastated. 'You know there's over a thousand calories in one curry?'

'There's a bit left if you're hungry.'

He recoils. 'God, no.'

I sink down onto the sofa, the bottle still in my hand. *He doesn't get it. It's not his fault he doesn't get it. Be nice.* 'I'm sorry, Martin. I'm upset, I'm not being very nice. I'm just . . .' I sigh. 'What did you expect me to say? We have nothing in common.'

'Yes we do!'

'You can't be serious? You're obsessed with healthy eating and the gym. I just had four thousand calories and a two p.m. nap.'

'We both like *The Walking Dead*.'

'Oh, great!' I stand up and wave the bottle in the air. 'Let's get married! Let's have a *Walking Dead* themed wedding and teach our children to fend off zombies and spend our retirement years watching reruns.' The champagne is swimming straight to my head. It is *completely* his fault that he doesn't get it.

Martin is twisting a rose petal between two meaty fingers. 'Well it's not a *bad* idea . . .'

'It's a fucking terrible idea!' I screech. Martin flinches. Why am I so horrible? I can't decide between consolation or attack; I'm flitting between the two. 'I know this was meant to be lovely, and I've ruined it. I'm sorry. But you must realise that we're not compatible? At all?'

Martin ignores me, taking the plates and shuffling dejectedly into the kitchen. I grab my tobacco tin from the bookcase, roll a cigarette and light it from one of the candles on the coffee table. I crack open the window and lean on the windowsill, taking deep drags and watching a pigeon peck at a fried chicken leg on the street below. Isn't that cannibalism? A chicken is a bird, and so is a pigeon. Does it even know what it's eating? Of course it doesn't. But then, if I ate a monkey, would that be cannibalism? Although we're not the same species as monkeys, are we? Could a human get pregnant from a monkey? Could a chicken get pregnant from a pigeon?

'For god's sake, please don't smoke inside.' Martin has returned, drying his hands on a tea towel.

'Could a chicken and a pigeon have a hybrid baby?'

He stares at me blankly. 'Put it out.'

'It's my apartment, Martin, I'll do what I like.'

'It's not yours, it's the landlord's, and there's no chance we'll be getting the deposit back if it stinks of smoke.'

'*I'll* be getting *my* deposit back because I'll fumigate it before I leave.' I don't even know what fumigating is. I think the smell of Brussels sprouts might require something a little stronger, though. An industrial, post-apocalyptic chemical clean, perhaps. Or just demolish the entire building. It's probably the only solution.

'You know for every one of those you smoke you're losing ten minutes of your life, right?' He looks quite proud of this little factoid he's produced. Note to self: if by some horrific turn of events I end up marrying Martin, I must smoke fifty a day to shorten the pain.

'Could a monkey get me pregnant?'

He flinches. 'So you're saying I'm a monkey now?'

'What? What are you even – no, but could it?'

Martin glares at me and thunders into the bathroom, slamming the door behind him. I must Google that later. I'm sure they can't – I'd have heard about it, wouldn't I? Martin wouldn't know, anyway. He doesn't even know where Canada is.

I'm deflecting. I know I am. I'm being mean and antagonistic and thinking about avian cannibalism instead of trying to have a civilised conversation about what the hell just happened. I can't process it, though, because the future that flashed in front of my eyes when I saw that ring was so terrifying, so totally the opposite of what I ever imagined for myself, that it made me sick. I want to go back in time and slap 25-year-old me. *You do* not *want marriage and children. Do not talk to the man with the alluring eyebrows. Walk out of the club and go and get a pizza.*

I take a final drag and throw the butt out of the window, taking care to miss the pigeon having his evening feast. I love pigeons; I think they're hilarious. They just trot around with half their legs missing and sit on lamp-posts not giving a shit and judging everyone. Martin hates them – yet another thing we can't agree on. I can hear him having a poo in the bathroom. That seems like an appropriate chain of events: propose, get rejected, contemplate re-using champagne, have a shit. I feel really romanced. What a lucky girl I am.

I down the last few dregs of the champagne from the bottle and pick up Martin's glass, which has hardly been touched. I imagine him picking out that bottle, buying the rose petals, carefully lighting each tea light. Guilt rises up from the pit of my stomach like vomit. I need him out of here. I look around the room, which is full of reminders of his existence. A stack of protein shake sachets at the end of the dining table, his phone charger neatly coiled by the wall, dumb-bells next to the TV. I want my space back. I want my evenings in front of *Hell's Kitchen* with a pizza and a bottle of wine. I want to stretch my legs across the entire bed and not have to breathe in his night farts. Why did I ever think this was what I wanted? How much time have I wasted?

He doesn't want me, anyway. He can't possibly be happy with me. We don't laugh, we don't cuddle, we don't have sex. We don't even *talk*. Martin just wants a wife; the carbon-copy, socially-approved life, ticking off all the milestones at exactly the right time. Excellent body in mid-twenties: check. Well-paid career at twenty-five: check. Centrally located apartment at twenty-six: check. Engaged at twenty-seven is just the next appropriate 'to-do' item. He doesn't think too much; it's just convenient for him that I happen to be here to ask.

The bathroom door opens and Martin is standing there, holding a hair I must have missed in the plughole earlier.

He opens his mouth to speak.

'Get out.' The words come out before I have time to think.

'What? Look, Maggie, it's not hard to just put these in the bin—'

'Get out, Martin.'

He steps out of the bathroom, looking over his shoulder.

'Not out of there! *Out!*'

'Out where?'

'Out of the *door*. Out of the apartment. Wherever. Just leave, please.'

29

'What do you mean?' He frowns.

'I mean I want you to go. I don't want to be with you anymore. I don't want you here anymore. I don't want you. So just go.' I can't believe I'm saying this. I can't believe I'm finally doing this. It's an injustice to him, to have left it this long, to have let it get this far. I could do this better, I could have done this better a long time ago, but if I stop to consider his feelings I'll never get through it.

His mouth hangs open. 'Where is this coming from?'

'Martin, if you have to ask that question, then you *really* need to get out.'

'What have I done?'

'It's nothing you've *done*, it's what you are. You're so different to me. We're not even slightly compatible. I feel suffocated by you, I'm not happy. I'm sorry. I'm sure you'll find someone lovely, who gets you and likes you and wants to eat chicken and beans every night for the rest of her life. But that's not me, Martin, I'm really sorry but it isn't. I need you to go.'

He looks hurt, and for a moment I regret it all so much. I feel like I should just give him a hug and apologise and stick an episode of *The Biggest Loser* on for him. Go back in time, say yes, let him smother me forever. Have the stable life with the husband and mortgage and sacrifice happiness for pure misery.

'I haven't finished washing up.'

That moment is gone.

'I'll do it. Please, Martin.' I'm getting frantic now. What if he doesn't leave? What if he stays here and refuses to get out and I'm stuck with him forever? Who do you even call about that? Is there an ombudsman?

He stares at me for a second, and then walks into the bedroom. I follow him and watch as he starts slowly and methodically placing everything he has ever owned into his suitcase, folding each item precisely as if he's going to a business meeting in Dubai. *Hurry uuuuuuup.* I can't watch this; every second he's still here is making me want to rip off my own skin. My friend Sophie always talks about *The Ick*, that feeling when you like someone, but then you notice something off-putting about them, and then just being near them makes you cringe. Unfortunately for me, I think that moment came two months after we met.

I head back into the kitchen and grab a bin bag. I throw everything of Martin's I can see into it as quickly as possible. This is quite therapeutic, actually, literally binning him. A few of my mugs remind me of him, so they go in as well. And that wall hanging he once said he liked. The radish in the fridge. The tea towel he just dried his hands on. And a nice sprinkling of rose petals to garnish it all off.

I drag the bag into the bedroom. He's on the floor, zipping up his case.

'You can pick up your weights another time.'

'Or you can just post them to me.'

I'm going to ignore that ridiculously expensive suggestion. He takes the bin bag from my hand and trudges towards the front door. I reach round and open it for him.

'Well, bye then, Martin.' I force myself to seal the deal. *Don't back down now. Keep pushing. Push until he's gone and then you can reassemble your mind and work out what to do next.*

'Bye, Maggie. Don't forget to water the bonsai.'

I decide not to mention that the bonsai is now rammed inside the bin bag he is currently holding, mangled and covered in protein powder.

I shut the door.

Somehow, I have half a bottle of wine in my hand. I've not even bothered with the glass; I'm just swigging it straight like some kind of tramp.

I'd hazard a guess that it's about three hours since Martin left, and in that time I have rather swiftly transitioned from euphoric tipsiness into full-on breakdown-wasted. I have a piece of paper in my hand, too, but I'm struggling to remember why. I roll and light a cigarette. *Cigarettes!* That's it. I write it down.

Obviously this isn't the first time I've had an all-consuming wave of panic about my cigarette habit. Facebook keeps slapping mini-documentaries on my newsfeed, with titles like 'the dangers of smoking' and 'here is what 100 cigarettes do to a clump of cotton wool'. It's like it *knows.* I've been smoking since I was sixteen, and I'm now twenty-seven. Eleven years. It was all fine when we were at uni, and we'd sit and smoke in the hallway of our disgusting ten-bed house in our dressing gowns, missing lectures. But slowly everyone has stopped smoking and started cooking and making money and settling down and talking about mortgages. Except me.

Anyway, I'm tired of trying to settle down and I'm quitting now, so soon I will be able to sit on my high horse and scoff at all the poor smokers and their boring husbands.

I roll another cigarette.

It appears I am creating a to-do list. I think I came up with the idea when I was looking at my phone. Emma Penton's Instagram, I think that was it. I want everything she has, so I have to make changes. Hence the list.

What else does Emma Penton have? She's skinny and looks good in a maxi dress. In fact, I've seen pictures of her painting her living room in 'Setting Plaster' pink, dressed in a huge nineties jersey and a pair of mom jeans, and she still looked three times smaller and more effortless than me. I take another swig of my wine. Skinny privilege is *so* unfair. Then again, so is male privilege, but I was born female so I'll just have to lump it. Unless I had a sex change? But I don't really want to be a man. I'm not sure I'd like it. All the rage and dangly bits and bloody constant erections. I've got enough going on as it is – I simply wouldn't cope.

I feel like I've drifted off topic. What was I thinking about? Oh, yes, being born a girl. A non-skinny girl. I wasn't born *fat,* though, was I? I write carefully. That's something I *can* change.

Emma's almost entirely muscle, too, but not in a beefy way. The woman basically lives at the gym when she's not going to sushi classes and trying cheese tea down some weird backstreet with Instagrammable neon signs. The gym is actually probably the reason she *can* have cheese tea. A tub of Philadelphia is not any healthier if it's dumped on a mug of Earl Grey, Emma. I scrawl my pen drunkenly across the paper again. For the past two years, exercise has been Martin's thing. Doing it myself felt like giving in to his regime. Now he's gone, I'll give it a shot. Maybe I could start with Zumba, or ballet or something. Become one of those people who post boomerangs of their workouts.

I'm nearly out of wine. I'm getting hungry again. I wish my mum was here to make me a cheese toastie. Or my nana. She makes a good ham butty. I haven't seen her in a while. I really miss her. My eyes well up and I shake it off. Now is *not* the time to transition into weepy-drunk.

Veri's coming over in a couple of days. Maybe I could try and get closer to her? I shudder at the thought. I do love hanging out with my brother, Charlie, though. Emma Penton has loads of pictures of her having cupcakes and visiting farmers' markets with her brother and her grandma. Anything's cool if you're cool. I take another slurp of my wine and then balance the glass precariously on the arm of the sofa, grabbing the pen again.

OK, good. I feel good. I'm happy drunk again! This list is the recipe for perfection. Follow the steps, and Emma Penton will appear. Looking a bit more like me, obviously. But not too much. Just so people recognise me. I squint at the piece of paper in front of me.

1. Stop smoking.
2. Lose weight.
3. Exercise.
4. See family more.

I'll start tomorrow. I drain the last of the wine and light one last cigarette. Oh god, work tomorrow. I can't cope with this. I can't spend another day in that place. I scribble one final item down.

5. Change your fucking job.

6

Jesus Christ, I'm going to be sick.

No, no I'm not. It's passed. Sort of. Maybe I've got the flu? I've never had the flu. People lose weight when they've got it, though, don't they? Maybe this is how I lose two stone and become 'bod goals'. I have been praying for this moment since secondary school. The illness that stops me eating.

Weirdly, though, the flu feels suspiciously like a hangover.

Wait. I'm remembering something . . . secret Sauvignon? I always keep a bottle of Sauvignon Blanc in the back of the wardrobe just in case Martin gives me an iota of time to myself. But no, I don't remember going in the wardrobe last night. Alvi's! My brain spits up the memory on request. I went to Alvi's corner shop and bought . . . a bottle of rosé. Oh, god. I vaguely remember shaking the last few drops into my mouth, Beyoncé's 'Run the World (Girls)' on repeat in the background. I polished off the lot. I'm such a fucking *mess*.

But I never usually drink at home . . . Martin won't even let the idea of a calorie into the apartment. I was definitely here, though. So I was able to drink . . . because Martin wasn't home. Yes, he wasn't here, I know he wasn't. Because he was out? No . . . he's never out. No . . . he wasn't home because . . . because I broke up with him! Oh my god, I binned Martin. It's all flooding back. Oh, thank the Lord Jesus our saviour.

I sprawl my legs across onto the cool side of the bed and sigh. The beer fear is at full throttle – every drop of guilt I had last night has returned, magnified to the power of ten. But I can't think about that. I have my life back. The world is mine to conquer. There is now literally nothing standing in my way. What shall I do with myself?

My phone buzzes on the bedside table. This is a failsafe way of determining my alcohol intake last night – a sober mind does not leave a phone on vibrate while it rests.

I reach out to grab it and wince as pain throbs in my temples. Bile is rising in my stomach in synchrony; a terrible orchestra of suffering. New WhatsApp message. I enter my passcode. My phone is so full of shit it takes about four hours for it to actually unlock and open. It won't even let me take photos anymore, the miserable little sod. 'Available device storage dangerously low' has screamed at me from the notifications bar for two months now. How can a lack of available space on my phone be in any way *dangerous*? The guy in charge of adverbs at Samsung needs a smack.

It's a message from Kelsey. 'Where the hell are you?'

Oh shit. Oh shit, oh shit, oh shiiiiiit.

It's a Thursday. I have a job. Small, mundane facts that normal people don't forget. Although normal people also probably don't sink enough wine in one night to fuel an Italian banquet, do they?

I throw myself out of bed, shove on my shoes, vomit in the kitchen sink and run.

'Sorry, sorry, sorry.' I sprint into the office and throw myself onto my chair, closing my eyes against the feeling of my own pulse drumming in my skull.

Silence.

I squint across at Kelsey with one eye. She is staring at me, her mouth hanging open.

'Have you been sick on yourself?'

'What? No, I don't think so.' I look down. I'm covered in reddish brown stains. *What?* I definitely got it all in the sink, I'm sure I did. And it was only a mini-vom, definitely not enough to create this war-paint effect I've got going on right now. It has also just come to my attention that I am wearing yesterday's clothes. I may also still be drunk.

'I don't . . . I'm . . . wait.' I dash out of the office and up the corridor to the bathroom, which is locked.

'Margaret?'

WHY LORD, WHY?

'Theo!' I spin round and smile, exposing my unbrushed vom-teeth to the world.

He looks me up and down shamelessly and his hand flies to his mouth. Subtlety is not his strong suit.

'Are you *unwell?*' He looks panicked, no doubt wondering if Romulus's condition is somehow transmittable to humans.

Before I have time to assess the situation and formulate a response, the bathroom door clicks open and Rachael steps out.

'Good morning, Theodore.' She flits her eyes in my direction and starts to stride towards the stairwell, her heels clipping on the lino. She slows down and stops for a second, before turning slowly and resting her gaze on me.

'Oh. My. God.' Her mouth is twitching at the corners.

I'm standing, the smile from earlier still plastered to my face, as they both stare at me in horror.

'I think I'm going to shit myself,' I say unexpectedly, and run into the bathroom, locking the door behind me.

Why the hell did I just say *that*? My defence mechanisms must have searched the archives for the absolute best thing to say to get everyone to shut up and leave me alone. Not saying anything and simply walking into the bathroom probably would have produced the same result. In any case, I'm now standing next to the toilet and I can hear Theo and Rachael discussing me at length through the locked door. Whatever.

I turn to face the mirror. Oh sweet baby JESUS. I am wearing the crumpled blouse and skirt I had on yesterday. More horrifyingly, however, are the smears of reddish brown covering my entire outfit. What *is* that?! I pull up a piece of the fabric and take a tentative sniff. Hmm. Definitely not poo. It smells a bit garlicky, a bit coriandery. Oh my god, it's the curry. I raise my eyes to my face and recoil in horror. Crusty brown flakes are tangled in my hair and there is an unmistakeable ring of lamb madras around my mouth. A smear of yellow korma sauce crumbles off my forehead as I touch it. It hits me that I must have stumbled into Alvi's dressed like this last night. I'll have to start forking out for Sainsbury's wine from now on.

I came to work covered in curry. This is the absolute low point of my life. It cannot get any worse than this.

What am I supposed to do? How didn't I realise that I was wearing yesterday's clothes? How didn't I remember that my bed was full of curry? How didn't I *notice*?

Ah, wine. You sneaky little bastard.

OK. Right. No time to wallow, must problem-solve. I can't sit in these clothes all day; that is not an option if I want to remain in employment long enough to file my personal injury claim. I can't go home again, not after I did absolutely nothing yesterday.

There's only one thing for it. I pull out my phone and fire off a text. Ten seconds later, no doubt fuelled out of her chair by the promise of hearing the details of my latest drama, Kelsey knocks on the door.

'Maggie? Are you OK?'

I unlock the door and open it an inch.

'I need your gym gear,' I whisper.

'What? No! Theodore says you've shit yourself. I don't really want that on my gym clothes . . .'

'I haven't shit myself!' I hiss. 'I had to get Theo off my case. It's curry. I slept in curry.'

'You slept in curry?' She presses her face to the gap in the door and scans me up and down with one bulging eyeball.

'Yes! I don't have time to explain, I need clothes. Give me your gym stuff.'

'I ran six miles in it this morning, it's all sweaty.' She grimaces, but I catch the slight smile on her face as she basks in her glowy, post-run freshness and compares it to my current situation. *Oh, good for you, Kelsey. You ran. You pumped your legs up and down like every human ever. Woop-de-fucking-do.*

Oh my god, this is not the point. *Stop being a jealous, malicious cow and problem-solve, Maggie!* 'I don't care. Please, Kelsey? I'll buy you new stuff!'

'God.' She sighs. 'It's all right, I don't want Primark's finest. Just wash them and give them back as soon as possible, OK?'

This is absolutely horrific. I have squeezed my size twelve (OK, fine, fourteen) body into size eight leggings and an XS sports bra. Both are white and my exposed flab is almost indistinguishable from the fabric. I look like a multipack of kitchen roll. There also does not appear to be a t-shirt or vest of any kind. I can't bear to go out there; my boobs have been squished so much that they are threatening to burst out from under my armpits. I am almost certain I will never be able to breastfeed after this.

The horrific stench of curry and alcohol is mingling with Kelsey's freshly squeezed B.O. and my stomach is threatening to add vomit to the mix. This bathroom is a hotbox of pain. I am so tempted to shove my curry clothes back on and run home. I could put on fresh pyjamas and just start again tomorrow. An image of my empty money sock swims into my mind. I can't risk taking another day off and losing this job. No. I have to suck it up (in, actually) and get on with it. Confidence is key.

I yank the window open and pull my cigarettes from my pocket. Something twitches at the back of my mind – another memory from last night – but I can't grab it. I smoke quickly, sticking my head out of the window and gulping in the cold morning air.

Before I can think, I bundle up my soiled clothes, hold them over my stomach to cover what little remains of my dignity and unlock the door. The musty air of the basement wafts through and I stop for a second, trying one last time to stuff my boobs into the bra, before striding down the corridor with purpose.

I make it back into the office and ignore Kelsey's sniggering as I plonk my blindingly white arse into my chair. I shovel my stinking clothes into my backpack and turn on my computer, feeling the unyielding lycra pushing on my vital organs and threatening to cause internal bleeding. Just five hours and forty-six more minutes of this and I get to go home and wash another woman's sweat out of my armpit stubble.

The latest steaming pile of turd to land on my to-do list is a product called 'NestWell', which promises pregnant women clear skin, energy and improved mental capacity whilst they prepare for the death of their social life and any other interests they may have had outside of Peppa Pig and wiping piss off the bathroom walls. Studies (funded by the pharmaceutical company who make NestWell) have found the drug to be seventy-eight per cent effective in fifty-nine per cent of cases. This maths is too much for me, both numerically and in terms of how utterly dire it sounds, so I transform it into 'NestWell has been tested on hundreds of women, with life-changing results.' I don't feel too much guilt writing this one, because a side-effect of chronic diarrhoea really could change your life for a while.

'Ladies!' Theo is at the door, clapping his hands like he's summoning a pack of huskies. 'Conference room, now, please.'

Calling a windowless cell containing a chipped IKEA table and several chairs with missing legs a 'conference room' is an outrageous overstatement that I believe Theo has employed to help himself sleep at night. But this is beside the point; I now have to walk into a room full of people whilst dressed like the Michelin man after an over-indulgent Christmas.

Kelsey and I make our way down the corridor and into the conference room, where Ben, Mohammed and Rachael are sat idly tapping on their phone screens. Theo is wrestling with the projector remote in the corner, stabbing it aggressively and waving it in the air. The projector begins to screech ominously.

Mohammed looks up. 'Christ on a bike.'

Ben and Rachael flick their eyes up from their screens and do a quick double take when they see me.

'Erm . . . Maggie?' Ben's mouth is hanging open and he looks quite concerned.

'For god's sake guys, have you never seen gym gear before?' I laugh. 'People wear it everywhere these days!' I aim this last comment at Rachael – I've seen her Instagram feed.

'Yeah . . .' she grimaces, 'but usually it, you know . . . fits.' She shoots a pointed glance at my crotch. I look down. Oh no. I'm rocking the world's most hideous camel toe. I'm standing here flashing a porcelain-white mould of my own genitalia to every single one of my colleagues. Kelsey has taken a seat and is eyeing me with horror; no doubt repulsed by the idea that the seam of her £60 leggings is currently threatening to render me infertile.

I grab my fanny, dignity now absolutely out of the window, and scurry to the last empty seat between Rachael and Mohammed. Theo, who is unaware of my recent show of public indecency, makes his way to the front of the room.

'Right, the projector isn't working so I'm afraid I'll have to do some on-the-spot stuff for you!' He titters, 'I knew my improv classes would come in handy one day; "nothing is for nothing", as Professor Aldman used to say!'

'Oh my god.' Rachael is leaning back in her chair with her hand over her mouth. 'What is that *smell*?'

'Yeah, it stinks. Is that B.O.?' Mohammed is sniffing the air like a dog. 'Jesus, who *is* that?'

For fuck's sake.

'It's these clothes, they're not mine, they're—'

'Ew, yeah, it smells like pasties!' Kelsey screeches, flashing me a half-apologetic look.

Bitch! That's *her* B.O. they're all inhaling, and she's just dropped me in it! She looks around the room nervously, checking that no one suspects her in the body odour witch-hunt she has inadvertently created. I've been framed.

'OK, people! Let's calm down please!' Theo taps his pen on the table like an angry schoolteacher.

We all fall silent, and Rachael makes a show of wrapping her pashmina scarf around her face like she's fleeing a burning building.

'Now,' Theo sucks in through his nose, 'you're probably wondering why I gathered you all here today.' Seriously, he thinks he's in a film. 'Before we get to the point, though, I'd like to thank you all for your well-wishes regarding Romulus and his current . . . condition.' He lets his gaze wander over to a card that he has displayed on the table, the words *IGUANA WISH YOU A SPEEDY RECOVERY!* emblazoned on the front. I don't get it.

'You're welcome, Theodore. I wish him all the best,' Kelsey simpers. That girl really will do anything to get to the top.

'He's stabilised slightly, you'll all be glad to hear, and ate three Brazilian vine leaves this morning.' Theo gives a watery smile to the room. 'As much as it pains me to move on, however, I need to discuss an upcoming event. As you are aware, we have a big client hoping to work with us on selling their newest range of post-menopausal drugs. This is obviously very exciting.' Is it, though? 'Coincidentally, there is a conference at the Wilcoxon Hotel next week to discuss the regulatory strategies and consumer behaviours of over-the-counter post-menopausal medication. I'm sure I don't need to tell you how useful this could be to us moving forward. Attending this conference and gaining the expertise of the attending speakers will give us a huge advantage, and will help us in proving to our new client that we have the knowledge to carry this partnership forward into the future.'

Oh my god, I'm so bored. I feel like someone has buried razorblades in my brain. My stomach gurgles ominously. Maybe I really *am* going to shit myself. Theo is absolutely loving the boring news he's sharing with us – he gets to go to a conference once every millennium, usually getting the information packs sent down afterwards from the big bosses, and he treats every invite like he's visiting Pierce Brosnan for Martinis and nibbles. The next week leading up to this is going to be hell. He's pausing now, revving us up into his big reveal.

I do wonder how PowerPoint could have come in useful during this meeting. Thank god the projector's broken.

'Now, I'm afraid I only have *two tickets* to this prestigious event.' He's wiggling with glee. Rachael sits up straighter and lowers the pashmina from her face, nodding interestedly. Rachael *lives* for networking opportunities. 'I have thought long and hard about this decision, and although this may surprise you, I have decided that the person I will be bringing along is . . .' He points his finger around the room like a radar, making a rising 'oooooooooooo' noise for suspense. Rachael, Ben and Mohammed are sitting forward in their chairs, practically wagging their tails and slobbering all over the table. Kelsey is filing her nails. I am trying to simultaneously remove my camel-toe and not throw up. 'Margaret!' Theo's finger lands on me and everyone turns.

'What?' I look up from inspecting my crotch.

'I know, I know, this is surprising! Margaret is the *last* person any of us would expect to be asked to attend an event of this calibre.' Everyone nods in agreement.

'She's not out in the field, Theodore. She wouldn't even understand any of it.' Ben pipes up helpfully.

'Yes I would!' I lean forward. 'I would! I've got a Biology degree.'

I'm quite excited by this – I've been chosen! Despite everything I said to Kelsey yesterday about not wanting to progress here, it does feel quite nice to be given a chance to do something different. Maybe Theo has picked me out as the next rising star!

I try not to think too much about whether that's actually what I want. *Just enjoy the moment, Maggie.*

'No, I didn't mean that.' Ben shakes his head. 'I'm sure you'd *understand* it, it's just . . . how would you *use* it?'

Is Ben aware that every word that comes out of his mouth at doctor's meetings is crafted by me? No, of course he isn't. Thinking about it, I'm really the *only* logical choice for this.

'Yes, yes, I know, an *unusual* choice!' Theo squawks dramatically, desperately trying to reclaim the attention of the room. 'But Maggie has very neat handwriting and I need precise minutes of every second of this. It's a *huge* deal.'

Oh. Right, good. How silly of me to think that Theo was handing me an actual opportunity. Educational certificates mean nothing when you can produce legible notes.

'Kelsey's your P.A., isn't this something she should be doing?' I must get out of this. Now that I've been branded note-taker, my enthusiasm has gone straight back out of the window.

'Oh my god, she doesn't even *want* to go.' Rachael is looking at me like I'm a particularly nasty smear on the wall of a public bathroom. How I would love to find something I feel so passionately about. 'I'll take notes! I can write neatly!'

'Yep, I'm happy for Rachael to go.' I smile at her. She gapes back at me.

'Excellent.' Rachael smiles and nods. 'She said I could go, Theo, did you hear that?'

Wow, it's quite a thrill having all this power.

'Unless Ben or Mohammed fancy a shot at it—' I start.

'No, no, I'll go! It's no problem, I'll go.' She scrabbles on the desk for a pen. 'What date was it, did he say?'

'LADIES!' Theo's voice has risen to a panicked shriek, such is his despair that we are not all riveted by his performance. 'My decision is final! Margaret, the conference is next Tuesday. I'll email you the itinerary when it comes through and you'll need to bring three large notebooks and eight pens. At least. Actually, make that nine.'

The sales team slump back in their chairs, Mohammed muttering under his breath about the 'injustice' of it all. I do not get paid enough for this shit.

'Right,' Theo is resigned now, his act has flopped. 'I'll be at my neonatal first-aid class this afternoon so just get on with whatever you're doing.' He shuffles dejectedly out of the room.

'Neonatal first aid?' Ben frowns. 'I didn't know he was having a baby.'

'It's for that bloody iguana.' Rachael is winding her pashmina around her neck with such force I'm surprised she can still breathe.

'Margaret,' Theo pokes his head back round the door. 'When we're all finished in here, would you freshen it up a bit?' He throws a bottle of Febreeze onto the table. 'It absolutely reeks.'

7

My first evening alone as a newly single woman. If we don't count last night, which I don't, because my philosophy is that if you can't remember something then it didn't happen.

I am sitting on the floor, wearing my biggest, ugliest clothes pulled straight off the maiden in the living room the moment I stepped out of the shower. I have scrubbed my body raw, put the soiled clothes of shame in the washing machine and I am watching the swirl of white Lycra spinning around with my curried blouse.

I am so embarrassed. What must everyone think of me, turning up to work like that? I almost miss Martin. I could have come home and ranted off to him about it, and he would have made me feel better.

Oh, who am I kidding? I wouldn't have told him, and if I had, he'd have only told me how much sugar was in all the wine I drank.

What shall I do? It's so long since I've had an evening to myself that I feel a bit lost, and I need a distraction because my mind is going into overdrive. I can't stop thinking about how much I despise my job. My first *real* job; when I was offered it I ran around for weeks telling everyone I was going to be a scientific writer and had visions of work socials and climbing the career ladder. Once the first month had passed I realised it was so boring that I couldn't be bothered to put the energy in to even try and progress. And where would I go? Into a sales rep position? Into a better paid, equally boring medical writing post with six times the responsibility? Even when I thought Theo was giving me my first break today, there was a voice in the back of my mind: *this isn't what you want.* I think the thing about a full-time job is that it's great in theory, but actually doing it is a real ball-ache.

Although . . . what if I *can* make something of this? Yes, I'll be at the conference to take minutes, but couldn't I network a bit? Schmooze around and see if there are any other positions going, something more exciting? I'm not sure it's exactly what I want, but anything's better than where I am right now, surely?

I feel shit, and when I feel shit I eat – preferably an equal mixture of carbs and fat. It's been a really successful coping mechanism so far. In the spirit of doing whatever the hell I want now I'm alone, I go to my old faithful Domino's app and create my very own signature pizza – pepperoni, pineapple and barbeque sauce with extra cheese.

I'm about to check out when I remember that I have literally *no money.* I can't use my money sock unless it's a Grade A emergency, and yesterday's curry has rinsed it almost dry. If I buy this pizza then I can't get tampons, and my boobs are in agony so that's probably going to be a necessity pretty soon.

Why is life so hard? I'm finding it difficult to think because I keep getting distracted by how fat and disgusting I feel. Today's humiliation has really brought my weight issue home; two years of living with Martin and his extreme health regime made me a secret eater. The woman at the Greggs next to work knows my name.

I should eat some poached eggs and spinach. Or some kale and crushed carrot. Emma Penton is always eating things like that – her Instagram is full of it and her body is on fire. I really need to try harder at being one of those clean-eating women; maybe even get a pestle and mortar so I can crush my own linseeds and take artistic photos of it sitting on my windowsill.

My mind twinges again with a vague shadow of a memory from last night. I can't grasp it.

I heave myself up and dig a pepperoni pizza out of the freezer, where I had hidden it underneath the frozen peas and ice bags. It's one of those Dr. Oetker Ristorante ones that look nice and crispy and only cost a quid. I slide it out of its packaging and all the cheese has shifted to one side, the pepperoni congregating in the middle. Tears spring to my eyes. Why is this happening to me?

I call Cecilia. As the closest of my three best friends, she is the one who truly knows how to talk me down. Plus she's a freelancer, so she *always* answers the phone. She picks up on the first ring.

'Maggie?'

'I broke up with Martin.' I'm sobbing now.

'Oh, great! Wait . . . you're crying. Why are you crying?'

'My frozen pizza looks shit.'

'Oh, Mags, I'm so sorry.'

'It's OK. Why is it always me?' Snot is running down my chin and I catch it with my sleeve.

'You're just unlucky. You always manage to pick the one where the toppings have migrated.'

'I know. It's so *unfair*.'

'Hey, come on. Get a Domino's. That always makes you feel better.'

'No money. I went to work covered in curry.' I'm giving her random facts now.

She laughs. 'What did Theo say about that?'

'Asked me to go to a conference with him.'

'Wow. That's great news, isn't it? You should cover yourself in food more often.'

'I don't want to go. He just wants me to take notes. I'm so *fat*.'

48

'Hey! Stop that. You're not fat, you're a beautiful, sassy, independent woman.' Someone shouts in the background. 'Yep, coming! Sorry, Mags, David's got tea on the table. Call you later?'

'Yeah, OK. Thanks C.'

'Shut up. Go and eat your pizza and listen to the *Mamma Mia* soundtrack. You know that makes you happy.'

'Will do. Say hi to David for me.'

'All right. See ya.'

Cecilia is so *nice*. Feisty, defensive and moody sometimes, but nice. She, Anna and Sophie have been my best friends for nine years now, and she's definitely the most mature of the four of us. She lives in a little two-bedroom terrace with her lovely boyfriend David and has loads of cute photos everywhere and potted plants. She's so together. I can picture her now, sitting at the dinner table and eating freshly made lasagne off quirky plates that don't match, talking about work and laughing as she sips her glass of £8 Chardonnay. She'll leave the rest of the bottle in the fridge for tomorrow night, too. She has self-control. My head throbs to remind me that I do not.

I slide my ugly pizza into the oven. It still stinks of last night's dry chicken and reminds me of my proposal. I almost forgot about that. I suddenly realise that Martin proposed to me whilst I had a prawn wedged in my hair; I found it in the shower earlier. How much time have I wasted being with Martin? How much time have I wasted *full stop*? Season seven of *The Office*, for Christ's sake, and I only started it two weeks ago.

I light a cigarette and stand by the window. God, my life's a mess.

I smoke slowly and sadly, looking out for the pigeon who doesn't appear, before heading into the bedroom to throw myself onto the bed and wallow. I nudge the bedroom door open with my shoulder and am greeted by what looks like the aftermath of an incredibly violent murder. My sheets are tangled in the middle of the bed, smeared with brown and red, and the stench is unbearable. For a moment I am shocked – *what the hell is this?* And then I remember the proposal, the curry, sleeping in the curry, humiliating myself at work, exposing my camel toe to everyone. How do I keep forgetting about all of this?

I strip the bed angrily. Thank god Mum convinced me to get a waterproof mattress protector (*in case you have an accident, darling, remember how often you used to wet yourself?*) as the curry has seeped through the fitted sheet and left vicious splodges that would have stained the mattress forever.

It's only after I have balled everything up and carried it through to the living room that I remember that the washing machine is full of other contaminated goods. I stand in the middle of the room, holding the bundle in front of my face and inhaling my shame, before shoving on my shoes and walking out of the front door. I make my way down the corridor, bed sheets trailing behind me, and down the stairs to the bin room, where I chuck the lot.

Fuelled by furious energy, I storm back into the bedroom and pull fresh bedsheets out of the wardrobe. I shake the fitted sheet out and, as it billows, a piece of paper wafts off the bedside table and settles on the floor.

I pick it up.

1. Stop smoking.
2. Lose weight.
3. Exercise.
4. See family more.
5. Change your fucking job.

The memory rushes back to me with force. A bottle of wine, Martin leaving, a new start, the despair.

A list. I made a list.

I gaze at it, slowly taking in each item. Every single thing seems completely undoable in the cold light of my hangover. I can't imagine stepping on a treadmill, eating salad or hanging out with Veri. And changing my job? I've just been given the opportunity to network, is now really the time?

I scrunch up the list and put it in my pocket. I was drunk; nobody follows through on drunk plans. How many brunches have I organised six vodka-and-cokes in? Hundreds. And how many have I attended? None.

Oh my god, my pizza. I run to the oven and get a burnt-pepperoni-scented steam facial as I fling the door open. The meat mountain in the middle is tinged black, and the crust looks like something you'd find in a bonfire pit.

No, be positive, I'm sure it's still edible. This is how they do it in Italy, isn't it? You get the black parts on it for extra flavour. I slice it up and it crumbles like ash, but this is a good thing – didn't pregnant women used to eat coal for the extra nutrients? I'm sure it's the same.

It tastes like a cigarette butt.

I flop onto the sofa and take out my phone, gnawing on a slightly less-black slice. Oh, look. Emma Penton is in Vietnam. She's standing on the beach, holding a crab, her taut stomach glaring at me.

Ugh. I pull out the list again and smooth it out on the table.

I've got to change *something.* I open my laptop and head to Amazon, feeling like a self-controlled millionaire because I cooked my own (inedible) food in the oven. I wonder if this is how Nigella Lawson feels every single day? Although she uses things like organic buttermilk and Tuscan truffles, so she's probably spending more than I am.

I type 'electronic cigarette' into the search bar. My brain battles with conflicting feelings. On the one hand, I am really, really not ready for this. On the other hand, will I ever be ready? I force myself to keep looking.

I've found a particularly cute-looking one which actually resembles a cigarette, sort of, and is only eight quid. I shove it in the basket quickly, before I can contemplate that there might be a reason it's so cheap, and have a look at the e-liquid stuff

I'll apparently be needing too. There are *so* many flavours, my brain can't cope. Lemon meringue pie, iced caramel latte, vanilla chai. Oh my god, they have blue flavour! I *love* blue flavour, like those ice pops you get from the corner shop. Three for £7, too! I add them to my basket, maximum nicotine content, and check out. Total price: £15, leaving me with £5 in my account – plenty to buy a box of Tampax Super. Excellent.

I suddenly feel lighter. This is a new beginning. Maybe once I've quit the cigarettes I can move on to exercising; become one of those inspirational people who document their journey from potato to ninja. I could start tumbling, or Parkour, and wear tiny sports bras and hotpants and not even my boobs would jiggle when I ran. Imagine what everyone would think of me then. The possibilities are now endless.

My computer pings with an incoming email. My order receipt from Amazon. I open it to get rid of the unread icon on my inbox and go to close it again when I stop.

Estimated delivery date: 5th April.

WHAT? Today is the 1st March. That's an entire *month* away. How can it possibly take so long? Are they sending it by carrier pigeon? Is a man hand-delivering it on foot from Moscow? What about the new life I had planned? The universe is ruining everything for me today. Why does all the bad stuff happen when I'm bat-shit hormonal?

I try to ignore the gleeful little voice in the back of my mind: *you don't have to quit for a while, then.* My mood lifts again. I am bolstered by the rush of making a change, whilst also knowing that I don't actually have to do anything *right this very second.* It's completely out of my control, really.

I get up and slide the rest of the blackened pizza into the bin, but as soon as I do, the sad, guilty voice in my brain gets a little bit louder, my good mood receding. I have to hold onto this positive feeling, I can't let myself dwell. But now I have no food, and it's like someone has snatched the crutch that was holding me upright from under my arm. I feel an urge so strong I can't see straight; I am alone and able to indulge and comfort myself as much as I want – no eyes watching. I can hide and get my fix and hate myself later, when the high has waned and the regret and self-loathing throb and strain against my waistband.

No. I can fight against this. I've done it in the past. I just need a distraction. Following Cecilia's advice, I shuffle an ABBA playlist on Spotify and try to think about my new, smoke-free future, postponed until April, when I will be ready and better and won't feel this way anymore.

'Mamma Mia' is the first song on the list. I try to get into the music, to absorb the happy beat, and for a second it works. I force myself to dance around the living room, singing along, thinking about Greece and boats and sunshine. But then, slowly, I realise they're singing about never learning, losing control, making the same mistakes again and again. I make my way over to my laptop to change the song and stub my toe hard on the coffee table. It feels like a sign.

I stab it off, grab a loaf of bread, a knife and half a tub of low fat cream cheese. I crawl into my unmade bed and cry.

8

It's Friday evening and I feel marginally better. I managed to get through the day without any further embarrassment, and now the working week is over. There's so much free time ahead of me for lounging around and hating myself.

I just have to get through a visit from Veri first.

It's three minutes to seven and if I know my sister, she will arrive precisely on time. There's actually a chance she's already standing outside, waiting for 7 p.m. to strike so she can press the buzzer with her long, annoying fingernail. I cast a cursory glance around the living room and throw a couple of mugs in the sink. It'll do.

As predicted, bang on seven, I buzz her up to the apartment. She storms through the door and throws her bag on the table.

'It's dark in here.'

'Hiii, nice to see you too.' I flick the kettle on.

She sets about tweaking the curtains, opening the windows and turning on the lamps. She's got a greater range of movement in her skirt suit than I have in my pyjamas. She has a home gym that she religiously pounds at five o'clock every morning. 'So, you're fine?'

'I'm fine . . .' I plaster a smile on my face. 'You really don't need to check on me.'

'Well,' she sniffs, 'I am very busy.'

'I know. Sit down. Tea?'

'Honey. No milk.'

I don't have honey, so I turn my back to her and plop a heaped teaspoon of sugar into her mug.

'Spoken to Charlie recently?' I try.

'Yesterday. He's fatter.'

She holds her hand out for her tea. I hand it to her and watch as she takes a sip. No comment. She's evidently not as clever as she thinks she is. I feel momentarily bad for the jolt of satisfaction I get from knowing she is also a complete fool sometimes. Yes, it's only sugar, but she is *oblivious*.

'So. You need to sort yourself out.' She raises her eyebrows at me.

'Oh, we're getting straight into it, are we?'

I grit my teeth and mentally check myself. If I rise to this, neither of us will get out of here unscathed. Also, Mum will go berserk if she hears one of us has thrown a mug at the other again.

'Look at yourself. Look at this place. You're not a student anymore, Maggie.'

I literally feel my heckles go up. 'I'm aware of that, thank you.' *I won't defend myself, I won't defend myself, I won't defend myself.* 'I'm making some pretty big changes, actually. Lots of things on the horizon.'

For fuck's sake.

'Oh?' She squints down into her cup of tea. 'This tastes funny. Is it Manuka honey?'

'No, no. Tesco.'

She sighs. 'You don't half buy some shite.'

We lapse into silence. I light a cigarette.

'You need to pack that in.'

'Yep. Like I said, I'm making big changes.' I lean on the windowsill.

She snorts. 'Looks like it.'

Sod it.

I dig around in my pocket and pull out the balled-up list. I throw it at her. She opens it and smooths it out, pushing her glasses down her nose. She looks about ninety, she needs to lighten up. *Don't be horrible, Maggie. She's your sister.*

'For god's sake.' She mutters, tossing it onto the table.

'What?'

'Well, what does this mean? That you've thought of all the things that are wrong with you but that you have no intention of changing?'

'*No.*' I'm reaching explosion point with her. Thank god I put the mugs in the sink. 'It's all the stuff I'm *going* to do.'

She picks it back up again and starts reading in a mocking, sing-song voice.

'Number one: stop smoking.' She stares at my cigarette. 'Great job, well done.'

'My e-cigarette hasn't arrived yet!'

'Number two: lose weight. Not difficult, stop stuffing your mouth with crap. Number three: Exercise.' She looks me up and down. 'Oh, I *agree.* Number four: See family more.' She laughs. 'I think you have bigger things to focus on than whether or not you've scrounged tea off Mum and Dad or not this week.'

'No, that's not—'

'Number five: change your fucking job.' She rolls her eyes. 'You don't need to change your job, Maggie, you need to actually get off your arse and put some effort in.'

'You need to *piss off.*' I bellow.

Silence again.

I close the window and scratch my eyebrow.

'Well, I've got a dinner to get to.' She rises from the sofa and takes her bag, throwing one last disdainful glance around the living room. 'I can't finish that tea, it's disgusting.'

I threw the list away last night. As soon as Veri left, I ate three packets of biscuits, screamed out of my bedroom window, tied my duvet around myself like a toga and chucked my resolutions in the bin. I tried *so* hard not to let Veri's thoughts about the list get into my head, but she has this effect on me. At thirty-two, she's the oldest of the three of us, and I'm so used to her being right that it's difficult to take what she says with perspective. I couldn't stop wondering whether this was just another silly, immature fad of mine – something everyone in the family laughs at over Sunday dinner.

I've calmed down a bit now. Once I crashed from all the sugar I slept for about ten hours, and woke up with a fresh (and guilty) perspective. I had a shower, ate some low-fat cereal and berated myself until I came to the conclusion that yesterday was a blip, Veri is a twat, and I need to start again.

I am now fishing through yogurt pots and microwave chip boxes to try and locate the list.

Eventually, when I am elbow-deep inside an empty tub of chocolate ice cream, my fingers brush against paper. I pull it out delicately by one corner and put it on the side. It has seen better days. Briefly, I consider writing it out again, but I don't trust myself not to delete things or give them caveats that make them easier for me, and I am still punishing myself for yesterday. I deserve a difficult path to perfection – I am too much of a disaster for it to be easy.

I set the hairdryer on the list for a couple of minutes. It looks like one of those early secondary school assignments where you'd dip your essay in tea and wrinkle it up to make it look like a war letter from the 1940s. I was always really good at those, although I rarely listened to the brief and just wrote love notes to my imaginary husband in Germany. *'What a vivid imagination you have, Maggie! Next time, could we try writing more about Hitler and less about your "dandy"? 3/10'* was the general response. Veri knew more about Hitler than the teacher did. That's probably why she's such a dictatorial bitch.

Fuck Veri, I think as I waft the hairdryer around the kitchen counter top. I can't deny that her dismissal of my vow to

57

spend more time with family hurt the most. Maybe she's half right, though; she has no interest in having a relationship with me, so why should I bother with her? And it's not exactly like she's in an enviable position, is it? All she does is work and turn her nose up at everybody. She can't relate to my situation at all because she's always made good decisions and had it easy. She makes about five times as much money as me and doesn't seem to spend it on anything other than pinstripe garments from H&M and going out for tea at Australasia.

Speaking of meals out, I'm supposed to be having tea with the girls tonight. My money situation is still dire – I don't get paid until Wednesday – so I did suggest on the WhatsApp group that we grab a sandwich from Tesco or something, but they laughed and thought I was joking.

In light of this issue, I immediately call my mum to see if she will give me an advance on my birthday money. Yes, I'm twenty-seven, no, I shouldn't still be getting birthday money and no, I certainly shouldn't still be asking my parents to bail me out. But this is an *emergency*.

'But your birthday is in *July*, Maggie.'

'I know that, but—'

'It's *March*.' She's speaking to me like I'm one of the five-year-olds she teaches.

'Yes, I *know*, but council tax was really high this month, and I've got nothing left.' Translation: I've burned all my money on wine, unnecessary ASOS purchases and Greggs.

'Council tax rates haven't gone up, have they? I'm sure you'll still be in the same band as you were last month?'

Dammit. Should have gone with the electric bill.

'Yeah, no, ours has because they've installed a chimney on the roof I think. It increases the value of the building.'

'A *chimney*? Whatever for?'

'The woman in the penthouse on the top floor just got a wood-burning stove. Selfish cow.'

'*Did* she? Well, you should take that up with the council! That's not fair at all!'

'No, I know, exactly. I'm on it; me and HMRC have been in conversation and I'm totally sorting it.'

'Well, good for you.' I can hear her clattering about with pots and pans and I sense that I'm losing her.

'So could I possibly borrow fifty quid? Just to see me through 'til payday? I'll send it straight back on Wednesday, I promise.'

'All right, darling. I'll send it over when I've made this béchamel. You keep hounding the council until they bring your tax back down, though – and go and pay a visit to that inconsiderate penthouse lady; what's she thinking installing a wood-burning stove in a city-centre apartment? It's outrageous! I don't want you dying in your sleep.'

Well, that's nice. I will absolutely not be heading up to visit the penthouse anytime soon. Mainly because nobody actually lives there at the moment, but also because anyone who does move there is about as likely to install a chimney as I am to lose five stone and make it in Hollywood.

I wish her well with her béchamel and promise to call tomorrow to speak to my dad before ending the call. My parents are wonderful people, really. My mum's a primary school teacher and my dad's a lawyer, and they live the middle-class dream in the leafy suburbs of Sale. I go home about once every couple of months and stay over, and my Mum cooks and feeds me wine while my Dad quizzes me on why I'm still paying vast amounts of money to live in the city and haven't yet had my first promotion. I think I'm a complete enigma to them; they just can't get their head around why I wouldn't want to get out of the rental market and tie myself down to a property and a never-ending mortgage, which, thinking about it, may possibly have contributed to my feverish persual of a committed relationship when I met Martin. They also don't get my lack of ambition – how can I not know what I want to do? My Dad cannot understand how anyone can *possibly* not know what they want to do with their lives.

'When your Mum and I were your age . . .' is his favourite phrase.

'When your Mum and I were your age, we got straight on the housing market as soon as we got married. It was so *exciting* to own our own place!'

'When your Mum and I were your age, we knew *exactly* what we wanted to do – and we helped each other get there!'

These statements generally don't go down well. More often than not, I will remind him that they got married at twenty-two, managed to buy their first house for about 20p and knew what their 'calling' was from birth. They also weren't faced with social media and its constant display of perfect lives which are better and more exciting than their own, and the crippling anxiety and indecision which comes with seeing every day what you *could* do, but having no idea where to start. Do I travel round Asia for six months? Do I aim to rake in enough commission to afford a luxury apartment? Do I teach English as a foreign language in Spain and fall madly in love with a man called José who will inevitably cheat on me and destroy my faith in men? How are you supposed to settle when so much is out there?

It doesn't help that my brother and sister are both successful, well-rounded and well-travelled. It's like two living, breathing counter arguments ruining my defence.

I usually take the tram back feeling like I've just had the foundations of my entire existence shat on, and vow never to go home again. Until my mum calls a few weeks later and says there's roast beef for dinner on Sunday and I rush back, pimping out my self-esteem for roast potatoes like the animal I am.

It's 3 p.m. and I need a shower. Unfortunately, the timer on my boiler doesn't work, meaning I have to turn it on two hours before I need a wash and wait for the water to slowly heat up. It then takes a further two hours to tame my hair, which is like a mane of frazzled pubes if I leave it without intervention.

I flick on the hot water switch; by my calculations I will be ready at exactly 7 p.m. This slightly clashes with my six-thirty meeting time with the girls, but I have the excuse that I'm a ridiculously disorganised and catastrophic individual, so they should be fine with it.

We're meeting at The Alchemist in Spinningfields, where one drink will soak up nearly a quarter of my funds for the evening, and then heading to Ibérica for Spanish food, where three meatballs on a side plate costs as much as I spend on my weekly shop. If I want to enjoy myself and not starve, I'll have to employ my 'expensive evening prep strategy', involving downing half a bottle of wine and eating three packets of crisps before I leave.

To avoid the inevitable time-wasting drama later, I head into the bedroom to pick out my outfit. The process goes as it usually does – I open my wardrobe, flick through my dresses as though something new might show itself to me, shut the wardrobe, open each drawer, rifle through my skirts, throw half of them on the floor and then leave the room. I have *nothing* to wear. Cecilia and Sophie always seem to turn up to every occasion in an outfit I have never seen before, and Anna mix-and-matches all her colourful skirts and tops to create a new, edgy look each time. I always try on all the clothes that I *know* don't suit me, in the hope that somehow something might have changed, before shoving on the jeans and vest top combination I've been rocking since 2009.

My phone vibrates constantly on the table with WhatsApp messages from the girls about this evening, and I flick through them idly whilst I half-watch an episode of *The Big Bang Theory* I've seen forty times.

Anna: MAJOR story to tell you all later :D

Sophie: omg stop, what is it?!

Cecilia: What have you done now? :'D

Anna: I'll tell you later over a cocktail, it's worth the wait I promise! First order of business ;)

Shit. I'll have to get there on time or I'll miss the original rendition of this fresh nugget from the gossip goldmine.

I step into the shower, which relaxes me in a way I imagine having thousands of tiny, freshly formed icicles pelted against one's bare skin might soothe the soul.

I wash quickly, forcing myself to stay under the water until I can no longer feel my face, before stepping out of the shower to begin my intense moisturising regime. Martin's disgusting deodorant (which actually smells very nice) is still sitting under the mirror, so I wedge it in the overflowing bin under the sink.

I pull out my cocoa butter and start lathering it up my legs, but my eyes keep wandering back to the deodorant can, forlornly peeking at me from its makeup wipe nest. I stare at it for a second, and then take it back out again and line it up next to my Dove roll-on. The image in front of me used to be all I wanted; the his-and-hers, the shared space, the casual indicators of a life gone *right*, with two people under one roof spraying their armpits in harmony as they groggily swerve around one another each morning. But adding Martin (who would hold the can precisely six inches away from his skin, as directed) as my co-star in the fantasy makes a teary wail wedge in my throat.

I put it back in the bin and slam the lid.

It's 6.45 p.m. and I am the only one here. I still haven't warmed up from my shower – despite cracking open the secret Sauvignon before leaving – and I'm nursing a hot cider alone at a table I've managed to bag.

My phone rings and I hold it against my shoulder, keeping my arms around the warmth of the mug. It's my brother, Charlie.

'Veri's here.' he says before I've had chance to speak.

'Christ.' I sigh. 'She's told Mum and Dad that I'm living in a cesspit and now they're worried sick, is that about the gist of it?'

'Bang on the money.' He lowers his voice. 'She's actually mental, you know? She turned up today with a photo of herself standing outside court after winning some appeal – some newspaper printed it – and she's only gone and hung it on the *wall*.'

I snort. 'She staying for tea?'

'Yes.' He coughs. 'I'm on the *phone*, Veri! It's Maggie. Fine, god, sorry Mags.'

There's a muffled scratching as the phone is passed over, and then my sister is speaking. I've been trapped.

'There's a bag of your old clothes here, Maggie. You need to come and sort them out, give them to charity or something. You can't expect Mum and Dad to just—'

'Oops, Veri, I've got to go. My friends are here. Speak soon! Say hi to everyone for me!' I end the call.

I feel a gulp of guilt drop down into my stomach. I should make more of an effort. I haven't cleared my clothes out. I haven't ticked any items off my list.

'Maggie, you're on time!' Anna wraps her arms around me from behind, resting her head on my shoulder. 'Jeans and a vest top, nice to see you're experimenting with your style.'

'Shut up.' I slap her arm. Anna looks amazing in a purple, floaty maxi skirt and black, sleeveless blouse. Tendrils of dark hair are escaping out of her loose bun and framing her face, which is flushed red from the cold.

She scoots into the seat opposite me and takes my hands across the table. She's always been a *very* touchy-feely person.

'I heard about Martin.' She gives me the type of eye-contact usually reserved for wedding vows or telling someone their father has died. 'I'm so sorry.'

I stare at her blankly. 'Are you serious?'

She breaks into a huge grin and throws herself back into her seat. 'Oh, thank *god*. I was worried you'd be all miserable and depressing about it.'

'Did you meet Martin? "Miserable and depressing" is his dictionary definition.' I feel mean saying it, but it's true.

She laughs. 'God, *two years*. How did you do it?'

'What, break up with him or cope for so long?' *Sorry, Martin. I really do wish you well.*

'Both. Tell me everything.'

Sophie and Cecilia choose this moment to squeeze through the crowds towards us, and as soon as we've all hugged repeatedly, complimented each other's hair and are cradling fresh drinks, I fill them in.

'Christ alive.' Sophie takes a long draw of her Martini. 'All that time and it was as easy as just telling him to piss off.'

'I know. Timing was a bit out.'

'I can't believe he *proposed* to you. How didn't you tell us this?' She's flushed from the drama.

'It's weird, it just hasn't registered with me as something significant. Guess that's a sign. It was so *not* what I wanted, or what I ever imagined a proposal to be like. It was awful, honestly.'

There's a pause as we all process this.

'So are you on Hinge yet?' Cecilia breaks the silence.

'Jesus, no. I'm just getting used to having the apartment to myself again.'

'You know you don't have to move in with them on the first night, right? That's not standard procedure.' Anna laughs.

'Fuck off. It wasn't the first night, and he only ended up camping at mine because it was easier to get to work. It's not like I ever *asked* him.' I shake my head. 'Anyway, I'm going celibate until Christmas.'

'Yeah, OK.' Sophie turns to Anna. 'Right, what's gone on with you? Tell us *everything*.'

'Well,' Anna puts her beer down on the table and leans forward meaningfully, 'I had a *connection*.'

'Oh, for god's sake.' Cecilia buries her head in her hands. 'Where was it this time, in Subway?'

64

'No! It was on the bus.'

We all groan. Anna has profound, spiritual 'connections' with people on alarmingly regular occasions. She says she can feel a person's energy when she locks eyes with them, and sometimes they just '*click*'. Five months ago, she had a moment with the man who ran the local chippy (Barry, forty-nine years old, bald) and ended up going back in there every day for two weeks waiting for him to acknowledge their chemistry. He never did, and she put on over a stone from all the battered fish, so she conceded that they had 'met at an unlikely time in their lives'. We assume that by this she means that if they had met twenty-three years earlier, when he was unmarried and twenty-six and Anna was four, they might just have hit it off.

'I'm serious! Just listen. I was getting on the V1 on Oxford Road, and as I showed him my pass he looked at me and I *felt* it. I really felt his energy and I know he felt mine too. We stayed like that, just gazing into each other's souls for what felt like forever.' Anna dabs at the corner of her eyes.

'That must have caused significant delays to the schedule. Bet the people at the next stop were fuming,' I offer.

'Well, yes, I suppose so. We would have stayed like that all day if it weren't for that selfish woman in a wheelchair crying about missing her hospital appointment.'

'Jesus.' Sophie looks disturbed. 'So, erm, how old do you reckon he was?'

She asks it casually but we are all holding our breath. Anna has yet to have a 'connection' with someone of an appropriate age. She skips our generation entirely every single time, developing infatuations with seventy-year-olds from Tesco or eighteen-year-olds in the college crowd at the bus stop.

'He's thirty-two.' She smiles proudly, knowing we can't argue with a five-year age gap.

'Aw, well done you! I'm sure he was lovely. Don't worry, you'll find the right one soon enough.' Cecilia pats Anna's hand and moves to get up to go to the bar. At uni, when Anna had her first 'connections', we used to encourage them; tell her to follow her feelings and go after it. Nine years later, though, there's been very little success and quite a lot of damage. We'd all like to avoid a repeat of the chippy man's effect on her cardiac health, so we brush it aside and try to move on.

But something seems different this time.

'Wait!' I shout, a little too eagerly, and Cecilia pauses halfway between sitting and standing. 'How do you know he's exactly thirty-two?'

Sophie raises her eyebrows in surprise. 'Yeah . . . how *do* you know that?' Anna has never once had an actual, real-life conversation with the victims of her infatuation, unless you count asking for salt and vinegar as a meaningful exchange.

'I asked him.' We all gasp. 'When we were in bed together.'

'Oh my *Gooooooooooooood*!' I scream.

Cecilia is standing fully upright now, screeching, 'What? *What?* WHAAAAAT?!' and flapping her hands around. People are staring. Sophie looks stunned.

'Shut *up*.' Anna's smiling coyly, 'He asked me for my number when I got off. This is it, guys.'

We all spend the next two drinks (donated to me by Sophie) getting progressively more vocal and excited about the fact that Anna has *finally* gotten laid at the hands of someone she actually feels something for and asking for graphic detail of every thrust. She is incredibly descriptive and we *love it.*

Two hours later and we are in Ibérica, irretrievably pissed and full of paella. The waitress has brought the bill and it comes to £283.98.

'We splitting this four ways?' Sophie reaches for her purse.

Anna and Cecilia nod. *Shit.* The girls had cocktails and ordered loads of tapas dishes, whilst I stuck to bottled beer and a small paella, counting the total in my head to make sure I could afford it. £284 divided by four is like, seventy quid? I don't have seventy quid. I have twenty-eight quid. Fuck, fuck, *fuuuuck.* This is so embarrassing.

Sophie catches my eye. 'Actually, guys, shall we just tot it up individually? We all had different things so it makes sense.'

Anna and Cecilia look at Sophie and then quickly glance at me and pretend that they didn't.

'Oh, yeah, definitely! Much better idea.' Cecilia grabs the receipt and starts tapping at her phone calculator, squinting with one eye.

This is so awkward.

'I'm sorry, guys. I'm so poor.' I can feel tears welling in my eyes and know that a beer meltdown is on its way.

'Oh my god, Mags, don't be so stupid! It's not right to split the bill when we've all had such different stuff.' Anna smiles warmly at me.

'Thanks.' I'm sniffling now. 'I feel so poor and fat and lost.'

'Nooooo!' They chorus.

'There is absolutely nothing wrong with you!' Sophie barks. 'You're funny and beautiful and fantastic, don't say things like that.'

'I just feel unhappy all the time. I had ideas of what being twenty-seven would be like and it just . . . it just wasn't like this.' For god's sake, I'm blubbing. 'It's six years since we graduated; you've all settled into careers and mortgages and relationships, or at least one of the above, why haven't I? I want to lose weight and get a job I love and wear gym clothes and walk up a flight of stairs without feeling asthmatic. Why aren't I doing any of these things?' I gulp. 'I don't even *want* to get married! I don't want a man. What if Martin has completely ruined me forever? What if I end up completely alone and join some kind of nudist cult or buy six ferrets or something?'

Cecilia looks at me worriedly. 'You'll find your way, love. You just need time. Maybe try being a bit more . . . proactive?'

There's a moment of silence as they gaze at me. I sigh heavily and pull the list out of my pocket, throwing it onto the table. All three of them physically recoil.

'What *is* that? Is that an old tissue?' Sophie peers at it. 'Why is it *brown*?'

'It's a list of everything I need to change about myself.' I flatten it out on the table and Anna picks it up by a corner, holding it out so they can all inspect it.

'Good for you!' Cecilia snatches the list out of Anna's hand. 'Stopping smoking is a great start.'

'I can't do the stopping smoking until my e-cig arrives.' I frown. 'I haven't tried any of them yet.'

'Well, if your mood's this low, why don't you start with the exercise? The endorphins are so good for the mind. Come to boxercise with me!'

'No cardio. Can't do cardio,' I whimper.

'What about a local walking group?' Sophie offers.

'Don't like the rain. Or creepy walking people.'

'Yeah, really, Sophie?' Anna grimaces. 'That's literally the most hideous thing you've ever said.' She leans forward and grabs my wrist. 'You *have* to try yoga. It's so calming. It's not cardio, either, but it's dead good for your body.'

'It's too expensive.' I'm being pathetic now, but I don't care.

'It's not! They do a beginners course at that Namaste place in the Northern Quarter, £50 for six weeks or something.'

'Maybe.' I sniff. That sounds like an all right idea, actually. I can imagine myself being all chilled and stretchy. I could be one of those people who does downward dog at sunrise and drinks herbal tea from a clay mug. Very *zen*. Hm. I'll think about it tomorrow.

The waitress is back and we all tell her how much we want to pay. I die of embarrassment momentarily and then we leave, standing outside in the cold March air.

'This was so good.' Anna wraps us all in a group hug. 'Let's do something next week?'

'Only if you don't turn up stinking like the number 46 again.' Sophie smiles.

'Excuse me!' Anna steps back. 'We would *never* have sex on the number 46.'

'Mmm, sure.' I laugh.

She shrugs. 'It's true.'

Cecilia and Sophie share a disbelieving glance.

'Only on the V1, V2 and V3.' Anna winks. 'The leather seats are easier to wipe down.'

9

The day of the conference. I'm freshly showered and dressed in a cream blouse and a grey skirt that doesn't fit but sucks me in like a dream. Theo strides down the corridor as I'm stealing four reporter's notebooks and nine pens from the stationery cupboard.

'All ready for the big day?' He looks me up and down with surprise. 'You're looking very smart . . .'

'Cheers.'

'. . . for once,' he finishes.

Excellent.

'It was touch and go whether I was going to make it today. I've had to leave Romulus with Bernadette again.'

I deftly swerve any slander of poor Bernadette. 'He's no better then?'

'No. He hasn't slept through for two weeks now.' He steadies his voice and sniffs hard. 'But I said, *no*. This is the most important day of my career so far –' God, that's depressing. '– and I *must* be at that conference.'

'Well . . . good for you.' I give him a tight smile and make to walk back to my office. I really don't have the energy for Romulus today.

'You grabbing your stuff then? Come on.' He pulls his car keys out of his pocket.

I freeze. 'It's only eight-thirty. I thought it started at ten?' Theo asked me to come in early and I assumed it was to prepare for the conference and print his notes (which he doesn't need, as he isn't speaking). I should have known better.

'It does! But we need to get there super early to make the most of the networking opportunities. Come on! All the croissants will be disappearing as we speak!' He strides up the corridor, leaving me to run after him with my arms full of books, dropping pens all over the floor.

As I sit next to Theo in his yellow Fiat 500, I get the distinct impression that this conference is important to him for reasons totally unrelated to career advancement.

'They do a real breakfast for us all, you know.' I *do* know, because he hasn't shut up about it for the past twenty-four hours. 'Waffles and blueberries and the like. And apparently the cookies are *to die for*.' He swerves around a woman walking over the zebra crossing to McDonalds and leans on his horn. 'Just *wait*, you bloody idiot! They'll still be serving McMuffins in two minutes!'

'I think that was a zebra crossing . . .' I look over my shoulder as the woman shakily makes it to the other side.

'Some people just cannot wait for their daily serving of saturated fat, can they? The state of society today; it's disgusting.' He grips his hands tighter on the steering wheel.

I hold onto my seat. 'So what were you saying about the breakfast?'

'Oh, yes. Apparently there's sausages, too! And roast chicken sandwiches on thick white bread for lunch. Loads of butter. Delicious.'

'What about your diet?' I ask tentatively. Theo has been on a diet his entire life, eating only grapefruit for lunch most days. He says Christopher likes a man with a lean physique.

He turns his head to me and glares. 'Have you ever heard of a cheat day, Margaret?'

'Look at the road, please . . .'

'A cheat day,' he continues, staring at me, 'is a day when you can eat whatever the hell you like. I live most of my days on raw vegetables and SlimFast. On this, the most important day of my life, I think I'm allowed a bloody *biscuit*, don't you?'

Theo's potbelly suggests he eats far more than raw vegetables and SlimFast when he's not being watched, but I decide to keep quiet.

'You know,' He takes a deep breath, 'when you get to my age, you go through great hormonal changes. My mood has dropped, my metabolism has slowed. To be quite frank, if that kind of turmoil doesn't justify the occasional treat, I don't know what does.'

Oh my god. Does Theo think he's going through the menopause?

'And if I'm honest with you,' he continues, 'sex just isn't what it was. They tell you things change over time, but there's this *dryness* I just can't seem to shift—'

'WILL ANNETTE BE THERE TODAY?' I shout. *Help me, please.*

'Annette?' Theo looks puzzled. 'Well, I'd hope so. She'd have a lot to learn from today, wouldn't she? That woman doesn't know her arse from her elbow.'

'She's so lovely, isn't she?' Annette is one of the other managers and I have no idea if she's lovely or not, having only heard about her through Theo. I just need to keep the conversation on track.

'Well, Margaret, "lovely" doesn't necessarily mean "competent employee". You'd do well to remember that.'

I do wonder if there's the tiniest hint of a compliment in there – is he saying I'm incompetent but lovely?

The rest of the journey is spent with me helplessly trying to dodge discussions about Theo's changing body and my career failings, and by the time we arrive at the hotel I am exhausted.

We enter the lobby and a tired-looking man in a pinstripe suit directs us to our 'suite'. I panic momentarily that he is referring to a suite with a bed in it, and clutch my rape alarm in my pocket in case Theo tries to lure me in there to ogle enviously at my labia or something. I am relieved to be led to a large, carpeted area with an empty buffet table and a registration desk full of name badges.

'Wow, some early risers!' A large, middle-aged woman beams at us from behind the desk. 'Come and tell me your names and I'll get you badged up.'

We head over and Theo signs the register and takes his badge, his eyes permanently fixed on the woman's gigantic cleavage.

I shuffle forward and take the piece of paper she hands me. My eyes flick across the title.

OTC Post-Menopausal Drugs Workshop Register

Oh, of course. This isn't a conference; it's a workshop. It's an educational workshop for people who give a shit about the bureaucratic awfulness associated with their jobs. The last glimmer of hope inside me dies. I am embarrassed to remember that I fell asleep last night imagining a representative from the BMJ turning up at the conference and offering me a real scientific writing post. The conference that doesn't even exist.

Theo is fastening his badge onto his lapel and gazing around the room. We are the only ones here (of course) – an hour early. According to the agenda I have just been given, the ten o'clock start indicated the beginning of 'coffee, meet-and-greet and registration' – the actual talks don't begin until 10.45. Nearly two hours from now.

I gaze at the shiny, empty buffet trays laid out on the table. Breakfast isn't served yet, either. Theo has been going on about the waffles here since last Thursday so I skipped my usual Special K in preparation for some serious binge-eating and I am *starving*. Middle-aged Cleavage Woman is speaking to one of the waiting staff, and he disappears momentarily before wheeling through a trolley full of coffee, milk and fifty different varieties of tea bag. I leave Theo to fiddle with his badge and grab a cup.

'You've not got any biscuits back there, have you?' I attempt a convincing smile but I must look ravenous and desperate as the waiter frowns and steps back.

'Breakfast is served at ten o'clock, madam.'

'Right, great.' I pour a coffee and stride away, trying to push down the hunger-induced irritation swirling around in my stomach.

'Excuse me, love?' Middle-aged Cleavage Woman holds out my badge. 'You forgot this.'

'Oh, sorry! Thanks.' She's really quite adorable.

I glance down at the professional-looking badge I am holding and feel a small swell of pride. My first badge! I feel quite important.

And then I see my title.

Margaret Gardiner
Minute-taker and assistant to Theodore Parbold

OK, no. No, no, no. Absolutely not.

My instinct is to run over to Theo, stab him in the eye with my badge pin and start crying. I push that instinct down.

Instead, I walk slowly over to where Theo is standing and smile.

'Theo.'

'Mmm?'

'Can I ask why my badge says *minute-taker*?'

He looks puzzled. 'Because you're taking the minutes?'

'But I'm a medical writer.' I struggle to keep my voice steady. My blood is boiling.

'Are you shaking? How much coffee have you drunk?' He eyes my cup.

'I haven't had any coffee. Yet.' I take a big gulp and try to compose myself. 'Can I change my title, please? And my name? You know I prefer Maggie.'

74

'Oh, Margaret. Let's not get into the particulars now, just try and do some networking and forget about it.' He pulls out his phone, already bored of our conversation.

'There's nobody here to network with, Theo.' I grit my teeth.

'Theo*dore*, please, Margaret.' He tuts, and then peers at me. 'Is it your time of the month?'

I look back into his eyes in disbelief. What goes on behind there? What on *earth* happened to him in childhood that made him this way? The surface of my coffee is trembling in my hand, *Jurassic Park* style.

'I'm going to get some fresh air.' I say, aware that this will further concrete Theo's theory that I am hormonally imbalanced. If I stay a second longer, though, I'll flip the buffet table and call him a twat.

I slump against the wall outside the foyer and roll a cigarette. I can't believe I just let that go. I'm half filled with self-hatred, half proud of myself for staying level headed. I don't care about this job, and I certainly don't care what a few people at a workshop think of my title. But I feel a heavy ball of disappointment sitting on my chest.

If I want to be able to keep paying my rent, I'm going to have to keep toeing the line. I'll have to keep my mouth shut, simper and fake my way through the day and never *scream* about how utterly, totally horrific I find it all. I've probably already landed myself in his bad books, just by causing a fuss over a title change. Maybe I should buy him a stuffed iguana and talk to him about cervical smears to get him on my side again. I take a deep drag of my cigarette, disgusted at the thought. I'm such a bloody sell-out.

I just need to calm myself down. I need an outlet for this anger that isn't snapping at people and squirrelling pizzas away like a pre-hibernation polar bear. I fish the list out of my bag along with one of the hundreds of minute-taking pens littering the bottom. I write:

6. Start yoga.

I take out my phone and search for the Namaste class Anna was telling me about. There's a six-week beginners' course starting tomorrow. The website tells me that the full £50 is paid in cash on the day of the first session. Tomorrow is payday. I book myself a place before I can think. There! I'm one step closer to ticking something off.

Someone coughs behind me and I turn, blowing a huge billow of smoke in their face as I do so. The fog clears and Middle-aged Cleavage Woman emerges, spluttering.

'God, I'm so sorry!' I grind my cigarette out on the wall and throw it on the floor. She looks at it worriedly.

'It's OK, love. Here.' She hands me my badge back. I go to protest and tell her that I must stand up for my rights and retain my pride, but I see that she has changed the text.

Maggie Gardiner
Medical Writer

I feel tears spring into my eyes.

'Oh,' I say.

'It's shit being young and working under someone who treats you like a skivvy.' She smiles.

She just said 'shit'. She is *so* great.

'Yeah.' I look down at my badge and blink rapidly.

'Keep standing up for yourself like that and one day you'll be doing what you love and running the show. Don't take any prisoners.' She pats me on the arm.

I look at her and feel a huge swell of gratitude and neediness – that is the kindest, most affirming thing anyone has said to me in *so long*. I want to ask her to take me home and tell me more nice things whilst she feeds me soup and strokes my forehead.

Before I know what I'm doing, I've grabbed her and I'm hugging her and crying on her shoulder. She's all warm and squishy and it reminds me of my nana. My lovely, lovely nana. I need to go and see her. I cry harder.

Middle-aged Cleavage Woman freezes for a second and then pats me on the back.

'Don't you worry. A bad day doesn't mean a bad life.'

I pull back and wipe my nose with the back of my hand. 'What about a bad *month*? Or a bad *year*?'

'Not those either.' She regards me warmly. 'We've all been there. Make the changes you can and accept what you can't control.'

I look at her in awe. She's a fucking *guru*. This is like meeting a wise old man in the desert who tells you how to solve all your problems. Except it's a sixty-year-old lady with gigantic boobs outside a Wigan hotel in the rain. Still meaningful.

'Come on inside now, breakfast will be ready soon.' She turns and I follow her back in (I might follow her home later, too) where Theo is tapping furiously at his phone.

Middle-aged Cleavage Woman smiles at me. 'Go on. I'll see where this food is up to.'

I glance at her name badge. 'Thank you . . . Barbara.' Barbara my sage. My saviour.

'I've had my badge changed, Theo.' I look him in the eye and try to channel my inner guru. 'I just wanted to tell you that it makes me feel quite inferior when you treat me the way you do sometimes.'

Theo looks up from his phone. 'Hm? Bloody hell, where is this breakfast? And where are all the people? I didn't give up my precious time to be here ALONE AND STARVED TO DEATH!' He shouts.

Sigh. 'I think Barbara is sorting it.'

'Who the hell is Barbara?'

'That lady over there. Are you hangry, Theo?' I am owning this calm approach. The type of approach one might use to appease a toddler mid-tantrum. I can be mature and I can rise above this.

'Hangry? Margaret, are you sure you're up to writing minutes when you can't speak?' He cocks his head. 'The female condition. Fascinating.'

'Hangry, Theo, is a disorder in which a person becomes uncharacteristically angry as a result of hunger.'

Theo's eyes rise slowly up to meet mine. 'No, it isn't.'

'Yes, it is. Google it if you don't believe me.'

He blinks. 'Oh my god. *Hangry*. This explains *everything*.' He covers his mouth with his hand. 'Is this a new condition?'

'It's been around for millennia, but it's only just been named.' I smile reassuringly. I'm not lying, really.

'Is there a *cure*?' He gasps.

'Yes.' I nod. 'Yes, there is a cure. Food is the cure.'

Theo squints at me suspiciously for a second. 'Really? Hm.' He glances over at the empty buffet trays. 'I suppose that does sort of make sense.'

I nod harder.

'Bear with me a moment, I need to call Christopher . . .' Theo turns away with his phone to his ear and clips towards the lobby. 'Christopher? It's Theodore. I just thought I'd let you know that I've been diagnosed with an incredibly *rare* condition, so the next time you tell me I'm being an *unbearable nightmare*, bear this in mind . . .'

Theo is still bellowing down the receiver when waitresses start emerging with steaming piles of waffles, sausages, bacon, eggs and beans. Jugs of maple syrup are placed next to huge, glistening bowls of berries and baskets of warm croissants. *Thank god.* For once, Theo was right and I am glad.

There is still not a soul in sight and I dread to think of the waiting staff getting offended at my lack of enthusiasm, so I grab a plate and start piling up. As I carefully balance my last sausage on top of my mountainous pile of food, I catch Barbara studying me with concern.

Oh, don't be one of those people, Barbara.

Surely she can understand that I've had a difficult morning?

Also, I've not made it down to *lose weight* on my list yet, so this is technically fine.

I carefully transfer my plate onto one of the tables lining the perimeter of the room and sit down. I pour maple syrup over the lot before tucking in. Lord, this is GOOD.

I've shovelled about half the portion down my gullet and I'm already contemplating seconds when someone sits down next to me.

'This is great, isn't it?'

I slowly raise my head up from where it has been hunched disgustingly close to my plate. Through my sugar-induced brain-fog I vaguely register a girl, about my age, with glasses. I swallow.

'Mmhm.' I glance at her plate and see that she has chosen a *single* waffle with a small handful of berries. Who *is* this weirdo?

'Oh,' she catches me looking, 'I'm trying to be good. Got to save myself for the chicken sandwiches and wine later on.'

'Wine?' My ears visibly prick.

'Yeah!' She laughs. 'No other way you'd get me coming to this kind of bore-fest.'

'My boss told me it was a *conference*.'

'Ouch. Mine told me it'd be a great opportunity for development.' She registers the look on my face and laughs. 'You believed it too, eh?'

I like this girl, small appetite or not. Saffron, her badge says. Personal Assistant.

'Have you seen that man going ballistic in the corner?' She nods her head towards Theo, who is too busy telling Christopher about his delicate emotional state to notice that the cure has been served.

'That,' I spear a sausage and point it towards him, 'is my boss.'

She grimaces. 'Jeez. My condolences.'

We finish our food and talk about our jobs as the room fills up. Saffron tells me how her manager is constantly trying to find new ways to aid Saffron's *personal development*, by sending her to countless events and workshops all across the country. She rarely gets any work done, and her expenses forms are a thing to behold, apparently. I tell her how I'm bored out of my tree and consider committing accident claim fraud alarmingly regularly to escape the daily grind.

We watch as Theo finally finishes his phone call and takes a plate almost as large as mine over to a table of women and starts chatting to them. I enlighten Saffron on the probable inappropriate topics of conversation Theo is choosing, and we laugh when the women slowly make excuses and move, leaving him sitting alone.

'I'd better go and get him. He'll be a nightmare on the way home if he doesn't get enough attention.' I stand up.

'Go do your duty. Hopefully see you in there.' She winks.

Maybe today isn't so bad. I've met Barbara with her sage advice and Saffron who, by the sounds of things, isn't exactly living the career dream either.

I get to Theo as he's sliding his final piece of syrup-drenched waffle into his mouth.

'Networking going well, is it?' I can't help myself.

'Bloody rude, the lot of them.' he says, sulkily.

'What were you chatting about?' I'm not sure I want to know the answer, but I really do at the same time.

'Really interesting stuff until they all decided to bugger off and sit elsewhere. I was actually asking them whether they thought the bacon here was organic. I told them about that research paper, do you remember, the one that showed that non-organic bacon was horrifically carcinogenic? And the hormone imbalances! I was *very* interested to hear their thoughts on how processed meat affected their oestrogen production.'

What better topic of conversation over a full English breakfast? 'So you thought you'd check if your theory was correct?'

'Yep. Not that they were interested in discussing it with me. Call themselves researchers.' He scoffs in the direction of the women, who are all sitting around a table several metres away and eyeing me with concern.

'Ladies and gentlemen,' a stocky man bellows from behind the badge desk, 'if you would like to make your way into the meeting room, this morning's presentations will begin shortly.'

We traipse towards the huge, open doors at the far end of the room. Theo strides on ahead, undoubtedly in search of a spot near the front where he can ambush the speakers at close-range. I lag behind and hope that he won't save me a seat so I can sit at the back alone.

'Hey,' one of Theo's unwilling counsel of ladies matches my pace and walks beside me, 'he's a very strange man, just be careful. Wave at one of us if you need saving at any point.' She gestures behind her to where her friends are walking close-by. 'We've all got to look out for each other when it comes to weirdos like that.'

'Thanks.' I smile, deciding not to tell them that I'll be sharing a tiny car with said weirdo all the way back to the office.

10

That has to have been the most boring morning of my life. It trumps even the most painfully slow days at the office staring at the computer screen and wishing for death. The first talk was the most tedious thing I have ever had to listen to and yet, somehow, each of the following presentations was more torturous than the last. My bum is numb, my hand is possibly permanently paralysed and my ears feel like they're bleeding from absorbing such mind-numbing information.

But now it's lunchtime and although I'm still full from the 3000-calorie feast I demolished this morning (and the two cookies I had during the coffee break) I am instantly revived because I can see *wine*. Time flies when you're pissed, or so I say, so my only hope for surviving the afternoon is to chug as much of the vino as possible during the one-hour lunch slot. I've got bladdered in far less time in the past so this is no challenge.

I stride to the buffet table, grab a glass of white and neck it with my back to the room before swiping another and striding outside to the main entrance. I roll and light a cigarette and sip my drink in the afternoon sunlight. This is a little bit like being on holiday in Spain, I think. I'm freezing and this is almost certainly Asda's table wine, but it's about as good as it gets under these unbearable circumstances.

It hits me again (probably at the same time as the alcohol starts to leak into my system) that I really do hate my job. Everyone has bad days at work, when they question whether they're in the right place, but I can't even remember the last time I felt properly happy. I feel like I've been running along with my eyes squeezed shut, not stopping to wonder why I constantly feel like someone's died and the world is against me. But what else could I do? I don't want to do a PhD, which is what *all* the good scientific positions require as a minimum, and I'm not even sure if I like science anymore anyway. I thought it was great at school when we got to look at gross models of the reproductive system and onion skin under the microscope, but now it's just so complicated and corporate and shit.

Although . . . I'm supposed to be changing my job anyway, aren't I? The list says so.

I'd like to be a detective, I think. But I don't want to start at the bottom and spend twenty years climbing the ranks only to be swamped by paperwork and never have time with my children (I watch a lot of police dramas). I'd love to be a lawyer, but I think I just like the idea of standing and shouting in a courtroom and having people fascinated by my quick intelligence. I'd absolutely hate doing all the work that comes before it.

The only thing I've ever actually really wanted to do is *write*. I've been writing since I crawled out of the womb; filling diaries and notebooks with random stories before having my mum find them and threaten to book me an appointment with the psychiatrist because of my 'disturbingly vivid imagination'. I went into medical writing because I'm good at stringing a sentence together and it matched my degree pretty well, but I'm so utterly disinterested in it that the idea of jotting down another drug-related sentence makes me want to drink myself into a stupor. Coincidentally, what I'm trying to do as we speak.

It's never really crossed my mind before that I could make money from writing for fun. Although . . . loads of people try to write books, but there's only one J.K. Rowling, isn't there?

What are my chances of actually getting something published? I can think right now of a million story ideas, but why put in the effort of getting one written if I'm only going to be rejected?

I'm putting effort into stuff I don't care about though, aren't I? Every single day I exert energy (albeit minimal) on drug write-ups, meeting preparations and research, and I don't even enjoy it. Imagine if I put that energy into doing something I loved; into writing something I cared about. I could actually, maybe, possibly be OK.

I've drained the last of my wine so I head back inside for a refill. There's still forty-five minutes before we're due back in, so I grab myself another glass and sit in the corner to do some Instagram scrolling. Balls to networking – I'd rather make connections with my nana's boules club than any of these people.

All the skinny girls on social media keep posting about this new tea that's supposed to help you lose weight and sleep better. I don't need help sleeping – I take three naps a day sometimes – but weight loss I could certainly do with. Apparently it's full of antioxidants, which make you feel 'zen' and 'chillaxed' and suppress appetite like a dream. I'm going to ignore the logic alarm going off in my head and imagine for a moment that this could actually be true. I could just drink tea for every meal and perhaps indulge in half a peach in the evening and I'd be a size six in no time. It's £20 for a box of twelve tea bags. You're supposed to drink one cup every morning, noon and night, which by my calculations means that it'll last me four days. I won't have to buy food, though, which is a bonus, and maybe four days is all it takes? I pop a box in my basket and set an alarm to remind myself to check out when I get paid tomorrow. I flatten the list on my lap and scribble:

7. Do tea detox.

'Not indulging in the chicken butties?' Saffron is back. I bury the list in my pocket.

'Still full from breakfast.' I rub my stomach. 'Reckon I could wrap one in a napkin and shove it in my bag for later?'

'Don't see why not.' She laughs. 'This wine is going down a treat.'

'I'm using it as a sedative so I can sleep for the rest of the day.'

'Don't you have to take minutes?'

Shit. Forgot about that. 'It's fine, I'll just type up the slides tomorrow.' I lift up the huge plastic wallet of PowerPoint print-outs we've all been gifted with.

'Plan. Another glass?' I nod and she goes to grab us another round. 'Bloody hell, this is my second already.' She plonks the glasses on the table.

'This is my fourth!' I say a little too loudly, and take a huge gulp.

'Oh my god.' She's laughing her head off. 'You're hilarious.'

'It has been said.' I'm really feeling it now. I must have drunk more than half a bottle in twenty-five minutes. Not quite reaching my record, but pretty damn close.

'So what do you want to do?' She looks at me inquisitively.

'What?'

'What do you want to do? When you eventually quit?'

'For a job, you mean?'

'Yeah. I think I'd like to paint, probably.'

'How do you know I want to quit?' I lean forward and stare at her. 'Are you *psychic*?'

She cackles. 'Don't think so. You've just been making it pretty clear how shit you find it all – and hey, I don't blame you – so there must be something else you want to do.'

'I think I want to write something. Not minutes. No more minutes.' I lean back in my chair and sigh. 'I'll write, you do the illustrations.'

'So we're going into children's books?'

'God, no. Why can't adult books have pictures? I don't get that, why are we not allowed to look at pictures when we're older?' This thought has just occurred to me and it's distressing me hugely. 'How unfair is that?'

'You're so pissed!' She grins.

'Not pissed enough.' I down the rest of my glass and walk over to the food table, grabbing three thick chicken and mayonnaise sandwiches and wrapping them in a napkin.

'Hey, sorry, you can't do that . . .' A floppy-haired teenage waiter approaches me nervously.

'Why not? I haven't eaten anything and I'll be starving later.'

'I don't think you will,' he frowns.

'What? How would you know?'

'It's just . . . we all saw how much you had for breakfast. We're supposed to look out for people who take portions home with them. We don't make enough to cater for someone's lunch the next day.'

'Excuse *me*?' I am outraged. 'I'll have you know I'm quite peckish, actually. I've been allocated a lunch and I'll take one, thank you very much.'

He's silent, so I hold his gaze whilst I slowly lower the sandwiches into my handbag.

I turn on my heel and grab another glass of wine, sassing back to my table feeling very proud of myself and only mildly humiliated.

Saffron is in bits.

'You are something else.' She dabs at the corner of her eye and takes a deep breath to calm herself.

'I think I'm a bit fucked. Did Theo see me? My boss?'

'Nah. He's too busy schmoozing the woman from that regulatory authority thing.'

I close one eye and squint into the corner of the room, where Theo has backed a woman against the wall and is talking animatedly. Her eyes are flicking around her in search of an escape.

'Ladies and gentlemen! I hope you all enjoyed our famous sandwiches and are feeling refreshed and ready for some more fascinating talks! Once again can I ask that you make your way into the conference suite. Presentations will resume in ten minutes.'

I say goodbye to Saffron, grab another glass of wine and sway into the room, smacking my shoulder on the doorframe as I do so. I vaguely register people glancing at me as the wine sloshes over the side of my glass, and I give a dramatic 'whoops!', raise my drink and laugh. I'm so fun.

I find my way back to the round table I have called home for the past three hours of my life. We all had assigned seats so I didn't manage to escape Theo, but we are at the back. Small mercies.

It turns out that my plan has worked incredibly well. I've had six glasses of wine and I am basically sozzled, which means I don't actually have the mental capacity to dwell on how much time is left before I can go home. The heating is cranked up in here, though, which is making it really, *really* difficult to stay awake.

Some woman gets up on stage and starts droning on about her life and how she came to be here, which no one cares about, before delving into the world's most boring speech, titled 'Applying New Metrics for Measuring R&D Performance to Optimise Efficiency and Cost.' What even *is* that? More pressingly, why do all these people look so *interested*? There's a keen bean in the seat next to me who's scribbling pages of notes down faster than I can write my own name. I hate her.

I lean back in my seat and close my eyes for a second. Perhaps people will assume that I am deep in thought; meditating on the wisdom of efficiency optimisation. I'm actually thinking about the chicken butties in my handbag.

'Margaret!' Theo is hissing in my ear.

I peel one eye open and see that the woman on stage is *still* going on, speaking animatedly about performance measures. She is ten times more enthusiastic now than she was when she was speaking about her background and personal life at the start, which is really, really depressing.

'What?' I squint at Theo.

'Are you sleeping?!' He's livid. 'You haven't made a single note since we came back from lunch!'

'I was internalising the information.' I'm slurring a bit, which I'm sure isn't helping my case. I'm acutely aware that I'm behaving completely unprofessionally. I'm also acutely aware that I couldn't give a shit.

'Write down what she's bloody saying!'

'It's all in the pack they gave us.' I slide it across to him. God, I've never been so cheeky in my entire life. What has gotten into me? Is this what happens when you really, really hate your job? I'll have so much more sympathy for those people on the CCTV videos trashing their offices in future. You're just not yourself when you're trapped in hell, are you?

'Only the generic stuff! Not the *details*! For god's sake, I didn't ask you to come here so you could eat all the breakfast food and have a nap!'

Right. If one more person comments on how much I ate for breakfast I will *really* lose my rag.

'I was *hungry*.'

'Write!' He turns back to the front and clasps his hands in his lap, nodding earnestly at the presenter.

I take out my pen and write very, *very* slowly. I start writing what's being said, but it's so boring that my hand physically will not commit it to paper, so I write a background story for the woman on stage instead.

Susan, 43. Lives with her husband, Derek, and silently resents him for spending so much time making Star Wars *Legos in the garage instead of being with her. Likes to think she can cook, but only succeeds at bland pies and stews which Derek says he likes but secretly he wishes he married someone who made fajitas and was adventurous in the bedroom. Two children, both at university, who rarely come home because the atmosphere is as lively as a wet flannel and they're sick of hearing their Mum talk about efficiency and optimisation. She looks forward to Christmas because everyone is together, but she orchestrates it to such an extent that it becomes stifled and she always finds herself weeping on Boxing Day. Only ever has one glass of wine on a Saturday when she watches* Countdown. *Often masturbates over research and development policies.*

'OK, I think that's all I had to say today. Does anyone have any questions?' Susan (real name Julie, just checked the agenda) scans the room hopefully.

Oh, this moment. The moment the most hated person in the room makes themselves known. How can anyone possibly have a question about this? The only query I have is whether I'll ever be the same again after enduring such boredom.

The keen bean next to me raises her hand.

Oh, *fuck off.*

'Yes, you at the back?'

'Thanks, Julie. I was just wondering if you could clarify what role a research manager could play in increasing the efficiency of an R&D department.'

'Great question.' No, it really isn't. 'There are many things all of us can do. Using our resources wisely is obviously key, and this is particularly true of human resources, if you understand what I mean. Try not to go to the head of R&D with a query that could be answered by someone lower down, for example. In terms of the metrics, these often won't fall under the remit of a research manager's responsibilities, so the best we can all do is to be as efficient as possible during working hours. Prioritising our workloads appropriately, etcetera.'

'Right, great. I'd also like to know whether you think we're becoming *more* efficient in the pharmaceutical industry? And how we've achieved that if so?'

'Oh my god, who *cares*?' I blurt.

Every eye in the room swivels towards me and silence descends. Theo is staring at me, his jaw hanging open.

'Excuse me?' Julie is glaring down at me from her podium.

'Does anyone *actually* care about this? Anyone?' I look around the room.

What in Christ's name am I doing? I'm in too deep.

Oh well, go hard or go home.

'Come on, hands up if you give a flying fart about *any* of this.'

Someone at the front gasps. Slowly, everyone starts to raise their hands.

'Oh *really*? *REALLY*?' I scrape my chair back and stand up. Suddenly, I am so, so tired of everything.

'Sorry, who are you?' The keen bean has her arms folded smugly and is staring at me with grim superiority. I bet she has the same look on her face when she watches the *Titanic* go down.

'I'm Sally,' I lie. I might be three (actually, make that twelve) sheets to the wind, but there's no way I'm ruining my entire reputation with this little outburst. I just need to *do* something, to prove a point, to shout and get it all off my chest and unleash that frustrated, angry monster that's been living inside me for months. I'm already feeling the regret to come.

'Her name is Margaret Gardiner,' Theo pipes up. Oh, thanks a *bunch*, Theo.

'Right, Margaret, do you have something constructive to say or are you just here to make a scene?' Julie looks around the room and earns a few shocked sniggers from the audience.

'I'm just . . . I can't believe any of you are actually interested. This is, hands-down, the most boring day I've had in my entire life. I refuse to believe that any of you are enjoying this.' I'm scanning the faces around me hopefully, but no one seems to agree. 'There has to be more to life than this, surely?'

A few people are shaking their heads, most of them are gazing down into their laps.

'Whilst I'm reluctant to waste my breath explaining this to you . . . Margaret, was it?' Julie purses her lips. 'What we do is actually *very* important. Perhaps if you looked outside your immediate little bubble you'd see that all of this has an effect on everything else that happens in the pharmaceutical industry.'

Murmurs of agreement ripple around the room.

'Yeah, you're a saint, I get it. This is *abysmal*. If sitting here is making you all feel titillated then go ahead. You're all a bunch of squares.'

'You're incredibly rude. Nobody is forcing you to be here. Feel free to leave and let everyone else get the most out of the day.' Julie's eyes bore into me.

There are two of her up there now. I should have stopped at four glasses. I slide down into my seat, defeated.

'No you don't.' Theo stands up and grabs me by the elbow, hoisting me up onto my feet. 'I'm so sorry, everyone. I'll remove her now.'

'*Remove* me?!' I screech as he drags me towards the door, bashing me into people's chairs and knocking glasses of water over. 'This is so BORING! I'm leaving of my own accord!'

This statement might be more profound were I not being forcibly yanked across the room in front of everyone.

I point my free hand at the keen bean at my table. 'You need to get a life! Go drink some vodka and take a pottery class!'

Theo hurls me through the door and I stand on the other side, breathing heavily.

'Nine a.m. tomorrow. I'll have a HR rep present.' He says.

He pushes the door and as it closes I catch sight of Saffron, slumped in her chair, holding her stomach and absolutely pissing herself.

11

Oh, I've really done it this time. I'm going to be seriously reprimanded for this. I am sitting on the bus, gazing out of the window miserably. My stomach is gurgling with anxiety. I got home yesterday as the last dregs of alcohol were still coursing around my bloodstream. The buzz had given way to quite severe anxiety and depression by then, so I ate all the chicken sandwiches, a box of cheese twists and half a tub of Häagen-Dazs and watched *Elf* until I fell asleep.

I mentally create another list; one which documents all the drama I've managed to get myself into in the past seven days.

1. Ruining the worst and only proposal of my life and rendering myself single: tick.
2. Turning up to work stinking of booze and covered in curry: tick.
3. Flashing my camel toe at the office: tick.
4. Huge drunken outburst at research workshop: tick.

Although number one feels more like an achievement than a fuck-up.

I sink down into my seat and groan. I want to disappear. I wish the bus would just keep driving until it hit the coast and then I could swim to France and start a new life in Paris. Although we're heading northwest, so we'd hit the wrong side of the country and I'd have to swim to America. Ireland is too close, too similar. I'm not sure I'd make it to the States; I haven't swum in four years and I was never very good at it.

It takes all my strength to reach out my arm and press the 'STOP' button. Depressing that small red square is a metaphor for me accepting my fate and lighting the fuse for the destruction of my life. Work will be unbearable once Theo has finished with me; everyone will know what I've done and I will never hear the end of it. I'm so *stupid*.

I dismount the bus and do a funeral-procession-speed walk up to the building.

'Morning, love.' Leonard the security man is awake and looks at me with pity. This is the first thing he has ever said to me. Word has already got around, then.

'All right, Leonard.' I bow my head and hurry down the stairs to the basement.

It is completely silent down here. I check my phone: 08:57. Typical, Theo can't even turn up on time to bollock me.

I head into the 'conference room' to prepare for my fate. A small, elfish woman is sitting at the table.

'Oh, hi.' I smile awkwardly. Who the hell is this?

'Hello! I hope you don't mind, I'm here for a meeting and no one seems to be around so I just thought I'd sit here and wait.'

'Oh, no problem. Do you want a brew?' I gesture towards the collection of chipped mugs in the corner. Theo's pixelated face stares back at us from one of them, the words 'live each day as if it's your LAST' screaming out from underneath.

'No, thanks. I've already had my daily allowance of caffeine!' She laughs and nods towards the takeaway coffee cup next to her. 'Those Starbucks Americanos are way too strong.'

'I know! They always give me palpitations. Stick with the lattes, the extra milk helps for some reason.' I'm an expert in this field.

'Good shout, I'll remember that in future.' She smiles at me warmly.

'What meeting are you here for? I'll call my boss and find out where he is.' I take my phone out of my pocket, already dreading hearing Theo's voice.

'I'm meeting Theodore Parbold and one of his employees. I'm from HR.' She lifts her lanyard up and wiggles it.

Fuck me. I've been making small-talk with my destroyer.

'Right-o!' I say, backing out of the room. 'If you don't mind waiting here . . .'

I shut the door heavily behind me and jog over to the toilet. Like hell I'm calling Theo. The longer she has to wait, the more incompetent he seems.

I hoist myself up onto the windowsill in the cubicle and light a cigarette. I haven't prepared anything for this meeting, aside from the eighty-four comebacks and sassy comments I devised in the shower this morning. Now I'm here, though, they all seem a bit much. 'You touched me in my private areas', for example, might be a tad excessive.

I'm trying not to panic about what I've done. I've never been so openly rude and hostile to people before. And I'd been so calm and collected earlier in the day! Everyone must think I'm such a mess. My head throbs with shame and anger at myself. Everybody knows you shouldn't drink when you're sad, angry or completely dissatisfied with your life.

Maybe I'll be suspended. That wouldn't be so bad, would it? You get paid if you're suspended, I think. It'd be like extra annual leave. I haven't got any left and the tax year isn't up for another month, so maybe this is actually a blessing in disguise? I could book a cheap flight and get paid to swan around Amsterdam eating brownies and taking photos of canals.

Actually, this is an excellent idea. Of course I regret what I've done, obviously I do, but isn't life all about flipping a negative situation on its head and making lemonade? I have to make this happen. I mustn't be too apologetic or they'll let me off; I must be repentant but with an air of 'a couple of weeks off would make me see the error of my ways' about me. This is a positive career step, I'm sure of it. It's even on the list – 5. *Change your fucking job.* That could be interpreted as 'change *something about* your fucking job'. Suspension is change, isn't it?

Plan devised, I jump down from the windowsill and bounce back to my office. I'm just scrolling through SkyScanner when Theo pokes his head round the door.

'Good morning, Margaret. Meet in the conference room in five minutes?' He looks jubilant, but is trying to hide it with a mask of regretful disappointment. He is relishing in my pain.

'Good morning, Theo. Yes, no problem.' I smile as though I don't give a fuck in the world.

I give so many fucks I think I'm going to be sick. I need this trip to Amsterdam. Or maybe Greece . . . I could drink little cocktails in the sun and shag a brooding local in a donkey barn, like something from *Mamma Mia*.

I pop a mint in my mouth before realising that having it roll around in there during this tense moment probably won't do me any favours. *Spit that chewing gum out, you look like a slob!* My mother's voice screeches through my subconscious. I quickly crunch it and fish the little pieces out of my teeth with my tongue as I stride to the conference room.

'Morning!' I beam as I open the door. 'Oh! You're here to see *me*?' I feign shock as I glance over at the HR lady. 'Gosh, silly me. I just didn't put two and two together at all!' I give what some people would describe as a 'hearty chuckle'. I hate those people.

'Sit down, Margaret.' Theo is shuffling his papers on his desk as though there might be something relevant in there. It's probably just a list of 1001 interesting things about iguanas. I sit.

'So, Margaret—' HR lady starts.

'It's Maggie, actually.'

'Oh . . . are we not here to meet Margaret Gardiner?' She murmurs to Theo.

Ooh, interesting. A case of mistaken identity? Could this work?

'She likes to call herself Maggie but her name is *Margaret*.' Theo purses his lips.

OK, nope. Plan B it is.

'Yeah, Maggie. Slaggy Maggie they used to call me at school.' I lean back on my chair nonchalantly, trying not to engage with the acute shame I'm feeling. *Suspend me, suspend me, suspend me.*

'Oh . . .' HR lady raises her eyebrows and looks down at the table.

'See,' Theo hisses, 'this is the type of behaviour I'm talking about. Totally inappropriate.'

OK, I might have taken the wrong tack. I'm making myself look completely unhinged. Although maybe that will work in my favour? You can't discipline someone with obvious mental health issues – it's unethical.

'Right, let's start this properly.' HR lady straightens up and clears her throat. 'My name is Evelyn Sachs and I'm here at the request of Mr Parbold to observe this meeting and ensure that everything is done properly. As a part of human resources, it is my job not only to look out for what is good for our company, but also for the people in it. So let's hope this can be a productive and professional interaction.'

'Thank you, Evelyn.' Theo places his hand over hers and she looks at it like it's on fire.

'Yes, *thank you*, Evelyn.' I shoot her a glance that says *I know your pain, my hand has been your hand, he's the mental one, not me.* She looks away.

'Margaret, I have asked you to come in today because I think your behaviour over the past week has been incredibly erratic.' Theo's voice is squeaky with power. His excitement is vibrating around the room. 'I let a few things slide but your performance at the conference yesterday was inexcusable. I simply cannot let that go without disciplinary action.'

OK. OK, good. Disciplinary action = suspension. Suspension = holiday.

'I'm sorry.' I say, playing the victim card. 'I've been very stressed recently and I've not been handling it too well.'

'Mr Parbold tells me you got incredibly drunk and accosted several people at the event?' Evelyn frowns.

'Accosted? No! I said a few things . . . inappropriate things, I suppose, but . . . I had a couple of glasses of wine, and—'

'A couple!' Theo scoffs. 'She had an entire bottle to herself!'

I hate you, Theo. I hate you and your excellent attention to detail.

'I don't think it was an entire bottle.' I say calmly.

'Six glasses! *Six*! In an hour!'

'I think six is a stretch . . .'

'Six glasses is actually *more* than a bottle! She was absolutely legless!'

'Honestly, Evelyn, it was a couple. I'd had a big breakfast too so I handled it well.' I smile.

'She had more than a bloody big breakfast. You could feed an African village for a week on the number of waffles she had!'

'Four waffles would probably only feed a small village, Theo. And probably only for a day . . .'

'She said,' he takes a deep breath, 'she said there *had to be more to life than this*. Direct quote.'

'I don't remember those being my *exact* words, Theo. As I said, I've been very stressed . . .'

'Stressed about *what*?!' Theo looks around incredulously. 'You don't have a mortgage or children, your responsibility here is next to nothing—'

'Mr Parbold,' Evelyn interrupts, 'I have to remind you that it's completely inappropriate to be commenting on or asking about your employee's personal life. If Maggie wants to discuss it, that's her choice, but—'

'I would rather not discuss it, thank you.' I fake a catch in my throat and look down at the table sadly. I try to pretend

97

that his comment about mortgages and children hasn't just struck a nerve I didn't know I still had.

'No, come on! If you're going to embarrass me in front of people, some very *important* people, may I add, at least have the balls to say what it's about!'

'Theo, I—'

'Tell us! Share all! What is *so* unbearable for you that you can't behave like a normal human being?' Spittle flies from his mouth and lands on the table in front of me.

'Honestly, Evelyn—'

'Why did you say it, Maggie?! Come on, why did you say all those *horrible* things?'

'Because it's fucking true!' I scream.

Silence descends upon the room.

Theo leans back in his chair, shaking his head.

'I mean . . . it's partially true. It's how I felt in that moment . . . I felt like it was all a waste of time, which it was, really . . . I felt depressed, maybe . . .' I'm scrabbling back to the mental health card in the hope of some leniency. 'I've been stressed and depressed and I felt it was true. I'm sick of it all.'

This part is not really a lie. I am pretty sick of all this.

Evelyn coughs. 'Well. I think there's some action that needs to be taken here. Mr Parbold, whilst I don't agree with the way you have handled this situation, I think the fact that there are issues with Maggie here is very clear. Before we defer to your judgement as manager, let's first ask Maggie herself what she thinks a solution to this problem might be.'

They both peer at me. Evelyn with a look of interest and expectation, Theo with a look of 'whatever you say is going to have no bearing on my decision whatsoever'. He's *really* mad at me.

'I think I need a break. Some time to get myself together, maybe. I can't carry on like this, I know that. I need to get my priorities straight and I don't think I can do that without some distance to reflect.'

Wow, I'm impressed with myself. That was bloody good. I can even feel that I've managed to make my face look sad. Well done, face.

'OK. If that's all you want to say, we can now ask Mr Parbold what his decision is as resolution to this issue.'

Theo sits up straight. He has just been handed the gavel and is absolutely in his element. Decide my fate, almighty Theo. Please give me my holiday.

I bet he's going to make me come in tomorrow. He knows how much I don't want to be here and actually making me work would be the perfect punishment for the humiliation I caused him yesterday.

'I don't really see any other solution than the one I am about to propose, I'm afraid.' He gives his stack of paperwork a sombre look. His amateur dramatics classes really were worth the fortune he paid for them. Perhaps if Christopher were here now he would see that it was worth sacrificing that kitchen extension for this very moment.

'I suggest termination.' Theo's gaze meets mine.

YES.

'OK.' I smile sadly. 'I'm sure after a few weeks I'll be back and better than ever. How long do you suggest?'

There's a small pause in the room and I glance between the two of them.

Wait. He did say suspension, didn't he?

'Termination, Maggie, would mean the end of your employment here. It would mean you wouldn't be coming back.' Evelyn gives me a sympathetic frown.

'WHAT?' I stand up. 'Termination?! I'm mentally ill!'

'We can all bloody see that,' Theo mutters under his breath.

'No! I have rent to pay! He can't do this, can he? Couldn't I sue? Isn't this . . . what do you call it? Wrongful dismissal? Discrimination?' I'm pleading with Evelyn.

'Unfortunately, this decision is down to Mr Parbold. His accounts of your behaviour at work, which have been backed up by your colleagues, suggest that you have been erratic and unprofessional and that is more than enough to justify termination. You'll work the four-week notice period and be paid for that, but then it will be time to go.' She grimaces. 'I'm sorry.'

'The amount of inappropriate stories I could tell about *you*, Theo . . .' I seethe across the table.

'We're here to discuss your behaviour at the moment, Miss Gardiner.' Evelyn says coolly. 'If you have any issues with Mr. Parbold's conduct, I urge you to meet with me and discuss it. You'll be here for another four weeks, so I'm sure we can make an appointment—'

'I think not.' I shove my chair under the table. 'You won't be seeing me ever again.'

'If you don't work through your notice period, you won't—'

'I've heard enough, thank you, Evelyn.' I march over to the door and yank it open. 'Expect to hear from my lawyer.'

And I'm gone.

Oh no. Oh no, oh no, oh no. This is really, really bad. Catastrophically, terribly fucking awful.

I don't even *have* a lawyer.

Being out of that soul-sucking basement chamber is all I have dreamed of for so long. But in my dreams, I left with money. A compensation pay out, or some lottery winnings. Never in my wildest fantasies did I imagine I would be walking out with my hands empty into a future of nothing.

'CHRIST!' I bang my hand on the seat in front of me. The bus driver slows a little and glances behind him.

'Sorry. All fine here.' I give him a thumbs-up. Maybe I *am* mentally ill. Normal people don't do the things I have done.

And what now? This month's pay came through this morning; it'll cover my next rent, but then . . .

I'll be paid for another month though, won't I? I remember when Sophie got made redundant at her old place, they paid her for another month after they told her. Although that was redundancy, not termination . . . and I remember she kept working there for a few weeks after the news. Her notice period, I think.

Oh god. The notice period.

The notice period I just screamingly refused to do.

Meaning no more money.

Not even until I find myself a new job.

The cut-off for payroll was a week ago, so I should get paid for this past week, AKA the worst week of my life. But that won't even be enough to pay my council tax and electricity bill.

I'll have to get on the job hunt. This could be a good thing, actually, a *real* strike through number five on my list. I've got a good load of scientific writing experience under my belt now; maybe I can try for something better. Maybe I'll get a new office full of exciting, vibrant people who have things in common with me and we'll go out for drinks on a Friday and bitch about our managers and everyone will neck each other and it'll be all dramatic like something from *Love Island*. As long as they don't have mortgages or children or any adult responsibilities whatsoever. I'm sure they won't, though. They'll be fun city-dwellers, living the high life and snorting coke off the Slug and Lettuce toilet cisterns. I won't partake in that part, but I'll definitely have a go at the necking.

Yes! I sit back happily in my seat, smiling like a mad woman, willing myself to stay sane. This is a good thing! I was miserable there, wasn't I? This is exactly the kick up the arse I needed. In fact, maybe my subconscious forced me into this. I've been acting up massively; maybe I was secretly trying to mess up so badly that Theo would make the decision for me, push me in the direction I needed. Maybe I have internalised the list. Perhaps the list has become my fate. Maybe I don't even need to *do* anything; destiny will just push me towards perfection.

This is excellent, it really is. If I tell myself it's excellent, it definitely will be excellent. I'll get applying as soon as I get home. Experience with a pharmaceutical company on my CV is bound to do me favours, and I'm sure I can plead with Theo to write me a good—

Wait.

Hold the bloody phone.

I sit up in my seat. Evelyn's voice is swimming in my memory.

If you don't work your notice period, you won't—

Won't what? My stomach sinks.

I know what.

If you don't work your notice period, you don't get a reference. Everyone knows if you just flounce off and leave, your employer can just refuse to write a reference for you. Or they'll write a crappy one so no one else will ever have you.

I slump backwards across the seat next to me and groan. I feel tears welling in my eyes. I am such a *dick*.

'Are you OK, love?' It's the sweaty man who smells like compost, looming down over me. Does he live on this bus or what?

OK, I'm really not one to judge right now.

'Yeah. Just having a breakdown, I'll be fine.' I close my eyes and he slides back into his seat, muttering to the woman next to him.

My phone pings in my coat pocket and I reach to grab it and hold it above my face.

Calendar Reminder: Yoga - 6 p.m.

Pfft. I balance my phone on my stomach and sigh. Yoga is absolutely last on my agenda right now, particularly considering I'm impoverished and could become homeless. Money might not be able to buy you happiness, but standing in downward dog and breathing rhythmically through your mouth certainly can't pay your rent.

I need a rational voice in my head. Unfortunately, I don't seem to have one of my own, so I decide to call Cecilia.

'Hello?' She yawns loudly.

'Hey, C. Are you working from home today?'

'Yep, going mental but at least I'm in my pyjamas.'

'Fancy a visitor?'

In the split second before she answers, I realise how desperately I need to see her. I need her to make me a cup of tea and let me sit on her pretty sofa with the chunky blanket her nan knitted her and tell me none of this is my fault.

'Sure, come and save me from myself. I've come dangerously close to opening a Terry's chocolate orange more times than I'm proud of.' She pauses. 'Why aren't you at work?'

'I'll explain later. Be there in ten?'

'OK.' She doesn't sound surprised. 'But I'm not getting dressed for you.'

12

'I've fucked it all up.' I wail as I throw myself at Cecilia, who manages to catch me despite being half my size.

'Come on, come inside. What's happened?' She ushers me through her open front door and into the living room, where she plops me on the sofa. I launch into sobbing about my misfortune but she holds up her hand. 'Wait, wait, wait. Tea?'

I nod and she trots into the kitchen, all brisk efficiency in the face of a crisis. I grab a tissue from the handmade tissue box sitting on the coffee table. Half the sequins have fallen off but it took David two months to make so he won't let her throw it out.

I curl up on the sofa and hold the tissue to my face, absorbing the quiet calm of Cecilia's living room. It's a weird hodgepodge of IKEA furniture adorned with amateur items whipped up in David's art classes. A white Billy bookcase holds painted cigarette cases, wonky pottery and, weirdly, a bejewelled penis. Photos of the two of them litter every wall and surface; some framed in varnished pine and others in multi-coloured macramé. The combination always feels homely and comforting and I wonder, not for the first time, if they'll let me live here on their sofa forever. It's doubtful, though – I couldn't even promise to do any housework in return.

Cecilia wobbles back into the room balancing two over-flowing cups and a plate of biscuits on a rustic wooden tray, which slopes upwards at the end and only has one handle. By the time she places it on the table it's swimming with tea.

'Thanks, C.' I dab at my mug with another tissue.

'Right, come on. Tell me what's happened.' She leans forward and clasps her tea between her hands.

I fill her in on the whole shitty mess, shovelling biscuits into my mouth between words. By the time I'm finished I need another drink – preferably something a bit stronger.

'Have you got any vodka?' I smile weakly.

She ignores me and looks me dead in the eye. 'I think it's impulse control, Mags.'

'Impulse control?' I don't like where this is going. I don't want to be told there's something wrong with me, I want to be hugged and fed and assured that it's all Theo's fault. Why isn't she telling me it's all Theo's fault? I take the last biscuit off the tray and inhale it.

'You don't really think before you do stuff, do you? And hey, it's brilliant most of the time, we love you for it, but in some situations it might be worth just . . . holding back a bit?'

'Holding back?' I'm parroting now, because I don't under-stand what she means.

'Yeah. Like, maybe when something happens you could just stop for a second and think a bit. Then react.' She smiles encouragingly.

I blink. Impulse control. Do I not have impulse control?

Cecilia senses my confusion and grabs my hand. 'Like I said, it's definitely not a bad thing, Mags. It's who you are. You're crazy and reckless and you do what feels right in the moment – it's amazing. But when you do things like that at work . . . people just don't take it well. Especially if they don't know you.'

'Shit.' I put my head in my hands. 'I'm reckless. This is all my fault.'

'Nooo! Well . . . yes, sort of, but no!' She curls up next to me on the sofa. 'You're great, Maggie, and I'm only saying this because I love you. But you self-destruct when you don't think things through. Remember when we were at uni and you bought that expensive all-day-breakfast sandwich, and the first bit you put in your mouth had a chewy crust so you launched it straight in the bin?'

'Yeah. It bounced off the side and one of the sausages landed on Boring Bethan's shoulder.' I sniff.

'Well that's sort of what you do with like, everything. You react before you even check. Which works in some situations; you don't find it difficult to make decisions which is a really good attribute. But sometimes you miss out because you jump on your immediate response and don't consider any alternative options.'

My god, she's absolutely right. What if the rest of the breakfast sandwich had been soft and palatable?

'What do I do?' I whisper.

'Just stop. When you're about to make a decision about something important, stop and think whether it's normal behaviour in that situation or whether it's just what you feel like doing. Then just go for the normal thing.'

'OK.' I'm not sure I want to carry on talking about this, it's making me feel sick.

'Nice tray.' I nod towards the wonky, soggy mess on the table.

'Oh, don't. David's on woodwork at the moment.'

'Jesus Christ.'

'I know. It's furniture now. I've managed to slip pieces of his other stuff into the back of the cupboard, or in the skanky bathroom that no one uses, you know? But this . . . how do you hide a hand-carved bookcase?'

'Shit. It's worse than the papier-mâché.'

We both look up at the giant head sculpture sitting on the dining table. It's lobster pink, with electric blue eyes and tufts of matted blonde hair superglued to the top. It's grotesque, and it's supposed to be Cecilia.

OK, maybe it's not worse than the papier-mâché.

David is a freelance life coach, and clients are very, very scarce because a) who wants a life coach, we're not in California and b) he's completely bonkers and word has gotten around about Brenda and the cactuses.

Yes, this is an actual story.

Brenda was David's first client, who had an obsession with cactuses (cacti? I don't know). It was severely impacting on her quality of life because she couldn't bear to leave the house in case one of them got too dehydrated or something. David said something along the lines of 'come on Brenda, they come from the fucking desert, love' and told her to leave them for a week as a test. Brenda did as she was told and when she returned from a nice holiday in Skegness the cat had eaten every single cactus and died. Brenda has since been diagnosed with a learning disability which helped her swerve an animal neglect charge, and David was featured in an article titled '*Life Coaching: A Destructive Tool In The Wrong Hands?*' He hasn't had much business since then. With sweet FA to do most days, he spends the majority of his time at various art classes, learning a new craft every month and filling his and Cecilia's house with crap in the process.

'Just get rid of it.' I shudder, tearing my eyes away from the gaze of Cecilia 2.0.

'I can't. He was *so* proud of it. I can't even break it because he sees it as some symbol of his love for me, and its destruction would be the destruction of our relationship or whatever.' She sighs.

'What?'

'Don't even ask, Mags. It's bonkers.' She runs her hand through her short, blonde hair. 'Anyway, what are you doing tonight?'

'Oh, I don't know.' I put my mug back on the table. 'I was going to go to that yoga class but I think I'll just go home and eat fried chicken and cry.'

'See? This is what I'm talking about. You choosing the decision that's easiest but gets you nowhere.' She says it kindly, but it reminds me of what Kelsey said the other day.

That's why you'll always be stuck at the bottom, whilst everyone else makes an effort and actually gets somewhere.

She's right, of course. I always do the easy thing, or the thing that makes me happy or comfortable in that moment. I'm the friend who disappears on a night out, because in the middle of 'Mr Brightside' I realise I want a pizza and my duvet and walk out without going through the rigmarole of telling everybody. Instant gratification, I think they call it.

'Fine. Fine, fine, fine.' I stand up and spread my arms. 'I'm going to yoga. I'm going to sort my life out and get flexible.'

'That's my girl.' Cecilia rises from the sofa and wraps me in a bony hug. 'You're fab, Mags. You'll figure it all out.'

I head over to the door and shove my shoes on, nearly toppling over and grabbing the nearest thing for balance.

'What the hell is that?' I jerk my hand away from the tall sculpture. Long, gnarled wood twists upwards, and antlers shoot out in every direction from the top. It looks like a destroyed beach umbrella with a death curse.

'It's a hat stand.' Cecilia stares at her feet.

'A hat stand?'

'Yes.'

'How many hats do you own?'

'Two. My beanie and that horrible one I wore to my cousin's wedding last year.'

'So . . . why do you have a hat stand?'

'I told you, David's into woodwork now.' She gazes at it sadly.

'Oh my god. Are those real antlers?'

'No. He carved them. Oak, apparently.'

'Jesus, Cecilia, you can't carry on like this. It looks like something from a cabin-based horror movie.' I swallow nervously.

'I know. Do you want it? If I told him you'd taken a shine to it I'm sure he wouldn't mind—'

'Absolutely not.' I interrupt. 'No way.'

She sighs. 'All right.'

I wrench the door open and step out into the cool air, desperate to get as far away as possible from the monstrosity inside.

'Chin up, enjoy yoga and call me later, yes?' Cecilia smiles.

'Only if you promise to do something about the hunting shed your house is becoming.' I pat her arm sympathetically. She'll never take action. She'll say nothing until one day she wakes up to find her bath is made of silver birch. 'See ya.'

I give her one final squeeze and head down the garden path.

OK. Yoga. I can do this. Everyone can do yoga, can't they? It's not like a marathon. I've never heard of anyone coming back from a yoga class and saying, 'God, that's completely wiped me out.' No. Ninety-year-olds do it, fat people do it, homeless people do it at the cathedral. It's for everyone, isn't it? I'm part of everyone.

I am climbing the four flights of stairs to the studio and breathing with some difficulty. I'm only at the second floor. Is this the warm-up? Why isn't there a lift? I thought they were a legal requirement now; it's not very inclusive to not have a lift. What about our diverse and accessible society? Some people need lifts, what if I were in a wheelchair?

Oh, shut up, Maggie. You're overweight and lazy, not disabled.

I grasp the handrail and pull myself upwards, step by step. After an embarrassing amount of time I arrive at the top and pause outside reception to get my breath back. God, I feel like I've done enough now. That's more exercise than I've had in weeks – I'll sleep well tonight. I'm very tempted to go home. I'm peering through the glass panel in the door and I can see incense and an impossibly thin man with dreadlocks surrounded by cushions behind the reception desk. He's swaying and slapping the table in time to a beat I can't hear. Christ.

I take my hand off the door handle and go to turn around, but an image of the list swims into my mind.

Come on, Maggie! Resist the impulse!

I force my feet forward and open the door. Dreadlocks turns his face towards me and breaks into a grin.

'Well, hello you!'

Wait. Do I know him? I swear I've never seen him before.

'Hello!' I smile extra-enthusiastically. If it turns out he doesn't know me he'll just think I'm keen.

'Who do we have here?' He beckons me over to the desk. OK, so he doesn't know me, and he's talking to me like it's my first day at nursery. Is it too late to pretend I'm in the wrong place?

'I'm here for the beginners' yoga course.' I force myself to say. Trap myself in my circumstances so I can't back out.

'Wow. *Wow.*' He claps. 'This is amazing. This is the first day of the rest of your life, I LOVE it.' He whips a piece of paper out from the drawer with such speed I wince. That's a recipe for paper cuts if ever there was one.

'Ha. Yes.' What else can I say?

'I absolutely, completely and utterly adore this moment. Do you feel it? This one, this moment right here.' He gestures to the empty space between us. An awkward second passes whilst he closes his eyes and inhales noisily. 'You're starting your journey and you don't even *know* it. Your first experience of yoga.' He gazes into the distance. 'I remember my first time.'

I watch him lick his lips. 'Great! OK, wonderful. So do I pay here, or—?'

'Yes! Yes. Just fill in your details and then we'll process the payment.'

I take the paper and go to turn around.

'And *then!*' I turn back. 'Your journey of mind and body begins.' He claps again.

I scuttle into a corner where I sink myself into a beanbag. I'll never be able to get up from here. Am I actually about to part with £50 for the privilege of climbing those stairs five more times and dealing with that nutter every week? Oh good lord, what if he's the teacher? I will not be able to cope.

I distract myself by turning my attention to the form.

Name, age, address etc.

Gender identity. Female? Girl? Woman? Slightly masculine at times? What's the correct answer? I scribble 'female' and move on.

Spiritual identity. What does that *mean*? I write 'undecided'.

Divine motivation (if applicable). Not applicable in any sense.

I scan the rest of the form and scrawl 'N/A' next to every optional question. I attempt to haul myself up from the cushion and succeed at finding myself on my hands and knees, my paper crumpled in my fist. Rising ungracefully to my feet, I stumble back over to reception.

'Nice Cow.' Dreadlocks winks.

'Excuse me?'

'Your Cow position over there. Great warm-up.'

'Oh. The doggy style thing I did?' I blush immediately. How I wish I had a filter.

'Oh no, the doggy style position is known as the 'cat'. The back is arched with the buttocks in the air.' He takes my form and smooths it out, then files it away without looking. Thank god.

'I guess I'll learn the technical terms soon.' I smile weakly, tapping my pin into the card-reader he's holding out to me. It beeps: too late now.

'Yes! In exactly five minutes! If you want to go through there, the studio is on your left. There's a rack for shoes and socks at the door.' He reaches forward and grabs my hand suddenly. 'Enjoy it. Live it. Breathe into it.'

I wrench my hand out of his and run through the door to the left, checking over my shoulder to see him staring at me with misty eyes. Holy fuck.

I peel my socks off and stuff them inside my shoes. My toenails are chipped. Actually, scratch 'chipped', they're less than fifty per cent polish at this point. Hopefully no one will look. I push the door to the studio open and I'm pleasantly surprised to find a bright, airy space with pale wooden floors and whitewashed walls. It does feel quite relaxing.

There's one woman here already, sitting in the middle of the floor with her eyes closed. I don't trust people who choose a space in the middle. Who walks into an empty room and just plonks themselves right at the centre? Everyone knows you stick to the periphery unless you don't have a choice. In contrast to Dreadlocks on reception, this lady looks like she's just come straight from her corporate tower. Her hair is pinned into a chignon, she's wearing smart designer glasses and her lips are a vicious shade of red. Even her workout clothes are business-like; all black and skin-tight like a ninja.

'Are you here for the beginner's course, too?' I peer at her. She sighs and her eyes flutter open. 'Yes.'

She gives me a withering look and her eyes slide closed again. Rude.

I grab myself a mat and wedge myself into the corner, where I feel comfortable surrounded by walls. Plus, no one will be able to see my bum when I do the Cat position. Everyone's going to see *her* bum, the corporate bore. Also, isn't this supposed to be a beginner's class? What is she doing meditating like she already knows stuff?

Other people straggle into the room, finding spaces against the walls and fidgeting nervously on their mats. Like *normal* people. We're all essentially circled around Corporate Bore, and I feel for a moment as though we're about to watch her perform some interpretative dance for us.

We are saved from the crippling awkwardness by the arrival of another person, a man, who looks around self-consciously and then drags a mat and parks it next to me.

'Hi, sorry, is this beginner's yoga?' he whispers.

'Yeah. I hope so!' I whisper back. 'Why are we whispering?'

He laughs and his face explodes into the biggest smile I've ever seen. It's quite alarming. 'I don't know!'

He has really kind eyes. He's only about my age, but he has overly pronounced laughter lines, which immediately make me like him. He obviously spends a lot of his time happy.

'I'm Gary, by the way.' He murmurs, fiddling with the cuff of his pants. *Gary?* Didn't people stop calling their babies Gary in the seventies? I thought they'd be extinct by 2050. This guy will be a lone wolf.

Although who am I to talk?

'Maggie.' I smile and he returns it, shocking me again with the transformation of his face.

'Oooookaaaaayyyyyyy.' Someone breathes, and we look up.

Corporate Bore is rising to her feet with the elegance of a flamingo trained in ballet. She turns on her heel and regards us all calmly.

'Good afternoon and welcome. Welcome to our six-week beginner's yoga class.'

What is she doing? Why is she welcoming us?

Oh my god, is she the teacher?!

'My name is Altantsetseg.'

Her name is *what*?

'I don't expect you to be able to pronounce it straight away. It's my Buddhist name, and it means "golden flower".' She smooths her t-shirt.

OK, I full on thought she said golden shower for a second. That must happen a lot. Can I get a Buddhist name? I'd like a really edgy one.

Probably not.

'Over the next six weeks, we are going to go on a journey together. You will see your mind and body stretch and expand beyond your own expectations.'

I hope this is figurative. My body does not need to expand.

'Let's start by introducing ourselves. If we could each say our name and why we're here.'

The entire room bristles. This is the worst possible circumstance to be in. Trapped in a room full of complete strangers, about to embark on an activity of which you have no knowledge and which will probably make you look ridiculous, and asked to present yourself as a normal human at five seconds' notice.

'Let's start with . . . you.' She nods at a girl a few spaces down from me.

'Oh. Well, I'm Casey, and I want to get more flexible.' She reddens slightly.

Good girl, Casey. Set the bar nice and low. A name and a simple statement are now all that is expected of introducer number two.

'Hi everyone, I'm Jack, and I'm doing yoga because I want to improve my core strength and posture. I get quite a few problems with my back from time to time.'

OK, Jack, well done for ruining it for everybody. Firstly you've gone and given a greeting to the room, which no one else will want to do because it's *awkward*, and secondly you've raised the bar and now we all feel like we have to give as much detail as you did. The tension in the room grows as people scrabble in their brains for something interesting to say.

Gary is next. 'I'm Gary, and I'm here because I wanted to try something new.'

YES Gary.

Right, my turn.

'Hi, I'm Maggie. I'm here because I want to do something different and take myself out of my comfort zone.' OK, that'll do. 'I've been told I have a problem with impulsiveness and running away from my problems, so I'm trying to force myself to do something which makes me feel uncomfortable.' Oh, look, I'm still talking. Why am I still talking? 'I also just broke up with my boyfriend and keep eating and drinking way too much, so I wrote a list and I'm hoping this will calm me down a bit and help me shed a few of the family buckets off my thighs.' I jiggle my legs in demonstration. I need to stop. They're all staring at me. The silence is unbearable. 'Also because it seems fun. Not fun, I mean new. Enjoyable. Exciting? Yes. Something

114

like that. It seems great, absolutely great. OK, who's next?' My face is hot and my heart is hammering in my chest.

Isn't yoga supposed to be relaxing? This is ridiculous.

The rest of the room hastily introduce themselves, a slight sense of relief in their voices as they know they can't fuck it up any more than I did. Well, I took one for the team. That's something.

'Right, great, it's lovely to meet you all.' Altantsetseg scans our faces and avoids my eye. 'We'll start with a joint-freeing sequence. If we could all sit on our mats with our legs out in front of us.'

We spend the next half an hour copying her movements, which are bloody boring to say the least. A full minute of rotating my left wrist, followed by a full two minutes of moving my head from side-to-side. Have I signed up for a weird type of yoga? I didn't read the small print.

'OK. That was great. You should all feel nice and loose now.'

Gary splutters and Altantsetseg glares at him.

'Now we're going to try some rudimentary poses. I want you to practice everything we do today at home before next week, so pay attention to how we transition.'

She moves swiftly from sitting cross-legged into a doggy style (sorry, *Cow*) position. We copy.

'Now from Cow . . .' she arches her back, 'we go into cat.'

Dreadlocks was right, this one is definitely more doggy style. I mirror her movements. This is really easy! Feels nice on my lower back, too.

'Remember to breathe. The breath is central to our yoga practice. Focus on the body's movement and the breath's journey and clear your mind of other thoughts.' She inhales deeply through her nose.

Right. I alternate between Cat and Cow with each breath, matching her pace. I focus on the air entering my nostrils and my back stretching and contracting. Inhale. Stretch. Exhale. Contract.

115

Contract. Job contract. I don't have a job contract. How has this happened? How have I rendered myself unemployed in the space of a week? This time yesterday I was terrified I'd be getting a major telling off. If only.

I wonder what type of job I'll apply for now. Scientific writing is the obvious choice, but what about a fresh start? One I won't need a reference for in particular. I've already discounted detective work and lawyering. I do like the idea of working in a café. All the busy lives and the steam and the cosiness. I'd have to stand up all day, though. Maybe it's just the concept I like. I've never tried it, have I?

Shit. Concentrate! I've stopped breathing in time and my pace has quickened so I'm flipping my back up and down like an epileptic seal.

'OK, now we're going to bring our left leg forward,' Altantsetseg brings her left foot to the front of the mat, keeping her right knee on the floor, 'and then hold our knee and twist the body gently.'

Ooh. That sort of hurts, but in a nice way. My abs and legs are aching already. What's this called? I can't remember. The proposal position, I'd call it. The exact position Martin was in a few days ago. I cringe into myself. That ring was so pretty. But I could have bought one myself if he'd paid half rent like I asked him to. God, I'm glad he's gone. I haven't even thought about him really. Isn't that mean? Is it horrible of me not to have thought about him?

My legs are shaking like crazy. How much longer is she going to keep us here? I feel like I'm going to topple over any second and start a domino effect across the entire room. *Don't stop now, Maggie, come on. Keep it going. This is how you improve. Don't embarrass yourself in front of—*

Shit. I really need to fart.

Hold it, hold it, hold it!!! I'm willing it to retreat with every cell in my being. I've never clenched so hard in my life. It'd probably be a silent one, I'm in a pretty exposed position, but there are people everywhere – I'd never get away with it. Oh god, help, please. Don't let me become the yoga farting cliché.

'OK, now switching legs and bringing our opposite foot forward.'

Good. I can suck it up whilst I switch legs. Just need to bring this knee backwards . . .

Brrrrrrrrp.

Oh my lord, no.

My arse has let rip mid-transition.

The gaseous cat is out of the bag.

Every eye in the room has turned to me.

I feel a heat rise from my chest and prickle at my face. Fuck, fuck, fuck. I can still hear the fart ringing in the silence of the room. I could blame it on Gary? Look at him and scoff in disgust? No, it's too late. I'm bright red; my face has incriminated me.

I hover in silence, one leg trembling awkwardly beneath me. Slowly the fart spreads, and people's faces scrunch up around the room like a Mexican wave.

I run.

13

I've bloody well done it again, haven't I? I've let impulsivity take over and legged it. Although, to be honest, what type of sick freak would carry on enjoying their yoga lesson whilst the rest of the room rhythmically inhaled their anus gas? Not the kind of person I'd want to be associated with, that's for sure.

Well, that's fifty quid down the pan. Excellent.

Why are we all so judgy about farts anyway? Literally *everyone* does it. I saw the way Altantsetseg looked at me – like she doesn't sit on the sofa and let rip like the rest of us. Probably even more so, considering the amount of lentils I bet she eats.

I feel utterly miserable. I'm traipsing back home via Market Street, gazing into the shop windows and wondering when the next time will be that I have a steady salary and can actually buy stuff. It's just so unfair. I've brought it all on myself though, really, and that feels even worse.

The chuggers are out in full force this evening, and an obese man on a skateboard is playing 'My Heart Will Go On' on the banjo. You wouldn't think it would work, but it sort of does, and people are dropping money in his hat like there's no tomorrow. The human statue of the day appears to be Winston Churchill – although he looks like he's been on rations and has dropped a good five stone.

Oh, and here are the vegans. Standing outside Boots in a circle, wearing anonymous masks and holding MacBooks showing videos of animal torture in the meat industry. Wonderful, now I feel better.

I stop and watch for a second. I don't have anywhere to be, do I? A man tries to hand me a bible and I shrug him off. Jesus, these videos are horrible. I'm watching one about chickens and I can see the eyes of the man behind the mask boring into me. Is he willing me to become vegan through telepathy? It's freaking me out, so I grab a pamphlet and carry on home.

I can't get the image of that poor chicken out of my head. Is that what happened to the one on the fajita pizza I was going to have for tea? But chicken is *so nice*. And steak. Imagine a life without steak. Actually, that's vegetarians, isn't it? Vegans can't even eat cheese! I feel sick at the thought.

As soon as I'm back in the apartment I sink onto the sofa and pull out the pamphlet. It's quite interesting, actually. There are lots of cute baby animals on every page, which I definitely like. The idea of someone beheading and eating them makes me really upset, and I start crying for the second time today. I knew this happened, of course, but I imagined all the lambs frolicking in pasture until someone shot them painlessly without any warning. I didn't realise they lived crammed together, covered in their own shit until they were murdered painfully. I wish I didn't know this.

Through the blur of my tears I spot the title of the final page. '*Health Benefits*.' Hmm. Interesting. I wipe my eyes and read about how much healthier being a vegan is. Come to think of it, I've never seen a fat vegan. How can you get fat when you live on beans and broccoli?

I gaze down at the podge creeping over the waistband of my leggings. I've tried the Cup-a-Soup diet, the lemon water diet *and* the SlimFast shakes, all since New Year. I actually think I've put *on* weight, because I was usually so starving after a day of consuming nothing but water and powder that I tended to go home and stuff myself with a family-size Iceland lasagne.

I go on Instagram and type in '#vegan'.

This food actually looks . . . really good! Pizza is apparently still doable, and banana bread. And is that macaroni cheese? *How?*

OK, there's a lot of avocado here. Like, an obscene amount. I'm not sure I like avocado, but apparently it's a mandatory requirement for vegans. Like believing in God if you're a Christian, or doing your dissertation if you want a degree. You can't be a vegan if you don't eat a minimum of one avocado a day.

Everyone on here is so skinny and vibrant. This woman allegedly ate a huge bowl of chickpeas and bread for lunch and is now padding about in a thong looking like the Queen. If the Queen was a sexual goddess.

Some of these people look better than Emma Penton. Bloody hell, imagine! What would my world be like if I could be even healthier, skinnier and more vibrant than Emma-bloody-Penton? Nothing would ever be difficult again. The idea is incomprehensible, like trying to imagine what aliens might look like.

I'm going to do it. I'm going to be a vegan. This is a sensible life decision for me and the planet. And surely it can't be that hard?

I smooth my list out on the coffee table, accidentally ripping one of the corners off in my excitement. I write:

8. Go vegan.

And then I draw an arrow to number two: lose weight. The two go hand in hand, surely. I scan my eyes down the rest of the items and realise that I've already, technically, achieved one of my goals. I draw a thick, straight line through 6. *Start yoga.*

I did it! I actually made a plan and stuck to it. The farting is a distant memory; I am immensely proud.

My eyes find *7. Do tea detox*, and I suddenly remember the box of it sitting in my online basket and tap to checkout. Maybe I could become a new influencer, pairing tea with vegan recipes and losing loads of weight and being hot as shit. Teaganism. No. That doesn't work.

It makes sense to cook something non-vegan for tea, my last supper, seeing as I don't have any avocados in the house at the moment. It's surely worse for the poor animals if they're brutally killed and then not even eaten? Their death completely in vain? Yes, it definitely is. I'll have my chicken fajita pizza and we'll start in the morning.

Right, breakfast is a struggle. My cereal appears to be vegan, but the four pints of semi-skimmed in my fridge most certainly are not. I could have toast, but butter is definitely just as bad as milk, and I don't even know where to begin with Nutella. I settle with dry cereal and some stale seeds that Martin left behind. It is utterly vile and the Special K flakes are sucking all the moisture out of my mouth. I'm washing each mouthful down with huge glugs of tap water and trying to pretend that it's milk and that everything is fine. Everything is not fine.

The apartment is an absolute state. Only eight days since I booted Martin out of my life and it's in a complete mess. He hasn't contacted me, which is unsurprising but is also giving my ego a massive pummelling. *I* kicked *him* out, isn't he supposed to be begging me to take him back? He asked me to spend the rest of my life with him, and then walked (well, was pushed, really) out of the door and never looked back. I don't want him back; I'm just about starting to acclimatise to life on my own again. But I do believe I at least deserve the courtesy of some 2 a.m. drunk texts I can smugly ignore.

God, I'm such a bad person. I don't want to be one of those girls who gets nasty with their exes. I want to rise above it all and wish him well, and I really do wish him well. I want him to be happy. But I do feel a little put-out that he isn't pining after me. I don't want him, I just want his attention.

And his cleaning skills.

The floor is really bitty. Lots of little crusty things in the carpet. How did that happen so fast? I wasn't a big cleaner before Martin, but I don't remember things getting this rank this quickly. Maybe my standards are higher now? I'm so used to living in pristine conditions that I notice the slightest bit of dirt. And I'm so used to doing nothing to maintain said pristine conditions, that I just assume things tick over quite nicely with minimal effort.

That is obviously not the case.

I can't be doing with this. I need to get out of this shit hole. There's no way I can stay here all day getting pizza crumbs between my toes. I could clean, but the hoover is really heavy and I haven't got the energy after forgoing my usual milky breakfast.

I'll go and visit Nana, that's what I'll do. Get one step closer towards ticking another item off my list. A couple of digestives and a lavender-scented hug and I'll be right as rain. Better give her some warning first though, or she'll get muddled and won't have time to make me any butties.

Half an hour later and I'm on the tram out of Manchester, heading towards Altrincham. Nana offered to come and pick me up from the station when I told her that no, of course 'Mummy wasn't bringing me', but I reminded her that 11 a.m. on a Thursday isn't exactly peak kidnapping time. I did worry that she might wonder why I wasn't at work, but I'm not entirely sure she has her days of the week straight at the moment. Right now she'll be flying around the house polishing all her porcelain figurines and turning the gas fire up to an unbearable temperature for my arrival.

I hurry off the tram and into the rain-soaked streets of Altrincham town centre. Nana lives in a little terraced house two minutes' walk behind the market hall. She's lived there since she got married and the entire place is like a shrine to my long-dead Gramps. It's a bit creepy.

I walk tentatively up to the front door and knock loudly. All the stone out here is covered in mould; it's a death trap.

'Nana!' I cry out as soon as she opens the door, launching myself into her woollen bosom.

'My goodness!' She laughs and holds me at arm's length. 'Is that my Marge? You've gotten so big!'

She is the only person I let get away with calling me anything but Maggie or Mags. It's always Marge or Margie, although the other month she accidentally called me 'Margarine'.

'I only saw you a few weeks ago Nana, I don't think I've grown since then.' I rub her arm. What does she mean, I've gotten *big*? 'Let's get inside, it's freezing.'

The heat smacks me in the face as soon as I'm over the threshold. A stifling, talcum-powdery wave of epic proportions. The first bead of sweat has formed on my top lip before we even reach the living room.

'Now, what are we having? A nice cup of tea?' She potters through into the kitchen and I follow her.

'I'll just have a glass of water, please. Let me get it.' I take the mug from her hand and fill it from the tap, gulping it down. I'm dehydrated after thirty seconds in here.

'Use a glass, love!' She pulls a crystal tumbler from the cupboard and fills it for me. 'Are you sure you don't want a milky brew?'

'Nana, if I have a cup of tea I think I'll die. It's far too hot in here. Are you drinking enough?' She's wearing two jumpers.

'Oh, if I drink too much I need the toilet, you know that!' she chuckles.

I think that's sort of how it works, isn't it? I decide against the argument we've had a thousand times. I take over the tea-making and sit her down in her armchair, setting her drink down on a coaster that has a photo of my Gramps' face on it. I never really understood the concept of coasters with faces on them – who wants to slam a boiling hot beverage on top of someone they love? Of course you could get ones with faces of your enemies instead – that could work. Theo springs to mind.

'You've got some new things, have you?' I reach over to a cushion with 'Enid & Bernard' painted across it in italics. It's very soft and very weird.

'Oh yes, don't you think Bernie would have loved it?' She takes it from me and hugs it to her chest.

I would be feeling quite dewy-eyed in this moment if it weren't for the fact that Gramps would have absolutely detested every single thing in this room. 'Military clinical' was his general style, and Nana knows that better than anybody. Sometimes I wonder if she does this as a little 'fuck you' to the heavens. A *can't stop me buying cushions now, Bernie* kind of thing.

'I'm sure he would, yes,' I lie. 'So how have you been?'

'Well, you know. Not good. Never good. My back's been playing up again and this cough –' she coughs to demonstrate, as though the word might need explaining, '–will not bugger off, it just won't.'

'Oh dear. Have you been to the doctors?'

'I live at the doctor's, love! Doctor Fashid, he's called. Absolutely useless.' She shakes her head.

'Well!' I say, interrupting the flow before it inevitably gets racist. 'We'll find you a new one. Now, where are your lovely biscuits?'

She claps her hand over her mouth. 'Oh my goodness. I forgot the lovely biscuits.' Her eyes fill with tears.

'Don't worry!' I wave my hands about, trying to convey that I'm not absolutely heartbroken by this statement. I live for Nana's lovely biscuits.

'It's almost lunchtime anyway,' she sniffles, 'how about I make you some ham butties?'

Oh god. I've just remembered. I'm vegan now. How can I live without Nana's ham butties? This is a travesty. Maybe I could start again tomorrow? No! This is what I always do, I never stick at anything. I will see this veganism through if it kills me, which it may well do if I can never eat a ham butty again.

'Extra butter and no crusts, Margie?' Nana has made her way into the kitchen and is laying out thick slices of white bread on a plate.

124

'Oh, erm, Nana . . . there's something I need to tell you.' I follow her through and gently hold her wrist to stop her taking a seventh slice out of the packet.

She peers up at me with watery eyes. 'You're in trouble, aren't you?' She slaps a piece of bread onto the counter. 'I bloody knew it! I knew that Benjamin would ruin you!'

'What? Nana, I broke up with Ben when I was sixteen. I'm not pregnant, I promise.' I think Nana last had full control of her faculties when my Gramps died in 2006, and in her mind we are all in the exact same situation as we were back then. I am united with Bonkers Ben as long as my grandmother walks this earth.

'He's not asked you to marry him has he?'

This is going to take some time.

'We're not together, Nana, I'm single. There are no men, no marriages, no babies.'

And also no job. No need to mention Martin, the failed proposal and my current career-decline. No need for that at all.

'Oh.' She smiles at me and reaches for the butter knife. 'Well then, we've no need to worry, have we?'

'Nana.' I take the knife and she meets my gaze. 'I'm vegan.'

'Oh my goodness.' She reaches for a dining chair with a trembling hand and steadies herself. 'Oh, Margie.'

'It's fine, Nana, really—'

She takes my hand. 'How do you know?'

'Erm, well, I suppose you reach a point where you just *know* you need to do something, and—'

'When did you find out?' She's gone white. This is not the reaction I was expecting.

'Find out? Well, last night I—'

'Oh, Margie. My lovely Margie. I'm so sorry.' She pulls me in and rocks me from side to side.

'Calm down, it's not a death sentence!'

'Isn't it?' She pulls away. 'Well, I don't know much about these things, of course. But modern medicine these days is so advanced . . .' She sinks down into the chair, lost in thought with tears dripping down her cheeks.

Oh dear. She thinks I'm dying, doesn't she?

'Nana, do you know what vegan means?'

'Oh, I can't keep track of all the illnesses and ailments people are coming down with at the moment. Victor up the road died last week, he had a lump up his bottom! Isn't that ridiculous? Couldn't he have just gone to the toilet and passed it out?' She wipes her nose. 'Everything kills you these days.'

Christ, poor Victor.

'Veganism is when you don't eat any meat. Or butter, or eggs and things.'

Nana looks at me for a second, and then bursts out laughing. 'You little tyke! You had me going there for a second!' She tuts and gets up, unwrapping the ham with her back to me.

'No, Nana, I'm serious. I don't eat those things anymore.' I take the ham and put it back in the fridge. The lovely, lovely ham. Goodbye, my lover. Goodbye, my friend. I'm sorry, Nana.

'No meat? And no butter either?' Her face starts to take on an alarming shade of red. 'Silly girl! What else is there to eat if not meat and butter? You'll starve!'

'Beans?' I murmur sheepishly.

'Beans!' She wails.

'And avocado?' I try.

'What? What on earth is an avmorado?' She looks confused now, dazed.

'Nana, come and sit down. I'll make you another cup of tea and get some lunch for us.'

'I'm just so disappointed in you, love. I thought you made better choices than this.' She starts crying again.

This is too much. She's actually crying harder now than she was when she thought I was dying. How charming is that? My demise is nothing compared to the idea of me living a life devoid of a proper British roast. Marvellous.

I decide to leave her to calm down whilst I get some beans on toast sorted. No butter for me, and the impending dryness already makes me want to throw myself on the gas fire. I'm putting the plates on the table when Nana walks in, smiling widely, our previous conversation forgotten. Thank god for the early stages of dementia.

'Well, isn't this a treat!' She sits down. 'I love beans on toast.'

I decide not to remind her that the word 'beans' almost gave her a stroke twenty minutes ago.

'Now, I can see you've got quite a big portion there, Margie.' She nods towards my plate. 'Have you seen how little our Suzannah is now? She's absolutely beautiful. Credits it all to portion control.' She gets up and shuffles into the living room in search of something.

Suzannah is my cousin, two years younger than me and, whilst she's always been ever-so-slightly overweight, she's also always been a nob. The kind of self-obsessed, see-through lip-gloss and chewing gum, hair to her bum, major Snapchatter kind of nob. Always so much more polished than me, and even with the extra pounds her body just fits her better. It is a real pity that she has the personality of a cross between a sheep and a dishcloth, but nobody else sees that, do they?

'Look!' Nana is thrusting a photo under my bean-crusted nose. Suzannah appears to have dropped about two stone, and is looking absolutely fucking radiant. She's the kind of girl that doesn't smile for pictures, and squelches up her filler-lips even for a family photo. In this particular picture she's managing to look seductive whilst holding a friend's baby against her exposed cleavage. It's obscene, it really is.

'Good for her.' I murmur, shovelling more beans into my mouth.

'Portion control, she says it was. That's how she did it!' Nana swings her gaze towards my fourth slice of toast.

Portion control, my arse. If you can call the SlimFast shakes, raspberry ketone tablets and protein powder mix she's been epileptically documenting on Instagram portion control, then I obviously know nothing.

And *yes,* before you say it, I *did* buy all my SlimFast shakes from her earlier in the year. She was convincing! And I hadn't actually realised it was a pyramid scheme until it was too late. It doesn't matter now anyway; I'm a healthy vegan and I mustn't dwell on the past.

I move Nana onto less self-esteem-destroying topics whilst I do the washing up, and then gather my things to leave. As I'm putting my shoes on, Nana presses something into my hand. I try to hide my disappointment when I see that it isn't a tenner, but a small potted plant.

'Aw, thanks, Nana.' I smile weakly.

'You're sad, love. You need a little brightness in your life.'

And then I really do start to cry.

I cried all the way to the station, I cried on the tram, I cried all the way home and now I'm crying some more.

At first I thought I was crying because I really did need that tenner, but then I looked at my tears collecting on the leaves of the plant nestled in my lap and realised that I was crying about a million other things instead.

How unfair is it that horrible, vapid Suzannah gets to be skinny and pretty whilst I'm sitting here with an actual *personality* and a belly like a Hartley's jelly cup? How did Cecilia get an amazing job where she gets to work from her lovely home all the time, when I got a 2.1 in Biology and she got a third in Media Studies? Why has Anna managed to find the love of her life on the V1, whilst I'm moving from one failed shitfest of a relationship to the next? And when did my lovely Nana get this forgetful?

I don't hold back on my self-pity session. I sob and snot all over the potted plant (which I've named Veronica) until I reduce myself to heaving hiccups and a sick, lightheaded feeling. Finally rising from the sofa, I carry Veronica through to the kitchen and set her on the side whilst I make a cup of tea (no milk, promise!) and shovel half a sharing bag of Kettle Chips into my mouth. The salt-and-fat rush buoys me. I need to snap out of this. 'The past cannot be changed, the future is yet in your power', I saw on Instagram earlier. An 'unknown' (aka made-up by someone unimportant) quote against a night-sky background. I must try to internalise this bullshit.

Firstly, I make a promise to Veronica that I will not let her die. I will measure the success of my life against her survival. Veronica has got a huge load of pressure on her now. If she gets a fungal infection I'll probably top myself.

Next, I take the first step in ticking *3. Exercise* off my list. I join the gym. The gym seems like a really great place to be right now. Emma Penton basically lives there, and I don't think I follow a single other person on Instagram who doesn't seem to spend fifty per cent of their week on a cross-trainer. I can become one of them! Then everyone will think I have it completely together. I could even go and just relax in the changing rooms in gym wear. Take a few selfies, maybe. You don't actually need to see people running to think they're fit and dedicated – they just need to look the part. But no! If I'm going to do this vegan thing and get skinny like *Fucking Suzannah* then I'll need to actually exercise as well.

PureGym is only eighteen pounds a month, and no contract, which is useful as I'll probably need to cancel it before the second direct debit is due, what with the joblessness etc. Martin is based at the Salford Quays branch so there's no chance I'll bump into him, either.

Still reeling at the idea of exerting myself physically, I then make a promise to myself that I will go back to yoga and face the farty music. I cannot afford to be fifty quid down for nothing, and crossing it off my list feels like a bit of a cop-out if I've only been once. I will also stick at this vegan thing, no matter how many ham butties I am offered.

I then phone Trafford Council and make the weary woman at the end of the phone *promise* to send someone over to de-mould the pavement outside Nana's front door. I will not live with myself if she slips and dies from smacking her head on one of the terracotta plant pots with Gramps' initials on it.

Finally, I make the most important resolution of all: to write something. I can't keep pretending to be interested in science anymore, so I need to put my energy elsewhere. I'm going to start a blog. If nothing ever comes of it . . . fine (I will die). But I need something in my life that channels me. Oh my *god*, I hate that I just said that. I need to stop watching *Keeping Up With The Kardashians*, it's seeping into my lingo. There's another resolution for me.

Of course, I'll need a job in the meantime. My chances of becoming a successful writer would be greatly impeded by starvation or homelessness. No reference means a complete change of career path for me, but I was probably never getting back into the drug-selling world after my workshop performance anyway. I get on indeed.com and set up an account, before speed-applying to about eighty random jobs that pay by the hour. Casting my net wide.

I'm watching *Ru Paul's Drag Race* and chain-smoking to reward myself for my life-changing action plan, when my phone rings. It's Dad.

'Hey, Dad.'

'Hello, poppet. How are you?'

'Good! Brilliant!' I enthuse. This is not exactly untrue – I'm embarking on a new life; that's good, isn't it? 'How are you?'

'All good here. Your mother and I were just wondering if you'd like to come over for Sunday lunch this weekend? I know you have work the next day, but we can drop you home. And Mum's bought a chicken.'

His booming, friendly voice is so warm and familiar, suddenly the only thing I want is to go home and be looked after. So much for my independent woman attitude – I want to be a baby again. I also feel like I could actually do with *seeing* people. Plus, with the out-of-bounds chicken comes roast potatoes, and everyone knows I'll do anything for a roast potato.

'Ooh, yeah, that'd be lovely! I was going to have a quiet night in, actually, so no plans. I have decided to go vegan, though, so I'll just eat the roasties.'

He sighs. 'You and your fads. All right, we'll get some extra veg in. Come over whenever you like. Bring Martin too, if he's free.'

I ring off quickly, a sick feeling swirling in my stomach. I'll have to tell them about everything – Martin, my job, the lot. It's not going to go down well. Unless I just . . . don't say anything? Pretend everything is fine and skirt around the subject? Is this what Cecilia would call a lack of 'impulse control'? No, I don't think it is. This is premeditated avoidance, it's not impulsive at all. It's actually the opposite – yes, I'm making the most comfortable decision and taking the easy road, but I've put careful thought and attention into it, which is exactly what she wanted me to do, isn't it?

Besides, it's all for the good of my family. If they thought I was jobless, boyfriendless and depressed, they'd be beside themselves (with disappointment, mainly) and I can't handle that right now.

So that's decided. I'll be a responsible adult and tell nobody about my current life issues. And when I'm successful and earning a good wage, I'll drop the bombshell and nobody can be angry with me.

It's a win-win situation.

I'm sure it is.

131

14

I spend the weekend cleaning the apartment for the first time since Martin left. I am actually baffled by how he found the time to keep all the tiny, insignificant areas of our living space grime-free. The underside of the tap, for example. I mean, how could he be *bothered*? I get a pang of nostalgia when I try cleaning the toilet roll holder like he used to, and I consider texting him.

But then I stop myself and realise how ridiculous I must look, crouching next to the toilet bowl, vigorously sawing a string of dental floss into the cracks of an object that literally *nobody* will ever see. The man wasn't normal.

The majority of my brain space is being used up thinking about what theme I should go with for my blog. Food blogs are popular, but they're also *everywhere*, and the only things I can cook are frozen pizzas and microwaved leftover takeaway. Maybe that's a theme in itself? No. Besides, neither of the above fit into my vegan lifestyle plan, so wouldn't it be a bit fake to be writing about them? Fashion is out of the window as I dress like a homeless person from the nineties, and I don't have a good enough camera to take photos of myself lying on top of Victoria Bridge wearing my latest 'haul'.

I found a new vegan range in Aldi on Friday; dairy-free mozzarella sticks and crispy bean burgers. All cooked from frozen. People have been going crazy for it on Instagram so I ran down there to grab some before it all ran out. There was a surprisingly large quantity of stuff left; I bought one of everything and they are honestly *amazing*. Who knew vegans could eat such delicious things? It's a brave new world and I bloody love it. I even consider basing my blog entirely on Aldi's vegan selection, but I'd probably run out of things to write about pretty quickly.

I go round and round in circles, taking breaks to smoke endless cigarettes and watch the pigeons on the street below, before Sunday arrives and I decide I need to stop thinking and do something.

Something like putting my new gym membership to use.

PureGym on Market Street is in a tiny doorway, wedged between New Look and EE, and the desire to run into Mango or Urban Outfitters and bury myself amongst the clothes is overwhelming. I put my blinkers on and drive myself through the door and up the narrow staircase.

There are three screens on my left, inviting me to join the gym. On the right are four pods with a keypad next to each one. People are beeping in and out like it's some kind of teleportation device. Maybe that's how it works? Enter the pod as a fat mess, leave looking like Jodie Marsh in her bodybuilding days?

Where is reception? Where are the staff? What do I do?! I bring the 'Welcome to PureGym' email up on my phone and read it for the first time. Oh, there's a PIN. I need to enter the PIN. I walk up to the nearest pod and stab in the numbers, watching in awe as the door slides open. As I step inside, the pod shuts behind me, and for a second I am sealed inside this little glass cylinder, wondering what will happen next. Am I going to be sucked up a tube like Augustus Gloop? I would definitely get stuck, and the Oompa Loompas would not rescue me because they would know what a greedy, chocolate-gorging mess I am. I'll be drowned in molten Cadbury's and it will serve me right.

Shit. I'm starting to panic.

Just as I'm about to scream, the door on the other side of the pod opens, and I am thrust into the loudest room I've ever been in. The noise of twenty treadmills going full-pelt is barely drowned out by the intense, bassy music pounding through the speakers. The air is so thick with sweat you can chew it, and the smell of feet is making me want to hurl. It's an assault on every single one of my senses. The customer service in this place is a joke – does anyone even work here? What does Martin *do* all day?!

I suddenly feel very exposed and very self-conscious. People must know I haven't got a clue what I'm doing. I can almost feel them all eyeing me. *Look at the newbie, what is she playing at?* I can't stand around or I'll look lost, but I don't know how any of this stuff works. It's so hot.

I need to find the changing rooms. I need to take my jacket off and get away from this music. I spot the ladies' across the room and make a bee-line, dodging glistening, red-faced humans as I go. Bursting through the door, I am met with a writhing sea of bodies in various states of undress. I don't know where to look. Someone is vigorously talcum-powdering their fanny in the corner and little puffs of it are landing on the benches around her. Squinting, I head towards one of the few empty lockers.

'Excuse me.' I squeeze between a woman who is sitting and texting, and another who is wearing a sports bra with a long, floaty skirt. She is obviously halfway between outfits, but it sort of works. I pull open the locker and carefully slide my jacket off, accidentally elbowing people in the process. This is *horrible*. I have never felt such a lack of personal space. I am suddenly met with a very strong desire to stand in the middle of a vast, open field.

I put my foot up on the bench and lean forward to redo my shoelace. As I do, floaty-skirt woman simultaneously whips off her sports bra and twists round to her locker in one swift movement.

For one, brief nanosecond, I am still pure. I am still innocently unaware of the trauma to come.

And then her boob slaps me across the head.

'Oh my god.' I clutch my face, rubbing at my stinging eye as tears leak down my cheek.

'Shit, did I catch you?' She's fastening her bra now. 'Sorry, they've a mind of their own!'

Sweet baby Jesus. I've just been titty-whacked. I'm pretty certain her nipple came into contact with my retina. This is akin to sexual assault, surely? I try to laugh it off but I am honestly traumatised. It was just so *unexpected*. I feel like I'm caught in the middle of an orgy I've changed my mind about; all bodies and sweat and fanny talc and no escape.

Against every screaming instinct in my body, I make my way onto the gym floor and position myself on the last remaining treadmill, still rubbing my sore eye. It takes me an embarrassing amount of time to work out how to make it start before I see the big 'GO' button in the middle and hit it. The machine jerks into action and I stumble forwards, trying to play it cool but misjudging my speed and ending up walking into the dashboard thingy.

God, this thing is so *slow*. Does it speed up by itself?

There's a picture of a man running, with a '+' and '-' either side. I give the plus sign a few taps and the machine gets faster. This is quite easy, actually! Admittedly, I haven't done any exercise yet, but using the machine is a piece of cake!

Right, time to crank this baby up a notch, get a bit of a sweat on. I hold down my finger on the plus sign until the screen tells me I am at a speed of 'twelve'. Whatever the fuck that means. Twelve what? Twelve footsteps per second? In any case I am now running faster than I have ever run in my life, simply because if I don't I will fly off the back. The man next to me is peering over worriedly, probably shocked by my rapid change in speed, but this is actually not at all difficult! In fact, I'd almost go as far as to say I'm enjoying it!

I'm pounding my feet down and pumping my arms by my side, and all I can think about is putting one foot in front of the other. I can feel my ponytail whipping across my neck, and for the first time in weeks I am completely in the moment – serenely free. Who knew I was a natural runner?

My breath is getting a little shallower now, my thighs burning a bit. But this is good! Pain is gain, which is useful because there is a sharp, stabbing sensation beginning in my lower right abdomen.

This is fine. This is absolutely fine. I'm not actually sure when I last took a proper breath, as my lungs appear to have collapsed, but I am still moving, which means I am still alive. I cannot imagine even childbirth being worse than the pain in my stomach right now, but this is what exercise does, isn't it? Every marathon runner crosses the finish line looking like they've been hit by a truck. It's *supposed* to nearly kill you, that's the thrill of it.

OK, I'm actually not sure if this is normal anymore. I've just seen several twinkling stars creeping into my vision, and I'm certain I didn't spot any special effect lighting when I came in here. I can hear my broken throat rasping for air, and I think, somewhere in the distance, someone is moaning.

I think that person might be me.

Through the descending blackness I scramble for the minus sign, holding my finger on it and willing myself to stay conscious as the treadmill slows and the pressure on my chest lightens a little.

'Are you OK?' A personal trainer is leaning against the front of my machine. Where did he come from?

'Yes . . . yes, fine . . .' Every word deprives my body of oxygen, and my chest screams at me to shut up.

'You sure? You were sort of growling a bit.' He frowns.

'Yep! I . . . just not used . . . such long distances . . .' I manage.

He squeezes between the machines and peers at my dashboard. 'You were only running for one minute and thirteen seconds.'

136

Is he serious? That can't be right, surely? I've just nearly died!

'Felt like . . . an eternity.' I'm calming a little.

'If you want to start running, start slow. Try some hills, get your heart rate going,' he taps a '+' sign on the other side of the machine, and it tilts upwards slightly, 'then flatten it out again and jog at a much slower pace. I'm talking eight, max.'

'OK,' I say, slightly pissed off. For all he knows I could be a triathlete, just having a bad day.

'I'm Pete, call me if you need any more advice.' He saunters away.

I am aware that the over-exertion has made me self-conscious and defensive, and that I should probably just take it easy for a minute and follow Pete's advice. *But no, piss off, Pete. I'll show you how much I need your help.*

I get my machine back into a fast walking pace and slam my finger down on the incline button. The machine tilts backwards at an alarming rate, and my phone slides from its holder and flies towards me. I reach out to catch it but I am marching at such a gradient that my balance is off, and it clatters down onto the floor. I try to straighten up and stumble backwards, screaming, as I realise I'm about to fall from the almost vertical drop I am hiking up. I flail my arms forwards, scrabbling for the dashboard and catching the bright red stop button with my palm.

The treadmill lets out a wailing alarm sound and stops immediately.

But I keep going.

I soar forwards into the void, only stopping when my head collides with the front of the machine. I crumple into a heap at the bottom of the treadmill, almost certain that I am dead.

'Oh my god, is she OK?'

'What happened?'

'She's really red . . . is that a sign of anything?'

'She'd be pale if she was dying, so I reckon she's all right.'

'How would you know, Darius, you idiot?'

'Lisa, will you shut your mouth for once in your life?'

I open my eyes and ease myself to my feet. A sea of people part in front of me and I smile weakly.

Pumped-up Pete breaks through the crowd. 'Excuse me, please, thank you.' He stops in front of me. 'Let me get you an ambulance, you've a nasty lump on your head.'

'I'm fine. Fine, honestly.' I push through people and hurry towards the changing room, ignoring the protests behind me.

I grab my stuff and head towards the exit, the crowds of people already dispersed back to their machines. Pete catches up with me as I'm stabbing my PIN in the door.

'I really think you should be seen. You had a pretty rough ride on that treadmill.'

'Yes, well, thank you, Pete, but no. I feel fine, it was nothing.' The door flashes red and I sigh, entering the eight digits again.

'I noticed you didn't exactly take my advice.' He smiles.

'Yeah, not too great at the whole listening thing.' I stab at the keypad, which has just rejected me for a second time. 'Oh my god, how do I get *out* of this place?'

Pete reaches over and taps on the keys and the pod door slides open.

'Thanks.' I smile sheepishly at him, feeling guilty. He's actually quite sweet. I really should stop being such a horrible cow to everybody.

'Next time you come in, I'll show you how to get started. If you'll pay any attention to me, that is.' He laughs.

The pod door closes and for some weird, inexplicable reason, I smile again at Pete and salute him.

I salute him.

Why? I don't know.

He frowns slightly and gives me a half wave, before heading back over to his next client.

For the second time in five minutes, my face flushes crimson.

I am such a bellend.

*

Four hours later and I have just about recovered. I am showered, dressed and waiting at the tram station for the next one to Sale.

On reflection, I don't think my first gym experience was *that* bad.

Yes, I was assaulted by a boob.

Yes, I nearly died on the treadmill.

No, I didn't actually do more than four total minutes of exercise.

But let's look at the positives! I *went,* didn't I? I pushed through, despite every cell of my being wanting to go home and eat Supernoodles on toast. I actually ran for the first time in *years*. How mental is that?! I pull out my list and review it.

1. Stop smoking.
2. Lose weight.
3. Exercise.
4. See family more.
5. Change your fucking job.
6. ~~Start yoga.~~
7. Do tea detox.
8. Go vegan.

Technically, I could cross off numbers three, four, five and eight. I have essentially done all of these things. I hover my pen over *3. Exercise*. It feels cheap, almost, to cross it out. Like I'm cheating. As for numbers four and eight, I did see Nana, and I haven't actually eaten any animal products for a few days, but this is supposed to be *long term*. Otherwise I'd be able to strike *1. Stop smoking* out every morning because I haven't had a cigarette for eight hours. And I haven't changed my job yet, have I? I've just lost it. As much as I want them to be, they are not the same thing. I put the list back in my pocket.

The tram finally pulls in and it's practically empty, so I spend the first two minutes of the journey traipsing the carriage and looking for the seat with the least offensive stains on it. By the time I've put my headphones on and chosen a playlist to match my mood (mildly depressed with an air of false optimism), we are pulling in to Cornbrook.

'Maggie?'

I freeze, hoping I can get away with ignorance by hiding behind my music. Someone slides into the seat beside me and shakes my arm.

'Maggie?!'

I stay facing the window, until I realise how tapped I must seem to not be reacting to aggressive physical contact, and then slowly turn my head. It's the girl from the conference (workshop). Shit, what was her name? Sadie? Saskia? I've been staring at her for quite a while now, and she looks a bit freaked out.

'Saffron!' I cry, suddenly remembering. She jerks backwards at my sudden outburst.

'I thought it was you! Are you OK?' She frowns.

'Yes! Sorry, god, I must look crazy. I'm really out of it today. How are you?' She probably thinks I'm pissed again. I didn't give the best impression last time.

'Oh, poor you. Good, thanks, yeah. Nothing's changed, still touring the country on my mission for research enlightenment.'

'Ah. Same old, then?' I forgot how funny this girl was.

'Yeah, pretty much. Anyway, I'm *so* glad I bumped into you, I've been dying to know what happened after you got dragged out of that room. It's literally all I've thought about since, like, "whatever became of that mental drunk girl who said all that stuff we were all thinking?"' She laughs.

'It definitely wasn't what *everyone* was thinking.' I'm laughing too now. It's quite hilarious imagining it from her perspective. 'I got called into HR the next day and lost my job.'

'NO.' Saffron stops laughing and covers her mouth with her hand. 'Seriously? They chopped you, just like that?'

'Yep. I doubt they'll be serving wine at the next one. There's always one that has to ruin it for everyone.' I pretend to bow in my seat and she laughs again.

'Well, I'm glad you can see the funny side. I'm guessing you haven't found anything else yet?'

'Nope, applied all over the place so it's just a waiting game now.'

She thinks for a second. 'You know, we've just had another PA position open up. I know I act as though going to all these workshops is a nightmare, but it's been amazing for my CV. You'd be working for a different guy anyway. He's lovely.' She smiles encouragingly.

Oh my god. This is like fate. I need the money and I need something to do with my days. It's as if Saffron was put on this tram to save me from all my problems. This is an amazing opportunity! I'd be mad to say no, wouldn't I?

Although . . . back into the drugs world. More conferences, more stuck-up sales reps, more sitting at a desk all day browsing Amazon for material possessions to fill the black hole in my life (which I'm actually still doing – must put a stop to that soon). I suddenly realise that losing my job wasn't necessarily a bad thing. It's spurred me on to think of what I really want to do, and now I know, I don't think I can face taking a defeated step back.

I get the feeling I'm about to make a huge mistake.

'I don't think the pharma industry is for me anymore, to be honest.' I say eventually, hammering the nail into my own coffin. 'Thank you so much for the offer, though. You were the only thing that made that conference – sorry, workshop – bearable. I'm really grateful for you trying to help me out.'

Saffron smiles and reaches for my phone. 'Take my number. Call me if you change your mind.' She pulls her rucksack onto her back and stands up. 'And for the record, I wish I had half the balls you've got. I really hope you find that writing job.'

141

My eyes fill as I watch her get off the tram. She is literally *so nice*. It'd be fun to work with her. I stare down at her number, now saved in my phone.

I promise myself I will not change my mind.

Mum throws open the door before I've even had a chance to knock.

'Darling! Wine?' She yanks me inside.

'Yes, wine, please.' I break free of her grip and kick my shoes off. I'm still preoccupied by my conversation with Saffron, and being in the House of Great Expectations is already filling my brain with rational thoughts. Career, career, career, scream the walls in here – the tribal chant of my childhood. Am I insane? Why in god's name did I turn down the opportunity of another job when I'm practically penniless? I suddenly remember I still owe Mum £50. Shit.

'Mum.' I follow the clinking of glasses into the kitchen, where my mother is pulling an ice-cold bottle of white from the fridge. 'That fifty quid you lent me the other day . . .'

'Oh, darling, don't worry about that. Give it to me whenever you've got it. In fact,' she hands me a glass, 'see it as an early birthday present, like you said. I got Ricardo some sunglasses the other day so it's only fair.'

'You bought sunglasses for *Ricardo*?' I take a sip of my wine. SO good. Why does wine have to be so bloody good?

'Yes! Isn't that funny? He'll be here soon.' She takes her drink over to the worktop and starts emptying an M&S gravy sachet into a jug.

My stomach sinks. Ricardo is Veri's Westie; spoilt, energetic and apparently, now in possession of his very own pair of Ray-Bans. I adore him, but his presence is, obviously, always paired with my sister's. The other night at my flat wasn't a one-off; our relationship is consistently icy and only thaws once a year – after seven glasses of Baileys at the end of Christmas Day. Last year she uncharacteristically confided in me that her left boob was significantly larger than the right one, and things have been even weirder between us since then.

'So Veri's coming, too?' I whinge.

'Yes.' Mum catches my eye. 'Oh, for god's sake Maggie, don't look at me like that. She's your sister. You need to sit down and sort it out.'

'There's nothing to sort out. We've never got on.' I slide myself onto a bar stool and start drawing a penis in the condensation on my glass. Veri and I are completely different people. She is serious, driven and competitive, whilst I am careless, scatty and perpetually floundering. In her opinion, each of my personality traits is a cardinal sin, and she takes every opportunity to remind me what a huge failure I am. I internally reprimand myself for showing her the list the other night. It's ammunition for her campaign against me; the one she has been waging since I entered the world. I am used to our dynamic, but her impending arrival is making me sweat, because today I need to lie, and you *cannot* lie to Veri.

As if reading my mind, Mum turns from her mixing. 'How's work, love?'

'Good, good.' I feel the heat rushing to my face. Why am I being so obvious?!

'And Martin?' She peers at me. 'Where is he today?'

'He's gone for Sunday dinner with his mum.' The pre-rehearsed fib slips out of my mouth smoothly. See, I can do this!

'Abandoning us for his own family, is he?' My dad's voice cuts across the room.

'Hi, Dad.' I stand up and give him a hug. 'How are you?'

'Well, very well. You girls! Drinking without me?' He gets himself a glass from the cupboard. 'You still giving that career ladder a good climb? Any promotions on the horizon?'

'Oh, John, leave her alone. She's only just arrived!' Mum slaps him on the arm.

'I like to keep abreast of what she's up to. I'm an excellent father, you know.' He winks at me and I laugh.

143

'Well, not much to report.' I say, desperate to change the subject. 'I've started yoga classes, though. That's fun.'

I'm sure some people class farting in a room full of strangers as 'fun'.

'That's a bit bloody hippy of you, Mags.' Dad creases up his face.

'She's always been crackers, though, hasn't she?' My brother's voice carries through from the doorway.

Why can't people in this house congregate all at once? Why do they need to keep dripping in one by one? It's unnecessary.

'Piss off, Charlie.' I stand up and give him a big squeeze. 'I didn't know you were here.'

'I live here, so, duh.' He rakes his hands through his messy hair. 'How's my absolute disaster of a sister?'

'Dunno, she hasn't arrived yet,' I quip.

'Touché.' Charlie saunters over to the fridge and pulls out a beer. He's looking a bit tubbier than when I last saw him, and he's wearing tracksuit bottoms with a disturbing looking stain down the crotch.

'It's yogurt.' He says quickly, catching my glance.

I crinkle up my nose. I *really* hope it's yogurt. Seeing a jizz stain on my own brother's pants during a family gathering would be the final bloody straw.

Charlie and I have always had a close relationship founded solely on banter. I actually think we've managed to get through the entirety of our lives without once having a serious conversation. He's a doctor, and is so laid back I actually wonder how he's done it. I can imagine him looking at a paralysed car crash victim and shrugging, 'be all right.'

The way he's knocking that beer back suggests something has him riled this evening, which is unusual. But asking him about it would involve talking about our feelings, and we must not even *consider* going there.

I watch as Dad rummages around in the 'shit' drawer, undoubtedly in search of a 'bastard pen', and Mum chastises

Charlie for not putting his bottle cap 'in the bin, where it lives', because unfortunately there's 'no magic cleaning fairy under this roof'. This is good – it feels nice. I'm spending time with my family like a normal person; like Emma Penton. I already can't wait to strike through number four.

Sudden barking erupts from the hallway. Ricardo flies through the kitchen door and skids across the tiles like a possessed mop, landing at my feet vibrating with excitement. I would kill for the energy of a dog. Ricardo is five now, which is, what, thirty-five in human years? I'm only twenty-seven and I can't even be bothered to blink half the time.

'For *fuck*'s sake, who left their shoes in the middle of the hallway? I've just nearly *died*.' Veri strides through the door with a face like a smacked arse. I actually don't remember a time when I've seen her with anything *but* a face like a smacked arse, so maybe that's just how she is. Oh my god, what if it's a condition? What if she's been trying to smile all these years and we've all just thought she's a miserable cow?

'Verity, darling.' Mum scoops her into a hug, and her face smooths from rage to expressionless in one quick movement.

Nope, she's a miserable cow.

'Maggie.' Veri nods at me across the kitchen and raises an eyebrow. 'Still working for the drug lords?'

Shit, shit, shit, shit, shit. Straight off the bat. Now that she's seen the list, she's going to see straight through me if I lie. Ever since we were little she'd sniff me out of a fib in two seconds flat, even if it was something really insignificant, like whether I'd eaten the last Müller Corner, or whether it was *actually* my turn in the front seat because Charlie had smacked me with a water pistol and Mum *said* I could.

She literally knows absolutely everything. It's a skill that has been of great use to her in life, and now she destroys people in a courtroom all day.

'Maggie? Hello? Still working or what?' Veri is plopping ice into a glass with her back to me.

'Yup.' I keep my answer short, hoping she'll move on.

She turns slowly, her eyes squinting together, until she's facing me head-on. My heart starts thudding. Seriously, if she looked at me like that during a trial I'd admit to anything. No wonder she's so successful.

'Just like her dad, this one!' Dad claps Veri on the shoulder, breaking her psycho-gaze. 'Always asking about work. It's a sign of intelligence that, you know.'

Veri smiles and leans her head on Dad's shoulder. Actually, she can smile, I remember now. Only for Dad, though.

I knock my wine back and grab the bottle from the fridge, filling up my glass.

'Right!' Mum claps. 'Dinner's ready, go on through.'

We trundle through to the dining room, Veri still nestled in Dad's armpit.

'Don't you think that's *weird*?' I murmur to Charlie.

'Of course it's weird. *She's* weird. They're both weird.'

'You know that's your father and sister you're talking about!' Mum hisses, following behind with bowls of steaming food.

I take a roast potato and pop it in my mouth.

'Margaret!' Mum seethes.

'Shit, that's hot.' I mumble, grabbing the bowls from Mum's hands and taking them through into the dining room.

'. . . and so I said, "Your Honour, has my colleague even *heard* of the Offences Against the Person Act 1861, section thirty-six?" and the room just *erupted*, honestly it did, we had to break early for lunch.'

This sounds like an absolutely thrilling story of Verity's, so I decide to sit at the other end of the table.

'Dig in, dig in!' Mum places a steaming chicken in the middle of the table.

Ohhhh my god. That chicken smells like all my favourite childhood memories, all my hopes and dreams, every sunny Sunday. All that is good in the world.

'Pass us your plate, Mags.' Charlie holds up a moist strip of breast meat on the end of a fork.

'No thanks, I'm not doing meat at the moment.' I reach for the potatoes and shovel three heaped spoons onto my plate.

'Steady on.' Veri raises an eyebrow. 'There's no point being vegetarian if you're only going to eat masses of fried food and put even more weight on.'

'Verity! Your sister is fine as she is.' Mum passes me the broccoli.

'Piss off,' I mutter, feeling a prickling in my eyes and my appetite giving way to a sick feeling in my stomach. I *hate* myself for reacting like this. I hate the way she cuts through me every time. I look down at my stomach, sitting softly on the top of my thighs. She's right, of course. I am overweight. But I don't need to be reminded. I don't need to be made to feel shittier than I already do.

I fork green beans into my mouth at record speed as the conversation goes on around the table. I fill my wine glass up two more times before I'm pissed enough to not to care and join back in.

'Killed anyone this week?' I nudge Charlie, who has eaten three platefuls and is on his sixth bottle of Becks.

'Yup. Guy died whilst I had my hand down his throat.' He smiles at my expression. 'He had been stabbed forty-six times though, so I might not be entirely to blame.' He reaches for another ball of stuffing.

'Jesus, Charlie. How much are you planning on eating?' Veri rolls her eyes.

'What is this, Veri, a fat-shaming party?' I snap across the table. 'Don't bother coming next time if you're only here to judge everybody.'

'Maggie.' Mum murmurs.

'Well, she does have a point.' Dad puts his cutlery down. 'You've put on a bit in the past few months, Charlie.'

'And how many beers are we on now?' Veri folds her arms. 'That must be your seventh?'

Charlie scrapes his chair back. 'Control your own life to the point of non-existence, Verity. Just keep your critical fucking nose out of mine.' He storms out of the room, beer in hand.

'Oh, well done, Veri. Brilliant work.' I smile.

'Come on, that wasn't Verity's fault. He's very sensitive at the moment.' Dad pats Veri on the arm.

This is driving me insane. I open my mouth to inform the room that Veri is the biggest, most virginal bore the world has ever seen, but my phone rings in my pocket.

'One second.' I go out into the hallway. Unknown number. I pick it up anyway. 'Hello?'

'Hi, is this Miss Gardiner?' A local accent. Probably Bolton? Definitely a call centre.

'Yes.' I get ready to hang up.

'Hi, this is Darren, from Frederick's on Deansgate?'

Frederick's? Frederick's the *bookshop?* What are they calling me for?

Oh my god, what if they've finally checked the CCTV from 2006 and seen me running off with that pencil-end rubber shaped like a chicken? I didn't *want* to nick it, but I'd used all my pocket money at McDonalds and—

Oh, shit, he's still talking. I've missed half of it.

'I'm sorry, could you repeat that, please?' I try to keep my voice level.

'I was saying, you applied for a sales assistant position?'

God, did I? I haven't got a clue. I'm pretty sure I applied to be a senior accountant at RBS, too.

'Er, yes, yes I did.'

'Great. I'm really sorry for the late weekend call, we've had a manic week and we needed to sort interviews before tomorrow morning. Can you make Thursday at 9 a.m.?'

'Yes, of course,' I stammer. I don't trust myself to speak any further, the wine is turning my S's funny.

148

'Fantastic. Just come into the shop and tell one of the guys behind the counter that you're here for interview. They'll tell you where to go.'

'Great, thank you, Darren.'

I put the phone down. Bloody *hell*. A job interview. Working in a bookshop. I *love* the idea of working in a bookshop! The smell of books is my favourite smell ever. And they don't know about the rubber! My criminal record will remain clean. This is exciting! I'd better put it in my phone calendar or I'll forget by tomorrow.

'Who was that?'

I jump. Charlie is sat at the bottom of the stairs in the dark.

'Jesus Christ! What the hell are you doing there, you freak?' I wander over and squeeze in next to him.

'Escaping.' He sighs. 'I really need to get my own place.'

'Yeah, you do. Scrounging off Mum and Dad at the age of twenty-nine. Not cool.'

'I pay rent!'

'Yeah, like a hundred quid a month. And no bills or food.' I poke him.

'Pfffft.' He rakes his hands down his face.

'What's up with you, anyway?' I try. It's as close to a personal question as I can get. Something is wrong, I can tell, but we don't want to get all *serious* about it.

'I could ask the same of you.' He stands up and steadies himself on the bannister before turning back to me. 'But I won't.'

15

'That's good, right?' Anna peers at me over the unnecessarily large menu.

'Yeah, it's good. I've always loved books.'

'Well, good for you. I'm really happy for you, Mags.' She reaches over and grasps my hand.

'Yeah.' Sophie smiles weakly. 'If it's what you want.'

'I know it's a step down. But I wasn't being paid much more than minimum wage at my old place, and hopefully the team will be better. And I'll get to check an item off my list.' I close my menu and prop my head up with my free hand. 'Anyway, I haven't even been interviewed yet.'

'I'm sure you'll get it.' Anna smiles and finally releases me. 'Have you told Cecilia?'

'Yeah, she's happy about it.' Cecilia is at one of David's amateur exhibitions. She invited us and we politely declined, which she completely understood. 'Wish I could fucking decline', were her exact words.

'Right, drinks.' Sophie looks around for a waiter. We're in Barbara's Tea Rooms off Canal Street. There's bunny rabbit wallpaper, dim lighting and mismatched crockery. It is really *not* my cup of tea, ironically enough.

'Hello!' The jolliest, most enthusiastic man I have ever seen has descended upon our table. 'I am so sorry you lovely ladies have been waiting so long!'

He starts describing everything on the menu in unnecessary detail. Apparently they cold press their coffee themselves in the back room, using barefoot bearded men, no doubt. He's in the middle of telling us how the tea is steeped for *exactly* three minutes and twelve seconds when I can bear it no longer. 'Just a double gin and slimline tonic, please.'

He raises his eyebrows at me and scribbles on his notepad. 'Right.'

'Rosé, please,' Sophie says. 'Any, large, thanks.'

'God, rough day, Soph?' I laugh.

'And for you, madam?' The waiter interrupts me back and side-eyes me, before turning back to Anna.

'Just an orange juice.' Anna closes the drinks menu as he swishes away, muttering 'a side of manners with that, perhaps?' under his breath.

'You forgot the vodka, Anna.' Sophie waves her hand to get the waiter back, but Anna pulls her arm down.

'No, I'm not drinking.' She rubs her eyebrow.

'Erm . . . what? Why? Are you on antibiotics?' I lean forward and lower my voice. 'Because you know it's bullshit that you can't drink on them, right? I've done it loads.' I peer at her. She's flushed. Maybe she really is ill?

'It's not that.' She sighs. 'I wanted to tell you all together, but David's crochet extravaganza screwed that one up.'

'What?' Sophie looks stricken. 'Oh my god, what?'

We both know what before she even says it.

'I'm pregnant.'

There's a silence as we process this and my stomach drops.

She's *pregnant*?

Oh my god, NO.

This is just not happening.

For the next nine months, nay, *eighteen years*, there will now only be three of us out drinking together. And even if she does come out, she'll have to bring a screaming miniature human with her. Babies are not pulling props. Anna's life is over. So is the current set-up of my friendship group.

And, although I barely let myself admit it, it twinges at a nerve that I really didn't think I still had. I had let go of that image of what my future looked like. The image I had when I met Martin. The world has been showing me examples of it being OK to be alone, admirable to be independent, laudable to be owning it whilst flying solo. The concept of the strong, single, put-together woman that is plastered all over my newsfeeds is my new focus, but Anna's situation is bringing old feelings back to life.

This is the worst news ever.

My only consolation is that Sophie's face isn't exactly radiating happiness, either.

Neither of us has reacted yet. One of us needs to say *something*, but what? Are we supposed to pretend to be happy about this? Is *she* happy about this?

The haughty waiter appears from behind a gigantic queen of hearts card to my left. He slops our drinks down on the table and storms off again. He's evidently been stewing over at the bar.

'It's OK. It was a shock, but I've accepted it. I want it, even.' Anna murmurs into the awkward silence.

'Are you sure?' Sophie looks like she's going to be sick.

'Yeah. Yeah, I'm sure. Brian's going to move in with me.'

For a second I think she's already named the baby, and is referring to his arrival in some weird, 'new lodger' style format. That would be so Anna.

But who would name a baby Brian?

'Brian the bus driver?' Sophie queries.

'Yes.'

'You don't get many thirty-two year olds called Brian,' I muse.

'Well that's not exactly important, is it?' Anna snaps.

We return to silence, Sophie and I a little shocked by Anna's outburst. In all the time I've known her, she has never been rattled like this.

'Are you OK? Like, really OK?' I reach for her hand, offering the comfort she would give me, but which makes me feel creepy and perverse.

'No.' A fat tear lands squarely in her glass of juice. My brain briefly contemplates how many tears would need to go in a glass of OJ before you tasted the saltiness, but then I remember that this isn't at all relevant and there are more important things to consider.

'Oh, Anna.' Sophie curls her arm around Anna's shoulder.

'He's not thirty-two.' She gulps. 'I'm not ready to be a mum.'

Which of these facts do I address first? My head desperately wants to know how old Brian really is, but my heart knows I need to comfort my friend.

Oh, *fine*, my heart wants to know how old Brian is too.

'How old is he?' My hand is getting really sweaty in hers, and I don't know what to do with it. She's clinging on for dear life, though, so I don't really have a choice. To ease my own tension, I start circling her wrist with my thumb, but that feels really romantic and weird so I stop immediately.

'You'll be so angry.' She sniffs.

'We won't. We promise, we won't.' Sophie looks at me. We probably will, to be honest.

'He's fifty-eight,' Anna whispers.

Oh my *fuck*. That's older than my dad. Older than *her* dad.

'Jesus.' Sophie catches my eye again.

'I know, I know. He told me he was thirty-two, I wasn't lying, I promise!' She's crying again.

OK, I know some men look good for their age, but a twenty-six year difference? Is she blind?

'You don't have to have this baby, you know,' I remind her.

'I know I don't. But I will.'

'OK, well you don't have to live with Brian. Not if you don't want to.' Sophie squeezes her arm.

Anna looks up. 'But isn't that the right thing to do?'

'Well, do you love him? Do you want to be with him?' It's a shame it took me two years to be so rational about my own relationship with Martin.

'I don't know. Maybe? He's friendly. He has really long nose hair, but nearly no hair left on his head. And he always makes jokes about TV shows I've never seen. He wants to get the full box set of *The Clangers* for the baby when it comes. What the fuck is *The Clangers*? And how many *Carry On* films did they have to bloody make?' She's shrieking a bit now.

'Can I get you anything to eat, girls?' Moody McGee is back, and he's softened his tone a bit. He's probably been hiding behind the pillar in the corner listening in to the drama.

We reject food (no vegan options – this is proving to be really, really limiting), order more drinks and get back to Anna's hormone-addled turmoil.

Together we whittle it down, and we figure out that Anna wants the baby (sort of, she's sure she'll love it when it's born . . . i.e. after it's ripped her vagina in two and left her with a stomach like flooded-house-wallpaper) but she isn't sure if she wants Brian. I'm pretty certain she *definitely* doesn't want Brian, but she's not drinking so she's less easy to convince.

Anna decides she's going to tell Brian that it's too early to move in together. She'll keep dating him and he can go to all the scans, but no cohabiting just yet. This seems wise.

As we pay the bill and put on our coats, Sophie and I slightly tipsy, Anna grabs us both into a group hug.

'You're the best friends in the world,' she breathes into my shoulder.

'You'll be the most amazing mum, babe.' Sophie plants a kiss on her head.

'With your support, maybe.' She smiles and pulls away. We trundle out into the glaring daylight of the street, and say our goodbyes. Anna turns to leave, but spins back round again.

'I completely forgot!' She beams. 'You'll be godparents, won't you?'

*

I cannot be a godparent. For a start, I don't believe in God. Secondly, I don't believe in children. Well, I know they exist, I just don't believe in them in the way one might not believe in giving to charity. It's not for me, I don't want to hear about it. So the words 'god' and 'parent' combined are making me want to move countries and find a new set of infertile friends.

I *used* to believe in children. It used to be all I ever wanted, before Martin. But I trained myself out of that little aspiration and now I want nothing to do with them.

All sorts of terrifying thoughts are filling my head. What if the baby hates me? What if I have to babysit, and I accidentally kill it by putting too many blankets on it? What if it's a boy and Anna asks me to change its nappy? How do you clean a baby's willy? I wouldn't even know how to clean an *adult*'s willy.

Oh god, I'm drowning in this.

I'm back at yoga after spending the last five hours sobering up and having mild panic attacks over unborn babies. I've done the forty thousand steps again (they weren't as hard this time, but still nearly killed me) and I'm sitting in lotus position breathing deeply. There was a sort of murmur of silence when I entered the room, if that's possible. I decided to offer no explanation or apology for my early departure last week and, being British, no one mentioned it.

'Pst.' Gary leans slightly towards me, his eyes still closed. 'Clench your bum.'

'Shut up, Gary,' I murmur, earning a loathing glance from Altantsetseg, who has clearly not forgiven me for ruining her zen last week.

I try to relax into the position, and I find myself surprised that it is slightly less difficult today. My head is still swimming with thoughts of babies and willies, but they are fainter, somehow. Easier to blur away.

155

We move slowly, breathing into each movement, and we finish in the cactus position: flat on our backs, elbows at right angles by our sides, eyes closed. I feel quite deeply relaxed by this point, and I inhale the pine and incense scent of the room slowly, appreciative of its fart-free aroma.

'Maggie.'

I snap my eyes open. Gary's face is looming over me, his gigantic smile almost tearing his face in two.

'Yes?' I sit up and notice that we are the only two people in the room.

'You were snoring.'

'No, I wasn't!' I feel heat rise to my face. For Christ's sake, I'm going to be asked not to come again at this rate.

'You were. We had to end meditation early because no one could concentrate.' He holds out his hand and I grab it, hauling myself up.

As we leave the building, I am aware that I feel looser, more relaxed. I feel quite . . . good? It's a strange sensation.

Gary offers to walk me home as it's dark by now, but I decline. I only live five minutes away, and as I round the corner and wave goodbye, I feel a tiny swell of happiness in my tummy that I've got a new friend; someone to share this tiny portion of each week with.

I let myself into the apartment, thinking about how absolutely magic yoga is. My teacher might be a fun sponge but she's obviously doing something right; my mind feels really focused, like I'm on that Ritalin drug they give to kids with ADHD. Maybe *I've* got ADHD? I'll have to Google the symptoms later.

I think I'll start meditating every morning. I don't have anything else to do, and it might help me to get more out of my weekly classes. Sort of like revision, maybe? I pull out my list and write *9. Meditate,* before downloading a couple of apps and vowing to start tomorrow.

I suddenly remember my interview, and my heart thumps in my throat. I swallow it down, urging myself to keep my positive, relaxed mindset. I really want this job. I'm in desperate need of the money, I need the full-time hours to fill my days, and the prospect of free books is too good to resist. I could be one of those girls who sits in cafés, surrounded by battered paperbacks, chunky glasses on the end of my nose. What an amazing Instagram story I could have. People could see me go from 'Messy Maggie who lives on the sofa' to 'Quirky Maggie who works in a bookshop'. Imagine that combined with my meditation, too – I'd have a really bohemian nerd vibe going on.

It's not forever, though, is it? I still want to write. I still want to sell my *own* books.

I need to start this blog. I grab the list again and add:

10. *Start blog.*

Once again my mind rakes over the possible subjects I could write about. I've discounted every single one, and I'm starting to think there's nothing I can specialise in, nothing I can offer. What do I know – biology? Nobody's interested in that. Bars in Manchester? Already done, and I'm hardly a critic, just a borderline alcoholic. How to totally fuck everything up? No. Nobody would read it.

Or would they?

Hang on a second. People generally write about what they know, don't they? Ex-policemen write about crime solving, social workers weave heartbreaking tales of child abuse. I sit up straight and ask myself again: *what do I know?*

The answer suddenly so clear, I suck in a sharp breath.

This.

This is what I know. Being twenty-seven, with no idea what I'm doing and royally fucking up everything around me. I've been doing it my entire life!

With a huge rush of excitement, I pull out my laptop, open it up and begin.

Two hours later I sit back, exhausted. I have clumsily navigated WordPress and created a cute, blue website for my blog. With all the widgets, fonts and sidebars that the free version of the website will allow, it looks pretty bloody good. I've uploaded photos, modified my background and set the order in which I want my posts to appear – reverse chronologically.

I have also written a grand total of 0 words.

I slap my laptop shut and stare up at the ceiling. It's late, and I'm wondering why I've decided to do this now instead of preparing for my interview tomorrow morning. Is this part of the condition Cecilia tells me I have? Putting off something I need to do until I'm faced with something even less appealing and more imminent? I'm an imbecile, honestly.

I half-heartedly rifle through my wardrobe, pulling out a black pencil skirt and a white blouse, both of which make me look like a maître d'. As an afterthought, I throw my gym kit into my rucksack. I'll go after my interview so I won't obsess too much afterwards.

I climb into bed and close my eyes, drifting immediately to sleep.

16

I gasp awake. I am drenched in sweat, my heart pounding. Light is seeping under the curtains as I check my phone: 7.12 a.m.

Swinging my legs out of bed, I pad to the bathroom and turn the shower to cold, scrubbing the sweat from my neck. I spray the cold water directly in my face, urging away the fug, until my mind clears and the anxiety begins to fade.

Right, I've got this. I've totally got this. I am going to smash this interview.

I try a power pose in the mirror, but my towel falls down and my boobs swing around like loose ferrets as I scrabble to get it.

Feeling as though I've left what remains of my modesty and dignity in the bathroom, I pull on my clothes and put some neutral makeup on, scraping my hair into a topknot which makes me look like Kim from *How Clean is Your House*, and not in a good way. I ram my feet into my mum's old court shoes. We're the same size, but she has skinnier feet. 'Chunky toes', my dad calls me.

I hobble out of the apartment and begin the eight-minute walk to Frederick's. Another bonus of getting this job would be the complete removal of my morning commute. All things considered, what I'll lose in pay I'll make up for in bus fares, not to mention lie-ins, so really I'd be winning, wouldn't I?

The entrance of the shop looms in front of me. All the lights are off, and I'm suddenly terrified that I've got the wrong day. I try the door – locked. Why is nobody here?! I check my watch.

It's 8 a.m.

It's eight o'clock! I'm an hour early!

Why am I so utterly incapable of doing the simplest of things?

I storm past the shop, enraged at myself. Throwing myself into Pret A Manger, I sulkily order a latte and a bacon barm, only remembering how low I am on funds as I tap my card on the reader – parting with the cost of a small flat in Rusholme to pay for my breakfast.

I sit down by the window and unwrap my sandwich. I snap a photo from above and add a flattering filter which makes the bacon look like it's just had a facial. It smells good – almost too good – and I lift it up to my mouth slowly, ready to savour the first bite.

And then I remember.

I'm vegan.

I gaze at the greasy, white barm filled with crispy bacon and the full-fat, milky latte sitting in front of me.

I bump my head down onto the table, a guttural groan escaping from my mouth.

'Are you OK, madam?' It's the guy who served me.

'I'm vegan!' I wail.

He pales. 'Oh my god, I'm sorry. I thought you said a bacon barm and a latte? It's mad in here this morning, seriously, I'm so sorry.'

'No, it's not your fault. I forgot I was vegan,' I moan.

'You forgot you were vegan?' He frowns at me.

'Yes. I forgot.'

He looks irritated now. 'Well, then I'm not sure what we can do about that really . . . if you ordered the bacon and latte, you'll probably have to stick with it.'

The guy's manager is glowering over at him from behind the counter, annoyed that he's chatting during the morning rush.

He shoots an apologetic look over his shoulder and makes to move away, but I can't bear the idea of abandoning my vegan mission. Nor can I bear the idea of paying for another breakfast, or going without one.

'I told you I was VEGAN!' I screech at the guy's back, earning a sudden hush from everyone in the room.

'Jason!' The suited manager scoots around the counter, marching over to my table. 'Have you served this woman incorrectly?'

'She forgot she was vegan!' Jason protests, his face flaming.

'How could I have *forgotten* I was vegan? How can anyone *forget* the suffering of animals?' I grab the barm and pull out a piece of bacon. 'This pig *died* and you think I *forgot* that?'

I'm getting a bit too into this now. A droplet of fat just landed on Mr Manager's tie.

'Absolutely not, madam. Please excuse my colleague. I'll bring you a vegan breakfast and an almond milk latte – it was a latte, wasn't it? – immediately.' He scoops my food off the table and marches Jason into the back room. 'How many times do I have to tell you, Jason, vegans are lawsuits waiting to happen . . .'

After some angry scuffling in the back, Jason returns with a new barm, filled with avocado, and a frothy, nutty-smelling latte.

I feel a bit bad, actually. It wasn't really Jason's fault. In fact, it was entirely the fault of my hangriness and stress.

'Hey, Jason.' I peer under his hat. 'I'm really sorry about that. When I get my new job, I'll give you a one quid tip every time I come in.'

He raises his red, spotty face. 'Oh *great*. If I keep my job, you can take your shitty tip elsewhere.' He strides away.

Well, that was *rude*. That bollocking from his manager was probably a long time coming. Imagine if he'd spoken to a *normal* customer like that? I've probably just done the company a favour.

Feeling morally restored I tuck into my barm (delicious – not bacon, but delicious) and scroll through Instagram on my phone for a while. I'm so massively jealous of some of the things I'm seeing, it makes me sick. How has Sarah Gleaves managed to keep a completely flat stomach when she's already had two kids? And how is she affording the Bahamas when she's a Juice Plus ambassador? Maybe I should become a Juice Plus ambassador. I'm not sure many people are aiming for the podgy-chic look this season, though, and I'd rather not be in any more competition with *Fucking Suzannah*. I reply to a few of my group chat messages – Anna is going for her first scan and wants me, Cecilia, Sophie and Brian there. That sounds like a completely relaxed and normal time to meet the new, fifty-eight-year-old boyfriend.

I wonder if we'll have to have a baby shower for Anna. I mean, we definitely will, won't we? But how does it work? Can none of us drink, or is it only her? I really hope it's only her. Cecilia can organise it as long as she doesn't let David do the décor.

I load up one of the meditation apps on my phone. Opting for 'waves of calm', I shove my earphones in, slurping my coffee as I listen.

This woman's voice is quite nice. A bit nasally, but nice. I can hear a little click at the back of her throat every time she does a 'c' or a 'g', like she needs a glass of water. It's fine, though.

Ow! I've missed my mouth and sloshed coffee in my lap. It's this stupid woman's fault, why did she tell me to close my eyes?! Surely she should give a pre-warning? Like, 'don't listen to this meditation around hot beverages'? It's just irresponsible. I wonder if I could sue?

She's telling me to breathe out all the negative stuff, and inhale all the good things. I'm trying, I really am, but I can't stop focusing on her clacky voice. She's got some weird American accent, what is that? The spiritual one, something quite neutral. The type of accent that would belong to someone who has a hypnotherapist for absolutely no reason.

OK, I can't do this anymore.

No, Maggie, stick with it! I settle further back into my seat, ignoring the woman's request that I 'sit up straight and comfortably' – that's a paradox, surely?

'Your breath is your inner voice,' she murmurs. 'Listen to it. But do not respond. Just watch.'

What's the point in having an inner voice if you can't chat back to it? I do as she says anyway and try to observe my breath. At first, my breathing goes all weird and I try to correct it; making my inhales shorter and my exhales longer, battling a few dizzy, panicky, oxygen starved moments before righting it again. It's never this hard during yoga; Altantsetseg never taught us this. It's completely impossible to think about your breath *without* thinking about your breath. Eventually I find myself falling into a natural sort of rhythm, and I relax slightly. As soon as I stop focusing on my breathing, though, my mind wanders. I realise I've got a chunk of avocado in my tooth and resist the urge to pick it out. I wonder what the price difference is between the normal latte and the almond milk one.

This is bullshit.

Ten times angrier than when I began, I rip my earphones out and open my eyes. Jason quickly diverts his gaze from where he's obviously been staring at me, perplexed.

I dab at the puddle of coffee sitting in my lap and thank god that my skirt is black. I should wear black more often – it's evidently useful for more than just interviews.

Oh my god, my interview!

I stab the home button on my phone: 09:01.

I'm a minute late and I'm sitting in Pret, fishing avocado out of my teeth and trying to meditate.

What the fuck is wrong with me?

I leap up, sending crumbs flying across the room. Weaving between the tables, I shoot a parting glance at Jason, who no longer looks angry but deeply, deeply concerned. This is exactly why I'm so careful to always be on time – if I take my eye off the ball for just a *second* it all goes to shit.

I hurtle down Deansgate, flimsy whisps of frizz escaping from my bun and damp patches seeping through the armpits of my blouse. I burst into Frederick's and find a sales assistant loitering by the science fiction.

'I'm so sorry I'm late, I got here an hour early so I went to get breakfast in Pret but there was a bit of a drama because of the bacon, and then I tried to meditate to prepare for this but I must have lost track of time because her voice was so *clacky*—'

'Sorry, who are you?' She squints.

It takes me a second to respond; I'm so riled up I'm not actually sure what the answer is. 'Maggie Gardiner, interview, at nine?' I breathe, finally.

'Oh!' She laughs. 'Don't panic, we only just finished putting the shutters up, you're fine.'

I sink with relief into the seat she offers me and try to think of some answers to questions I might be asked. I haven't actually prepared for this, at all, and it might have been better to start thinking about these things quite a few days ago. Or, you know, whilst I was sat in Pret causing drama and meditating. I can't even remember what I've got on my CV. I've barely had a second to reflect before a short, stocky man with a buzz cut swaggers out of the back room and heads towards me.

'Margaret Gardiner?'

'Yes, hi, that's me, hello.' I clumsily get to my feet, catching my bag as it slides off my lap and yanking my skirt down at the back. I shake his hand and watch as he leaves it hanging by his side for a second, fingers splayed, before discreetly wiping it on his pants. I am quite sweaty.

'I'm Darren, the store manager, do you want to come on through?' I follow him into a tiny, cluttered office and perch on a hard, wooden chair at his desk.

'Sorry we kept you waiting. As I said on the phone, it's been a manic few weeks.' He smiles and sinks into the much nicer seat opposite me.

164

'Oh, no problem at all. I thought I was late, to be honest!' I giggle. Why did I say that? Now he's going to think I've got no concept of time and that I'm an unreliable and not-at-all-punctual individual. My stomach starts knotting.

'Right.' He offers a weak smile. 'So it's just me today, I'm afraid. I usually bring a sales assistant in too, but we're crazily understaffed.'

'Looks like you'll have to hire me then!' I joke, regretting it immediately.

'Let's see how you do, shall we?' He turns a page in front of him. 'So you've got a pretty good Biology degree, and you just left a nice position with one of the lower-level drug companies. Why are you wanting to work at Frederick's?'

Bloody hell, that's direct. Isn't that a bit offensive? Assuming that a job with a drug company is 'better' than a job in a shop? In any case, I have no idea how to respond because I'm a dick and I didn't think of how I was going to explain any of the situations I've got myself into over the past few weeks.

'Well, I always thought I liked biology. I mean, I *do* like biology, I find it really interesting. But I love books even more, and I guess I didn't think about that when I finished my A-Levels. Working with books didn't even enter my mind as an option. But working in the drugs world is terrible. It's just this sell, sell, sell mentality and it doesn't fit with my values.' That sounded all right, didn't it?

'You know we have a pretty big "sell, sell, sell" attitude here, too?' He raises an eyebrow.

Shit. Selling books. I forgot this was a corporation, too, and not just a cosy, paper-scented place to relax in.

'Oh, of *course*. But I believe in books. I can't tell you how much I love books. When you sell a book you're selling someone an *experience*, you know?'

'And when you're selling drugs, you're selling someone the chance at health and a better life, no?' He's being antagonistic now, but this time he actually doesn't know what he's talking about. I'm on the upper foot here.

'I'll have to partly disagree with you there actually, Darren.' I sit up in my seat. 'I was primarily charged with condensing all the complicated medical information into positive "scripts", so the sales reps could go out and sell what we were offering. The majority of our product base was weight loss supplements. Granted, they all had evidence behind them, but they were sold at extortionate prices – very much for the benefit of the company and not the patient. Or, I suppose in some cases, the NHS, which is struggling as it is. Many of their active ingredients could be found in foods too, so you're buying a £5 meal sachet when you could get the same nutrients from a head of broccoli.' I shift uncomfortably, suddenly realising that the skinny tea I've ordered fits this exact description. 'When you sell a book, you don't feel bad. You're selling pleasure, aren't you? It's a choice, an addition to your life, not a fundamental necessity to be able to live normally. There's no exploitation, I guess.'

Bloody hell, I didn't even know I felt like that.

Darren holds his hands up. 'You know more than me about pharmaceutical sales, I can't argue with that.' He laughs. 'So it says here that you have previous retail experience at . . . Fashun Shoes? Is that how you pronounce it?'

Yes, Darren, I spent a month at Fashun Shoes in Sale town centre when I was sixteen, before I stopped going in and ran off drinking vodka and smoking with my friends instead.

'Oh, yes. That was a wonderful little shop, very quirky.' Translation: they sold leopard print prostitute heels and fake Ugg boots and the entire place stank of plastic. Imagine Primark's shoe section, and times that smell by 8,000.

'And what kind of responsibilities did you have there?'

Making tea and coffee, stealing the occasional pair of shoes and being ignored by all the people who actually worked there?

'Assisting customers, putting purchases through the till, opening and closing the store – all the usual stuff.' I never even got near the till. Or a customer.

'All right.' He lets out a whistle through his nose. 'And you were a member of your university's book club?'

'Yes. I hosted our meetings several times. It was my favourite part of the university experience – getting to read fantastic books and meet new people at the same time.'

I don't know if the University of Salford even *had* a book club.

Darren flashes me a smile, two pointy incisors making him look like a hyena. 'Okie dokie. Just a hypothetical situation question now. Can you tell me about a time when you disagreed with your superior and how you handled it?'

I start to sweat.

Of course, Darren. Quite recently, I went to a workshop and events transpired that made me feel belittled and overlooked. I responded to this professionally and maturely, by downing a bottle of wine, heckling a data management woman and calling everyone in the room a square. This precise incident has shown me the importance of not getting plastered during working hours, and has taught me the invaluable skill of submitting multiple job applications as a consequence.

'Ooh, I hate these questions,' I laugh, buying myself some time. 'Errrrm. Let's see . . . well, we had sales reps as I've mentioned, who were above me in pay grade and status. One particular sales rep was quite rude and derogatory to me at times and we disagreed on the principles of the job I was doing. I handled this by taking her to one side and explaining how her remarks made me feel, and how I didn't think it was contributing to a good team atmosphere in the office. She was mortified and apologised, she hadn't even realised what she'd been doing, and we got on really well after that.' I smile.

What a load of shit. What actually happened was that I screamed 'skank' at Rachael in the bathroom one morning after she told me a monkey could do my job better than me. Thinking about it, it's possible that all these little episodes might have contributed to Theo's case for dismissing me on the grounds of 'inappropriate behaviour'. Hmm.

'It sounds like that was handled pretty well.' Darren taps his papers against the desk. 'Well, I think I know everything I need to – thanks so much for coming in.'

He rises and holds out his hand, and I shake it again, imagining him scrubbing my sweat off in the bathroom as soon as I'm gone.

'Thank you for your time.' I smile.

'We'll be in touch.' He opens the door and I walk out into the shop. I hear the soft thud of his office door behind me, and I'm alone.

The shop is quiet and smells, as Frederick's always does, of newly printed paper and fresh coffee. I wander the aisles and flick through autobiographies, niche historical fiction and number one bestsellers.

I dip my head into a Charles Dickens, breathing in deeply, and hope against hope that it was enough.

17

I spend the next three days going to the gym, binging Netflix and organising the apartment. I get twelve job rejection emails, each of them automated – 'unfortunately your skill set was not deemed fitting with the current needs of our company', or some such bullshit. On Saturday morning, my electronic cigarette arrived, way earlier than the email said it would. I spent an hour staring at it, willing myself to open the box, before shoving it in a drawer and rolling one with tobacco instead.

Apart from going to the gym, my contact with the outside world has been limited. I've muted the group chat; all Anna's baby talk makes me feel like I'm going to vomit, such is my despair at the idea of god-parenthood and slipping back into my old obsessions. In fact, I've only used my phone to scroll endlessly through Instagram and Facebook, feeling sharp stabs of envy and depression every time someone's good news is shared. Emma Penton is back from Santorini and has just landed a job as Head of Marketing. My thumb is stiff and aching from constant scrolling, I'm eating everything in sight and having two naps a day out of sheer boredom.

I don't think I'd quite realised how much I wanted this job at Frederick's. Not only for the money, or for something to do with my days, but also for the ego-boost – for knowing that someone could like me enough to give me a job. By Sunday night I am at my wits' end. Had this been a standard nine-to-five position, I could have calmed myself down with the knowledge that everything closed down for the weekend. But this is retail; I was even offered the interview on a Sunday night, for god's sake.

I'm staring at the wall, smoking endless cigarettes and chewing my fingernails to shreds when my phone pings.

It's a notification from WordPress – someone has commented on my blog post from Saturday morning. My first one – all about my gym experience.

I'd written it carefully, letting my hands move without thinking too much, before editing and re-reading countless times. It was good – I thought – and I'd managed to gain a few likes and about ten followers since I published. I click on the comment.

NRJogger *Who reads this drivel? Sounds like you need to get yourself a life and something more important to think about.*

I blink. Even though I'm alone, I'm smacked by the heat of shame rising up my chest and to my face, my eyes filling with tears. I feel exposed and ridiculous.

Stupid, I tell myself. *I'm so fucking stupid.* How could I have thought that I could write and people would actually like it? What did I expect, that I'd put my fingers on the keyboard and become an international sensation overnight?

I feel sick at the thought that someone, somewhere on the planet, has read my words, smirking, thinking how ridiculous I am. I've put myself out there and I've been mocked, publicly, as a result. I suddenly want to delete all traces of myself on the Internet, to completely disappear.

Slamming my phone onto the table, I stand up and start pacing the room.

Breathe, breathe, breathe.

I'm trying to swallow the wedge of embarrassment down, but it clags in my throat. I have never felt so ashamed in my entire life – not when Barney Dalton lifted up my skirt in primary school, or when I suddenly got my period in my boyfriend's dad's cream-leather BMW, or even when I faceplanted the pavement on a first date and then vomited up a tree. It feels different, somehow – completely raw – because this is all I've ever thought I could do, and someone thinks I'm terrible at it.

How is everybody else so completely amazing at everything they're doing? Head of marketing, freelancer, world-traveller. They don't even seem to try and they're smashing every goal. Is it even what they want? Because this is what I want. This is what I want and I can't even do it. I bet everyone thinks I'm such a ridiculous failure.

I feel panic rising from my stomach, and I pull open the window to let the cold March air wash over my face. As I'm leaning out I notice Veronica, sitting on the windowsill, her leaves furled and brown.

This is all too much.

I sink down to the floor, tears suddenly dripping down my face. A sensation of absolute, concentrated shame and disappointment consumes me. How did I fuck up this badly? Being fired wasn't so bad when I thought I could try my hand at something else, but Frederick's don't want me and the one thing – the *one thing* – I truly believed was my calling has fallen flat. I've lost my friendship circle to a clump of cells, and I'll lose my apartment if I don't find the money to pay next month's rent. I've ticked virtually nothing off my list and am even further away from becoming Emma Penton than I was when I started. I can't even keep a potted plant alive – the potted plant my own grandmother gave me – that I swore I would use as a measuring stick for my own success.

Well, the verdict's pretty clear on that one, isn't it?

I stay crouched on the floor for a few minutes, until my thighs start to tremble, and then I do what I do best in any given crisis: I grab a gigantic packet of vegan chocolate-chip cookies, bury myself under the duvet and stare at the wall some more.

What feels like days passes, and I watch the light move across the walls and then disappear, replaced by the navy of the evening and the orange glow of the streetlight outside. I haven't moved an inch, except to insert biscuits mechanically into my mouth, but I've relived every fuck-up I have ever made, torturing myself with the cringe of shame squeezing my stomach every time. It doesn't stop me eating, though.

I am vaguely aware of my phone ringing, and I listen to it for a while before shuffling slowly back into the living room and picking it up without looking.

'Hello?' I sniff.

'Maggie? Are you poorly?' It's Mum.

'No. I'm sleeping, can I call you tomorrow?' I pull the phone from my face and hover my finger over the 'end call' button.

'No, Maggie, wait.' She sighs, and I put the phone back to my ear. 'Now, I don't want you to panic, but Nana's had a fall.'

'What?' Fresh fear surges through me. Not Nana, please not Nana. I'll move back in with my parents, never work again, never have any money, never have another boyfriend. Just please don't let anything have happened to my nana.

'She's OK, she's broken her hip but she's OK.' Mum sniffles a bit, and I realise she's been crying. How selfish am I? So wrapped up in my own stupid problems, I didn't even notice she was upset.

'Where is she? Is she in hospital?'

'Yes, she'll be in for a while. She's confused, but nothing life-threatening.'

'She was confused when I last saw her. I think she's confused a lot, recently.' I well up again, imagining how scared she must be.

'Yeah. I don't think she'll be safe to go back to the way she was living before.' Mum's voice breaks.

'You can't take away her independence!' I cry. 'You can't take away her house!'

172

'Nobody's saying we'll take away her house. But she may need some help, especially when she goes out. That pavement is deadly, it's a good job she landed on the grass or it could have been a lot worse.'

'She slipped on the pavement outside her house? Are you serious? I called the council over a week ago and they said they'd sort it the following Monday. They said they'd bloody sort it!' I'm crying again.

'Maggie, calm down. They obviously haven't sorted it. That doesn't change what's happened, though, does it?'

'No.' I sink down onto the sofa, defeated. 'Where is she? I'll get a taxi.'

'She's at Stepping Hill. She'll be in surgery soon though, love. Wait until the morning. Do you think you can get it off work?'

'Yes, yeah, of course. Is someone with her, though? Is someone looking after her?' I die a little inside at the idea of her alone and frightened in A&E, with no idea where she is or why she's in so much pain.

'I'm going there now,' she says tiredly.

'Are you OK, Mum? I'll come with you if you need me.' I want to reach through the phone and squeeze her until she pops.

'I'm fine, love. I'll pick you up tomorrow morning. All right?'

We say our goodbyes and I curl up on the sofa, trying to remember that Nana is in safe hands, surrounded by professionals who are used to confused, elderly people and will treat her with kindness.

I'm exhausted from the overflow of emotion, and I close my eyes, watching the pulse of my own disappointing blood thudding against my eyelids.

The phone is ringing again. I jolt awake, distantly noticing the smear of saliva across the couch cushion I've been lying on. The ringtone screams danger to me – reminding me of Nana, and I grab the phone with my heart racing violently. I don't want to know, what if it's bad news? What if these are my last few minutes of a life with Nana in it? I want to savour them, to block out any alternatives.

'Hello?' I pick up at the last minute.

It's Mum. She's in the car, she'll be here in twenty minutes.

I wash my face, recoiling at the puffy eyes staring back at me in the mirror. Never fall asleep crying – why does nobody tell you that? It ruins your face for days. I pat the bags under my eyes uselessly – they're going nowhere – and pull on some jeans and a jumper, spraying some deodorant under my armpits so I don't stink the place out. It's crazy how a serious life event can twist your perspective. For this small moment, for this crisis, I am not even remotely conscious of what I look like. It's OK to go to a hospital without showering though, isn't it? I'm not going to breach infection control? We probably covered this at uni, although I wouldn't know – I was drunk for most of my 'Bacteria and Infection' module.

Mum pulls up just after 9.30, and I jump in the car feeling light-headed, butterflies swirling around in my stomach. We drive the thirty minutes to Stepping Hill mostly in silence, both of us lost in our own thoughts. Mum pulls into the car park and turns off the engine, sitting back with her hands clasped on her knee.

'Is Charlie OK?' she murmurs.

'Charlie? Yeah, why?' The memory of his behaviour at dinner last week swims across my mind.

'Oh, it's nothing. He's different, recently, that's all. You saw him. Put on a bit of weight, stopped caring about himself.' She sighs. 'I'm sure he's fine.'

'I'm sure he is. Don't worry.'

'Well, if anyone had a clue what was going on in his head it'd be you.' She opens the door and steps out into the cold sunshine.

I'm taken aback by that comment. Is that true? I suppose Charlie and I are technically closer to each other than to anyone else in the family, but we laugh together, we don't cry together.

Besides, we barely speak at all recently, and he doesn't exactly share his thoughts abundantly. I'm pretty vocal about even the most minor inconveniences in my life, unless they involve things my parents would disapprove of, but Charlie seems to sail along without resistance. I don't know how he's feeling. No one has ever known how Charlie is feeling.

We squeak through the hospital corridors and I take a pump of every hand sanitizer we pass – there's no way I'm passing anything on to Nana. I wonder if I should drink some too, in case I've got a virus brewing in my throat. I heard about prisoners and alcoholic patients doing that. I smear some across my cheeks so I can give Nana a germ-free cuddle.

Mum rolls her eyes at me but says nothing until we are at the entrance to the orthopaedic ward. I go for the door but she blocks my path.

'Now, I want you to remember that she's had a nasty fall. Her face is pretty bad.' She raises her eyebrows at me. 'Do you understand, Mags?'

'Yeah.' I whisper. She's preparing me early so I don't over-react – it's a tactic she's employed since I crawled out of the womb and she realised how prone to dramatic outbursts I am. This will be a big test. I need to stay calm.

We move down the ward with the rest of the morning's visitors, and I slow as we reach the final bay. I'm not going to be able to cope with this, I'm not going to be able to hold it in. *Come on, Maggie, she needs you.* I swallow and step into the bay.

I don't spot her immediately; there are too many fluffy white heads propped up on pillows. I scan each one before my eyes land on the bed in the far-left corner. At first I don't think it's her. Her face is purple and black, one of her eyes the size of a tennis ball and swollen shut. But then I see her yellow cardigan and a lump rises in my throat.

'Hi, Mum.' Mum has gone over to Nana's bedside and is hugging her gently.

I'm still standing in the doorway, terrified. I can't do it, I really can't. I know as soon as she looks at me I'll break down, and that will make things worse for her. It'll make her upset, too.

Mum points over in my direction and Nana turns and sees me in the doorway. Her face breaks into a pained smile and she waves shakily. I take a deep breath. This isn't about me and how I'm feeling, it's about her. She needs to see familiar faces and people she loves.

'Nana!' I say brightly, striding over to her bed. 'What've you done now, hey?' I plant a kiss on her soft head.

'Oh, I don't know. I'm a silly bugger, aren't I?' She chuckles.

'You are! What're you like?' I squeeze her cannulated hand. She is absolutely covered in scrapes and bruises, crawling down her neck and out from under the sleeves of her cardigan.

'Now, Suzannah, let me tell you about the food here.' She flutters around on the bed for the menu.

'I'm Maggie, Nana.' *Fucking Suzannah.*

'Maggie? I know you're Maggie!' She tuts and smiles at me. I've got to hand it to her, she's an absolute pro at making her own mistakes someone else's problem. 'Silly billy. Now, when I booked they said it was just bed and breakfast, but I've been getting three meals a day!'

I eye Mum; she's staring at the floor and blinking rapidly. She's not coping with this, and that makes me feel responsible. I have to handle this for the both of us. I read somewhere that the best thing to do with dementia patients is to go along with their beliefs of reality. Contradicting them causes distress.

'Now I know you two, you're sneaky little sausages. Did you upgrade my booking as a surprise?' Nana grins.

'How did you guess?!' I laugh. 'We wanted to surprise you. You're too quick for us!'

She taps the side of her nose. 'When you bring up six children you don't miss a trick.'

I spend the next half an hour asking questions about Nana's hotel stay. There are gardens here, apparently, and a grand piano. There's bingo in the evenings and a tea dance on Sundays. Her and Gramps are planning on going to the next one. I well up a bit at that. I wonder if she's regurgitating a memory of a previous holiday. It's doubtless a happy recollection, and she lights up as she tells me all about it. What's the point in forcing her into the truth?

Visiting hours are over, and we stand up to leave, causing some upset when Nana wonders why we won't go for a walk down to the beach with her. Luckily she doesn't have a window nearby, so we tell her it's raining and that we're going back up to our rooms to get changed.

As I hug her goodbye, she holds me close and whispers in my ear. 'Don't worry about me. I'm not as lonely in here.'

18

I haven't slept well for worrying about Nana. How could it be that she's lonely? Actually, scratch that – how could it be that we hadn't *noticed* she's lonely?

When I think about it, it makes perfect sense, which makes it even harder to swallow. I feel guilty, mostly, for being so selfish. I always saw her as the matriarch; ever-present and strong, pottering around and doing her thing and perfectly content with it. Obviously, since Gramps died, I knew she'd be missing him, but she always seemed so warm and chirpy when we went to see her. I suppose I never stopped to wonder whether she was happy just for those moments; the moments she wasn't alone. Because you don't think about what happens when the door closes, do you?

I have spent the last few days trying to swat it away and stay strong. What use am I if I crumble? Besides, this revelation is so gargantuan that it's blurring all my other crises into insignificance. When I receive a text from Martin telling me he's seeing someone new, and that he wants me to meet her, I brush it off. I don't have time to be sad and whingey – I only have time to keep moving forward.

This is just classic Martin anyway, isn't it? Showing off the girl who *would* say yes. He never really wanted me. He wanted what

I represented – the fiancée on his super-toned arm, his female counterpart in the idyllic home. Whoever she is, I've no interest in meeting her. I do, however, need to get Martin's collection of weights out of my apartment. I'll think about that later.

As soon as I got back from the hospital I hit the gym, smacking my feet down on the treadmill until they wouldn't run any further. I managed a new record of fifteen minutes of solid running. Pete gave me a thumbs up as I left, and I felt pretty vindicated. Then I rang the woman from the council, *again*, and told her what had happened. She was mortified, as she bloody should be, and swore down on her nephew's life that she'd have it sorted before Nana got out of hospital. If she doesn't I will murder her nephew with my bare hands.

Joke.

Maybe.

It's Tuesday now, and I've been applying for jobs and practicing my mindfulness all morning. It's getting a little bit easier, but my posture still needs some work. I'm resisting the urge to scroll through Instagram and have instead downloaded a new book onto my Kindle. I'm three chapters in when the phone rings.

'Hello?'

'Hello, am I speaking to Margaret Gardiner?' It's a woman's voice.

'Yes?'

'Oh hi, it's Emma here from Frederick's. We're sorry it's taken so long to get back to you, Darren's been off sick but he's been reviewing candidates from home.'

My stomach somersaults. I hope it wasn't my sweaty hand germs that made him ill.

'No problem at all,' I say, with as much calm as I can muster.

'So we're really happy to tell you that you were successful at interview and we'd like to offer you the position of full-time sales assistant. You don't have to accept now, you can think about it, but do try to let us know as soon as you can.'

Oh my god. I've been offered the bloody job! I have to stop myself from asking what my staff discount will be straight away – that wouldn't come across well.

'I'd be delighted to accept!' I say, a little too enthusiastically. 'When would you like me to start?'

'Great! I know it's very short notice, but could you come in and do some shadowing on Thursday at 9 a.m.? Just for a few hours. Then we'll get you on some proper shifts.'

'Of course, that'd be great, thank you so much,' I gush.

As soon as I hang up I do a little 'whoop!' and call Cecilia. I feel an unquenchable urge to *show* her that I'm getting my life together.

'C? It's me, I got the bookshop job!' I screech as soon as she picks up.

'Aw Mags, that's great news! I'm really happy for you.' She sounds distracted.

'You OK?'

'Yeah, I'm fine! Why? Why wouldn't I be?' She laughs but it sounds false.

'No reason, just wondering. You need to come over and we can do wine and watch *Mamma Mia* to celebrate. When are you free? You could come over tonight?' I start picking stuff up around the room and tidying, the phone wedged on my shoulder.

'Oh, I can't tonight. I'm busy with David. I'll call you and we can sort it out. I've got to run, Mags. Congratulations again! Love you.' She puts the phone down.

That was weird. Wasn't it? Maybe I'm imagining things. I fire off a message to Sophie and Anna, but Sophie doesn't reply and Anna just says, 'Woo! Proud of you gal. Can't tonight but soon x'.

I sit down again, a little deflated. It's fine, there's plenty of time for us to celebrate. My phone buzzes. It's Anna again. 'Don't forget my scan next Tuesday, 3.30 p.m.!! x'. Oh good. I hope I'm not working. Actually, I hope I am.

Working! How exciting. I briefly remember that less than two weeks ago the prospect of working made me want to electrocute myself, but I'm over that now. I'm a new woman. A new, book-selling woman! Frederick's never gets really busy, either, it's always so calm. I'm sure I'll be able to spend most of my time curled up in the kids' corner, leafing through the latest paperbacks. If a customer needs me they can come and sit next to me and ask me whatever they want.

God, I hope we don't have to dust all those books. Surely they're not on the shelves long enough to get dusty? But what about those ones that are really difficult to shift, like *War and Peace*? I know it's a classic, but surely nobody actually buys that anymore? It's the kind of thing your uncle forces on you at Christmas, to show you how people used to live and how much of an ungrateful brat you are for not appreciating the straighteners your parents got you in the wrong colour.

Frederick's is a five minute walk from the gym, too! I can go when I finish my shifts. And yoga is only down the road, hopefully I can get out no later than half five on Wednesdays and run straight there. I wonder if it's too early to start making requests?

I grab a glass of water and neck half of it, chucking the rest on Veronica (who is now completely brown and crispy) before rolling a cigarette. I lean out of the window and take a few long, deep drags. I'm really excited! This could be the start of a brand new career for me. I might meet some authors, or agents, who I can pitch my book ideas to. Of course, that would require me actually coming up with a book idea, but maybe once they see my blog they'll suggest something of their own?

My stomach sinks a little bit as I remember the nasty comment on my latest post. It was such a cruel thing to say; I actually feel quite angry. What gives that arsehole the right to make me feel so terrible, to make me completely abandon something I really enjoy? It's one person's opinion, and they don't speak for everybody. The post has about thirteen likes now, why should a single comment override all that positivity?

I pull out my laptop and start a second post, the fire of defiance burning in my belly. *Fuck you, boring troll.* The words flow easily as I describe my vegan journey so far – how many times I've forgotten, how I've struggled with restaurant menus, how the smell of bacon has driven me to the brink. It's light and funny, in my opinion, and for now, that's all that matters.

Mum calls as I'm walking to yoga the following day, to say that Nana's hip is healing well, but mentally she is worse than ever.

'She's been kicking off at the nurses a lot, especially at night. Moonlighting, I think they call it.' She sounds tired.

'Moonlighting? Like, showing her bum to everyone?' I am horrified at the thought.

'No!' She laughs. 'Dementia patients get a bit crazy when the sun goes down, apparently. Sundowning! Sorry, not moonlighting, sundowning. She's just been trying to get out of bed, screaming that she's been wrongly imprisoned, asking where Gramps is. Stuff like that.'

'Jesus.' This is not good.

'Yeah. They're not going to let her go home until we've sorted out some support for her.'

'It's the hospital, she's not used to it. She needs to be around her stuff, her memories.' I suggest.

'I know, you're right. But we can't deny that she's not the same, even before all this happened. I think we should get her to move in with Charlie and your dad and I for a bit.' She sounds exhausted at the idea.

'Oh, god. That'll be torture for all of you. Don't we need to think long-term? She can't stay with you forever.'

'Yeah. But for now I just want her out of the hospital.'

'I get that.' It's too much to think about right now. 'All right, Mum, I've got to go. I'll go and visit her tomorrow afternoon after –' I nearly say after my first shift, but then I remember that my parents still think I'm working for Theo and I stop myself, '– after work.'

I put the phone down and head up the stairs to Namaste studios. Dreadlocks guy gives me a cheery wave and I wave back, genuinely happy to see him. He's weird, but he's welcoming. I'm starting to like him.

I'm early, but Gary and Altantsetseg are already here, sitting in uncomfortable silence. Well, the uncomfortable silence seems just to be on Gary's part – she's sat meditating and he's shifting his eyes around the room as though she's masturbating in front of him or something. Relief washes over his face when I walk in.

'Thank god you're here.' he whispers as I roll my mat out next to him. 'I'm not coming early again.'

I laugh. 'I can't cope with her at all. She's constantly pissed off. I thought yoga was supposed to make you chilled and all-loving.'

'Apparently not.' He smiles at me.

We walk down the street after class finishes, until we reach the corner where we usually go our separate ways.

'I feel really chilled and all-loving right now.' Gary laughs.

'Same. I'm really enjoying this, you know. More than I thought I would.' I take in the quiet streets, the steamy windows of the pubs. I feel inexplicably and completely un-alone, entirely un-self-conscious.

'Me too.' He catches my eye as I look at him and holds my gaze for a second. 'You up to much tonight?'

'Yep, only three more episodes of *The Office* left until I've finished the final season. It's a big night.' I smile.

'Ah, OK. Sounds important. Maybe next time?' He reddens a little.

Oh, shit, was he asking me out? I thought we were making small-talk; I'm so autistic with these things. God, what do I do now?

'Yeah, maybe next time,' I say eventually. 'Shall we swap numbers, though? Then we can make sure we arrive at the same time and avoid being alone with Alabama Slammer or whatever her name is.'

He throws his head back and laughs, his hair flopping back and exposing his creased-up face. 'Alabama Slammer. You're funny. Farty, but funny.' He clocks my glare and holds up his hands. They're big, I notice. 'OK, OK, I'm sorry. Yeah, let's swap numbers.'

I walk home feeling wired and buzzy. Was that a friendly invitation, or something more? Panic swirls in my chest. I can't get locked into another relationship. I can't even face imagining it. Fat-free dinners and long weekends and impromptu proposals. I take a deep breath. Maybe he just wants a friend. Christ, maybe I could *do* with a friend. And even if it's more than that, it's not like one date would swipe my independence, is it? Rational thoughts like that don't get rid of the butterflies swimming around in my tummy, though.

My first day at work. Shit.

I'm wearing black suit pants and a cream shirt. I assumed I'd be given an official Frederick's uniform and I was right; a girl called Anita has just thrust a crumpled, suspiciously not-new-looking polo shirt in my hand and directed me to the staff changing rooms. The dingy space is in stark contrast to the cosy, low-lit atmosphere of the shop; all metal pipes, chipped paint and fluorescent tube lighting. I sniff the shirt tentatively (it smells like bolognese) before taking a deep breath and wrenching it over my head. The top three buttons are done up, so it gets stuck on my nose, smears my makeup down my face and pulls all my hair out from its bobble.

I eventually unpop the buttons and manage to get the shirt on. It's a sickly green colour and it's *huge*, an XXL at least. I look like the winner of *The Biggest Loser*. I am disheartened to realise that I don't look cute, like other girls might. I don't look like a dainty model, swamped in her boyfriend's t-shirt. I don't look like Emma Penton. I turn away from the mirror.

Leaving my stuff under one of the woodchip benches, I head out onto the shop floor and make my way over to Darren, who is murmuring to Anita by the recipe books. He spins round when he sees me, and the girl hurries off.

'Maggie, welcome! I see Anita has given you your uniform.' He flashes those weird, pointy teeth at me.

'Yeah, it's a bit big . . .' I start.

'Well, it's our *newbie shirt*. All newbies wear that one until we're sure they're going to stick around, then we give them their own.' He looks at me proudly, as though this is the best idea anyone has ever had.

'Does it ever get washed?' I brave.

'Oh, no. Probably not. Nobody wears it for that long anyway. Now, let me find Beric and he can show you the ropes.'

I follow him round, feeling filthy and contaminated, until we find a weedy blonde boy crouched next to a table display.

'Beric, meet Maggie.'

The boy starts suddenly, trembling to his feet and staring at us with big, round eyes. 'I'm just doing the crime thriller stack . . . I'm nearly done,' he whispers.

'No problem, take your time,' Darren twinkles.

Beric flits his eyes from the display to me, as though he's weighing up the least dangerous option.

'I don't bite!' I try, feeling creepy as soon as it comes out of my mouth.

Darren booms with laughter. 'I'll leave you two to it. Good luck on your first day.'

Beric's eyes follow Darren to the back of the shop until he is out of sight. We stand in silence for a second.

'Want a hand?' I offer, getting on my knees and reaching for a book.

'No, it's OK. I'll sort it later. Come on, I'll show you around.'

Beric is really sweet, showing me everything I need to know at an unbelievable pace. I'm not really taking any of it in; he's rattling off really minute details until he's out of breath, his eyes darting around the room and never meeting mine. If I'd been paying attention, I'd know where the spare fuses for the staff kitchen kettle are kept. I tried to process it all for the first ten minutes but then I gave up, figuring as long as I knew where the toilets were I could ask about other stuff when needed. At midday, Darren seeks us out again.

'Got the gist of it all, then?' He smiles.

'Yep, pretty much, I think. It might take a few goes to get the hang of some things, but I think I'll be OK.'

He nods. 'Of course, of course. Rome wasn't built in a day, etcetera.' He turns to Beric. 'Now, Beric, I don't want you taking this the wrong way and panicking, but a customer has just tripped over an Agatha Christie from the stack you were doing earlier. Completely not your fault – I asked you to show Maggie around – but would you mind going and finishing it off now?'

Beric scampers off at an alarming speed, his knees trembling as he flees to the other side of the shop.

'God, is the customer OK?' I start. 'I feel awful, I hope Beric isn't upset.'

'Not a problem at all, she's absolutely fine.' Darren gives me a warm grin. 'These things happen. Here's your rota for the next fourteen days, see you tomorrow?'

'Absolutely.' I nod.

Darren heads off to the other side of the shop, where Beric is hurriedly finishing his stack.

'He's really nice, isn't he?' I turn to Anita, who is sticking 3 for 2 labels on a stack of paperbacks.

'Mmm.' She doesn't look up from what she's doing.

I keep watching her for a second, but she doesn't offer anything further. 'Well, I'll see you tomorrow then.'

When she doesn't reply I make my way to the back, grab my stuff and change my top. In a last ditch attempt, I offer Anita a wave on my way out of the main door. She hesitates for a second and then looks down again, ripping a sticker off the sheet with force.

That was weird, I think as I walk down Deansgate. Beric obviously has quite bad anxiety, he was so desperate to do everything right and give me all the information he could as quickly as possible. He evidently doesn't cope well with new people. I hope I can earn his trust; it'd be nice to have an ally who can tell me how I can get rid of my *newbie shirt*. It's really lovely how patient and kind Darren is with him too – Theo would have given him a total nervous breakdown by now. He went to speak to Beric a few times when he was alone and I was practicing something, checking everything was going OK. It's such a relief to finally have a nice, normal boss, who isn't interested in small talk about women's problems and iguanas. I've got a good feeling about this place.

19

After a long, hot shower I decide to go and see Nana again. I catch the tram to Altrincham and head to her house first to grab a few little bits that I hope might make her stay in the hospital a little less confusing.

I turn onto Nana's street and fumble in my bag for one of the spare keys she hands out at random, just in case she's in the garden and can't hear the doorbell. I'm pretty sure the majority of Greater Manchester owns one of these keys. Mine has a 'J' keyring on it – no idea why.

Nearing the house, it's obvious that the shit-for-brains council have done sweet FA about the mould on the pavement. It's still caked on, with three heavy smears across it where Nana must have fallen. The idea makes me feel sick. I stab at my phone and rest it on my shoulder as I wrestle the key into the front door.

'I'm calling about my nana's house,' I say once I've navigated the options and been put through, again.

I reel off my details and the man pulls up my previous conversations.

'Ah, yes. I see,' he murmurs. He's got a charming, seductive voice. 'This is logged in for tomorrow morning, so it's all being sorted.'

God, he sounds so sexy and reassuring. I feel an over-whelming desire to giggle and thank him profusely, but then I picture the smears in the mould and the fog clears. My grand-mother's safety is far more important than a man whose voice makes my fanny flutter.

'See, I'm struggling to believe that. Last time I called I was told that this would be sorted the very next day. It clearly hasn't been. Is this *"first thing tomorrow morning"* line just the go-to remedy for annoying callers?' I wander into the living room, distractedly studying items on shelves and wondering which I should take to the hospital. I rifle through the cupboards and look for some bathroom cleaner, wondering if I could take a stab at cleaning the pavement myself. But it's all the way up the street; it needs one of those spray jobs – the one with the backpack that makes you look like the decontaminators from *Monsters, Inc.*

'I can assure you that absolutely isn't the case, Miss Gardiner. We take this very seriously. I will personally make sure someone is at your grandmother's house tomorrow morning,' he replies.

'There better had be. I'll be calling tomorrow at midday to make sure—' I stop mid-way into the conservatory and gasp.

'Madam? Are you all right?'

Charlie is sitting on Nana's sofa, beer in hand. I end the phone call, Council Man's audio Viagra suddenly a distant memory.

'What are you doing here?'

'Charming.' Charlie looks up at me. His eyes are red-raw, I can't tell if it's from booze or crying. 'Why are you here?'

'Getting some stuff to take to the hospital for her.' I slump into the seat opposite him. 'Again, what are *you* doing here?'

He shrugs. 'Dunno.'

We sit in silence as I wait to see if he will offer anything further. When he doesn't I start to panic a little – we have never been at a loss for words with each other.

'Charlie . . .' I brave. 'You OK?'

His head snaps up as if I've slapped him. 'Yes.' He frowns.

I sit back for a second, and then reach out to touch his shoulder. 'You know, if you want to talk—'

'I don't want to fucking talk.' He swats my hand away. 'Just leave me alone, Maggie.'

I stand up, feeling like I've been punched. I've never seen Charlie like this. He's never *spoken* to me like this. What is his problem?

'Fine,' I say, grabbing the *Enid & Bernard* cushion from the sofa. I feel like I need to say something to diffuse the situation, to let him know I'm not angry with him. I can already feel the burning guilt of walking out of the room without offering some comfort. But I don't know what to say, and Charlie has resumed gazing glassily into his beer bottle. He doesn't want me.

I stuff the cushion in my bag with a couple of black and white photos from the TV stand, glance at him once more and leave.

Nana is propped up in bed, chatting to a healthcare assistant sitting at her side. The girl jumps up when I approach the bed.

'Hello! Are you Mrs Lawson's relative?' She beams.

'Yes, granddaughter.' I peer at Nana. She looks fine, so this can't be bad news, surely. Although it's hardly likely to be good, is it? Old people don't come into hospital and get special surprises. *Guess what, we've reversed her dementia and brought her husband back from the dead, isn't that lovely?*

'If we could just have a quick word . . .' She leads me onto the corridor and motions to a girl on the other side of the bay, who comes and sits next to Nana.

'As you can see, Enid is being specialed.' She cocks her head in sympathy.

'Specialed?' I repeat dumbly. What the hell is specialed? Like, special needs? Does Nana have an undiagnosed learning disorder? Or does she mean special treatment, because Nana is so lovely? I'm not sure it works like that, but it'd be nice, wouldn't it?

'Yes. She's having one-on-one supervision, around the clock.'

'Like a suicidal person?' I bleat, my mind running at a thousand miles an hour. 'Oh god, has she tried anything? Has she tried to end it all?'

'No, I—'

'Keep the bloody pills away from her, and the carrier bags. She once told me if they cancelled *Emmerdale* she'd take six paracetamol and put a Sainsbury's bag over her head.' My voice has risen to a shriek. The girl holds my arm.

'This is a hospital. Drugs are strictly controlled, she wouldn't be allowed near any paracetamol unless she was prescribed it. Enid isn't suicidal, she's just very confused.' She releases my arm and gives it a little pat.

'Oh. Oh, yes, I know that. But she doesn't need *watching*. She just thinks she's on holiday, it's best to leave her be. She's a very private person.' I smile, relieved that nothing new has come to light.

'Well, she keeps getting out of bed because she forgets she's had her hip replaced. It's really dangerous, if she puts weight through it or – god forbid – falls, it could really set her recovery back,' she says.

'Jesus Christ, thank god you're keeping an eye on her then!' I squeal, suddenly grateful for 'specialing' and the manpower it must cost this hospital. 'Thank you. Really, thanks for looking out for her.'

'That's what we're here for.' She gives me one more beam and a pat and scurries off to chide an old man who is getting his penis out in the next bay.

I take over from the girl sitting next to Nana, who looks more than a little pissed off at having her chance to sit down literally ripped from under her feet.

'Marigold!' Nana holds her papery arms out to me.

'Maggie, Nana. Not Marigold.' I give her a gentle hug.

'Marigold who works in the corner shop?' She frowns. 'Has she been chatting my Bernie up again?'

This is going to be exhausting.

'Nope. Everything's fine.' I reach into my bag and pull out the cushion and the photo frame.

'I recognise this!' She chuckles, grabbing the cushion and inspecting it. 'Whose is this? It's got our names on it! Isn't that funny, Bernie?' She turns to her left and blinks, looking around frantically. 'Where's Bernie gone?'

'He's just nipped to the toilet,' I risk, hoping she'll have forgotten soon. This is really, really bad. She was forgetful before, but this is next-level awfulness. I feel my eyes threatening to well up and blink fiercely, giving myself a mental slap. *Pull yourself together Maggie, for god's sake.*

I try to keep Nana on safe topics for a while; what has she been eating, does her hip hurt, who's her favourite nurse? She tells me she had chips and gravy on the ship's deck last night and is confused when I ask her about her hip, as if it's the weirdest question ever. She tells me her favourite nurse is Florence Nightingale.

When I prop the photo up on her over-the-bed table, she gets a little more lucid. 'Oh, look how lovely we looked. Me and my Bernie.' Her eyes fill with tears. 'In our little house there, aren't we?'

I nod because I don't trust myself to speak. She gazes at the photo for a long time before her eyes drift over to me.

'I don't think I can go back there.' She whispers.

'Where, Nana?' I'm preparing myself for the latest confabulation.

'Home. I'm scared.' Her top lip trembles.

I grab her hand and hold it to my cheek. 'Nana,' I kiss her fingers, 'you don't ever need to be scared. Please don't be scared.'

'Our lovely house,' she repeats, her eyes sliding back to the photograph.

'Nobody is going to take your house away.' I reassure her. 'You can go home soon and everything will go back to normal.' I'm saying this to convince myself rather than her; I'm pretty confident things will never be as they were.

'No.' She grips my hand tighter. 'No, Margie. I can't go back there, I'm not safe. I forget things, I fall over.' She pauses. 'I'm lonely.'

My heart breaks. This is the second time she's said this, so it must be true. It wasn't just a confused one-off. I don't want to believe it.

The idea of Nana not being in her cosy house anymore – of giving up that gigantic chunk of my entire life – fills me with such a huge sadness I feel like I'm going to be sick. That house has been a boiling-hot, saturated-fat-filled haven for me since the day I entered the world. Nana and Gramps have always been there, as solid and reliable as anything I've ever known. When Gramps died it was hard, but we always had that space to remember him, and the love of my nana in her warm home to welcome us in and care for us.

The sadness and heartbreak of losing that constant, however, is nothing compared to the gut-wrenching despair I feel at the prospect of Nana being unhappy. Of her being lonely. Afraid. Her safety and well-being must be a priority. She must come first, above my own sense of security and childhood nostalgia.

'Whatever you want, Nana,' I say eventually. 'Promise.'

She looks up from where she has been studying her hands. 'Hm? Where on earth has our Bernie got to?'

I stand up and plant a kiss on her forehead. 'Love you, Nana.'

20

The day of Anna's twelve-week scan.

I am so irrationally freaked out by the prospect that I consider cancelling. I don't want to see the bean-sized alien and be presented with proof that it exists – that my world is heading in the direction of babies and seriousness without my permission.

But Anna is my best friend; I need to be there for her. As I pull on jeans and a woolly jumper, I remind myself that I have six months until he or she arrives. I vow that I will use that time to get over my baby-phobia. Maybe there's a meditation track for it?

Walking back through to the living room, I notice the list on the coffee table. I almost forgot it. There are a few more things I can *definitely* cross off on here now. I strike the pen across the page and feel just a faint glimmer of satisfaction. I am a couple of steps closer to becoming Emma Penton. That's what I wanted, isn't it? I look at the rest.

1. Stop smoking.
2. Lose weight.
3. Exercise.
4. See family more.
5. ~~Change your fucking job.~~

6. ~~Start yoga.~~
7. Do tea detox.
8. Go vegan.
9. ~~Meditate.~~
10. ~~Start blog.~~

I still can't let myself cross out numbers three, four and eight. Not until I've stuck at them a little longer.

A car horn sounds outside, and I peer out of the window to see Cecilia sitting next to Sophie in her bashed-up Fiat Punto. Shit, shit, shit. I give Veronica a quick pat for good luck – her leaves are plumping up again, with new sprouts coming up at the base. She's not out of the woods yet, but she's getting there.

'Hey,' I say, as I squeeze myself through the gap behind the passenger seat.

'Hey!' Cecilia chirps. 'Are you excited?!'

'No,' I say sulkily.

'Oh, come on, Mags. Aren't you over this baby hatred yet?' Sophie turns in her seat to grin at me.

'Erm, nope,' I sigh. 'I'm terrified of killing it.'

'Well as long as you don't stab Anna or push her down a flight of stairs, you'd be pretty hard pressed to have an impact at this stage.' She starts messing with the radio.

'Yeah but after today it's real, isn't it?'

'It's been real for the past three months, love.' Cecilia laughs.

'Yeah, I know. Anyway, what's new with you guys? Give me the goss.'

I settle back into my seat and wait for the outpouring of drama – David's latest creations, Sophie's work crises. Sure enough, Cecilia starts ranting about the life-drawing class David has started taking, but not before there's a pause as they exchange a look they think I can't see.

Am I being paranoid?

'-and he keeps begging me to be his muse. Like I'm going to stand bollock-naked in a room full of dirty old men and sweaty art students with hairy armpits.' She laughs, but it sounds forced.

I shake the feeling that they're keeping something from me, telling myself I'm tired. I've been to the gym every day over the past week, and I've just pulled two long weekend shifts in a row at Frederick's. I'm burning the candle at both ends and I'm not used to it.

We get to the radiology department a few minutes late, and Anna is nowhere to be seen. The frog-looking lady at reception huffs as she tells us she can't promise we'll be able to go in because the scan is probably already taking place. I silently pray we can go home now.

'It's fine, I'll call her!' Cecilia taps at her phone. 'Anna? It's me. We're outside, can we come in? Yep. OK. Great. See you in a sec.' She shoves her phone in her pocket. 'She says it's fine, she's in room four?'

The receptionist glares at us for a second before jabbing her thumb down the corridor. We rush along, my stomach gurgling with anxiety the closer we get. This is everything I used to want, but after Martin I feel like it's the last thing I can imagine for myself. It's all too adult, too stale. I should be travelling Asia, shagging strangers and drinking Pinot Grigio until I vomit – why am I here? I try to remind myself that it's not me that's having the baby, it's Anna, and I can still do all of the above. I probably won't though – I'll probably just keep sitting on the sofa watching *Queer Eye* until I'm fifty.

That makes me feel a bit depressed.

Sophie knocks gently on the door of number four, and we hear Anna shout 'come in' from inside. The door opens to reveal a dimly lit room with a monitor in the corner and a trolley next to it, upon which is lying Anna.

With her fanny out.

We all stop where we are, mouths hanging open. Anna is lying back calmly, beaming, her knees bent and legs spread.

'Come in, guys! The radiographer will be here in a minute.'

We step into the room silently and close the door behind us.

'Anna,' I whisper. 'What the fuck are you doing?'

She frowns. 'What do you mean? I'm having my twelve-week scan!'

'Why don't you have any pants on?' Sophie is addressing the ceiling in an attempt not to see her best friend's exposed genitalia.

'I just *said*,' Anna rolls her eyes, 'I'm having my scan. That's why you're here?'

'Did the radiographer tell you to take your pants off?' Cecilia's voice is shaking now.

'She left me in here to get comfortable whilst she went to get something. Why? What's going on?' Anna looks panicked now, but has done nothing to cover her modesty. It's still there, staring at me.

'Babe, do you know what an ultrasound scan involves?' Sophie fiddles with the paper towel dispenser on the wall.

'*Yes.* It's like a smear test.'

I can bear this no longer and I let out a snort, which sends Cecilia and Sophie into fits. 'Have you never watched any TV, any films?' I choke.

'You know I don't like television!' She wails.

All three of us are bent double now, screaming with laughter. Cecilia is hyperventilating. 'Oh my god, oh my god . . .'

Suddenly the door opens and the radiographer steps in. 'Are we all OK in here? All comfortable, Miss—' She stops dead as she spots Anna and her naked flaps.

We had managed to contain ourselves as she walked in the door, but the look on her face sets us off again. I'm howling.

'Miss Watson, you can keep your clothes on for this. It's just an ultrasound.' The radiologist coughs and looks down at her clipboard.

Anna jumps off the bed. 'Oh my god. Oh my god. I'm so sorry.' She yanks her jeans on and sinks back on the bed. She stares at her hands for a second, her face crimson, before looking up and catching our eye. A small smile pulls at the sides of her mouth and her nose starts twitching. 'What a dickhead.' She bursts out laughing and sets us all off again, tears streaming down our faces. My stomach hurts.

'OK, ladies, shall we get started?' The radiographer has settled herself by her machine and is eyeing us with disapproval.

The door opens again and a bald, chubby middle-aged man scoots in. 'Sorry I'm late!' He pants, sweat beading on his upper lip. 'A homeless guy had a poo on the upper deck.'

'It's OK, Brian, come over here.' Anna holds out her arm.

Cecilia, Anna and I exchange a glance. Bloody hell, so *this* is Brian. Horny bus driver and father of Anna's child. Until just now, I was holding out hope that he was some kind of *Sex-and-the-City*'s-Big-Type god, all dark hair, brooding eyes and a deep, sultry voice. That hope has been squashed flat by Brian's gigantic belly. Perhaps he and Anna can share maternity jeans.

OK, that was mean. I need to calm down. I can't drown this out with judgemental thoughts.

The radiologist goes through some medical questions with Anna, and then announces that we are ready to start. Anna lifts her top, mercifully keeping her lower half buttoned up.

My stomach flips as the slimy gel is smeared over her exposed belly. Any minute now and the little bean will be on the big screen. I'm going to have to act excited – like this is the best thing that's ever happened to me – and not as though my entire world and social life is crumbling around me. Nana's house and my friendship circle, ripped from my grasp in one miserable bastard of a week. I'd called Mum when I left the hospital and told her how much worse Nana was, how she'd told me she was scared to go home. Mum ended the call saying that she would research options, so the wheels are firmly in motion.

Deep breaths.

'OK . . .' says the radiographer, 'if you look here . . . you can see baby's head.'

There is a gasp of 'aww' around the room, and a small choke from Brian, but I keep my eyes firmly planted on the floor. I can't look.

'And here are baby's feet!'

More aww-ing, a few sobs, Anna's voice whispering, 'it's got my dodgy toe.' More staring at the linoleum for me.

'Maggie,' hisses Sophie, 'just look, it's beautiful.'

'And if I move a little over here . . . there! There it is, there's baby.'

I lift my eyes from the floor and force myself to look at the monitor. On the screen is a fuzzy, moving, black-and-white mass of shapes and shadows. Everyone is squeezing Anna, who is mesmerised by the screen. I force myself to look more carefully, and then I see it.

A tiny little baby.

Curled up in Anna's tummy.

My eyes prick with tears. I feel a strange sensation wash over me and wait for the roar of unfairness and hopelessness, but it doesn't come. Like a fog has lifted, I realise I'm not crying for myself. I'm not crying because Anna has what I want, or because her pregnancy is taking away everything I've got. I'm not crying because she is pushing me back into my old mindset of wanting a husband and a baby and stability. I'm not crying about any of that, because it doesn't matter. I'm crying because of that tiny little bean-baby, because soon he or she is going to come into the big, scary world. That baby is going to pop out into a crazy, dysfunctional family dynamic, with the most mental godparents and a father who could be its grandfather and a mother who reads signs in tea leaves and believes in 'connections'. That baby is going to be so fucking *loved*.

And I realise, suddenly, that I am neither jealous nor resentful. I am just happy. Happy for Anna, happy for Brian and happy for us.

'How lucky are we?' I find myself whispering.

'What?' Cecilia looks at me in shock.

'We're so lucky. We've got a new little human joining our group.' I walk over to Anna and squeeze her hard.

'Christ, Maggie, are you hormonal or what?' Anna laughs.

The radiologist tuts at Anna's language. 'Shall we take a picture of baby for you to take home? Would Mum and Dad like one each?' She's diplomatic. She senses that the photo of this little foetus won't be going on the fridge in Anna and Brian's lovingly shared home.

'Yes, please. A picture of Nugget for both of us.' She smiles wistfully.

'Can we have a photo of Nugget, too?' I say, adopting the new McDonalds-themed nickname for the baby.

'It's a maximum of two per scan, I'm afraid. You can get copies made at camera shops.' The radiologist sets about rotating the scanner, trying to find the money-shot of Nugget.

'Pout, queen, work iiiiit,' Sophie drawls.

We walk out, Anna and Brian cooing over their freshly printed photos. I ask if she can make me a copy and Anna puts her arm round me and gives me a kiss on the cheek. 'Of course I can.'

'I see we have a woman transformed,' laughs Sophie. 'I didn't expect that reaction from you, Mags.'

'Neither did I. It's just so . . . lovely, isn't it?' I'm welling up again.

Cecilia pats me on the arm. 'Come on then, home time.'

We bundle back into the car after saying goodbye to Brian and Anna, and twenty minutes later we're pulling up outside my block.

'Thanks for the lift, C.' I undo my seatbelt. 'What are you two up to for the rest of the day?'

There's an awkward pause again, unmistakeably this time, and they look at each other quickly. 'Oh, I'm going back to work,' Sophie says hurriedly.

'Yeah, I've got stuff to do at home.' Cecilia shoots me a quick smile.

'OK . . . well, I'll see you soon?' I jump out of the car and wave them off, trying to keep the happy baby bubble intact in my stomach.

But I can't deny it anymore.

Something is up.

It's one week after Anna's scan and I'm stacking the shelves of our new 'Foreign Romance' section at the end of my shift, wondering whether Nana could live at Mum and Dad's indefinitely, when my phone buzzes in my pocket. We're not really supposed to have phones on the shop floor, but as long as Darren (or a snitchy customer) doesn't see then it's basically fine.

I pull it out and see a WhatsApp from Kelsey.

Staff night out next Friday. Going to Common Bar in Northern Quarter. Would be great to have you there? ☺

I feel a little stab of irritation. This is the first time Kelsey has contacted me since I left. We were never best friends, but she was the closest thing I had to support in that place. I assumed since I'd ruined my own reputation she was keeping a wide berth, not wanting to be tarnished with my filthy brush. There's a part of me that wouldn't blame her for that, although that doesn't mean it stings any less. But maybe I was wrong? Maybe she did want to see me, but hadn't known what to say. And now she's reaching out; offering a way back in. I can't say I'd ever want to be bosom buddies with her, but it does feel nice that I haven't been forgotten.

I shove my phone back in my pocket, and feel hot breath on the back of my neck.

'Maggie.'

I spin around to find Darren smiling at me.

'You know our phone policy.'

'Oh god, sorry, Darren. My grandad is really ill so I thought I'd better keep it on me in case of emergencies. I'm really sorry, it won't happen again.' I purposefully don't use Nana as an excuse in case I jinx her. Gramps can't die twice, can he?

201

'Well of course, that's absolutely fine. Just let me know next time, please? No problem at all though, you're new and these things happen!' He pats me on the shoulder. 'I hope he's better soon.'

He wanders off across the shop, straightening books as he goes.

Beric sidles over to me. 'Are you OK?' He murmurs.

'Yeah, thanks Beric. Darren's so understanding. I can't tell you what a breath of fresh air it is after my old place.'

Beric flinches, his eyes wide. 'Yeah.'

'Honestly, my ex-boss was *so* dysfunctional. Well-intentioned, I think, but nuts. You're living the dream over here.' I laugh.

'Mmm.' He helps me stack the last few books.

'You finished now?' I ask.

'Yeah.'

'Shall we go and get a drink?' I try. I'm so desperate to know what's going on with him. He seems like he could do with a friend too, and I could use a pint.

He hesitates for a second. 'Sure.'

We head out onto Deansgate and into The Coach Inn, AKA the biggest dive pub the world has ever seen. It's a multi-tiered monstrosity with swirly carpets, dark brown sticky tables and upholstered seat pads. It's also a Wetherspoons, though, which means everything's cheap. We settle into a corner with our drinks and Beric visibly relaxes, his body slumped.

'So,' I say, cutting straight to the chase, 'is everything OK?'

Beric smiles and makes eye contact for the first time since I met him. 'Sure, how're things with you?'

'Good, yeah, settling in.' I stop myself going into detail about how much I'm enjoying the job. He's so visibly relaxed, it strikes me that his behaviour at work isn't his personality. It's a reaction to something. Maybe he's one of those people who can't handle hierarchical environments? 'I hope you don't mind me saying, but you're different when you're not in work.'

'What do you mean? We've been here two seconds.'

'No, I know. Sorry, I don't want to be presumptuous. I just wondered if maybe you wanted to talk about it. You seem really anxious at work, especially when Darren's around.'

At the mention of Darren's name, Beric's eyes flit around the room and a bead of sweat appears on his forehead.

'It's fine. It's nothing,' he says.

'If you don't want to talk about it, it's fine. But you don't seem to speak to many other people at work. I thought if there was something going on I might be able to help, you know. A shoulder or whatever.' I don't know what I'm offering, really. Nosiness and empathy are my driving forces right now.

Beric pinches the skin on his hand over and over again. Eventually he stops and looks at me defiantly. 'Darren's a dick.'

'Oh.'

I must look shocked because Beric starts trembling again. 'Don't tell him, please. Oh god, please, I shouldn't have said that.'

'Beric, it's fine. I'm not going to say anything, I *promise*. I just haven't seen that, so I'm trying to figure out what you mean. Maybe you can tell me? If you want to.'

He picks up his drink and it sloshes over the side of the glass.

'Like I said, you don't have to talk about it—'

'All right.'

I wait, watching him fight with himself. He looks at the table, blinking rapidly, before taking a deep breath and sitting up straight.

'I started here about a year ago. I was at a dead end, pretty much. Let go by my old job, rent to pay, my girlfriend was pretty high-maintenance so I needed a steady income. I got the job and I was so happy, honestly. I couldn't wait. Darren was amazing at first, so supportive. Even when I made mistakes he'd say, *these things happen*. I thought I'd struck gold. But then everything changed. I'd been there about three months, I think, when it started.' His eyes fill with tears. 'I'm sorry, I've never told anyone this before.'

'It's OK. Take your time.'

'At first it was just little whispers here and there, we'd be at the till on our own and he'd say something nasty under his breath. I thought I'd misheard. Then there were notes. Little things in my locker. Threats, you know? Then he turned everyone else against me, nobody spoke to me anymore. He told them things about me, things that weren't even true, that he wouldn't know anyway. And now, if I mess up, he makes me do stock check with him at night and he trips me up, mixes books I've already organised, hides stuff so I have to look for it. I tried telling Anita but she said I was mad, told me to see someone.'

Beric shakes his head and gazes into his drink. He's not shaking anymore.

I can't speak for a second. I'm trying to reconcile that version of Darren with the one I know; the charmer and understander. I'm also trying to imagine how that must feel – to be so subtly and systematically undermined and broken down, until you're living in terror every day, a shell of yourself.

'Beric,' I say, eventually. 'I am so, so sorry that you've gone through this. I know you don't really know me, but I want you to know you can trust me. I promise you can trust me. Do you believe me?'

He looks at me for a second. 'Yeah. Yeah, I believe you.'

'Good,' I say, shifting in my seat. 'Now, we need to do something about him. I'm going over there right now.'

'No!' Beric is alarmed. 'No, don't. We can't be impulsive about this.'

Impulsive. There's that word again. It's been following me around for weeks. And here is yet more proof that I don't know any other way to resolve a situation than acting on my immediate feelings and blowing up. I guess it's time to test myself.

'OK, you're right. Let's be calculating. What do you suggest?'

'I don't know.' Beric stares gloomily at the table. 'I can't lose my job.'

'What would happen if you lost your job?'

He looks at me as if I'm stupid. 'Well, I wouldn't have any money, would I? I need to pay my rent.'

God, I can relate to that. It's terrifying having the burden of rent resting squarely on your shoulders, especially when you have nobody else chipping in. I'm almost glad Martin never contributed – losing my job and boyfriend in the same week would have been so much harder if I wasn't already used to paying for everything myself.

'And the high-maintenance girlfriend?' I smile.

'She's long gone.'

'Then what's the issue? We can't be so terrified of losing our jobs that we never stand up for ourselves, Beric. There are a million jobs in this city, we'll find another one. Do you have any savings?'

'Yeah.'

'Then fuck it!' I grab his hand. 'It's worth the risk, isn't it? And take it from me, if this goes tits up, you *will* find your feet again.'

Beric blinks. 'OK. OK, let's do something.'

I grin, an idea forming. 'I say we collect evidence, report him to HR, and fuck him. And we have a bit of fun while we're doing it.'

'How do we collect evidence?' He looks overwhelmed.

I wink. 'I'm glad you asked . . .'

21

I have the next two days off, so I go to the gym, do some shopping and write another blog post. I've had no more nasty comments from trolls, and quite a few likes now, so I'm feeling pretty good. I tried to give Sophie a call to tell her about Kelsey inviting me to the work do, but she didn't pick up and hasn't texted me back. Cecilia has been distant too, and Anna is completely wrapped up in baby-world. I have to force myself to think rationally; I'm sure they're just busy with life and work and domestic dramas of their own.

But why aren't they talking to me about it?

I start to wonder what I've done wrong, going over every interaction with them in my head. Is it because I work at Frederick's now? Do they think I'm irresponsible for stepping off the career ladder? No, of course not, they wouldn't sack me off for something like that. I bloody hope they wouldn't, anyway.

Maybe I cringed everyone out with how emotional I got at the baby scan? But they're used to my outbursts and fluctuating moods, and besides, they were odd with me before all that. I called Saffron in the end, apologising for burdening her with my issues but explaining that I needed someone to offload to. She was amazing; talking me through it, making me laugh, making it all seem easier. I feel better, but my mind keeps circling around what I could have done to upset everyone.

I'm stewing on this as I walk to yoga. People look at me strangely and I realise I'm acting out conversations in my head, and my face is moving in response. I get to the bottom of the vast set of stairs up to the studio when my phone rings.

'Hello?' I lean against the door frame and light a cigarette, grateful for the respite before the big climb.

'Hello, love.' It's Dad.

'Hi Dad, you all right?' It's a while since I've spoken to him; all my correspondence has been with Mum and about Nana. Oh god, what if this is about Nana? What if he's calling because Mum's too upset to come to the phone?

'Yes, all good here.' He breezes. 'We're organising an Easter lunch, would you like to come?'

Phew. 'Easter was last weekend, though?' I spent it eating buckets of pasta, watching *Catfish* reruns, drinking schnapps from last Christmas and feeling a bit depressed.

'I know, but Nana was in hospital, wasn't she, so we postponed. She'll be out soon and once she's settled in here we're going to do a nice big roast.'

'Wait, so Nana's definitely moving in with you guys?' I'm relieved. I've been constantly worrying about her going into care. I've seen enough Facebook shaming videos to see what horrible things go on in nursing homes.

'For the time being, yes. We've asked Charlie to find his own place. He needs the push. We'll find something more permanent for Nana once she's properly on the mend.' He sighs. 'So, this coming Saturday? Does that work for you?'

'Yep,' I say immediately, knowing I have no plans.

I end the call and bound up the stairs. This feels so much easier now, but the tightness in my chest is still holding me back, just like it does at the gym. I need to stop smoking.

Dreadlocks guy (whose name is actually Frank) lights up as I walk in and scoots around the counter to wrap me in a hug.

'Hello! I'm always so glad when you come back.' He grins at me, a little piece of spinach wedged between his two front teeth.

'Hi, Frank,' I say, a little uncomfortable with his familiarity but also sort of used to it.

'Your penultimate lesson. Are you loving it? Is it everything you dreamed it would be?'

I ponder this question for a second. When I started here, I dreamed that yoga would make me a sexy, flexy Instagram influencer. That hasn't happened, obviously, but I do feel different. I feel calmer, more in control. Although I'm sure I'd feel even *more* in control with a body like Emma Penton's.

The thought doesn't hit as hard as usual.

'Sort of.' I smile.

'Then go forth, child of the universe, and connect with the earth beneath your feet!' He pushes me towards the studio and I stumble to the shoe rack, contemplating how I can feel the earth when we're three storeys up.

Everyone is here already except Altantsetseg, so I grab a mat and squeeze in next to Gary.

'Hiya.' I give him a nudge.

'Hey.' He glances at me and fiddles with his mat. He was a bit strange with me last week too, and I wonder what I've done. Why is everyone being off with me?!

Altantsetseg eventually arrives, giving off serious negative vibes, and angrily leads us through our sequences. She really isn't cut out for this job.

As soon as we finish, Gary leaps up and goes to put his mat away. I scamper after him.

'Do you want to go and get a drink?' I ask, my heart hammering. It's one drink, it doesn't mean he has to be my boyfriend. We're just *friends*. Yoga friends. It's normal to get a drink with a friend after doing a joint activity, isn't it?

His eyebrows shoot up. 'Oh.'

'Oh, god, sorry, is that weird?' My face flames.

'No! No, it isn't. Sorry, I just – well, I assumed you didn't want to hang out with me. Outside of here, I mean.' He looks at his feet.

'What? Why? Because I said no last time?' This is so awkward.

'No, it's . . . this is going to sound really stupid. It's just that you never texted me, so I thought . . .'

Oh, shit. I completely forgot we swapped numbers. We were supposed to coordinate our arrival so we wouldn't have to be alone with Altantsetseg.

'God, Gary, I'm sorry. I completely forgot. I'm a bit useless at the moment.' I run my hands through my hair.

'No, seriously, I'm sorry. I just assumed . . . never mind. Of course I'd like to go for a drink.' He smiles.

We go into La Viña round the corner and get a table by the window. It's dark in here and there are candles on every table. It's making me a bit horny.

'So,' Gary says as soon as our drinks arrive, 'what's going on with you?'

'Ugh, where do I start?' I realise that I haven't ever really spoken to Gary about my life, so there's a lot of ground to cover. I decide to pick one minor thing we can discuss without needing miles of context and history; explaining the whole sorry mess would just be overwhelming for him.

'Well, I got fired a few weeks ago, and it was a pretty messy situation. I never really got on with anyone there, except this one girl, and she's just invited me to work drinks next Friday.' I roll my eyes. 'It's bothering me, I don't know why.'

'Wow, easy problems to have.' He smiles.

'Oh, trust me, that's the tip of the iceberg. My least problematic problem.'

'So why are you even worrying about this? You hate them all, don't go. Simple.' He takes a sip of his beer.

My phone chimes and I pull it out from my pocket. It's another text from Martin, asking me to meet him and his new girlfriend for drinks on Friday night. What is wrong with him? How is that a normal thing to suggest?

Gary is looking at me, waiting for me to reply. I come back to myself, remembering what we were talking about.

'I don't *hate* them. But it's weird. Part of me really *wants* to go. I feel different recently, now a bit of time's passed. I think it'd be nice to see them all and just behave however I want, because I'm not worried about losing my job anymore. Does that make sense?'

He laughs. 'You just want to give them all a piece of your mind, basically?'

'I don't know. Maybe? Or maybe just show them I'm better off now I don't work there. I didn't exactly behave impeccably.'

'Oh god, give me an example.' He leans forward.

I start by telling him about Theo and his strangeness, and the whole thing comes tumbling out – the curry clothes, the sporty camel toe, the drunken conference showdown. All of it. By the end Gary is shaking with laughter and I find myself laughing too.

'You are the most interesting person I think I've ever met,' he says eventually.

'You know, it's strange. I felt so terrible about all those things. I felt really ashamed. But now I'm looking back and it's just *funny*. Nobody died, except my dignity, career and relationship, of course, but it's good. I feel like it's been good for me,' I laugh.

'I feel like I'd be happy just sitting here and listening to your stories forever. You've got a real way of telling them.'

I feel myself physically shrink away from the flirtation. 'They're all true, unfortunately.'

'Go on, tell me some more.' He rests his head in his hands and I feel like I've been given centre stage to talk about *everything*, so I do.

I tell him about Nana, my brother's weird behaviour, my new boss Darren. How I've made a list, gone vegan, how I want to quit smoking. I talk about the gym, my friends being weird with me, Anna's baby scan. It all comes pouring out and he is a captive audience, offering laughs for the funny parts and consolation for the sadness. It feels weird to be offloading to someone I barely know, but in a way it feels like the easiest thing in the world – this guy has no pre-fixed ideas about me, he's easy to open up to. I could mould my past and my present to sound wonderful to impress him, but I don't. I tell him everything exactly as it is.

And he's still sitting here.

'God, sorry, I feel like I've gone on about myself all night.' I check my watch; it's already 10 p.m.

'Hang on, backtrack a sec,' he scratches his chin and I panic, wondering which part has made him second-guess his opinion of me. 'What do you mean, you wrote a list?'

'Oh.' I wasn't expecting him to flag that part. I feel my face flame. 'Well, there's this girl – on Instagram – and she's just so . . . perfect, I guess, and I just felt like I so totally *wasn't* perfect . . . I don't know,' I'm babbling. 'I made a list of all the things I could change to be more like her.'

Gary's eyes widen. 'That's ridiculous.'

'Well, no, when I say it it sounds ridiculous, but in practice—'

'No way.' He shakes his head. 'You should never try to be someone else.'

'But she just seemed so much happier, and *better*—'

'How do you know? You don't even know her. She could be a really miserable, terrible person in real life.'

'No, I do know her. She's— oh, never mind, it doesn't matter. Sorry. I've rabbited on enough, you must be bored.'

'This has been the best night I've had in a very long time.' He smiles and his face breaks open again. 'You can really tell a story. Fuck the list, you should write a book.'

I open my mouth to tell him about my blog, but it's something I'm not ready to share yet. NRJogger is still in the back of my mind, along with the shame and fear of not being good enough.

211

Eventually we leave, and I make him promise me that next time we hang out I can hear *his* monologue, The Story of Gary, even though suggesting a next time fills me with something fearful I can't put my finger on. He promises.

We hug goodbye and I feel a little frisson of excitement as he pulls me close to him. Fuck – I can't fancy him. I'm not ready, I've not got the mental space. I suddenly feel trapped and pull away quickly. As I turn to leave he touches my arm.

'Go to the work do on Friday. If nothing else, it'll make another great story.'

I pause for a second, taking in his crinkly eyes.

I can't do this, I really can't. Can I?

I take a deep breath.

'Only if you come with me.'

22

I've bought a set of scales with my first paycheck from Frederick's. Last time I weighed myself was at Cecilia's house a few months ago, when I'd escaped the worst dinner party of my life (due entirely to Martin giving a full nutritional breakdown of every item Cecilia served) and hid in the bathroom for ten minutes. David had adorned her scales with obscene amounts glitter and star confetti, which was all well and good until you stepped off and left evidence of your recent weighing all over the house like a crime scene.

I was twelve stone four pounds. This hit me pretty hard, as the last time I'd weighed myself before that I was eighteen, and nine stone ten. Whoever said people lose weight at uni is a big, fat, fucking liar.

So now I've been running most days and I've gone vegan, I'm expecting a pretty dramatic result. I don't feel like I *look* any different, but you never notice it on yourself, do you? We all have a distorted view of what we look like, everyone knows that. I'm sure I'm nearly down to my old weight.

I take a deep breath and step onto the scales, praying that eighteen-year-old me will emerge on the screen.

12st 03lb.

What?

A *pound?* A fucking *pound?!*

I step off the scales angrily and wait for them to go back to zero before stepping on again; maybe it's because they're new, they need time to get accurate.

12st 04lb.

I jump off quickly, horrified. The number is growing by the second. What is this?!

I stomp out of the bathroom in a rage, livid at life. How is it possible that I've been working this hard and it hasn't paid off?

Shoving a sweet potato brownie (surprisingly good) in my mouth, I go into the bedroom to get changed into the new dress I've bought for the staff do tonight. I'm just wrenching my t-shirt over my head when the buzzer goes.

'Hello?'

'Delivery for Margaret Gardiner.'

What? I haven't ordered anything, I don't think. I send him up anyway and a few seconds later he raps at the door.

'Sign here please.' I do, and he thrusts a box in my hand before slouching off.

This is so exciting! Maybe it's a present. Something from Mum, maybe? Or a gift from Gary, maybe a little flower arrangement or a necklace or something . . . no! Stop it, Maggie, you weirdo. This isn't the 1920s.

What if it's a threat? It's got my name on it but I don't recognise any of the sender details. What if someone's got it in for me, Theo perhaps, and is sending me a giant explosive, or a bag of glitter I'll never be able to hoover up, or a *stink bomb?!*

I open the package tentatively, just in case I activate whatever is inside, and am mildly disappointed when I finally get it unwrapped.

It's my weight-loss tea.

Well, maybe this is how I'll shed those extra pounds! Granted, it's only a four-day supply, but if it's as good as Kim Kardashian says it is then that's probably all it takes.

I make a cup and head back into the bedroom, balking a little at the smell the teabag is producing. It's a heady mixture of feet and mushrooms. That's probably how it works, though, isn't it? Makes you feel so queasy you never eat again.

My dress looks really good, actually. I stand and turn from side to side in the mirror, wondering when the last time was that I went out for the evening in something that didn't have legs. I send a picture to Saffron and she pings back immediately: 'Slay, queen! You look incredible!'

I feel feminine and sassy, and a little jolt fires through me at the thought of Gary seeing me dressed up.

I'm going to do simple hair and dramatic makeup, I decide, and show Theo, Rachael and the rest of them that my life without them is just dandy, thank you very much.

Gary will be here in an hour to pick me up, so I run my shitty hoover around the apartment half-heartedly, tugging my dress down every time I bend over. Then I load up a YouTube tutorial for winged liner, neck my tea, gag and head into the bathroom.

Ten minutes later, I step back and take in the scene in front of me. I look like I've been punched. Worse still, one of my flicks is pointing directly sideways, whilst the other extends alarmingly up, merging with the end of my eyebrow hairs.

I scrunch my face up and let out a long moan, but that makes me look even uglier so I slam the laptop shut and set about scrubbing my face raw.

This stuff will *not* come off.

It simply will not.

I'm on my third makeup removal product, having exhausted soap and micellar water, and my eyes are still ringed with black. It has travelled under my eyes, giving me huge, grey bags and making me look like an extra from *The Corpse Bride*. My shitty attempts at 'sweeping strokes' are still firmly attached to my eyelids, the middle of them hollowed out, like a tea stain.

I contemplate nail polish remover, but settle on more scrubbing with a cotton pad and some toner. By the time it eventually comes off I've aged myself about fifty years. My eyes are puffy and red and I look like a pig.

Gary will be here in ten minutes, so I quickly slap on some foundation and an entire bucket of concealer, along with a bit of mascara and some red lipstick. Not OK.

I am just shaking my hair out of its bobble and coming to terms with the fact that it will have to stay *au naturel* (frizzy and limp, all at the same time) when the doorbell rings.

'Sorry, I tailgated someone into the building.' Gary smiles sheepishly. He's wearing a deep maroon shirt and smart jeans. I want to eat him and, simultaneously, slam the door in his face. 'Have you been crying?'

'Don't ask, please.' I usher him inside with my head bowed, begging the swelling to go down. 'You look lovely.'

'Thanks. Not too shabby yourself.' He holds out a bottle of wine and I lunge on it far too enthusiastically.

'Bad day?' He laughs.

'Good day, bad hour.' I crack open the top and pour us two large glasses, my hands shaking. God, I'm nervous.

'How you feeling about tonight?' He says as he sinks onto the sofa. I sit opposite him on the armchair.

'Weird. I don't really know.' I hope he thinks I'm anxious about seeing everyone, and not because of him.

I've been feeling good about tonight. Of course, there's a part of me that wants to show all of them how fine I am; how well I've landed on my feet. But there's another part that really hopes they discussed inviting me and wanted me there, actually looked forward to seeing me. I've imagined them welcoming me back, giving me the chance to apologise for embarrassing them, and maybe even apologising to me for treating me like an underdog for so long.

I'm jiggling my leg up and down and I force myself to stop. He's going to think I'm nuts. He wouldn't be wrong.

'I like your apartment.' He scans his eyes across the overflowing bookcase. 'You really love to read, huh? Nick those from work?'

'Nope, all bought with my own hard-earned cash.' I raise my glass.

He wanders over and pulls out a battered copy of *The Catcher in the Rye*. 'God, I remember reading this at school. So depressing.'

'Do *not* insult J.D. Salinger under this roof.' I poke him in the leg.

'You know this was censored in the USA for ages. They thought it was communist propaganda.' He flips it over in his hands. So he's funny *and* intelligent. Interesting.

'It's one of my favourites.' I take it back from him and slide it back into place before he can open it and see all my weird margin scribbles. 'All that rebellion and crisis of identity. I love it.'

'It speaks to you?' He smiles and tucks a frizzy hair behind my ear. 'That doesn't surprise me.'

It's really, really hot in here.

I duck from his gaze and cough unattractively, wandering over to the window and swinging it open. I think the makeup remover chemicals have gone to my head.

'So, you promised to tell me about yourself.' I take a deep breath and turn around. Gary is watching me with a small smile, his head cocked.

'What do you want to know?' He sits down again.

'Everything.'

'Well, my name is Gary. I'm twenty-eight years old. I'm a software developer. And I hate my parents for calling me Gary.'

'Me too!' I say shrilly. 'I mean, for calling me Margaret.'

'*Margaret?*' He almost chokes on his wine.

'What did you think Maggie was short for?'

'I don't know . . . MagBeth?'

'. . . MagBeth.' I laugh. 'Mag*Beth?*'

We're both laughing now, that kind of silent, shaking laugh where you're staring at each other, tears gathering in the corner of your eyes.

I calm myself and take a sip of my wine, sighing. 'So, software development. Is that . . . interesting?'

'I think it is, obviously. But you probably won't.' He grins.

'Hey! How do you know?' Does he think I'm thick?

'Nobody does, really, unless you're really into it. It's all numbers and algorithms and code.'

I am silent for a second. 'No, that sounds pretty boring to be honest.'

He laughs, his face almost splitting in two. He has such a *huge* mouth. 'Told you.'

'So where do you live?' I ask. I'm always nervous about asking people this question; it has such potential to sound stalkerish, people can get a bit weird about it. I'm not asking for his address, though, am I? Just his general area.

Thinking about it, I'd quite like to see his *general area*.

No you wouldn't, Maggie! That would lead to shagging and mortgages and engagement rings and that is not *what you want!*

'Just behind Piccadilly. Not the Northern Quarter, the shit part.'

'Can't be as shit as this.' I gesture around my dull, decaying living room.

'You'd be surprised.'

I pour us another glass of wine and take it with me as I get my shoes and jacket together. I transfer the contents of my bag into a different one, receipts and all. Who are those weirdos who can be bothered to clean out their handbag? I've got a receipt from 2014 that jumps from bag to bag with me, along with an old tampon wrapper and an unused piece of chewing gum. It's like an archaeological dig of my life.

'Shall we go?' I down my wine and Gary does the same, moving away from the window where he's been looking at the street below.

'I love your amaryllis.'

'My what?' I blush. Why does that sound like a pet-name for a fanny? Surely he wouldn't tell me he loved my fanny at this stage in the evening? He hasn't even seen it yet. *Yet* – Jesus Christ, why won't my brain behave?

'Your plant here.' He points to Veronica. 'It'll have flowers soon.'

'Oh.' I blush even harder at my own assumptions, even though he doesn't know what they were. Thank god. I guess I was right, in a way though. He loves my flower. Ew, I hate myself. 'What's it called, again?'

'Amaryllis.'

'How do you know that?' Nana knows loads of stuff about plants, I should have asked her really. My knowledge extends to being able to tell the difference between a daffodil and a daisy.

'I was really into gardening when I was younger. Don't laugh!' He says when he sees my face. 'Every flower has a meaning, I think it's interesting.'

'What does that one mean?' I ask, finishing tying the lace on my brogues and opening the front door. I stand out in the corridor and he follows, shutting the door behind me.

'Worth beyond beauty,' he says.

We walk through town and past the crowds of post-work drinkers, swarming out onto the pavements to light cigarettes while their bosses buy the rounds. We're turning the corner onto Edge Street when someone grabs my arm.

'Maggie Gardiner?'

I look at her for a second, because I can't believe my eyes. It can't be.

'It's me! Emma Penton. From school?'

Oh my god, it is. It's her. She looks . . . different. She's wearing a gorgeous A-line skirt and a loose blouse with white trainers, and tiny, pretty tattoos are dotted around her wrists. But her makeup is cakey around her forehead, and her hair is lank and greasy.

'Emma!' I squeal eventually. 'Hi! How are you?'

'*Amazing.*' She nods aggressively. 'Really, *really* good.'

'Great!' I smile at her. She's swaying on the spot. Is she pissed?

'Head of marketing now.' She smiles and her eyes lose focus.

'Good for you, congratulations!' I grin harder.

'Been to Santorini. Going to South Africa next month. With my boyfriend. He's a lawyer.'

'Sounds lovely.'

'Got a lot of followers now.' She hiccups and looms towards my face. 'Have you seen?'

'I have! Congratulations.' My face hurts.

'What are *you* doing now?' She squints.

'Oh, well, I'm working at Frederick's, actually—'

'*Amazing!* Listen, I'd love to chat,' she pouts, 'but I am *so* pushed for time. I'll check your Insta – do I follow you? – then you don't have to tell me everything *right this second.*' She laughs. 'Do you have Twitter? LinkedIn? Let's connect!'

'Oh, yeah. I do.' I feel an embarrassing urge to impress her, to prove that I'm not failing as badly as I seem to be. 'I've got a WordPress blog as well, so there's loads of things on there—'

'Mmm, yep, wow. Anyway, babe, so lovely to *see* you.' She wraps a skinny arm around my neck. 'Can we meet? Brunch? Something? Text me.'

And she's gone, staggering up the street, going over on her ankle as she scurries around in her bag for her phone.

Gary raises his eyebrows. 'I didn't know you had a blog.'

I don't say anything. I feel sick and cheap, like I just gave my virginity to a guy who didn't give a fuck about me. I haven't told *anybody* about the blog, and there I go blurting it out to her: *like me, like me, like me.*

I keep watching her as she rounds the corner, a tag hanging out from the back of her skirt.

Gary coughs. 'No offense, but she seemed like a bit of a twat.'

I look up at him, taking in his kind eyes and big mouth and floppy hair.

'Yeah, she did, didn't she?'

Common Bar is absolutely heaving. As we walk inside, I get that exposed feeling that comes with entering a bar and looking for people you know in the crowd, aware that the people you're searching for could be watching you. I can tell you now, it's especially bad when the people you're looking for think you're a basket case. I get a strong urge to hold Gary's hand for comfort, but that would be wildly inappropriate.

It's in situations like this that I'm glad I smoke. A reason to sneak outside and escape the throngs for a while. My hands flutter towards my cigarettes. Gary leans into my ear. 'Breathe, MagBeth.'

I'm hit by a renewed surge of confidence and a swell of gratitude; how lucky am I? It's so good to have such a supportive new *friend*. I emphasise the last word in my head, trying to condition my mind into believing what I want it to. Part of me feels this might be a mistake, though. Introducing him to all the people who hate me – and potentially exposing him to my ridiculous behaviour that seems to emerge whenever I see them – is probably not the best setting for a second date. *Date!* There I go again.

I spot the back of Kelsey's head in the corner and grab Gary's arm, dragging him to the bar. We manage to catch the bartender's eye and I order two pints and two shots of tequila, which we knock back immediately.

'Dutch courage sorted, come on. Where are they?' Gary grabs his pint and scans the room, as though he'll be able to spot them.

'In the corner,' I shout over the music and he drags me over.

Theo clocks me first.

His eyes widen and his mouth drops open. He immediately nudges Rachael, who is sitting to his left, as though I can't see him.

'Hey, guys.' I smile and squeeze onto the end of the bench next to Kelsey, who looks at me nervously.

'Hi!' She gives me a half hug and turns back to the table. Rachael is eyeing her suspiciously. Everybody else murmurs their greetings and stares at their drinks, the conversation halted by my arrival.

Oh, good. This is nice.

'I'm Gary,' Gary says and shakes everyone's hand, smiling as they all look at him incredulously. 'Maggie's friend.'

'*Hello.*' Theo leans forward enthusiastically and grabs Gary's hand. '*Such* a pleasure.'

'Hi, Theo,' I interject.

He narrows his eyes, reluctantly releasing Gary. 'Good evening, Margaret.'

'I wanted to apologise.' I don't even know I'm going to say it until it's out of my mouth. But I need to, I realise. Theo treated me like a second-class citizen, and I embarrassed him in front of fifty important people, potentially damaging his reputation forever. I might not have given a shit about my career, but he cared about his, and it wasn't fair.

'OK.' Theo leans back and appraises me, loving being the victim. Did I expect any less?

'I'm so sorry about the way I behaved. All of it. It was completely unprofessional and I didn't think about you and your reputation, only about how unhappy and angry I was. I was wrong and I'm sorry.' I look him dead in the eyes, hoping he knows I mean it.

He blinks. 'Unhappy?'

'Well, yeah. Obviously.' If he starts going on about mortgages and responsibilities and other 'reasons to be unhappy' again I will scream.

'About what? I was giving you a chance!' He squawks, his face colouring.

'A chance? You took me there as your minute-taker!' *Calm down, Maggie.* I have to be careful not to get back into this. I've apologised, I can't bring it all back up.

'Don't you think Kelsey could have taken minutes?' he says, 'Or Rachael? Or anyone, really?'

'But you said you needed me because of my neat hand-writing . . .'

'Oh, for god's sake. You thought that was the only reason I asked you to come?' He looks around at everyone incredulously.

'Well, it's what you said, so . . .'

'I thought you were serious about making something of yourself as a Medical Writer. I thought you could network, get some good information to improve your pieces.' He shakes his head. 'But you just *flipped*.'

'But—' I stop myself. Have I been completely stupid? Was I so wrapped up in how miserable I was, so blinkered by my determination to hate that job and everything it stood for, that I couldn't see when someone was offering me an opportunity that other people would have killed for? I'm a complete tool.

'Theo, I had no idea. I'm so sorry. I just . . . I thought . . . you know what? It doesn't matter what I thought. Thank you for giving me that chance. I'm sorry I ruined it.' It takes everything in me not to lean across the table and shake him, ask him why he couldn't have been more straight-forward; hug him, apologise for misunderstanding. It's confusing.

'I hated letting you go.' He looks me in the eye for the first time. 'You were a good worker when you weren't having one of your moments.'

My brain rewinds to the day I was fired. Theo was in his element, wasn't he? He loved it. I'm sure he did. Didn't he? Could it be that I've misinterpreted everything? That his anger at the HR meeting wasn't because he was sick of me and couldn't wait for me to leave, but because he was so frustrated that I'd put us both in that awful position?

There's nothing I can say, so I nod, and for a moment, peace and understanding pass between us.

'Hormones, hey? They make you do the craziest things.' He sighs, and I laugh my head off. In another world, with a different dynamic, I'd probably have adored Theo.

Ben asks what I'm doing now and I fill them in, appreciating their attempt at masking their horror when I say I'm working in a bookshop. They tell me nothing has changed at the office, but that my replacement will be starting on Monday. I don't feel sad. That chapter ended a long time ago for me.

Theo checks his phone and jumps up, scooting out of his chair and striding across the bar. Gary takes his seat.

I turn to Kelsey. 'I haven't heard from you in a while.'

'Ugh, I really wanted to avoid this conversation.' She crinkles her eyebrows together.

'What do you mean?'

She runs her hand through her hair. 'All right, I'm just going to come out and say it. It's just – and don't take this the wrong way – I couldn't let you hold me back anymore, Mags. You hated that place so much it was contagious. You were determined to fuck it up for yourself, one way or another. And when you left like that . . . I didn't want it to affect me. I know that's selfish. I decided to make a real stab at things over there, you know? Stop crying and applying for other positions and actually give it a go. There's another sales rep vacancy opening up next month.'

I expect to feel offended, or upset, but I don't. I never wanted that life, and if she had to let me go to get it then I can't blame her. 'I get that. You've got your goals. I really hope you get it, I mean it.' I squeeze her arm.

She leans her head on my shoulder for a second. 'Sorry, Mags.'

I gaze around the room and spot Theo standing by the bar, talking to an absolutely gorgeous man in an expensive-looking jumpsuit. I vaguely catch the words 'Romulus', 'illness' and 'heartbroken'. That poor sod.

Rachael makes a joke and Kelsey laughs too loudly. Gary raises his eyebrows at me across the table. I'm happy; I've behaved really well and acted on impulse a total of zero times. Gary has no idea I'm secretly absolutely crackers.

I glance over at the bar again. Jumpsuit man is on his own, staring warily at Theo, who is now speaking to a group of women in the corner. Good god.

'Another drink, Mags?' Gary raises his pint glass to me. I *love* that he just called me Mags. It means he's comfortable with me. Although . . . is he *too* comfortable? What does he want from me?

'Yeah, I'll come with.' I squeeze out from the table and Kelsey immediately darts out after me, squeezing closer to the sales reps.

'Well, that was a real treat.' He nudges me as we walk across the room.

'I can't believe I made you come here with me,' I say into his ear. 'A fun night out watching a girl you barely know apologise to her ex-boss.'

We end up standing next to jumpsuit man, who does a double take when he sees me. 'Oh my god, that dress is *so* gorgeous on you.'

'Oh, thank you! I saw it on Instagram. It's only Primark.' Look how nice people can be! This evening is going really well.

'*Love* the Insta inspo.' His eyes drift over to Theo again.

'I saw you got cornered by Theo before,' I say, nodding towards Theo and his latest terrified harem.

'Pint again, Mags?' Gary pokes his head back from where he's been leaning over the bar.

'Yes, please.' I turn back to Jumpsuit Man. 'He's bonkers, honestly, watch out. You do *not* want to get involved. How long did he talk about his bloody iguana before you managed to get rid of him?'

I'm grinning up at the man, but he isn't laughing. In fact, his face is darkening a little.

'What?' he says quietly.

'That man? The one who's obsessed with iguanas and periods? Over there?' I point to Theo again. Even as I'm speaking my stomach is sinking. Something is wrong here, I need to shut up.

'That *man*,' He hisses through gritted teeth, 'that *obsessed, bonkers guy*,' little pieces of spittle are collecting on his lip, 'is my *husband*.'

I am silent.

Oh my fuck.

What have I done?

'And that *bloody iguana*,' he jabs a finger in my face, 'had a name. His name was Romulus, and now he's *dead*. Have some fucking respect.'

The silence stretches on. The man (who I now know to be Christopher, how *lovely* of Theo to introduce us when we came in) is glaring at me like I'm Ian Brady.

'Christopher!' I scream, eventually. 'How wonderful to meet you!'

He throws me one more venomous stare and swishes away, marching over to Theo and muttering in his ear.

'Here you are!' Gary turns round with our drinks, his timing on point.

'We have to go.' I take my pint and throw it down my neck.

Gary follows suit. 'I'd ask why, but I'm learning to just go with the flow with you.'

I drag us both out of the door and onto the street, where I clumsily roll a cigarette and take deep, long drags. Grabbing Gary's arm, I jog down the street and past the window of the bar, where I can see Theo gesticulating wildly at the table as everyone searches the room for me.

'OK.' We stop in a side street and Gary bends over, panting. 'It's killing me, you have to tell me what just happened.'

'I insulted his iguana. It's dead now.' I dab at the concealer that has started melting from under my eyes.

'OK, fair enough.' Gary curls his arm around my shoulder and I lean into him, suddenly realising how long it's been since I've had someone hold me. This doesn't mean anything. I have a say in this. I can stop it at any point.

We stroll up another side street, which is the perfect setting for an undetected murder, before veering left onto Oldham Street, which is cluttered with smokers in huddles outside the bars. I roll another cigarette.

I flick the lighter and take a long drag, watching the crowds and feeling content nestled under Gary's shoulder. A woman laughs and it sounds like Cecilia and I smile, remembering the good times we have had on this road. Getting closer to one of the groups, I notice one of the women looks almost exactly like Sophie. And standing next to her is someone who is the spitting image of . . .

She laughs again.

It *is* Cecilia.

Why didn't they tell me they'd be out tonight?

I open my mouth to call to them, but I stop when a man walks out of the door of the bar and plants a kiss on Sophie's forehead. He smiles down at her and his thick eyebrows scrunch together. She gazes up at him and he leans down, pulling her into a long, passionate snog.

'Awwww,' croons Cecilia.

I freeze.

Gary stops and takes his arm from round my shoulders, frowning at me.

'What's up?'

I feel sick. My friends are out without me. Cecilia is here, swaying happily on the side of the road, whilst Sophie, one of my closest, best friends, kisses my ex-boyfriend. Kisses *Martin*.

I start to run.

'*HOW COULD YOU?*' I scream, skidding to a stop in front of their group. 'How fucking *could* you?'

Cecilia's hands fly to her mouth, her eyes wide. Martin grabs Sophie protectively round the waist as she reaches for me. 'Maggie, oh my god.' Her face is white. 'Maggie, I'm sorry.'

I feel like I'm dreaming. Is this really happening?

'Sorry?' I bleat. 'Sorry?' I can't process what's in front of me. We're here, on the pavement, where we usually would be

227

on a Friday night. But we aren't laughing or confiding; there's a bolt of uncomfortableness quivering around us. It feels so completely wrong. I swing round to Martin. 'So this is your new girlfriend, I presume?'

He gazes at the floor.

All those texts. It all makes perfect sense now.

'And you wanted me to *meet* her? What were you going to do, just turn up with her? *Surprise! Guess who!*'

'Maggie, I wanted to tell you. I just wanted to make sure it was real first. That I wasn't jeopardising our friendship for something that wouldn't even last.' Sophie's eyes are filled with tears now.

'So you'd have jeopardised our friendship for a guy if you were pretty certain, is that it? Well you've done a brilliant job of it all. Really, bravo.'

I'm so winded by this I can't think. I knew something was going on, but never in a million years did I expect this. My best friend and my ex-boyfriend; we broke up just over a month ago, for god's sake. It doesn't matter how little I ever felt for Martin, it's the principle. What's stabbing at me the most though, I realise as I'm standing shivering on the pavement, my closest friends huddled around me, is that Cecilia has not only covered for Sophie, but actively encouraged her to pursue this. Actively cut me out.

I jab my finger at Cecilia. 'And *you*. You chose her? I wouldn't have expected you to take sides, or even to *tell me*, but you excluded me. You didn't stay neutral. You distanced yourself from me and made me feel like I'd done something wrong.'

'I'm sorry. I'm really, really sorry.' She reaches her hand out to grab me. 'I just knew you'd overreact.'

'Overreact?!' I screech. 'What's an appropriate reaction to this kind of thing? Is there a forum I can consult? I'm sorry if I'm being a little bit too *dramatic* for you, Cecilia. A little bit too *impulsive* with my outburst. Am I embarrassing you? Is that what I am, just a big fat fucking embarrassment?'

I'm crying now, and Gary pulls me into him, stroking my hair.

'Oh, come on Maggie.' Martin steps forward tentatively, holding his hands out. 'You've moved on too, can't you let me be happy?'

'This isn't about *you*, Martin!' I screech.

'Why are you getting so upset then?' He frowns down at Sophie, completely nonplussed.

'No, it's not about you,' she says quietly, shrugging out from under his arm. 'It's about me. I lied and I'm so sorry.'

'I can't believe this is happening. How long has this been going on for? Were you seeing each other before we even broke up?' I glare at Sophie through my tears.

'No! I promise.' She reaches for me again and I step back, taking Gary with me.

'Don't touch me. I don't want either of you near me.' I detach myself from Gary and stride up the street, not caring where I'm going.

'Maggie, wait!' I can hear them all calling behind me, but only one set of running footsteps. Gary catches up with me and spins me round into a hug.

'Maggie.' He smooths my hair as I cry into his chest. 'Are you OK?'

'No.' I pull away and march towards home, Gary on my tail.

'Maggie, stop, please. You need to calm down.'

I keep walking and he follows me, a few steps behind, trying every so often to coax me into talking. We walk for twenty minutes but I keep up my speed, great stomping strides along the pavement.

'You need to calm down,' he says again as we reach the door to my building.

'Calm down? I need to calm down?' I throw my hands in the air. 'I lost my job, my grandmother's ill, I'm fucking up every last little thing around me and I'm so completely *stuck* . . .' I suck in a shuddery lungful of breath. 'And now I've lost my best friends. I've lost it all.'

Gary moves forward and holds my arms. 'But look how much you've gained. It might not be the stuff you had to start with, but it's something, isn't it? Look at everything you're doing! Life's chucking some curveballs at you but . . . you're surviving.' He shrugs.

'Barely.' I sniff, unwilling to hear anything that will force me out of my pity party.

Suddenly his face is so close, his liquid blue eyes sinking into mine. 'You've got me,' he breathes, and leans in until our noses are almost touching.

I can smell the warmth of his aftershave and the indescribable musk of boy. My heart thumps hard against my ribs.

'No,' I murmur.

He reaches his hand to my face and tilts my chin up. I stay transfixed as he moves his lips closer to mine, but before they touch I jerk from under him. I step backwards towards the front door. 'No.'

He stands, frozen, and watches as I put my key in the lock. His mouth opens to say something, but he just stares, wide-eyed and confused.

'No,' I say again, and I close the door behind me.

23

They haven't stopped trying to contact me, any of them. WhatsApp messages, missed calls, Instagram DMs – even a couple of emails when I turned my phone off. I have isolated myself, my only contact with the outside world being trips to the gym or my shifts at Frederick's, where I obligingly take the worst work in the back room just in case one of them comes looking for me.

I have felt completely lightheaded about it all; the crying and lack of appetite has made me dizzy, like I'm not really here. I don't eat all day, but as soon as I get home I stuff my face with bread and olive oil; huge vats of tomato pasta; multipacks of vegan cookies. After a couple of weeks of a gradual lessening of my dependency on food, I have well and truly relapsed. My distractedness is affecting my work. The other day I gave a child who was looking for a colouring book a copy of *Fifty Shades of Grey*. His mother went berserk.

I'm toeing the line, I can feel it. I just don't seem to care, which somehow makes me feel worse. I'm used to being full of something; rage, boredom, hate. I usually fuck it up for myself because I'm driven by some emotion or other, not because I'm empty of anything at all.

I'm sorting through some of our unsold sale items, packing them into boxes to send back to the publishers, and the methodical act of it is a nice distraction. My phone buzzes in my pocket and I go to check it isn't Mum, giving me news about Nana. I can't keep my phone off permanently, but I refuse to open anything from the girls.

It's a tweet I've been mentioned in.

@EmmaPenton92 *Ran into my adorable old friend @ MaggieG123 the other eve. She's writing a super cute little blog! Look at this one!*

And then she has retweeted my blog about starting the gym as a newbie. I'm almost certain she's done it out of pity, or even to mock me for going to the gym for the first time aged twenty-seven, but Emma has over 17,000 followers and the tweet has had 139 likes and sixteen retweets already. I check my WordPress statistics. 296 total views of my site in the last twenty-four hours. I feel my stomach drop. I did this. I told her about the blog and now I don't get to control how many NRJoggers see it and laugh at me anymore.

'Maggie?' Beric's timid voice comes from the doorway.

'Yeah, come in Beric.' I dump myself down on a box of hard-backs, sliding my phone back into my pocket. I'll process this later.

'You OK?' He stays standing, fiddling with the strap on his backpack.

'Yeah. You?'

'You seem upset recently.'

'I'm OK, honestly.'

'All right. We haven't erm – initiated our plan?' He looks at me from under his eyelashes.

Oh, the Darren Destruction Deployment. The big ol' DDD.

'I don't know if I'm in the mood for that today, Beric. I just—'

'You can't give up!' He says, with more energy than I've ever heard from him. 'You can't!'

'I know, I'm sorry Beric, another day?'

'No! We've waited weeks. He's only getting worse. I feel like I've got the balls to do it now, and I don't know how long that will last.' He rubs his eyes.

I look at Beric. I remember his demeanour when I started here, his shyness and anxiety. He's different, recently. More confident, more sure of himself. I hadn't thought that it could be because of our 'solution'. Maybe the project would give me more of a distraction, something to focus on outside of myself and my problems. I remember Darren threatening Beric. Darren making him feel like he was going mad. Darren turning everyone against him. I stand up.

'Let's do it.'

His face breaks out into a grin. 'I've got the stuff.'

'What time are you on 'til?'

'Close.'

'Me too. Come on, back here.'

We squeeze behind some stacked boxes of stickers until we are completely hidden from view. He pulls his rucksack out and rummages inside, pulling out bits and pieces and setting things up.

Ten minutes later and we are back on the shop floor. Darren spots me as I leave the back room and makes his way towards me.

'Have you managed to sort the unsold books?'

'Nearly.'

'OK, well, let me know when you're done. No rush, take your time.' He pats my shoulder and I'm dazed for a second; again trying to reconcile this kind man with the bully Beric tells me about. Part of me doesn't want to believe it.

I look up. Anita is staring at us from across the room, her face twisted.

I walk across the shop, relieved that Darren didn't suspect anything, and offer to help a lost-looking customer. I need a nice, normal human to converse with to distract me. I lead her to our recipe and cookbook selection and have a chat with her about our best sellers. Her daughter is vegan so she's giving it a try, too. I tell her about baked avocado and coconut bacon, as though I actually cook for myself and don't live off non-dairy, family-sized garlic breads from Tesco.

I bag up her book at the till and wish her good luck with her journey. She smiles and walks away, and the next customer fills her place.

'Maggie?'

Oh, god.

I knew this was coming. It was only a matter of time.

The worst has finally happened.

'Hi, Mum.'

She holds an Anne Tyler paperback in her hand limply, going to put it on the counter and then looking at it as though she's not quite sure what she's supposed to be doing.

'What – what are you doing? Here?' The book slips out of her hand and lands with a *thwack* on the floor, the corners of its spine dented. I feel suddenly sad; it's such a good read.

'How's Nana?' I say. Maybe if I get her distracted she'll forget I'm in uniform, on the staff side of the tills, and we can go and get a coffee.

'Maggie.' She sighs. 'Are you working here?'

Damn it. I forgot she was a perfectly sane human being.

I wonder if there's a real-life version of that spell they use in *Harry Potter*, where you just aim your wand at someone's eyes and they forget everything. Like what happened to Professor Lockhart down in the Chamber of Secrets. I think he was pretty much permanently disabled after that, though. Couldn't really do that to my own mother, could I?

Oh, I've just remembered. *Roofies!* Rohypnol! That wipes the memory, doesn't it? A real-life version of the *Obliviate* spell. I wonder where you buy a nice packet of Rohypnol. I could take her for a drink and slip it in her Pinot Grigio whilst she's in the bathroom. Although would it erase her memories from before she took it?

'Maggie?' I snap back to reality. Jesus Christ, was I really considering date rape drugging my own parent? What is *wrong* with me?

'Can we meet for a coffee? On my break?' I'd rather explain when Darren isn't watching me.

'Well, yes, when is it?' She bends down to pick up the book and slides it across the counter, catching my glances at my boss.

'Half an hour, in Costa?' I scan the book through and take her card.

'OK, thanks.' She takes the carrier bag and looks at me for a second. 'See you there.'

I smoke a cigarette round the back before sloping over to Costa, dragging out the minutes so I won't have much time to talk. Mum's sitting by the window and she waves as I walk in, moving her scarf off the seat next to her.

'Got you your favourite.' She pushes a cup towards me. Earl grey with vanilla syrup and hot frothy milk. Don't knock it before you've tried it.

'I don't drink milk . . .' I say regretfully.

'I know, it's soya.' I am momentarily surprised that she has remembered, but then of course she has. She remembers everything about me.

'Thank you.' I take a warming sip. 'I'll just say it all, and then you can speak. Is that OK?'

'Yes.' She sits back in her chair and I begin, intending to censor the worst parts of my behaviour but ending up including everything. I feel the pricks of emotion associated with each memory, and with telling it comes a sort of catharsis, my confession lifting a huge weight from my shoulders. When I'm done I sit back and sigh, checking my watch. Twenty minutes, that took me. I've only got fifteen left.

'Oh, Maggie.' Mum dabs a tear from the corner of her eye. 'I'm so upset.'

'I know, I've really messed it all up. I'm sorry.'

'No, love.' She reaches forward and clasps my hand. 'I'm upset you didn't tell me.'

'I didn't want you to be disappointed.' I'm welling up now. I didn't expect this.

She laughs. 'Darling, I could never be disappointed in you. Intrigued, bewildered, baffled – yes, but disappointed? No.'

'I'm ridiculous, aren't I?' I wipe my nose.

'You are a bit, yes. That's why we love you. Now, do you want to know what I think?' She lets go of my hand and sits up straight, ready to deliver her wisdom.

'Yes, please.'

'I actually think you've done something wonderful. You were miserable at work and you got fired, and no –' she shushes my protests, '– it wasn't under the best circumstances, but you carried on. Pretty much alone, it seems. You found another job. You were unhappy with your lifestyle so you joined the gym, you made attempts to quit smoking. You went vegan, started thinking more about what you were eating. Started yoga because you wanted a calmer outlook. Again, all by yourself because you had the gall to end the relationship that was making you miserable and refused to ask for help from anyone else. You had some horrible news about Nana and dealt with it, rallying to her side. Your friend got pregnant and that scared you, but you sucked it up to be there for her. And now they've betrayed you and you're flying solo again.' She takes a deep breath and leans forward. 'And you're *coping*, darling. You've had a series of shitty, rubbish events but you have taken them and moved forward, never giving up and still trying to improve yourself. Granted, you've created some of the turmoil yourself, but that's just you, love. When you're unhappy you rock the boat, no mind for consequences.' She cups my face with her hand. 'You didn't need a list, Maggie. You didn't need to try to be somebody else. You did this all by yourself.'

I'm openly sobbing in Costa Coffee now. I had been so focused on convincing my parents that I was still the half-successful person they thought I was, I hadn't considered just telling them everything and allowing them to support me. Yes, I'd shared bits with my friends, but with their recent distance from me and the Martin debacle, I had pretty much been alone.

Saffron has been an amazing, fresh perspective on things, but she doesn't know me well enough to give me complete support. Everything with Gary had been funny and anecdotal. All I really needed was for someone who loves me unconditionally to sit me down and tell me I'm doing fine. None of this is a disaster. I almost laugh because it's true – I'm still here, aren't I? Still breathing, living, experiencing. So what's the damage been, really?

'Thanks, Mum.' I lean over and crush her into a hug. I pull back as a thought hits me. 'What about Dad?'

'Oh, I'll talk your father round. He'll be fine.' She waves a hand in the air. 'Now, get back to work.'

'I think I'll just sack it off and come shopping with you.'

I laugh at the look of alarm on her face.

'*Joking.*'

I handle the rest of my shift well, feeling buoyed by my unearthed secrets, exposed and accepted. I'm pulling the shutters down at 5 p.m. when Darren comes over.

'Where's Beric?' he asks.

'In the back? I'm not sure.' I keep my finger on the button and watch as the shutters crunch to the ground.

Darren goes into the back room and I stand for a while, pretending to fiddle with the lock. I can't leave Beric here alone with him. After several minutes Beric emerges, scanning the room until he spots me. He holds up a shaky thumb. 'Bingo,' he mouths.

24

I wake up on Sunday feeling like my chest has a dumb-bell on it. This is happening almost every morning now. Ah, the degenerative powers of tobacco. I shuffle into the kitchen and make a huge black coffee, eyeing my rolling pouch on the side table. Strange how right at this moment, after eight hours without nicotine, it feels like the only thing that will make my lungs feel better is a freshly lit cigarette.

I force myself to walk past and settle down on the sofa, loading up my blog. Since I've been ignoring everybody I've found it easier to just leave my phone in the bedroom and write instead. I click onto my WordPress stats, distracted by how much I want a cigarette, and then freeze. *What?* I close the browser and reopen it, heading back to the page. It's still there.

28,479 followers.

No. It's not possible. I refresh the page. The number grows: 28,481 followers.

What is happening?

I haven't checked my phone since I went to bed last night, when Emma Penton's retweet had boosted my count a little. Even *she* doesn't have the platform to amass nearly 30,000 new followers overnight.

I open a new tab and load up Twitter. 740 notifications. What the fuck is happening? I click through them. Comment after comment after retweet after comment. Where has this come from?!

And then I see it.

One particular retweet.

The one that must have started this entire thing.

@LanaCastoOfficial *Funniest thing I've read all week . . . this girl keeps it real.*

Lana. Fucking. Casto.

Only the biggest lifestyle blogger in the whole of the UK.

I let out an unattractive squeal, and then jump up from the sofa and start pacing the room. Lana Casto. I must be dreaming. That is quite literally the only logical explanation. I'll wake up in a minute with my fifty-two followers and questionable blog content, and I can begin my day as normal: invisibly. I glance down at my computer again as I pass. If my WordPress numbers were high, it's nothing compared to my Twitter following. Oh my god.

Lana Casto.

Despite being a blogger, I haven't heard of many others. But I have heard of Lana. She writes about decorating and cooking and gardening and what she gets up to on the weekends. She's unconventional – shaved head, weird clothes and not at all skinny. People adore her; she has over twelve million followers.

This is insane.

I am bursting with energy. I feel like I need to catch them all and trap them in a box, so they can't realise what a mistake they've made and unfollow me again. What if they all disappear? What if they're all sat there now, reading my writing and smirking at how awful it is? But . . . they've retweeted me, haven't they? They obviously like what they see. Maybe they don't . . . *hate* it?

I need to write something else, something more. I need to keep the supply coming while the demand is there. The demand!

For *my* writing! I punch the keyboard aggressively with my fingers, writing a new piece that comes straight from a place of new emotion for me; of excitement and acceptance and courage.

After my initial writer's block, recently I can't seem to stop finding new things I want to write about. I've kept a list on my phone every time a new idea comes to me and fighting my instinct to be impulsive is almost impossible – the result is always so much more interesting for people to read than if I've kept my mouth shut and behaved.

I have started to wonder whether I make my own drama. What Cecilia said about me being impulsive and not thinking things through was pretty accurate, and it's true that my behaviour has become more erratic since I got together with Martin, but what Mum said the other day hit closer to the bone. *When you're unhappy you rock the boat, no mind for consequences.* Do I generate my own turmoil to keep myself stimulated? It's probable. Looking back, a lot of my experiences have come from me *acting* rather than *reacting*, so it can't just be a case of me getting carried away in the moment. Take the conference, for example. I was frustrated and bored (and, yes, *slightly* drunk) so I caused a shit load of trouble for myself. And for what? Was I subconsciously trying to get myself fired? Trying to shake the stale packet of crisps that was my life to get something going? Maybe, in my mind, even catastrophic life events are better than being bored.

I write it all out, processing it as I go.

I'm really quite desperate for a cigarette now. I've had some soya yogurt and seeds (disgusting) and now I'm pacing, trying to keep my mind on my newfound fame and off my rolling pouch. I feel like I deserve a treat, but the fags seem like failure to me. If I can say goodbye to chicken nuggets, a sedentary lifestyle and a miserable career, why can't I ditch these? I pick the pouch up and turn it over in my hand. Just looking at it reminds me of every moment it's saved me from: awkward family dinners, stressful situations at work, boredom at home alone. It's something to *do*. I mean, the raging nicotine dependency I've developed probably doesn't help, but breaking the habit is definitely the most daunting concept.

I close my eyes and imagine lung cancer patients, people coughing up black phlegm at bus stops, thirty-eight-year-olds with croaky voices. All it does is make me feel anxious, and the urge to smoke gets stronger. On a whim I stand up, open the window and empty the pouch all over the street, watching the golden brown tendrils catch on the wind.

Fuck.

What did I do that for? I've just chucked about eight quid out of the window and now I'll have to go to the shop. My heart immediately starts hammering at the sudden inability to have a cigarette after – what is it now, ten? – hours without. I wasn't this desperate before I knew they were gone.

I do a mini-jog into the bedroom, intending to pull on a jumper and head straight out, but I stop myself in the doorway. If I go and buy cigarettes now, will I ever have the balls to bin them again? How long have I been telling myself 'next week' or 'on Monday' or 'when things get calmer at work'? Do I think I'm going to wake up one morning and find it easy to stop, just like that?

I open the bedside drawer and pull out the neglected e-cigarette. I've never even tried it. I read the instruction manual and set it up, feeling like a meth chef as I squeeze the liquid into the glass canister at the top. I take a tentative puff and cough violently. How is inhaling vapour harder on the lungs than smoke? Although . . . I coughed loads when I first started smoking cigarettes, didn't I? And the blue flavour is *amazing*.

I take a few more puffs and notice that whilst I'd still murder my own firstborn for a proper smoke, it has taken the edge off the craving. Good. Now I've just got to survive the day with my family with only this as my saviour.

I jump into the shower, wash my hair and brush my teeth. I contemplate telling my family about Lana Casto and my new apparent internet fame. What if I really am dreaming? What if I've actually, finally, completely cracked and it's all a hallucination? Or, worse still, what if NRJogger trolls me again and everyone realises he's right and it all comes tumbling down? In any case, my dad will only just be getting his head around my career/relationship/general life demise; I don't want to provide him with any false hope before even *I* know what it could mean.

No. I'll keep it to myself.

It's an hour later, as I am standing at the tram stop, that I realise I've forgotten the list. I don't think I've looked at it for a couple of days, actually. I can't remember whether there's anything else for me to tick off. I'll check later.

I'm looking good: hair straightened and wearing the same dress I wore to the work do the other night. I've decided to face my family dressed like a boss woman who doesn't take any shit. This feels like A-Level results day, when I showed my grades to my dad and he photocopied them with a piece of paper over the 'Mathematics – C' section before popping them on the fridge. Agh, the pressure. *No!* I am a fully grown, adult woman with a job and an apartment. I cannot let other people's judgement affect me. Unless it's positive judgement, then I'll take it and run.

The tram is three minutes away. I'm vaping like a madwoman, giving a really striking impression of Darth Vader. Vaping just isn't as glamorous as smoking, is it? I can't imagine Audrey Hepburn leaning coyly against the ticket machine, dragging noisily on an e-cig. No, it's just not the same.

Every carriage is bursting at the seams when the tram finally arrives, so I squeeze on and wedge myself under someone's armpit. Thankfully he's clean, so I inhale his deodorant and musky armpit smell and it makes me horny and sad. It reminds me of Gary. I still haven't spoken to him. I just don't know what to say.

'Bloody hell, Maggie, we've got to stop meeting like this!' I wriggle uncomfortably to my left, swiping a small child with my rucksack, to find Saffron's head poking between the tangled mass of limbs clutching onto the pole.

'Saffron!' I laugh. 'Are you following me?'

'You got on after me, so maybe you're the stalker.' She winks. 'How's things?'

I wince as the tram doors open and a torrent of people hurtle past me, quickly replaced by twice as many cramming on. I use the in-between time to dislodge myself from the armpit and grab onto the pole, facing Saffron.

'Good! Yeah, not bad.' I say. 'How are all the unnecessary workshops going?'

'Same old.' She rolls her eyes. 'Fredrick's going well?'

'All good, got my staff discount.'

'Amazing! Free books.' She grins. I feel a flare of satisfaction at the first positive reaction to my new employer. Saffron lowers her voice. 'Any drama?'

I roll my eyes. 'Of course. I'll fill you in another time.'

'No!' She forces the old lady to let go of the pole as she reaches over to poke me. 'You can't do this to me!'

'I'll tell you soon, promise,' I laugh. 'Anyway, this is me. I'll see you around?'

'Text me!' She calls as I'm spat out onto the platform. 'Let's drink!'

I wave over my shoulder and start the walk to my parents' house.

Saffron and I have been talking more recently, but I've been resisting getting too close out of a strange, misplaced loyalty to the girls. Maybe we should go for that drink.

Maybe it's time for some new friends. Mum takes it a step further this time, opening the door with a glass of wine already poured and forced into my hand. 'Darling.' She envelops me in a half-armed hug, ensuring both our glasses are protected from the intimacy. She pulls back and puts her face close to mine, looking me in the eye. 'Are you OK? How are you feeling?'

'Fine?' Has someone died or what?

'Good. Good. Now, I've sorted it all with your dad. Nobody's angry in the slightest. We're all *very proud.*' She takes me by the elbow like I'm infirm and gently leads me into the kitchen.

My entire family are sat around the island, drinks in hand and solemn expressions on their faces. Only Ricardo zooms over to me, quivering with excitement at my arrival. I might just lock myself in the bathroom with him all evening.

'Hey, fishy fart.' Charlie stands up and gives me a hug. He looks terrible, half a stone heavier than when I last saw him, sunken and swollen at the same time. It seems we are brushing over our meeting at Nana's house. 'Chin up.'

Dad scoots round the island and rests his hands on my shoulders. 'You'll succeed one day with something. Don't give up.' He pecks my head.

Great. Moving.

'I mean, I don't see a future in books, personally.' Verity raises an eyebrow at me. 'It's all electronic now. Give it ten years and paperbacks will be archaic. Then what'll you do?'

'Veri!' hisses Mum. 'We said *supportive.*'

'There's a basket under this chair!' Nana is hunched in the corner in the cosy seat, covered in blankets.

'Hi, Nana!' I rush over to her and kiss her powdery head. 'How are you?'

'Lovely.' She beams. 'You know they've stopped selling torpedoes at the offy? Maureen's Derek's had a right hissy fit! And not a dicky bird about those papers, would you believe?'

'Gosh, unbelievable.' I nod.

'To Maggie!' Mum blurts, raising her glass.

'Why?' I hold my glass in the air, too. 'Why to me? I've got a different job, that's all.'

'And you're really giving it your best shot!' Cheers Dad, taking a swig of his wine.

'OK, whatever.' I take a gulp too. Pity is better than hostile disappointment, I suppose. 'How are you settling in, Nana?'

'Wonderfully. The staff are delightful.' She winks at me and I laugh.

'Cheek on you!' Charlie throws a balled up tissue at her and she catches it, chuckling.

'She's doing well, aren't you, Mum?' Mum smiles. 'We've put her down here, turned the other living room into a bedroom.'

'Couldn't give her the nice spare bedroom seeing as Charlie refuses to move out.' Veri glares across the kitchen.

'Oh, and the fact that she'd struggle up the stairs with a brand new hip didn't factor in at all, did it?' Charlie retorts.

'And the goats come round at dawn!' Nana enthuses, lost again. 'Absolutely ruin the lawn, they do. Such chirpy little things.'

There's an awkward silence as Nana stares into the distance.

'Anyway!' Dad booms. 'Where's that lovely belated Easter lunch?'

'Easter was weeks ago,' murmurs Nana, and we all exchange surprised glances.

'Lamb's just resting.' Mum catches my eye. 'Don't worry, I've got some weird nut burgers for you.'

We all settle ourselves in the dining room, putting Nana at the head of the table with the 'special plate', the one with the pink flower on that we used to fight over every mealtime. Charlie once slapped me in the eye with a teaspoon he wanted it so badly. Then he turned fourteen and would proudly announce that flowers were 'gay' and he was 'over it'. I'm still not over it.

Veri slides into the seat next to me. Wonderful.

'Just to warn you, I'm going to eat many, many roast potatoes,' I announce. 'No comments or I'll sit on you.'

'Oh, shut up and pass me the wine.' Veri leans over and drags the bottle across the table, filling her glass and mine. Charlie cracks a beer and sighs. Everyone's in a bit of a mood and hitting the booze in defiance. Aren't family traditions wonderful?

'Dad, this Malbec is divine.' Veri swirls her glass.

Tastes like velvety, alcoholic blood to me, and not in a good way. Then again, a good bottle to me is anything not on the bottom shelf at Tesco.

'Isn't it just? We tried it at Hawksmoor the other week and loved it.'

'Then I found a crate in Costco and I thought, it's fate! So I bought it.' Mum walks in carrying a huge roast lamb. 'I got ninety-eight toilet rolls, too, so you can both take a few home.'

'Thanks,' me and Veri mutter simultaneously.

'You'll need those, Mags. Remember when you got the shits in Crete?' Charlie says.

'Tuck in!' Mum waves the gravy boat, keen to shut down the diarrhoea conversation before it begins.

I eat potatoes and vegetables and heaps of tomato ketchup to wash down the dry, crumbly nut burger I presume was bought from Waitrose's organic-vegan-suicide section. I'm on my third glass of wine as we're sitting back, staring at our empty plates in front of us in silence.

'Jesus, I am *so full*.' Charlie burps.

'I'm not surprised,' Veri mutters.

'Aw, and there was me thinking we'd got through the entire meal without you being a bitch.' I smile. Mum opens her mouth to bollock me but Nana says she's tired so she fusses away to help her into bed.

'Got to take this.' Dad says, producing his screeching phone from his pocket and marching through to the kitchen. 'Gardiner speaking.'

It's just us three, now. It's never just us three, because Charlie and I generally point-blank refuse to be left in a room alone with Veri.

There's a long pause.

'You ever notice how all our names end in *-ee*?' I try.

'What?' Veri sloshes more wine into her glass.

'Ver*ee*, Charl*ee*, Mag*gee*.'

246

'Verity, Charles and Margaret. Not similar at all.' She sniffs.

'All names belonging on a 1960s Coronation Street set.' Charlie opens his next beer with his back teeth.

'Aw, no, Charlie's nice. Timeless.' I nudge him. 'You're the lucky one.'

'You talk some absolute shite, Maggie.' Veri rubs her temples.

'You always have to be so nasty, V?' Charlie glares past me.

'I might be nasty but at least I'm not a mess.'

'What's that supposed to mean?'

'Look at you – what's happened to you over the last few months?' I'm surprised to hear a slight undertone of concern beneath the hostility.

'Nothing.' Charlie chugs half his beer down in one.

'You're drinking like you've three livers.'

'Oh, and you're not? It's OK to drink fifty units when it's a *divine Malbec*, is it?'

I pull out my e-cig and take a deep drag, ignoring Veri's protests. A couple more hours of this and we'll all go our separate ways, get on with our lives with no idea what the fuck the other's problem is. I ache a bit as I think of it; the guilty tram-ride home, wishing I'd said something, wishing I'd tried to get to the bottom of this stupid, tangled rift between us all. Veri is an impossibly deep mine of defensiveness, but she's my sister and societal convention says I have to try. God knows she won't. And Charlie . . . I don't even feel like I know him anymore. We've all three of us survived on bitter remarks and witty banter for twenty-seven years, but it feels like we've lost the chance to have a real relationship. But how to make them talk?

The hazy image of Christmas and Veri's uneven boob situation swims into my mind and I jump up from the table, interrupting the bickering.

'Oi!' Charlie yells as I pluck his half-empty beer bottle from his hand. I swipe mine and Veri's wine glasses too and march into the kitchen, both of them hot on my tail. Dumping everything on the draining board, I go to the cupboard and pull out a sticky bottle of Baileys and three little crystal glasses and stride into the living room, setting it all down on the coffee table.

'Sit.' I order, and they do, on separate sofas. I can't choose sides, so I get the floor, as it has always been. I pour our drinks and hand them out, noting that the Baileys has curdled slightly and hoping nobody says anything. They take their glasses in silence and sip obediently.

'Right.' I take a deep breath. 'What the fuck is going on?'

'What, me?' Veri raises her eyebrows as I look at her. 'What's going on with *me*? Have you seen him?'

'Both of you!'

'I'm the same as I always am.' She sulks.

'Exactly! You're always horrible. What's wrong with you?' I neck my drink and pour another.

'There's nothing wrong with me!' Veri snatches the bottle from me and drinks straight from it.

'I might be wrong,' Charlie says, 'but I'm pretty sure you're not *actually* a bitch.'

'What does *that* mean?'

'I think you're just insecure or something. You just can't be this mean. And you can turn on the charm for Dad no problem. There's a chip on your shoulder for sure.' He sits back smugly, content with his diagnosis.

'I'm not drunk enough for this.' Veri clamps her lips together and folds her arms.

'Look. You two have it made. There is literally *no* reason for you to be miserable. What's going on?' I implore.

Charlie sighs. 'I just can't talk to you two about this stuff. It's weird.'

'Have some more Baileys.' I pour him another glass. 'And start.'

'Why are you so interested anyway?' Veri scowls at me. 'Just leave us to it.'

'Because I care about you, weirdly enough. It's bad enough having Nana rapidly dwindling without having to worry about

248

you two as well.' I raise my arms in surrender. 'Excuse me for having an emotional investment in my family members.'

'I know it'd be easier if I just told you.' Charlie sighs and rubs his eyes. 'You know, like, spoke to you when stuff was going on. Because we're close, aren't we? But not in *that* way. Not emotionally.'

'But can't that change? We're older now. I'd really like it if we could depend on each other when times are shit. Look at Nana's fall, none of us even spoke.' I only realise it's true as I say it; only realise how little support I've garnered around myself during all this crap as I'm faced with two potential saviours who also never ask for help. 'I've seen you since then, Charlie, and it wasn't comforting, it was horrible. Is that normal?'

'Normal isn't necessarily pouring our hearts out all the time,' Veri sniffs.

'I'm not saying it is. But when stuff's going on, wouldn't *you* like to have us to talk to? Just a little bit?' Ricardo patters over to me and flops into my lap, and I bury my head in his furry tummy.

'I don't know what advice *you* could give me, Maggie, to be perfectly honest,' she sneers, but her heart isn't in it.

I sigh. 'OK, I'll share my shit first. What's Mum told you?'

'That you quit your job to go and work in a bookshop,' Charlie says.

'That's it?'

'Yeah, because you love books so much or something.' Veri rolls her eyes.

Wow. Kind of don't want to share my depressing life story anymore; that version sounds much better. I'll choose something else.

'Well, the other evening I was on my old work's night out, and I walked through the Northern Quarter afterwards. I saw Sophie and Cecilia, and Sophie was kissing Martin. Remember Martin, my ex? She was kissing him and Cecilia was cheering her on. Turns out Anna knew as well. Haven't spoken to any of them since.' I lean back on my elbows, waiting for their reaction.

'Isn't that, like, your entire friendship group?' Veri frowns.

'Yup. Poof, gone.'

'Wait, is this before or after you chucked Martin?' Charlie sits up.

'After.'

'Oh, let it go then. He was a drip, anyway. Couldn't keep up with you.'

I feel a bit warm inside at that. He couldn't keep up with me. I'm like Effy from *Skins*.

'But they've betrayed me, haven't they?'

'I guess they have. But stuff like this happens all the time; if they're sorry you should just put it behind you.' Charlie sips his third glass.

'Actually, no. If my friends did that I'd never speak to them again,' Veri says, a renewed fierceness in her eyes.

'What friends?' Charlie murmurs.

'*Anyway*,' I interrupt. 'Veri, your turn.'

She sighs. 'I don't even know what to say. There's nothing *wrong*.'

'There's been something wrong as long as I've known you.'

'I don't know.' She stares into her glass. 'I honestly don't know. I can't put a word to it.'

'Well . . . is it something physical? Or . . . or, you don't like seeing us? Or you don't like coming home?'

'No, I like coming home. I do, honestly. I think . . . I don't know. I feel . . . alone.' She shakes her head. 'I'm talking shit.'

'No, no, you're not.' I'm desperate to keep this going. We're on the verge of a breakthrough, I'm sure of it. We have *never* spoken like this. 'Alone in what sense?'

'Well, you two have your cosy little club. You both have friends, partners sometimes. It sometimes feels like I don't have anybody at all.'

Charlie leans forward. 'But you go to all these dinners! All those nights out.'

250

'Work stuff. Politics. Not one real friend among them.' She sighs. 'I think that's why I'm so nasty sometimes, you know? I feel so angry and defensive. I don't want people to think I'm unravelling.'

'But maybe the defensiveness actually makes the problem worse,' I muse. I can completely relate to her anger and snappiness. I'm mean when I'm unhappy, and I see it in myself. It makes me sad that I couldn't see it in her, couldn't read that there was something going on under that veneer.

'I know. I know my attitude doesn't help and I've brought it on myself.' She slurs a little. The Baileys is working its magic.

'Well, we're here for you, aren't we, Charlie? We can all go out together and do stuff, it'll be fun!' I smile, but I am trying to wrap my head around the fact that she was jealous. Of *me*, of all people. I am hit with the realisation that actually, from the outside, my life might not look so bad. I suppose it depends what you focus on.

'I'm not saying I want to hang out with you both,' she mutters, her face flushing.

'Oh, you don't?' Charlie raises his eyebrows. 'OK. We're not good enough apparently, Mags.'

'Apparently not.' I cover my mouth in pretend shock. 'Looks like it'll be just the two of us next month then.' I have no idea what I'm alluding to, but Charlie catches on quickly.

'Mmm. Shame for Verity to miss out on Alton Towers, isn't it?' He shrugs.

There's an almost imperceptible movement from Verity.

'What's up, Veri?' I smile innocently.

She glowers at me. 'You *know* how much I love Alton Towers.'

'Aaaah!' Charlie throws himself onto her sofa. 'I knew it! Bloody come with us then!'

Veri laughs and slaps Charlie across the head. 'Maybe.'

'You have to stop being mean, though. They don't let grumpy bastards on Oblivion.' I say.

'No promises.' She flashes me a half-smile.

'Starting now, by the way. No more negative comments for the rest of the night.'

'Fucking hope the night ends quickly then.' She sees my expression. 'OK! Fine. For the rest of the night. But only if Charlie talks.'

'There you go, Charlie. All our problems solved if you'll just spill.'

His body slumps down and he sighs again. He's sighed so many times this evening, I could make a musical montage. 'It's honestly so difficult to talk about. You won't get it.'

Fucking hell, I hope he's not dying. I really, *really* hope he's not dying.

'Try us.' Veri says.

'Fine. But you asked for this. The baggage that's going to come with this.' He looks me dead in the eye. 'I'm gay.'

There's a silence.

Charlie flits his eyes between me and Veri, colour rising in his cheeks.

'Well? Say something!' He puts his head in his hands. 'I knew I shouldn't have told you. Bloody Baileys.'

'Wait, what? Is that it?' Veri looks at me. 'Is that seriously it?'

'This is why you've been so unhappy?' I jump up from the floor and throw myself at him. 'Charlie! I can't believe it. I mean, I can – you're obviously gay, we've known longer than you probably have – but I can't believe you didn't want to tell us!'

'*I* can't believe you thought that would be an issue.' Veri is shaking her head. 'Have you just sat on this forever?'

'Pretty much.'

That makes me *so* sad. My funny, lovely brother has driven himself insane and nearly given himself diabetes and/or alcohol poisoning because we didn't create the right emotional environment for him to be himself. I'm ashamed.

'I am so sorry.' I'm crying now, wine and Baileys hurtling through my system. 'I should have pushed you harder to tell me what was wrong. I mean, I knew this. You knew this too,

252

right, Veri?' She nods. 'It was just . . . I never thought it was something to discuss.' I stare at the arm of the sofa, trying to find the words. 'It just *was,* you know? Part of you. But I didn't realise you were so worried about it. We all should have been there for each other. We've failed each other.'

How much have I neglected, being so absorbed in my own problems? How much have I *missed,* more to the point, in the lives of the people around me? Not once did I take my head out of my own arse to consider anyone else and what they might be going through, and by the sounds of it it's been worse for them than it has me.

'No, you haven't.' Charlie shakes his head. 'How could you have known? And we're all to blame, aren't we? I had no idea you two were going through stuff, either.'

'You know, I've been thinking . . .' Veri stops herself. 'No, never mind.'

'No, go on, what?' I poke her leg.

'Your list thingy. You seem . . . happier.' She catches Charlie's confused expression. 'Mags made a list of everything she hated about herself. I don't know, maybe we could do the same? It might make us feel better? Like, Charlie, you could write 'stop eating shit' and 'get my own place and stop being a scrounger', then maybe—'

'No.' I interrupt. 'No, don't do that.' I don't know why I suddenly feel like this is a bad idea. Something in me just knows that I don't want them documenting and obsessing over the things they loathe themselves for. I wave my hand. 'Didn't work. Just the new job.'

'Hm. You seem a *lot* better, though.' Veri's eyes lose focus for a second as she stares at the wall.

Suddenly, she grabs her glass. 'In any event, this is a happy occasion. To being gay!'

'To being gay!' I scream, euphoria rising in my chest as I finally, for once, stand on the same side of the fence as my sister. And it's not even Christmas!

Charlie pauses. This is still new for him; he's spent so long not saying those words, that it doesn't come easily to blurt them out and toast to them. He looks at us both and takes a deep breath.

'I'm fucking gay!' He cheers, the burden of his secret lifting slightly from his shoulders. 'I'm so obviously, wonderfully gay!'

We sit back and giggle. I wipe my nose with the back of my sleeve.

'Now I've got to tell everyone at work. And Mum and Dad.' Charlie winces.

'They love you, Charlie. They'll accept anything with time.'

'Dad can't even accept that you work in a bookshop.' He raises his eyebrows. 'Sorry, but he can't.'

'Not surprising, really—' Veri starts, before clamping her lips shut and shaking her head in apology. 'Sorry, sorry.'

'So?' I say, realising that I actually don't care. 'You can't be so worried about disappointing him that you don't live your life the way you want.'

There's a small silence as we sip our drinks, all of us pretty smashed by this point.

'Is there a guy on the scene, then?' I try, but *scene* comes out as *ssshene*. Thankfully, drunk understands drunk.

'Hey, there might be a man on my ssshene,' slurs Veri.

'Really?' I sober up momentarily. Did she not say two minutes ago that she didn't have a boyfriend? 'Who?'

'Roger. One of the senior partners. We're just shaggin'.' She hiccups.

That seems to be it.

We start talking about my friends again, what I should do, back and forth until I can barely remember why I'm angry with them in the first place. We're debating forgiveness when Nana pokes her head around the door.

'Goodnight, scallywags!'

'I thought you went to bed ages ago, Nana?' Charlie says.

'Did I? Oh, I can't remember.' She shakes her head.

'Night, Nana.' I sway to my feet and give her a kiss.

'Night, love. Make friends, won't you? Life's too short.' She potters through the door and we sit back down.

'God, imagine what she'd say if she knew I loved cock.' Charlie giggles.

We jump as a chuckle comes from down the hallway. 'Don't we all, darling!'

25

My mind is blown. I feel, clichéd as it is, like I've just woken up, or had a blindfold removed, or been transported Matrix-style into an alternate universe where everything is just so . . . *clear*.

The word *lonely* reminds me of GP surgery adverts; old women who look like Paul McCartney sitting with blankets on their knees, watery eyes gazing at the camera and the words 'BE A FRIEND THIS WINTER' emblazoned underneath.

It reminds me of IT geeks in basements, prisoners, playground bullying and struggling single mums.

It doesn't remind me of my sister, or my brother, or my Nana.

It doesn't remind me of *me*.

I'm moving around the kitchen, sweeping a growing pile of dust from one end of the tiles to the other. I can't be lonely, can I? I lived with Martin for two years, I was *never* alone. Sometimes, the only time I had to myself for weeks on end was my bus journey to and from work.

But what about Charlie? He comes home to Mum and Dad every evening; home-cooked meals around the table, questions about his day. But *he* was lonely, wasn't he? Because he was pretending. He was compromising himself. Maybe, when you're hiding who you are, you're the loneliest person in the world.

I sweep the dirt into the dustpan and shake it into the bin. I had Martin. Martin, who made it completely impossible for me to be myself. Was I lonely, too? I think of Charlie and the beers. Is that what I do with food? Hide away and eat, smothering the frustration and isolation I don't even realise I'm feeling? Or was it my only respite from the constant pretence? The only time I could say to myself, *no, actually, I don't like poached salmon and edamame beans, thank you very much*?

Is that why I fucked it all up? I pull a hair out of the bathroom sink. I'm certain that Mum was right, that I rocked the boat to make a change, but was it also a cry for attention? A sort of 'see me, please' expression of myself that I was unable to show at home? Although it pains me to say it, it fits with Cecilia's theory: I was increasingly more reckless after I met Martin.

But my own feelings aren't the only things I've been blind to.

I take out a piece of paper and bullet-point everything that wasn't as it seemed.

- Theo was giving me a chance.
- Emma Penton is probably just as much of a mess as the rest of us.
- Sophie was seeing Martin.
- Veri needs us.
- Charlie is gay (this was evident from birth, but it being the reason for his depression was a huge shock).
- Darren is secretly a bullying ballbag.
- Nana was lonely and afraid.
- Nana is also potentially a filthy little minx.

When I've written it all down I stare at it for a really, really long time. It all makes sense on paper. But it makes me wonder: what if my perception of *everything* is skewed? Not only in the way I've been so blinkered by my own issues, but in how I see life in general? Perhaps disasters aren't always write-offs. Maybe being skinny, or chic, or having a million followers isn't everything. Maybe we all just need each other.

I pull out my laptop and write a new blog post, spelling it all out for myself and processing as I go. I reflect on my loneliness, my misconceptions, how I was so blind I couldn't see that Theo was good and Darren was bad, Martin was killing me and my best friends were betraying me. It's more personal than anything I've written before, and I feel exposed, knowing that my now 38,754 followers are about to see a side of me I have never even shown my closest friends.

As soon as I hit publish, I am filled with intense, nervous energy. I have laid my soul bare; I can't sit around here waiting to see what the world thinks. I jump up from the sofa and throw on my running gear, grabbing my keys and slamming the front door behind me.

I suddenly feel excellent. Like really, really great. The sun is shining, it's feeling warm for the first time this year and the stomach cramps the skinny tea gave me have finally eased up. The vegans are in a circle outside Boots again, MacBooks flashing images of sheep butchering this time. I run up to the one I think I saw last time. I can't be sure it's him because of the mask, but he's in the same position.

'I turned vegan because of you!' I shout happily.

The soul-penetrating eyes that have seen too much animal slaughter crinkle and he pulls his mask off his face. 'Really?' He grins. He's in his forties, with long hair and a star tattoo on his cheek. Basically exactly what I expected.

'Yep! I read your pamphlet.'

'That's great! I'm so happy.' He genuinely looks it, too. I wish him all the best and trot off up the street, into the dark and pounding world of PureGym.

I'm finishing my run when Pete, the personal trainer who witnessed the undignified catastrophe of my first visit, comes over. 'You've really improved. I'm impressed.' He raises an eyebrow.

'Thanks, Pete. Followed your advice in the end, actually.' I wipe a droplet of sweat out of my eye.

'Great news!' He smiles and I clock how attractive he is, in that carbon-copy Instagram-influencer personal trainer kind of way. 'Maybe you'd let me train you sometime.'

'I'm piss-poor, Pete, you're wasting your breath.' I smile.

He sighs. 'Bloody difficult, here. People come because it's cheap, they don't want to fork out for personal training.'

'I'm sorry. Must be hard.' I cock my head in sympathy. 'Can you answer questions for free, or is that chargeable, too?'

'Fire away.'

'I've been running for weeks now, and I've gone vegan. But I've not lost any weight.'

'What's your diet look like?'

'Vegan? Like I said.'

'Yeah, but what do you eat?'

'Veggie stuff. Vegan pizza. Vegan mayo. Vegan bacon and soya yogurt. Lots of avocados.' I say smugly. Try and argue with *that*, Petey.

'See, that's probably where you're going wrong. Just because it's vegan doesn't mean it's low fat or low sugar. You're probably getting just as many calories, if not more. Avocados are *full* of fat.'

I stare at him.

Is he serious? I've been eating avos like apples.

'I can't believe it,' I whisper.

'What's your alcohol intake like?' He tries.

'Jesus, look at the time. I've got to go, actually . . .' I edge past him and move towards the changing rooms.

'Wait, remember you've got to think about muscle gain, too. You've been running and you'll have gained muscle on your legs.'

I spin round. 'Well that's *definitely* what it is then!' I grin. I knew it wasn't the endless bottles of wine and deep fried falafel bites.

'A pound of fat is the size of a grapefruit, a pound of muscle is the size of a tangerine. So maybe you weigh the same but feel slimmer?'

'Wow, you know what, I think I do!' I am delighted. 'That is *so* interesting, Pete.'

'Friend of mine over at the Quays branch told me that one.' He smiles.

'Bloody hell, his name wasn't Martin Peel was it?' I laugh.

'Yeah! No way, do you know him? What a great guy.'

And suddenly, just like that, Pete is a wanker, too.

'Ex-boyfriend. Massive twat.' I give Pete a thumbs up. 'See you later.'

The weather is too beautiful to go home, so I grab a soya latte and sit in Albert Square, watching people pass by in the sunshine. My phone is full of yet more unread messages from the girls. I haven't opened the chat since it happened. I have a flick through Instagram; more holidays, more new clothes, more promising face creams. I feel my mood drop an octave. The strange thing about social media is that even when your brain is telling you to close the app, put your phone down, your thumb just keeps on going. Like you're not in control of your actions; eyes wide, fixated on the stream of shit you don't want to be seeing. Comparing, comparing, comparing. As if seeing other people's wonderfulness will somehow make you more wonderful, or push you to hate yourself so much you change everything about you.

That particular thought hits a little close to home.

I scroll down some more and come across a picture of Anna showing off her tiny baby bump. My heart twists. We've shared everything for seven years, the three of us. I always imagined us being those lairy middle-aged women in town, screeching over pornstar martinis, bitching about our husbands and match-making our grown-up kids. The idea of not being around for this amazing moment in Anna's life, sharing it with Sophie and Cecilia, makes me want to cry. Is one mistake really worth throwing away everything we've ever had? Haven't I made my fair share of those?

On a whim, I fire off a text to Saffron, taking her up on her offer of drinks. She replies immediately, suggesting Friday night at La Viña. I get a weird flash of guilt as I remember the last time I was in there; laughing with Gary about my life choices. I can't explain why I haven't spoken to him. He didn't do anything wrong. In fact, he did everything so completely *right* that it now feels hard to justify my running away from him. I was just so caught up in the hurt and embarrassment of the Sophie and Martin situation and the fear of being trapped with another man, on another life trajectory that didn't fit with who I thought I was, that I panicked – I had to get away and be on my own. He messaged me a few times over the following days to check if I was OK. I never replied. I feel like I've left it too long now; he'll have realised what an unstable nutjob I am and will have put me straight in the bin, adding me to the list of could-have-beens. The list of lucky escapes.

I know that a text won't suffice, and I suddenly feel like I have to see him. I have to apologise and explain why I cut him off so abruptly. I don't know where he lives, but there's a chance he'll be at yoga tonight. During the last session of our six-week intro course, Altantsetseg advised us to start attending the weekly beginners' classes every Tuesday. Tonight is the first one. I wasn't planning on going – it's £8 a week – but it's a small price to pay if it means I can make amends.

I head home to grab a shower and change into some fresh exercise gear, leaving again as soon as I'm ready. I head towards yoga, nerves swirling around in my stomach as I prepare what I'm going to say to Gary. I need to make him see that it wasn't his fault, he didn't do anything wrong. I just hope he'll stick around to listen. What if he takes one look at me and runs out of the door? Or worse, hears me out and still decides he wants nothing more to do with me? I suppose I'd understand; we've never had an encounter where I haven't done something ridiculous. I probably bring unwanted drama into his life. Nothing is normal around me.

Although what do I even want from this? His friendship, or something more? My heart flutters. I can't walk in there without an answer in my head, but I know I'll never really have one. Not until I've tried.

I walk into reception with five minutes to spare, and Frank lights up.

'I knew you'd come back! I just *knew* it!' He runs over and holds me again, pushing my face into his flaky dreadlocks. I swallow.

'Hi, Frank! Yeah, I thought I'd come and give it a try.' I prise myself out of his scrawny arms and root around in my purse, putting £8 in small change on the counter. 'Anybody else from the beginners course here?'

'Not sure.' He says, opening the till. 'Your friend Gary didn't come to the last session though, did he?' Frank sees right through me. 'Maybe he doesn't know it's on.'

My heart sinks. Frank's right – Gary didn't turn up to our final session. Although maybe he got the email Altantsetseg sent round? I can't give up hope.

'Right.' I give Frank a pat on the arm and head into the studio, breathing deeply against the anxiety as he murmurs blessings and encouragement behind me.

I take my shoes and socks off slowly, delaying the moment I have to walk in. I hope I can settle myself in just as the class starts, giving me all lesson to think about how I'm going to approach him if he's here.

At one minute to, I push open the door and keep my head down, grabbing a mat and placing it in one of the spaces I can see through my limited, floor-gazing vision.

'So, if we're all here?' It's Altantsetseg again. Part of me hoped for another, less psychopathic teacher, but I find that another part of me is glad. She did teach me well, even if she is terrifying. But this isn't the point; I'm not here for the yoga. As we start our first poses (a bit of Cow, a bit of Doggystyle) I take a few sneak glances around the room. There are more people in here than there were on our course – about twenty – and I can't see him.

We stand up into Warrior One and I use the heightened vantage point to look more closely. I can't see through to the left of the front row, so I lean to the side, peering through the bodies. Keeping my arms stretched above my head, I edge myself an extra inch, but it's too much. As I feel myself toppling, my brain makes a quick calculation and decides that the priority is holding the pose, impressing Altantsetseg, as opposed to throwing out my arms to catch my fall.

I land square on my side, arms still raised above my head like they're chained that way, my ribs singing with pain as they take the brunt of the impact. Altantsetseg hovers over me.

She sighs. 'Maggie.'

'Hi.'

'Are you all right?'

'Yep.' For some reason I'm still holding the pose, laid out on the floor like one of those aerial-view baby photos.

She reaches out her hand and I take it, rising ungracefully to my feet. Everyone is staring. I would be, too, to be honest.

'You hit the ground pretty hard. Go and rest up. Come back next week and take the lesson you paid for today. Frank will sort it.'

I nod and she pats me on the arm, her hostility towards me given way to raw, baffled pity. I put my mat away, feeling every eye on me. As I reach the door I turn round and scan the sea of faces one last time.

He isn't here.

Frank gives me a cup of weird tea and sits me on another beanbag I dread trying to get up from.

'You poor mite. Does it hurt?' He strokes my hair.

'Yeah, but it'll be fine.' I smile and awkwardly lean my head to the side, away from his hand, but he follows my movement and keeps going. It would be quite soothing if there wasn't a heady mix of B.O. and furniture polish emanating from his clothes.

'I'll do Namu Myoho Renge Kyo for you.' He closes his eyes.

'What?'

He sways slowly from side to side, breathing deeply, before starting to murmur slowly under his breath.

'Sorry? I can't hear you?'

'Namu Myoho Renge Kyo, Namu Myoho Renge Kyo,' he chants quietly.

I stare at him. What is happening? He's showing no signs of stopping. Is this supposed to make me feel better?

'Frank?' He continues chanting. 'That was nice, I think I feel better now.'

He gets louder. My eyes dart around the room. What do I do? Would he notice if I left? I can't get off this fucking beanbag quietly, though. Should I join in? He's repeated it so many times I know the words off by heart. It's a real earworm.

'Frank.' I try again.

'NAMU MYOHO RENGE KYO, NAMU MYOHO RENGE KYO!' He's practically screaming now, his head swaying rhythmically like a cobra. Oh my god, why is this happening to me? Why is this kind of shit *always* happening to me?

He lets out a final, ear shattering blast of his chant, before snapping his eyes open and grinning at me.

'Oh. Hi.' I am taken aback by the sudden break of his trance. 'That was . . . good.'

'The essence of Buddhism.' He sighs and holds his hands in prayer. 'That each of us, at any moment, has the ability to overcome any difficulty, to transform our suffering.'

Jesus, it's only a bruised rib.

'How lovely.' I smile and rise to my feet. 'I must be off now, thank you, Frank.'

'Wow!' He clasps his hand over his mouth.

'What?' Please, god, not another chant.

264

'The grace! The poise! The strength!' He's dancing a little jig around the room.

'Frank, I—'

'When you first came here, you couldn't get off that beanbag!'

I stop and look down. Bloody hell, he's right! I've just got up from the beanbag in one swift movement, no awkward all fours or pushing with my hands.

'You're so much stronger.' He cups my face between his hands. The smell of furniture polish is *really* strong.

'You're right!' I'm excited, too. 'I can't believe it!'

'Go forth, child of the universe.' He moves to the side, allowing me to pass. 'Go forth and love yourself!'

I wave goodbye, not wanting to speak in case I open up another spiritual chat, and scoot out of the door. I feel like I've just passed some kind of test. Maybe the beanbag is a metaphor for my problems: I've risen above them without struggle. Just like Frank's chant!

Or maybe, just maybe, all the running and yoga is finally paying off.

26

I'm on my way to La Viña to meet Saffron. It's Friday and town is packed, but she's already texted me to say she has a table so at least I know once I've dodged all the screaming half-naked students, I can sit down and rest my old bones.

'*You* don't know *anything* about my situation!' A girl is sitting on the floor crying, her makeup smeared across her chin. She's screaming at another girl who's swaying above her. 'Just because you've got the *tits*, you think it's easy for anyone to go viral on YouTube but it's *NOT*, Cassie! It's fucking *not*!'

Christ, it's only 7 p.m.

I scoot past them as Cassie starts recounting the various times she's had to flash a nipple to get a like. La Viña is the next door on my left and I hurry inside with relief. I spot Saffron immediately, sitting in the corner, a bottle of wine chilling in a bucket on the table.

'Hi!' I give her a hug and squeeze onto the stool opposite her, nodding towards the wine. 'How much do I owe you?'

'Oh, you thought this was to *share*?' She frowns awkwardly, and then laughs. 'Kidding. I thought white wine might've been a bit of a sore point, but I don't reckon you're the type to get all PTSD over it.'

'You know me so well already.' I hold my glass out as she pours and there's a moment of silence as we take a long sip. 'Amazing.'

'Better than The Wilcoxon's finest?' She smiles.

'Hmm, now I wouldn't go that far.' I rest my glass on the table. 'So how are you? How's the job?'

'You first! How're the books? What's the drama?'

'The books are great, but my manager is a dick. *Again.*'

'No, really? What is with your luck?' She scrunches up her face in sympathy.

'God knows. Me and this guy I work with have a plan though.'

'Oooh, a *plan*. Tell me more.' She leans forward conspiratorially.

I fill her in on everything: Darren's multiple personalities, his treatment of Beric, how nice he is to me. I explain our plan; how we're going to do it and when. She loves it.

'That is the most badass thing I've ever heard.' She grins, then pauses and creases up her forehead. 'It's weird . . . I read this story online about this girl who had the exact same situation. Like, in a bookshop and everything.'

'Really?' My heart starts hammering in my chest. This is sounding familiar. She can't be talking about my blog. She really can't.

'Yeah! It was like . . . big on the theme of loneliness, which was actually really interesting. I'll send it to you. All about misconceptions about people; family, friends, bosses. Her boss is a total psycho like yours. The one she had before that was really eccentric too, just like Theo.' She narrows her eyes at me.

Balls.

'Oh.' I try to force a smile but it sticks on my flaming hot face. 'Weird.'

'Twenty Fucking Seven, it's called!' She clicks her fingers. 'It's a blog.'

'Sounds interesting.' I have to tell her I wrote it. Either I tell her, or she thinks I've read it too and copied the story, which would just be mortifying.

'You're twenty-seven, aren't you?' She cocks her head, smiling.

'Yeah.' I bury my face in my hands. I feel embarrassed, somehow. I should feel delighted that people are reading my work, but it still feels exposing and cringey.

'I fucking knew it!' She shouts. 'Oh my god, Maggie! I knew it! You're the blog Lana Casto shared! *You!*'

'Agh, shut up.' I keep my head down.

'Maggie!' She prises my hands from my face. 'Maggie, it's *amazing*. I can't believe it!'

I laugh. 'Stop it! It's just a little blog.'

'But it's incredible! It's so funny and relatable and real, honestly. I'm actually in shock. I'm shook.' She's shaking her head, laughing. 'I love that blog *so* much!'

Wow.

This is actually really, really nice. It's a great feeling. Someone who knows me has read my writing, not knowing it was mine, and *loved* it.

Shit, am I actually good?

'Stop!' I grab her hands. 'Thank you, thank you, thank you, but stop. Drink some wine and tell me about you. Please.'

'Only if you promise to keep writing that stuff. It's hilarious.'

'I will,' I laugh. 'Now tell me, how's work? How are the workshops?'

'Well . . .' She sighs theatrically. 'I wouldn't know.'

'What? Have you stopped going to them?'

'Not exactly . . .' She clasps her hand over her mouth and murmurs. 'I quit.'

'You *what*?'

'I quit!' She shouts, raising her arms in the air. 'I quiiiiiit!'

'No you didn't!' I smack her on the arm, noting the waiter tutting at us as he passes. 'No way, have I rubbed off on you that quickly?'

'Yeah, you honestly have.' She smiles. 'It's not the most interesting story, to tell you the truth. Last Tuesday I got caught in loads of traffic getting into work and it was pissing it down.

I got to my desk late and completely drenched. I just broke down, I was so sick of everything.'

'I know that feeling well.'

'Yeah. Anyway, Dana, my boss, came over and asked me what was up. I told her I was upset and she was really kind, really thoughtful. She asked me to come into her office.' She takes a deep breath. 'And once we got in there she handed me these pamphlets. Like, all these leaflets for more training events, said maybe it'd take my mind off everything. I just looked at her for a minute, trying to squish down what I *knew* I was going to do. And then I just screamed: I fucking quit.'

'Oh my god.'

'I got escorted out by security.' She giggles. 'I felt quite bad about it, you know? It really wasn't her fault. She was great. I just couldn't do it anymore and I exploded.'

'That's incredible.' I'm impressed. That is *so* something I would have done.

'It's all thanks to you, really.'

'What do you mean?'

'I just couldn't stop thinking about how ballsy you were at that workshop. And how you turned down that shitty job I offered you, even though you didn't have anything else. You sort of just decided to sack it all off and never look back, didn't you?' She grins. 'And then I read your blog, obviously, and that just clinched it. But I didn't know it was you. Weird, isn't it? You're like my guardian angel or something.'

'Guardian angel.' I muse. 'Coincidence, probably. But it is weird how we keep running into each other. You know, you were the first person to react positively to my new job? The first person, and I barely even knew you. How sad is that?'

'That is sad.' She drains the last of the wine into our glasses. 'I don't know, I think sometimes people pop up and have a massive effect on you. Do you know what I mean?'

I do know what she means. When I started university I was at a pretty shitty low – I'd just broken up with my boyfriend,

Bonkers Ben, was terrified of moving out of my family home and was riddled with that eighteen-year-old feeling that all your problems are the biggest thing you'll ever face. I met all my friends and they just changed me. I felt more at home than I did at my actual home. Saffron has changed me, too; it's been great getting to know her and even better knowing I had a companion in my misery – a companion *full stop* – once things blew up with the girls. It's strange to think that I've been that person for her, too. *Me*, the least enviable person on the planet.

'Yeah.' I nod. 'People do tend to pop up and shine a bit of perspective just when you need it, don't they?'

Suddenly I'm thinking about Gary.

'Go on, tell me.' Saffron raises an eyebrow. 'Who is it?'

'I swear to god you're psychic,' I laugh. 'Just this guy I met recently. He helped me through some shitty stuff and I sort of blew him off, even though I didn't really want to.'

'So you're not speaking anymore?'

'He tried to text me a few times. I didn't reply because my head was in a bit of a state. I think it's too late now.'

'Nah, of course it isn't. If he's as nice as you say he is, he'll understand. Especially if you had a lot going on.' She signals the waiter to bring us another bottle. I'll be feeling this tomorrow.

Gary is nice. And I feel pretty confident that he would understand. 'So should I text him, do you reckon?'

'Yes!'

Ooh, I've just had an idea. Any idea after half a bottle of wine is never good. Right on cue, the waiter brings another ice-cold Sauvignon Blanc to the table. Well, after a full bottle I'll hardly care whether the idea's a good one or not anyway, will I?

'OK, I think I know what I'm going to do. I'm going to text everyone I've been ignoring.' I reach for my glass and catch Saffron's confused expression. 'Oh, remember the part in my blog post about my three best friends being in a conspiracy where one of them was getting off with my ex-boyfriend. Long story. Yeah, I haven't spoken to them, or the nice guy, ever since. So I'm going to text them all and tell them to come to my apartment and we can have it out.'

'What, all of them at once?' Even she looks alarmed. 'You don't do things by halves, do you?'

'I can't be bothered with individual discussions.' I drain my glass. This is suddenly feeling like the best plan ever.

'Go on then, text them,' Saffron says mischievously.

I pull out my phone and start a WhatsApp group with Cecilia, Anna, Sophie, Gary and, god help me, Martin. He still needs to pick up his weights.

Hey guys. Can you all be at my place at midday on Sunday, please? We need to talk.

I show Saffron.

'Love it. No emojis, straight to the point.'

'Pour me another.' I hold out my glass. 'No regrets.'

By midday on Saturday my hangover has waned enough for me to drag my arse out of bed and into the shower. I remember very little about last night after I sent that group message, but vague images of me and Saffron dancing down the street, arm in arm, reading everyone's replies and singing 'Fuck You' by CeeLo Green keep swimming into my head. I woke up, strangely, with zero remorse.

Beric messaged me at 9 a.m., inviting me to his house so we can review our plan and choose our method of implementation. I dry myself off and shove on some comfy, black clothes: ninja-style. It feels appropriate given I'm on my way to the brief of a top-secret mission.

On the tram I have a scroll through Facebook and Instagram, but my eyes keep glossing over and my mind keeps wandering. Eventually, I shove my phone in my bag and pull out the list, but I can't focus on that either, so I stick to gazing out of the window and wondering what I'm going to say to everyone tomorrow. I could cry, but it makes me look like an albino frog and Gary will be there, so I'd better keep it together. Maybe

I'll put across a fierce, boss-woman image. Would he be into that? I could rehearse a really eloquent speech, then say it really casually like it's off-the-cuff. The girls would notice I was blagging, but Gary definitely wouldn't.

Who am I trying to impress here? Shouldn't I be putting all my energy into reconciling my friendships? No, I realise. It's them who should be trying to reconcile with me. Not that they haven't been – they've messaged and called and emailed and DM'd every single day. But it's still not my problem. I'll leave it in their hands; let Sophie panic about what she's going to say, let Cecilia bake one of her trays of apology brownies, then watch the joy slide from her face as I remind her I'm vegan. They can make the effort. The only person I've got to make amends with is Gary.

They've all replied, affirming they'll be there. I haven't read over their responses in the sober light of day, but there was a lot of grovelling and *thanks for giving us the opportunity to explain*, etc, etc, etc. I seem to remember Gary's response being short and curt – either he's angry with me or he has no idea why I'm inviting him to something. We knew each other for a few weeks and then it ended, maybe that's that in his mind. Time to move on.

I jump off the tram at Burton Road and walk the long distance away from the pretty hipster bars and artisan restaurants and towards the shittier backstreets of the area. Beric's is a basement apartment located under a beautiful semi that has long been neglected, and is covered in mould and dead foliage. I feel quite curious as I ring the doorbell, wondering which category of Didsbury-dweller Beric falls into. Given his fears of joblessness and tales of unaffordable ex-girlfriends, I'm assuming it's the 'struggling' kind.

Beric answers the door wearing a loose kaftan and, as far as I can see, absolutely nothing else.

'Hi!' He is enthusiastic on his own territory, away from Darren's gaze. 'Come on in!'

I give him a smile and raise my gaze to the ceiling as we pass over the threshold. I'm pretty sure I saw a couple of pubes poking through the flimsy beachwear, and I'd rather not let my eyes probe further.

'Sorry about the state of the place.' He leads me through his door and downstairs into the basement, where everything is alarmingly and inexplicably painted orange.

'Don't be silly, it's lovely. I like the orange,' I try.

'Do you? Do you really?' He looks delighted. 'I did it all myself. It really brightens the place up, doesn't it?'

For the first time I wonder if it was a silly idea to get myself locked in a basement with a kaftan-wearing man I barely know.

Oh well, too late now.

'All the stuff's in my bedroom, I'm afraid,' Beric says, in exactly the voice a rapist would use if he was trying to lure you into his assault den.

'No problem,' I reply, with absolutely no regard for my own personal safety.

We pass through a tiny living room (orange) where a small window is situated high on the wall, letting minimal light in through the partially drawn curtains (orange). Beric leads me through into his room, which consists of an unmade single bed (orange) and a giant desk (mercifully for my retinas, brown).

'Take a pew.' He plops himself into the desk chair and gestures towards the bed, whose sheets look like they haven't been changed in months.

Possibly years.

I perch, ignoring the suspicious stains and curly, dark hairs that don't match those on Beric's blond head. It's a pube-y kind of day.

'I like your desk,' I say, because I really can't think of anything else.

'Thanks. I found it in a skip.' He clicks the mouse on his desktop a few times. 'Right, I've put it all together. It's taken me a while, but I think it's pretty much perfect.'

'Amazing. Let's go through it?' I attempt to lean forward but I'm already precariously balanced on the edge of the mattress and my abs can't handle it. I stand up and lean over his shoulder.

Beric clicks around and we review our work, wincing and laughing in equal measure. I didn't have any suspicions that Beric was lying to me, but now I *know* it's all true.

'If we can pull this off, it's going to be legendary.' He grins. 'Maybe we should film it? Get it viral?'

'Hmm. Maybe,' I say. I take over the mouse and click around a bit more, going over some of the details and high-fiving Beric when we get to something good. 'Right, let's have a look at the online roster and see when he's next in.'

I swipe the mouse down and hover over the Google Chrome icon.

It all happens very quickly.

My finger depresses the button of the mouse at the exact moment that Beric rises rapidly out of his chair, his arms reaching forward.

A noise comes out of his mouth, primal, almost, as the browser window springs to life.

Slow-motion, it seems, his hand makes contact with mine, taking control of the computer.

As I'm drawing breath to scream, a giant, extremely HD image of a woman being shagged up the bum fills the computer screen.

Beric clicks off it.

The desktop appears innocently, and then there is silence.

'Oh,' I say.

'I'm sorry,' he says.

'Don't be.' I scratch my eyebrow. 'It's completely natural.'

The look on that woman's face was about as natural as a McDonald's chicken nugget. I don't think I will ever forget it.

'So. I'll see you on Monday, then?' I brush some wayward pubes off the legs of my jeans.

'Yes. Yes, I'll see you then.' He stares at me, almost defiantly, determined not to be embarrassed. I mean, he knew the porn was there when I came in, didn't he? He freaked when I went to click on Chrome. Fair enough, forget to clear your history, but come *on*.

'Goodbye, Beric,' I say, and for some reason I do a small curtsy.

''Til next time, Maggie.'

I walk slowly out of his bedroom, through the orange maze and out into the hallway, where I lean against the woodchip walls for a second.

Fucking *hell*.

I have no problem with porn, no problem at all. Apart from the objectification of women, the coked-up actors and unrealistic body image portrayal, I think it's a perfectly normal thing to like. I'm no stranger to it myself.

But there is something slightly unnerving about being slapped in the face by a full-screen anus when you're least expecting it.

It does something to a person, it really does.

I walk to the tram stop in a state of stunned traumatisation, wondering how I'll ever look Beric in the eye again. We just shared a moment that I wouldn't wish on my worst enemy.

To distract myself, I look up when Darren is next in work and make a few phone calls to really set the plan in motion. By the time I'm back home I've almost forgotten all about it. I shove one of Tesco's stuffed red peppers in the oven and am just settling into a documentary about female serial killers when my phone rings. It's Veri.

'Hello?'

'Hiya.' I wait for her to say something further. Nothing.

'You OK?'

'Yeah, yeah.' She goes silent again. I never speak to Veri on the phone if I can help it; she either makes your skin itch with awkwardness or shouts at you for something.

'Did you need something, or . . .?'

'No, no.' I let the silence hang this time. 'I'm just updating you. We've found Nana a home.'

'What?' My throat constricts.

'Well, she found it herself, actually,' Veri sighs.

'What do you mean, *she found it herself*?'

'She disappeared the other day for ages, honestly it was about three hours. We called the police and everything.' Wonderful that they didn't call *me*, I think to myself, but then again I'd have thrown myself in front of a tram if they'd told me something like that, so probably wise. 'She came back right as rain, makeup done, handbag swinging on her shoulder. You know, how she used to be?'

'Yeah.' I smile, remembering, the panic subsiding a little.

'Said she'd been to visit one of the care homes back in Altrincham. She got on the tram by herself and everything,' Veri says incredulously.

'Are you sure she was telling the truth? I mean, that she didn't just *think* she'd been there?' It's not an unfair question; she thought she was on a cruise ship a few weeks back.

'We checked it out. It's legit. *Shady Forest*, it's called.'

'*Shady Forest?* That sounds horrible.' It sounds like the kind of woodland where *things* happen. "Gave Tom a blowjob in Shady Forest last night", for example.

'It's amazing, Maggie, honestly. Looks like a hotel. Fresh flowers every day, huge gardens. She's really taken with it.'

'Well, there goes our inheritance,' I think out loud.

'Maggie! That's *not* the point.'

'No, no, of course it isn't. Obviously.' I'm already mentally saying goodbye to my round-the-world self-discovery voyage. 'Are you sure she's not doing this because she feels like she's a burden?'

'Mum said that.' Veri laughs. 'She really didn't want her to go. Nana turned round and said that she couldn't bear to stay with us a moment longer because the noise of lovemaking was keeping her up all night.'

'Lovemaking?! Jesus, she really has lost the plot.'

'That's what everyone else thinks, but Charlie's room is above the living room where she's sleeping . . .' The sentence trails off and I gasp.

'No way! You think Charlie's got a boyfriend?'

'Of course he's got a boyfriend! Why do you think he's gone all depressed about being gay *now*? Obviously it's because he's met someone.' She tuts like I'm dim. Good to see the old Verity is still swimming around in there.

'This is *amazing*.' I am delighted. 'When can we meet him, do you reckon?'

'Not soon, Maggie. Leave him to figure stuff out first. He needs to come out to Mum and Dad, for a start.'

'He still hasn't done that?' I guess it's his choice. He'll know when he's ready. 'Does he seem happier, at least? Have you seen him?'

'Yeah, he really does. I think telling us might have helped, you know?'

You're welcome, I think.

'Yeah. Well, good. I'm glad. I'm really happy for him, too.'

'He's not such a fat shit anymore, either.' She says.

For god's sake. Just as I was beginning to enjoy our conversation.

'I've got to run, Veri. Myra Hindley is up next and I don't want to miss it.' I unmute the TV.

'What? OK, whatever. Speak to you soon.' She hangs up.

I feel strangely buoyed by that conversation. I don't think I've ever had such an intimate, friendly chat with Veri. It almost feels like we could start to be friends.

I check on my dinner and attempt to get back into my programme, but I can't concentrate. It's a strange feeling; I'm usually completely at home in front of the TV. Could it be because I haven't exercised in a couple of days? Surely not, I never used to exercise and I got along just fine.

Well . . . that's not exactly true. I was a complete fucking mess, to tell you the truth.

277

I get the sudden urge to run, like when I wake up in the morning craving nicotine like a junkie. On impulse, I turn off the oven and the TV and shove on my gym clothes, heading straight out of the door and into the darkening evening.

What is happening to me?

27

I slept like a dream last night, all things considered. At the gym I managed 5km without stopping in twenty-five minutes – if you'd have told me I'd be doing that three months ago I'd have spat in your face. Switching to the e-cig has made such a massive difference, even I'm surprised. I mean, anyone would expect that stopping coating your lungs with tar would improve your cardiac health, but still – the benefits are staggering.

On my way back I did a guided walking meditation, which was really relaxing until I realised that loping down a pitch black side-street with my eyes closed probably wasn't very safe. I put my keys between my fingers like Wolverine just in case anybody tried to rape me or steal my brand new reusable water bottle. People have been eyeing it enviously ever since I bought it – I accidentally left it on the treadmill the other day and some scrawny cow tried to walk off with it. I screamed at her to buy her own planet-saving equipment and she dropped it like a hot potato.

Everyone's going to be here soon. Martin is going to be back under my roof, noticing the limescale on the showerhead, clocking the crisps and biscuits on top of the bread bin. After finally managing to get him out, I almost can't believe I'm willingly letting him back in. And with Sophie, too. Looking at them both and knowing what they've . . . *done* together. What if it's too much?

I can't let myself panic about it, so I spend a couple of hours composing a new blog post about the awkwardness of sharing an unplanned porn moment with an acquaintance. There's not much to be said (it's horrifying, end of) so I keep it short and to the point. The response to my loneliness post has been incredible; my follower count has soared and I've had so many DMs from people telling me how my words struck a chord with them, how once they thought about it, they realised that they were lonely, too. It felt good. A weird, unusual kind of good – one I haven't felt before. Like I'd had an impact. Like I'd helped.

Of course, I've had the odd troll telling me I'm a fat waste of space with a personality disorder, but I just tend to read the first line of those and then block and delete. I can't waste any more time worrying about what other people think of me – there are just too many other things to think about.

At bang-on midday, the buzzer goes.

Without speaking through the intercom I let them up, hoping it's not an axe murderer for the first time in this building's history. That would be just my luck. It takes whoever it is an age to get up the stairs, but when they do, the knock at the door is timid. I swing open the door, assuming that anyone with an axe would just chop the whole thing down anyway.

It's all of them.

Sophie, Martin, Cecilia and Anna are all standing in the doorway, forlorn, desperate smiles on their faces.

'Hey, you.' Anna pulls me into a hug but I stand rigid, arms by my side. Now that they're here I don't know what to say. Seeing Sophie and Martin in front of me, together, has brought that gripping anger back up with huge force. I'm paralysed by it.

'Come in,' I say eventually, once Anna has released me.

They traipse past me slowly, funeral-procession-style, heads bowed. They all stand awkwardly in middle of the living room, except Martin, who is inspecting the bookcase.

'Sit down, please.' I keep my voice level, determined not to freak out and throw something. Having him back in here, checking for cleanliness, is sending my stress levels through the roof.

'Can I just say something before we start?' Anna sinks back into the sofa and holds her tiny bump. 'I knew what was going on, I've already told you that. I won't deny it. I hope you'll forgive me.'

'For god's sake, Anna, stop being such a martyr,' Cecilia snaps.

'No.' Sophie leans forward. 'She did know about me and Martin, but as soon as she found out she said we had to tell you or she would. And we didn't, and I'm sorry.'

'You didn't tell me either, though, did you, Anna?' I ask.

She looks down. 'I told them I wouldn't speak to them until they told you, or it stopped. Then I said I'd tell you, but I didn't. I just didn't want to cause any drama. I'm sorry.'

'It's OK,' I find myself saying. She stayed out of it and she tried for me, it seems, and she is pregnant. I can forgive her for not wanting to get involved.

'It is?' Cecilia stands up. 'Oh, thank god.'

'Woah.' I hold my hands up. 'I mean it's OK that Anna didn't tell me. You two are a completely different story.'

'Come on, Mags. It's time to let it go.' Martin moves towards me, his thick eyebrows knotted together. 'I'm sorry, but we're in love.'

'Oh my god, Martin, this is not about *YOU*!' I scream suddenly. 'How many words does it take to get the message in? I. Could. Not. Give. A. Fuck. About. What. You. Do.' I jab my finger into his chest.

He takes a step back. 'Calm down, please. You're overreacting again.'

People talk about 'seeing red', but I don't think I've ever experienced it until right at this moment. I know I'm being horrible, and I'm saying things that will hurt him. I spent so long pretending to be happy, pretending to be OK with my lot, and I'm too angry to pretend anymore. 'I'm not overreacting! I'm not! I didn't invite you here so you could dust the bookcase and tell me how much you love my best friend. I invited you so we could sort this out and MOVE ON!'

'Maggie, come on—' Sophie touches my arm.

'No!' I shake her off. 'You were the worst thing that ever happened to me, Martin, including myself. I've done a fair few things to fuck up my own life, but at least I kept it interesting. You kept me stale. You kept me boring and grounded and you squashed the fire out of me.'

Aaaagh. The relief hisses out of me like steam. I've hit the nail on the head without even realising it. It wasn't his fault, but he anchored me. And then he slept with my best friend, so he deserves to hear the truth.

He blinks and looks around the room for backup, and finds none forthcoming. 'You're being dramatic again.'

'Get out.'

'What?' He frowns.

Is this déjà-vu? I had this exact conversation two months ago.

'GET OUT.' I grab his arm and march him to the door, throwing him onto the corridor as well as I can, nearly pulling my arm out of its socket.

'Wait!' He shouts, suddenly. I pause with the door half open. 'Maggie, wait.'

His face is ashen. Well, I suppose this is it. This is the moment Martin apologises for everything he's done. It's about time. I fold my arms and look at him expectantly, my foot wedging the door open.

'I need to get my weights.'

Unbelievable.

I leave him holding the door and stomp into the bedroom, where I begin dragging his weights across the floor and out into the corridor. It's a real task, to be honest, and by the time I get to the heaviest ones I'm sweating, grunting like a rutting hog as I pull with all my might, crouched and red-faced. Nobody offers to help, but I do get the impression that they're probably quite scared of approaching me at this particular moment.

Weights finally strewn across the corridor, I slam the door in his gawping face and walk back into the living room, throwing myself onto the sofa as the girls watch on in horror.

'Did you just throw him out?' Sophie glances at the door worriedly.

'Not the first time.' My voice is muffled by the cushion I've buried my face in.

'You did invite him, Mags,' Anna says.

'I thought I'd cope with it. I thought he might have changed; that maybe he'd have thought about what he'd done and apologise and we could get over this.' I raise my head. 'Tell me how it started.'

Sophie runs her hands through her hair and straightens her back. She's obviously rehearsed this. 'We bumped into each other at the gym the day after you broke up. You know I go to the Quays branch? He needed someone to talk to, so we went to the pub, and it all went from there really. He's so sweet Maggie, honestly.'

The audacity she has to tell me what Martin's personality is like almost makes me chuck her out, too.

'I know you're upset, Mags. I know you're angry with us, I completely understand,' Cecilia pipes up. 'But acting on impulse and chucking him out into the corridor like that was too much.' She looks nervously towards the door as though Martin is a child I have just thrown out of the window.

I sit up straight. 'I *am* impulsive, C. You know that, she knows that, we all fucking know it. I've tried toning it down, I've tried being normal. It's not for me, I can't do it.'

'Of course you can. You just need practice.'

'No!' I shout, rising again. 'I can't and I don't *want* to! I like being me!'

I realise as I'm saying it that it's actually true. I *do* like being me. I like being weird and unpredictable and not thinking before I do things. It gets me into trouble but it keeps me going. I have stories, I experience things, I meet people, all because I run at things head on and don't listen to anybody else.

'She wouldn't be Maggie if she wasn't absolutely bonkers,' Sophie says, smiling.

I don't reply.

'Mags. I can't tell you how sorry I am. I really can't.' She drops the grin and her eyes fill with tears. 'I can't imagine losing all this.'

'You're still with him though, aren't you?'

She drops her head to her chest.

'Even after all this, it's worth it?' I choke. I know I felt nothing for Martin. I know I was desperate to have him gone. But the point is that she *knows* it was wrong. She knows she could lose me, and she's still going ahead with it.

'I can't justify Sophie's actions, but I can apologise for mine.' Cecilia reaches for me and I back away. 'I just got caught up in it. I thought I had to take sides. I stuck by Sophie when I should have stayed in the middle, and I'm so, so sorry for that. I'm sorry for cutting you out.'

'I really needed you,' I sob.

They look at me, tearful and silent. The buzzer goes again.

'I'm not letting him back in,' I say to Sophie. 'He wants a wife, Sophie. We weren't in love, you know? We never were. He wants a wife and the perfect, fairytale life. If you're happy with that then go ahead, be my guest.'

Sophie hesitates before going over to the intercom to deliver the news.

'Me and Brian have been thinking about names.' Anna strokes her bump again, trying to bring some niceness into the hostility.

'That's good.' I lean on her shoulder. I have no more anger towards Anna. Cecilia watches us from the other sofa. 'Which is your favourite?'

'Jetaime,' she whispers, visibly melting.

I have no appropriate response for this. I pretend I haven't heard. 'How are things with you and Brian?'

I'm expecting to hear more slander of the age-differences, more turmoil on the home front with the foetus edging closer to becoming a baby every day.

'Amazing.' Her eyes shine. 'I think I love him, Mags. I think he's going to move in.'

'Maggie?' Sophie calls.

'He's not coming in!' I shout.

'No, it's someone called Gary? I think he was on the group chat with us?'

Oh god.

Oh god, it's Gary.

I forgot I invited Gary.

I make my way to the door. I am extremely conscious of the fact that I look like a boiled pig after all the crying. It seems like every time he comes over here my eyes are almost swollen shut.

He emerges from the lift, stepping over the weights self-consciously. My heart does a little flip. I really like that about him, his normalcy. He's nicely confident, he has something to say for himself.

He isn't Martin.

He stops in the doorway and looks at me, pressing his mouth into a line. 'Hey, stranger.'

'Hiya,' I say.

I want to hold my arms out, to give him a hug, but things need to be said first. I stand aside and let him pass into the room full of people he doesn't know. He doesn't say anything, just takes a seat at the tiny dining table in the corner and studies his hands.

'Everyone, this is Gary.' I gesture towards him and the girls nod. 'I wanted to have you all here at the same time so I could sort this all out at once, but you guys arrived first and it got a bit out of hand.'

'I don't know how you could do that to someone.' Gary looks up at Sophie. 'Your best friend.'

'I don't think we need your input, thank you,' Cecilia glowers. 'Who are you again?'

I always forget about Cecilia's temper. She's a nightmare when she's backed into a corner.

'You didn't see how upset she was,' Gary says.

Sophie starts crying again.

Cecilia grabs her. 'We're sorry. We're so sorry, but everybody makes mistakes.'

Gary shrugs. 'Not like that, they don't.'

'Anyway.' I pause. 'I wanted to speak to you about how I treated you.'

'How you treated me?' Gary frowns and glances over at the girls. 'Here? Now?'

'Yeah. I just want to get it all out, right now. I'm sorry I ran away from you. I was . . . I wasn't in a good place, I suppose. I thought I was coming out of the shit-storm and I felt sucked back into it for a moment. That doesn't excuse me not texting you back, I know you must be angry, and I'm sorry. I just didn't know what to say, how to excuse myself. It was a shitty thing to do.'

'Sorry?' Gary looks incredulous. 'You're . . . you're sorry?'

'Yes. I really am. It might not be enough, and I understand that—'

'Wait.' He rubs his eyebrows. 'I thought I was coming over here to explain myself. I thought *I* was here to apologise.'

'Apologise for what?' What is he talking about?

'For trying to kiss you!' His cheeks colour. 'You were emotional and it was the worst timing. I felt awful, like I'd taken advantage or something.'

'What? No!' I stand up and everyone winces, presumably conditioned to enter defence mode whenever I raise my voice and make sudden movements. 'It wasn't the right time, of course, but I didn't hate you for it. I just . . . I just couldn't deal with it, at that moment.'

'Oh,' he says.

There is a silence as we look at each other. Anna coughs. 'I think we've got to go, haven't we?'

'What?' Sophie drags her eyes from where she's been fixated on me and Gary. I can practically see the popcorn crumbs down her top. 'No, we can't go. We need to sort this. I can't leave until you forgive me.'

'I can't do that right now, Soph.' I follow them as Anna drags them by the hand to the door. 'I need some space. I appreciate your apologies, but I need to think.'

Cecilia turns around and stares at me, her eyes wide. 'Please say we can move on from this.'

'I don't know.' I hold the door open. 'I need time.'

'We'll go.' Anna ushers everyone out of the door in silence. She hands me a small, white envelope. 'Open it later.'

I nod. 'Bye.' I close the door before I can change my mind. I thought I'd be able to forgive and forget this, and my gut reaction was to just let it go. It turns out my impulsivity works both ways – I make mistakes quickly and I'm quick to forgive them, too. But for now I need to step back. I need to really think on this one.

And then it's just me and him.

'So,' I say.

'So.'

He lowers himself onto the sofa and pats the space next to him. I sit.

'I can't believe we both thought we were angry with each other.' I snort.

'Bloody idiots, the pair of us.' He laughs and suddenly we are both laughing together, shaking our heads.

'So, you don't hate me?' I smile.

'Hmm . . . nope, I don't think so.' He edges a bit closer to me on the sofa.

'Well, that's a relief.' I scoot up a bit too, preparing myself to push against the feeling of entrapment and fear. It doesn't come. I couldn't feel less anchored if I tried. 'I must warn you, though, I am certifiably bonkers.'

'That might be an issue.' He dips his head slightly.

His face is close to mine. My heart flips, but my mind is clear. This is OK. This will only be what I want it to be.

'One more thing . . .' I murmur. 'Why were you so short on the group chat if you weren't angry with me?'

'I was angry with them,' he whispers. 'I couldn't believe you'd added me to a group chat with them all.'

He inches his face closer to mine.

'You're wild.' I can feel the heat from his lips. 'I fucking love it.'

And then he kisses me.

28

Veronica is in full bloom. Huge red and white flowers have emerged as I slept, their faces tilted towards me as I shuffle into the room, pyjama clad and happy.

Gary stayed for a cup of tea before heading home, leaving me to my evening and my thoughts. I like him (a shitload, to be frank) and we're going to see where it goes. I'm still not sure if I'm ready for a relationship, but it is what it is. Maybe we will take things slowly or maybe things will go no further; either way I'll be fine. I will focus on myself and let the rest come naturally, as additions rather than necessities.

I thought a lot about the girls last night. I opened the envelope Anna gave me; it was the ultrasound photo of Nugget. How can we not go through this life-changing moment together, a compact and supportive group, as we always have been? Their absence is like a physical pain; not just being with them, but speaking, messaging, laughing every day. It's hard. I know we'll move on from this though, at some point. We might not be the same for a while, but we'll come out the other side.

Something else has clicked in my head after my conversation with Anna. When she told me she was pregnant, I was convinced her life was over. She would be a mum now, forever tied to a man more than twice her age. Her youth had ended. It was so much the opposite situation of those glossy lives I saw on Instagram, the people I was trying to be and the life I had convinced myself I wanted. The high-flying worlds of Emma Penton and my brother and sister, who always outshone me. But who's winning, really? Anna is happier than I've ever seen her, Veri and Charlie were miserable and Emma Penton wasn't perfect at all. Maybe it really does have nothing to do with how things look on the outside.

I'm loading the washing into the machine and as I check the pockets of my jeans I find the list. It's torn and stained, but I can just make out the words and satisfied crossings-out across the page. I almost can't remember writing it, and it's hard to transport myself back to the mindset I had when this was all that mattered. But there's still a thumping at the back of my mind as my eyes travel down each item. I know I've changed, but wouldn't it feel better to have changed *and* be skinny, sleek and polished? Maybe it would. Maybe I'd be happier and more popular, maybe there'd be career opportunities jumping at me from every corner. Maybe my friends wouldn't have betrayed me in the first place, maybe I'd have coped better if they had. Maybe I wouldn't have lost my job, wouldn't have fallen off a treadmill, wouldn't have embarrassed myself time and time again. And maybe . . . maybe all of it would have happened anyway. Maybe if I hadn't been so focused on changing my exterior and chasing the idea of 'perfect', I'd have given time to the important things: accepting myself and nurturing those around me. Perhaps happiness isn't born from itemisation and the magnifying of flaws. And isn't a list really the *antidote* to impulsiveness and spontaneity and fun? To all the things I have struggled and fought and battled to love about myself?

There's a funny kind of irony in it, really: the woman for whom no one day ever goes to plan, embarking on a life change using a *list*. It's crackers.

Today is the day of mine and Beric's Darren Destruction Deployment. Darren is in as the shop opens, so me and Beric are planning on getting there at 10 a.m. We aren't on shift, but we have work to do. It's still early so I head to the gym, listening to my walking meditation in the daylight with my eyes open this time. Afterwards, I head into Tesco and grab some strawberries and vegan meringues (apparently made from bean juice, but I try not to think too much about this), and crunch on them with a cup of tea. I find I can eat more calmly now. I know there will be moments when I'm sad and a bucket of fried rice is my only solace, but my mind goes more quickly to calling my family, or asking Saffron to hang out, than to eating. Food isn't company, and nor are people who don't accept you for who you are. It took a while, but I've figured that out now.

Eventually it's time, so I get dressed and take the eight minute walk to Frederick's, spotting Beric standing outside as I approach.

'Hi.' He looks at the floor, beetroot. It seems being in this place has pushed him firmly back into his shell, and the porn atrocity probably isn't helping.

'Hello,' I say.

'She's not here yet.'

'She will be.' I look around me, trying to pick out who she might be from the crowded streets.

'You know the plan?' Beric raises his eyes to me for the first time.

'Like the back of my hand.'

On cue, a woman in an exquisitely tailored suit approaches and scans our faces.

'Beric Johnsson? Maggie Gardiner?' She says and we nod, shaking hands. 'Shall we go inside?'

We walk nervously into the shop. It's almost completely devoid of customers, and I spot Darren over by the counters murmuring to Anita. I lead our party over until we're right behind him, and then tap him lightly on the shoulder. He spins round.

'What are you two doing here? You're not on the rota for today.' He looks confused.

'This is Pamela Stones.' I gesture to the suited woman, who shakes Darren's hand too. She really loves a good handshake, this one.

'Right . . .' He looks a bit worried now, but turns on the charm, flashing those pointy little teeth. 'So what can I do for you?'

Before she has a chance to respond, Beric holds up his hand and reaches into his backpack. To the untrained eye, it could be quite plausible that Beric (small, put-upon, potentially unhinged) is about to pull an explosive from the bag. This goes some way towards justifying the horrified, panicked expressions of Darren, Anita and Pamela. Those expressions don't change when he produces a small electronic device and places it onto the counter.

'What is it? What's that?' Anita has edged further along the counter, and is breathing heavily.

'This is for you, Darren. Pamela, I'd like you to pay close attention.' Beric reaches a shaking finger forward and depresses a small button on the side of the device, earning an audible gasp from Darren and causing Anita to throw her arms over her head dramatically.

The recorder crackles into life.

'. . . *absolutely useless, Beric . . . You're working stock-check tonight, no overtime pay . . . What have I told you about trying to tell people? They'll never believe you . . . Everyone thinks you're mental, you know that, don't you? . . . Looks like somebody knocked the Sci-Fi stack down, you'd better go and pick it up . . . You're a waste of space . . . Try to tell anybody and I'll make sure you're never employed again . . .*'

I reach forward and press pause. Pamela looks horrified. Darren has gone an alarming shade of white, his undereyes sunken and grey. He looks dead.

'Mr Farraday, is this how you speak to your employees?'

Pamela takes the recorder and holds it close to her chest. 'Is this how you treat them?'

'I . . . I . . .' Darren gawps like a fish, his mouth opening and closing like an idiot. 'He doesn't do his work properly!'

'And you think that's an excuse to bully and manipulate him? To threaten him out of employment for your own satisfaction?' She glares at him.

'Who are you, anyway?' Darren raises himself to full height, his face regaining colour at an alarming speed. 'Get out of my shop.'

'We were introduced several moments ago, Mr Farraday. My name is Pamela.' She reaches into her bag and pulls out a curled up lanyard, flashing the badge on the end at us all. 'HR at Frederick's.'

Darren physically blanches. The amount of times his blood pressure has risen and fallen in the last two minutes is unprecedented. I almost feel sorry for him.

Almost.

'Mrs Stones!' Darren recovers and inexplicably holds out his hand again. I am reminded of my behaviour with Christopher in the bar the other week. If in doubt, just shout the person's name at them. 'I do apologise, I didn't recognise you. Would you like a cup of tea?'

Pamela narrows her eyes. 'It's *Miss* Stones, thank you, Mr Farraday.' Oooooh, BURN. I'm learning a lot from these badass HR women. 'And you're suspended, pending an investigation into abuse and misconduct. I'll keep this, if that's alright.' She slips the recorder into her bag and Beric and I nod, mute. Pamela takes Darren's elbow and guides him, stunned, towards the main door. He is silent. We did it! We shopped the bastard!

I look over at Beric. His face is slack with relief. He watches as Darren is led towards the door, and then his eyes flit beyond me, to Anita. I turn. Her head is in her hands; wet, noisy sobs escaping from her mouth. We rush over, one of our hands on each of her shoulders.

'I thought it was just me.' She gulps. 'I thought it was only me.'

I pull her into a hug and she snots onto my collar.

'I'm sorry I didn't help you.' She turns her attention to Beric. 'I didn't want things to get worse.'

Jesus, Anita too. Beric told me everything was perfect until the three-month mark. It wouldn't have been long until it was my turn.

Beric moves in to hug Anita and I edge away, leaving them to their shared moment. I watch as Darren leaves the shop. I feel a jolt of pride – I did that! I got that calculating, power-complexed wanker chucked out of here forevermore. And I did it through careful planning and well-timed execution, no impulse used whatsoever! I'm learning! Maybe I can be a calm, rational individual – not always, but sometimes? Perhaps I can be professional when it really matters, when real causes need fighting for.

Pamela and her detainee have reached the doorway.

It's no use, I can hold it in no longer.

'FUCK YOU, DARREN!' I scream.

Hmm, maybe not.

Joy of all joys! I cannot believe we did it. Beric was like an unleashed animal, springing into animation the moment Darren left the building. 'Pub?' he asked me, and I agreed, despite it being 10.30 in the morning. We got suitably plastered and ordered a Wetherspoons all-day breakfast, mine consisting of beans, mush-rooms and a roasted tomato – the establishment hasn't quite got itself up-to-date with the new vegan trends just yet.

Beric didn't mention the porn incident and neither did I – some things are probably best left unsaid. He did mention that he'd started seeing someone new, which will hopefully encourage him to change his sheets, clean his apartment and close all tabs before allowing visitors in. We discussed Darren and Anita at length; I always thought her quiet sullenness towards me was because I was new. Beric hadn't said a word to her since she pretended she didn't believe his story. He admitted that he probably would have done the same to her, when he was in the middle of it.

At 3 p.m. I staggered home, merry and elated, and watched *Father Ted* reruns until I fell asleep. It was a wonderful day.

It's Wednesday now – I had my first Darren-free shift yesterday. Things are chaotic (in his defence, Darren did run a very tight ship) but the mood was high. Everyone was chatting and laughing and customers seemed to leave in a better mood than when they entered. It was mad but happy. A bit like me, I suppose.

I woke up at 6 a.m. today; lie-ins seem to evade me recently. As do naps, thinking about it – I don't really get tired so much anymore. I've got a decaf coffee perched on the armrest of the sofa, and the late spring light is filtering through the open windows, making Veronica sway.

I'm just reading through some of the comments on my blog – there are a *lot* – it seems I've hit the nerves of a lot of people with my eviction of Darren. Workplace bullying is apparently far more common than I'd thought, and people are inspired to take action. It feels good.

I'm going out with Gary later. We're going to see the new sex exhibition at the museum – apparently there's a real-life preserved vagina which I can't *wait* to see. I think maybe I'd like to donate my vagina to science when I die – let people have a good old gawp when I'm not around to be self-conscious. I've booked us tickets (it costs a lot to learn about the mashing together of genitalia, would you believe) but they need printing, so I'm going to forward the email to Ryman's and head over there to collect them after lunch.

I'm just scanning through my inbox for the confirmation email (it's surprisingly easy to find things when you stop ordering clothes that don't fit from ASOS and receiving 9,000 email updates per day) when I notice an unread message that came through last night.

Holy shit. This is just not happening.

Is this happening? Maybe I'm losing my marbles. It cannot
possibly be that someone has contacted me about representing
me and my blog. A real-life, bona fide literary agent, who probably reads fifty billion manuscripts per week and rejects ninety
per cent of them. *He* sought *me* out?! It can't be true. And all
because of Saffron?

I call her and she picks up on the first ring.

'You got the email, then?' I can hear her grin through the
phone.

'What the fuck, Saffron?! You never told me your brother
was an agent!'

'I didn't want to get your hopes up. I thought I'd show him,
and if he wasn't interested you'd be none the wiser. Someone
was going to pick you up eventually!'

'Oh my god. Is this a joke?' I laugh nervously.

'I promise it's not. He's good, you know. Are you going to
meet him?'

'Of course I am! Will you come with me?' I need a nervous poo already and we haven't even set a date to meet yet.

'No! You have to do this by yourself.'

She's right, of course. How would that make me look, dragging Saffron along to a business meeting? Because that's what this is, isn't it? My very first business meeting! About something I'm actually interested in!

'Thank you so much. Honestly, what you've just done for me . . . I don't know how I can express how grateful I am.' I'm almost crying.

'See what comes of it first. Then you can buy me a drink if he agrees to represent you.'

'I'll buy you a drink in any case. I'll buy you twenty. You're the best.'

'Just be yourself.'

She says goodbye and rings off. Jesus Christ on a bike! I feel like I want to run through a field of wheat, Theresa May style, that's how het-up and excited I am about this. I need to calm down.

Two seconds later, my phone pings. It's a picture from Saffron; a painting of a girl with frizzy hair, sitting at her computer and typing manically, steam coming from the top of her head. In the corner are the initials 'SC'.

'YOU ARE INCREDIBLE,' I reply. Her work is amazing. I am overcome with such a strong feeling of happiness for her, for her talent, and it shocks me. I can't remember the last time I saw someone do something wonderful and wasn't jealous and resentful.

I make a cup of tea and gaze out of the window, imagining all sorts of far-fetched scenarios. Me at the UK Blog Awards, giving my acceptance speech, dressed in a gown, Gary in the audience. My author profile – *Maggie lives in her rural Devon cottage, where she writes and looks after her dogs and chickens with her husband and three children.* Maybe even branching out into vlogs – that's what people do these days, isn't it? I'm not sure people would want my face on a screen, though. Probably best to stick behind the keyboard.

I'm getting ahead of myself, so I take some deep breaths and reply to Ross carefully, giving him my free dates and telling him I look forward to meeting him.

He pings back immediately and we decide on tomorrow lunchtime, at Pret A Manger.

Shit.

29

I haven't slept a wink. I spent all night tossing and turning, my mind raking over my meeting with Ross and the unspeakable trauma of last night's preserved vagina. I saw a penis, too. I think it's ruined sex for me forever. Even Gary couldn't cope, he tore up the leaflet as soon as we left and didn't speak for several minutes, his eyes wide and traumatised. Needless to say I will be burying my genitals with the rest of me.

I'm actually quite worried that I look stark-raving bonkers, which may very well be true. My hair is not cooperating despite a deep and expensive conditioning treatment, and my eyes are ringed with black circles that even the most industrial concealer is failing to remove. I had a major wobble when considering what to wear – I was really tempted to go for my jeans and vest combo, but that just wouldn't do for such an important event, so I stood in front of my wardrobe for twenty-eight minutes contemplating my vast array of unwearable clothes. Is a skirt suit too formal? Is a t-shirt too casual? I went with the suit, in the end. I can always say I'm meeting him on my lunch break. I'm going to give most of my clothes to charity this weekend – there is simply no point pretending I'm a chiffon blouse and maxi skirt kind of girl.

At 11.50 I'm sitting in Pret, a green tea in my hand. Jason, the pimply recipient of my pre-interview vegan outburst, almost fainted when he saw me in the queue. I gave him a reassuring look and dropped a pound in the tip tray. 'I got the job,' I smiled. He looked like he wanted to headbutt me.

I'm facing the door, and I start panicking about how I'm going to recognise Ross when he comes in. He certainly won't recognise me. I do a quick Google search of him, realising that I should have done this last night instead of painting my nails and hyperventilating, and pull up an image of a ginger man with a neatly trimmed beard. I set my phone on the table and zoom in on his face, scrolling around from eye to eye to beard to mouth to pass the time.

'Maggie Gardiner?'

I look up to find said ginger bearded man standing above me, frowning down at my phone. I quickly lock it and jump to my feet, knocking the table and sending hot tea coursing onto the floor. Jason sighs loudly and trudges over with the mop.

'Hi! Sorry, sorry, I was just – just looking at your face. Your picture, I mean. So I could recognise you, you know. When you came in. But you recognised me! That's great. Wonderful. Really great and wonderful to meet you.' I hold out my hand and he takes it, his eyebrows raised.

'I did a quick search of you, found your LinkedIn profile.' He sits down opposite me as Jason drags the mop bucket back behind the counter. 'Thought it might be useful to know a bit about you.'

'Oh, absolutely, yes.' I nod enthusiastically, wracking my brains for what utter shite and lies I have undoubtedly spread all over my LinkedIn profile. I'm almost certain I said I was a paralegal at some point.

'You're looking very smart,' he remarks.

'Just on my lunchbreak,' I breeze, no hesitations.

'I thought you were a sales assistant at Frederick's?' His brow furrows.

There is a pause.

I appear to have no response to this.

300

'So,' he says eventually, putting his briefcase on the table (a briefcase, I kid you not) and sliding out some papers. 'I've printed a few extracts of your blog to show you the parts I really like. The parts I think could sell.'

'Sell?' I'm confused. How can he sell what is already out there? 'You mean, like, putting advertising on my page or something?'

'No . . .' He sighs. 'I mean if you write the book.'

'The book?' I stare at him, dumbfounded.

'Did you look up my work, or just my face?' He smiles.

'Erm. Just your face, actually.' I feel myself going red. 'I'm quite new to this.'

'I don't represent blog writers. Well, I do, but only if they write a book.' He grins. 'I think it would be a great idea for you.'

'A book?' I say again. Bloody hell, writing a book is only my life's dream. No big deal, Ross. Just come in here and throw that at me like it's nothing. I scan my eyes over the posts he has highlighted. 'So like . . . my blog made into a book?'

'No, a collection of other anecdotes. The same style as the pieces you've already written, but completely new stuff. You have a real natural talent for writing funny, relatable material. Very contemporary and relevant. Just what the market is looking for at the moment.' He shuffles through his papers. 'I don't know if half the stuff you write is even true, but it gets a good response.'

'It's all true!' I say eagerly, wondering whether I'm doing myself a favour or making this man pity me for my chaotic life events.

'Well, you've got quite the following and a great platform to market it on. I think it could do well. If you use your Facebook and Instagram to publicise to people you know, too—'

'Oh, I deleted them.' I admit.

'You did what?'

'I deleted Facebook and Instagram. Sorry.' Why am I apologising? This isn't China, I can choose to have social media or not. I choose not.

301

'Why?' He looks baffled.

'They made me depressed. All that comparison, you know?'

'Right . . . well, that might knock our marketing strategy a little bit. Would you consider re-joining them?'

'Hmm.' I contemplate this. It took a lot of balls for me to finally uninstall those two toxic apps. Recently I found that I didn't even enjoy using them; the restless energy of constant scrolling and comparing. It almost made me feel mad, like I was trapped. I got rid of it all in one fell swoop last week and I've never felt happier. I'm reaching out and connecting through my blog, a medium where I can be 100 per cent myself, almost untouched by other people's ideals and faux-perfect lives, and it's infinitely more satisfying.

'I could use it on my computer, but I don't want it on my phone,' I concede. In all honesty, I can't imagine that my 500 Facebook friends and sixty-five Instagram followers would make a huge difference to the *marketing strategy*, but whatever he says.

He nods. 'OK. I assume you're still active on Twitter?'

'Yes,' I nod. Twitter I *have* kept. There's an incredible community out there, and I feel like I owe it to them to be involved, especially since they're the ones who retweeted my blog into oblivion and got me here in the first place.

'That's good.' Ross downs the rest of his coffee. 'Well, I've got to get to a meeting. I'll be in touch.'

'Great.' I want to ask when, like, will he call me? Should I keep my phone on loud? Does he like me? Have I ruined it by zooming in on his eye and throwing green tea everywhere? 'Please respond at your convenience.'

No idea why I said that.

'Take some time to think about what you want from your writing.' He scoops my work back into his briefcase. 'A little fact for you, though, if you're doubting the book route: it'd do well. Bear that in mind.'

He stands to leave and I shake his hand numbly, stunned by the speed of our meeting and the overload of information. I resist the urge to shout 'Yes! It's a yes! I want to write a book, say you'll represent me!' Some things really do need careful thought.

I sit back down and stare into the distance. I can't quite believe this is happening to me. I almost don't feel I deserve it, after all the shit I've done. Me – the unfashionable, abnormal catastrophe. But I do, don't I? I worked hard at this, and I love it. Why should I be undeserving yet assume that other people should get what they want? They were old Maggie's thoughts, and she's been shoved in the backseat.

A red, blotchy hand reaches across the table and slides a cup in front of me. I look up to find Jason, half a smile on his face. 'It's soya,' he says.

All the leaves are back on the trees now. I'm walking slowly to the tram station; there's no rush. I've realised that there's rarely *really* a need to rush – it's just what we do to keep ourselves motivated. Walk faster, barge through, get in the winning mindset. It's exhausting, honestly.

I take in a big lungful of air and try to ignore the faint tinge of dog-shit and bins. It's nearly summer! It's my favourite time of the year. The tram station is quiet on this Monday afternoon with everyone ferreting away in their offices. Only the elderly and odd are clambering on and off the trams – I place myself firmly and proudly in the second category.

With no Instagram or Facebook to distract myself, I spend the journey to Altrincham gazing out of the window and noticing things. The mismatch of houses squished by the sides of the tracks; the faint slash of green on the distant horizon; the smatterings of people going about their daily lives.

When I arrive I take a detour past Nana's house, just one more time.

I look up at the tiny stone terrace, almost identical to every other house on the entire street, save the 'For Sale' sign nailed to the drainpipe. I notice the little things that have always been a part of my life – the knitted doll in the upstairs window, the lion's head doorknocker, the lavender bushes in the tiny front garden. It's all so achingly familiar and comforting and the pressure of tears builds behind my nose. I let them fall, just for a moment, and then wipe my eyes and reach into my handbag, pulling out the list.

I gaze at it for a second. Who was this girl? The girl who wrote down all the things she hated about herself. I want to hug her, because really, she had spent so long pretending, that what she actually hated wasn't really her at all.

I crouch down onto the pavement, holding the list in both hands. I place it face-down in the smears of mould that the council still hasn't cleaned. I press gently, making circles, slowly at first, feeling the damp seep through the paper and onto my fingers. And then I start scrubbing hard, back and forth, until I see clean stone and the list is shredded and crumbled like wet toilet paper on the path.

The nursing home is *massive*. Honestly, I'd pay £2,500 a month to stay here. *Shady Forest*, ironically, doesn't seem to have an ounce of shade within a one-mile radius of its shiny new doors. It's a huge stately home set in a good few acres of fields, filled with benches and flowers and smooth, zimmer-frame-friendly paths. Around the perimeter of the grounds are thick, ancient oak trees, presumably to remind the residents that they aren't so old after all.

I walk into a spacious foyer with huge glass skylights and fresh flowers on solid-wood side-tables. At the check-in desk (sorry, reception, it really is hard to remember this isn't a hotel) a smartly suited woman beams at me.

'Good morning!'

'Hello!' I match her tone.

'Who are you here to see today?' She taps at her computer.

'I'm considering getting a room for myself!' I laugh.

'Oh, we only take over sixty-fives, I'm afraid.' She frowns sympathetically. Another sense of humour lapse – why is everyone so unfunny?

'I was joking, don't worry. Enid Lawson.'

She beams again and scoots round the glass-and-wood counter. 'Follow me, madam.'

Fucking hell, what *is* this place? We walk down an airy corridor, passing a colossal, intricately decorated dining room, with full tea service set at each round table. At the far end of the room, a long row of bi-folding doors open out onto a wooden terrace adorned with comfy, outdoor recliners, overlooking a duck pond. I wonder if they do cocktails. I may well visit more often.

Nana's room is at the end of the corridor. There's no name, just a shiny number 34, and that makes me happy for some reason. Like she's got her own apartment.

As we get closer, I notice a girl leaning against the doorframe. I sigh inwardly.

My cousin. *Fucking Suzannah.*

The receptionist drops me at the door and clips back down the corridor.

'Mags!' Suzannah lisps through her fillers. 'You look *gorgeous.*'

I smile. 'So do you, Suze.' And she does. She looks happy. I'm glad.

She scans me through her spidery eyelashes. 'You know, I could give you some more SlimFast shakes if you want a *big* change. Like, a noticeable difference. I'll give you a discount if you let me take before and after shots. Preferably in underwear, but a bikini is OK if you're self-conscious or something.'

'I'm good,' I laugh, meaning it more than I have ever meant anything. I'm *good.* Just like this. 'Come on. Let's go in.'

It turns out Nana has more than her own apartment. It's a bloody penthouse. There's a sitting room with brand new sofas, plush carpets and fresh roses on the coffee table. In a separate, spacious room is a dining table adorned with doilies and her favourite tablecloth, with a bedroom off to the left. From what I can glimpse she's got a king-size, with discreet buttons on the side to lift her up in the morning. Where do I get my hands on one of those? There's no kitchen, which doesn't surprise me – dementia and ovens are a fateful combination.

Nana is relaxing in a humungous armchair, looking pleased as punch. Mum and Dad are sitting on one sofa, Veri and Charlie on the other. Charlie is texting, a quiet smile on his face. He's lost weight and his colour has returned – he looks happy. Veri smiles as we walk in.

'Hiya.' She gives me an uncharacteristic hug.

'Hi.' I squeeze her back harder, the emotion of it all compelling me towards closeness. I pull away and glance towards Charlie, who is still besotted with his phone, and she raises her eyebrows.

'Well hello, my darling!' Nana pats the stool at her side and I take a seat, feeling like we're congregated for council around an ageing monarch. 'What have you got to tell us, then?'

'I have some good news.' I look around at their faces. They look intrigued, but warily so. It's understandable – I've never had actual good news before, at least not in their books. I haven't told them yet that Ross has offered representation – he sent the email through this morning after a month of agonising waiting. I filled the time with blogging – every moment I'm not at Frederick's I'm writing until my wrists ache. I love it.

'Can I ask you something first, Nana?'

'Anything, love.' She smiles down at me.

'Do you remember the plant you gave me, last time I visited you at your house?'

'Of course I remember! It was an amaryllis.' She nods.

'Do you know what amaryllis symbolises?' I hold her papery hand.

She smiles, her face crinkling. Her eyes meet mine and twinkle knowingly.

'Worth beyond beauty,' she says.

I look around the room. Mum is nestled into Dad's arm, her eyes closed, her face calm. Charlie looks up from his phone and grins at Veri, winking. Veri rolls her eyes and laughs, her mouth wide and happy.

'Yeah,' I nod. 'Worth beyond beauty.'

Acknowledgements

Unfortunately, I didn't have a huge amount of support while writing this thing, because I spent most of the time curled up on my sofa getting backache from typing at such a weird angle and refusing to tell anybody what I was doing. Nevertheless, there are a few solid champs who were privy to my secret life and let me go on about it endlessly over gin and tonics, until I ended up crying because I was certain it was all for nothing and anyway, gin always makes me cry.

Well, guys, all those boring late-night monologues were worth it, because now your name is published in a book, right at the back, in the section that ninety-nine per cent of people don't bother to read. You're welcome.

Zara. My number one sidekick and 'let's-go-to-Pizza-Express-I-got-a-Tastecard-with-my-Natwest-account' pal for nine whole years. Thank you for having bigger dreams for me than I did for myself, and for peppering me with questions about it all and making me feel more normal. Every woman needs a best friend as warm, generous, and selfless as you. You deserve the world; please don't ever forget that.

To my parents, thank you for not going ballistic when I said that I probably maybe didn't really like psychology or research (or anything that I'd spent eight years and £50,000 of government money on that I'll probably never end up paying back) that much anymore, and possibly potentially wanted to pack it all in and write things instead. Thank you for being kind and supportive and accepting and just *there*, always. Thank you also for croquet, roast potatoes, Scrabble and wine.

Tanera Simons, agent *extraordinaire* and lovely human being, thank you for believing in me and giving me the first inkling that I might have written something worth reading. Thank you for your patience with my questions, neediness and swearing.

Thank you to Phoebe Morgan, for lending your magical editorial brain to this book. Thank you for giving me my first book deal, making my life's dream come true, and being supportive and available beyond the call of duty. Thank you for understanding in the way only a fellow-author could do.

Thank you to everyone at Trapeze for their hard work and faith. To go from scribbling alone in a darkened room to having a team of experts tell you that you're not half bad is *everything*. This book wouldn't exist without you. Obvs.

Thank you my fellow members of the Core Four – Alex, Amie and Lauren – for the continued life-support network you have provided since Debbie ruined my life with a dirty Cup-a-Soup mug in 2015. We are none of us where we expected to be, but we are happy and generally smashing it, difficult bosses and snooty email trails aside. Thank you for rescuing me from many a meltdown and for putting up with my flighty tendencies. I am forever grateful to you all for signing me in to Professional Development seminars when I simply could not be arsed.

Patrick, thank you for keeping me grounded by insulting me every moment we are in each other's company. I am sure that one day you will leave your moody, too-cool phase behind and go back to being the adorable little sausage who cried over lost toy lizards, worshipped scorpion paperweights from Arizona and dreamed of BB guns instead of AllSaints t-shirts.

George, thank you for constantly, consistently, unapologetically being *you*, 24/7. To do what you feel and be who you want in a world that likes to tell you that it's wrong is a code nobody else I know has cracked. You inspire me not to give so much of a shit, and that is inspiration in its purest form. Also thank you for making me laugh by existing. I promise I'll never buy you a spoon for your birthday.

Finally, the biggest thank you to Stef. My best friend and Aperol Spritz dreamer, the kindest, most open-minded man I have ever had the sheer luck of meeting. Every day, even when I am moody and pessimistic (even then! Imagine!) I am in awe of the fact that I get to share my life with you. Thank you for pushing me to write, and for championing me even when you hadn't read anything I'd ever written. Your blind faith in me is testament to the person you think I am, and I hope one day to be half as good as you believe me to be.

Credits

Trapeze would like to thank everyone at Orion who worked on the publication of *This is Not a Love Story*.

Agent
Tanera Simons

Editor
Katie Brown

Copy-editor
Loma Halden

Proofreader
Laura Gerrard

Editorial Management
Lucinda McNeile
Charlie Panayiotou
Jane Hughes
Alice Davis
Jo Whitford
Claire Boyle

Audio
Paul Stark
Amber Bates

Contracts
Anne Goddard
Paul Bulos
Jake Alderson

Design
Rachael Lancaster
Debbie Holmes
Lucie Stericker
Joanna Ridley
Nick May
Clare Sivell
Helen Ewing

Finance
Jennifer Muchan
Jasdip Nandra
Rabale Mustafa
Elizabeth Beaumont
Sue Baker
Tom Costello

Marketing
Lucy Cameron

Production
Claire Keep
Fiona McIntosh

Publicity
Francesca Pearce

Sales
Laura Fletcher
Victoria Laws
Esther Waters
Lucy Brem
Frances Doyle
Ben Goddard
Georgina Cutler
Jack Hallam
Ellie Kyrke-Smith
Inês Figuiera
Barbara Ronan
Andrew Hally

Dominic Smith
Deborah Deyong
Lauren Buck
Maggy Park
Linda McGregor
Sinead White
Jemimah James
Rachel Jones
Jack Dennison
Nigel Andrews
Ian Williamson
Julia Benson
Declan Kyle
Robert Mackenzie
Sinead White
Imogen Clarke
Megan Smith
Charlotte Clay
Rebecca Cobbold

Operations
Jo Jacobs
Sharon Willis
Lisa Pryde

Rights
Susan Howe
Richard King
Krystyna Kujawinska
Jessica Purdue
Louise Henderson